Heretic Knight

HARBINGER OF LIGHT

LEMUEL V. SAPIAN

For information contact :

BRIMINGSTONE

PRESS

inquiries@brimingstone.online

Book and Cover design by Lemuel V. Sapian

ISBN: 978-1-953562-97-5

First Edition: September 2025

10 9 8 7 6 5 4 3 2 1

TABLE OF CONTENTS

Dedicated to Michelle

The Travels of John de Ontivero, 7th Baron of Breckington
1209 A.D.

Lords of Breckington
Barony Breckington in the Earldom of Devonshire,
Kingdom of England
1068-1191 A.D.

† - died young / without issue.

1. Lord Ricardo de Ontivero (1040–1093)
First Baron of Breckington, 1068–1093

A knight of Iberian birth, he was exiled from Toledo and
found honor in the service of Duke William of Normandy.
He fought valiantly at the Battle of Hastings and was
rewarded with lands in Devonshire. A just but stern ruler, he
laid the foundations of Breckington's manorial law and
castle works.

> **Spouse**: Ysabel of Rouen (1045–1102), of noble
> Norman blood
> **Issue**: Armand (heir), Irina

2. Lord Armand de Ontivero (1067–1132)
Second Baron of Breckington, 1093–1132

A lord of steady hand and quiet resolve. He strengthened the castle's defenses during the troubling times following William Rufus's death. He was remembered for his marriage to a Saxon noblewoman, symbolizing union between the conqueror and the conquered.

> **Spouse**: Editha of Wessex (1075–1141), a lady of Saxon lineage
> **Issue**: Roland I (heir), Edward (knight vassal), Owain†, Elaine†

3. Lord Roland I de Ontivero (1098–1151)
Third Baron of Breckington, 1132–1151

A pious and temperate baron, he was known for hosting monks and favoring Gloucester's abbeys to his own castle and estate. After his death, his heir Roger would be lost to an illness, but Roland I left his legacy strong in faith and diplomacy.

> **Spouse**: Marie of Gloucester (1106–1178), cousin to the Earls of Hereford
> **Issue**: Roger†, Gerald, Avelina, Gwenfyl

4. Lord Roger de Ontivero (1123–1154)
Fourth Baron of Breckington, 1151–1154

A brief and sorrowful reign. He fell ill and died in his thirty-first year, leaving no issue. His passing brought his younger brother Gerald to the lordship of the barony.

Spouse: Eleanor of Kent (1120–1167), daughter of a royal steward
Issue: None

5. Lord Gerald de Ontivero (1128–1176)
Fifth Baron of Breckington, 1154–1176

A strong lord who oversaw the barony during the early reign of Henry II. Known for his military acumen and for marrying a Galician lady of noble descent. Died in peace, having rebuilt the manor hall after a fire.

> **Spouse**: Joan of Galicia (1130–1195), niece of a Galician count
> **Issue**: Beatrice, Roland II (heir), Edwain†

6. Lord Roland II de Ontivero (1152–1191)
Sixth Baron of Breckington, 1176–1191

A crusader of high esteem, he joined King Richard's army and perished nobly at the Battle of Arsuf. His memory is honored with a stone cross at Breckington chapel.

> **Spouse**: Leonora de Castile (1154–?), kinswoman to the House of Trastámara
> **Issue**: John (heir), Isabelle

"Honor is absent, where faith is corrupted."

John de Ontivero
7th Baron Breckington

L'orgueilleux

May 2nd, 1209 AD

Shire of Devon, England

 he squawking of carrion birds pierced the afternoon sky, striking a discordant chord above the English road. They wheeled in slow circles, black silhouettes against the sun, descending to feast upon the dead below. Their harsh calls mingled with the metallic tang of blood that lingered heavy in the air. Beneath their circling vigil, eleven knights rode through the aftermath of slaughter—their armor catching the waning sunlight in cold flashes of steel. The clink of bridles and the creak of leather stirred the stillness as they wove through corpses sprawled across the road like broken effigies.

Lord John de Ontivero reined in his destrier, his dark eyes

sweeping over the carnage. Brigands, their bodies twisted in death, some clutching weapons even in rigor. The remnants of a desperate last stand. He breathed in the stench—sweat, blood, rot—and beneath it, the faint sweetness of wildflowers crushed beneath the dead. A cruel contrast.

He dismounted with practiced ease, boots sinking into the blood-damp earth. The blue and yellow of his heraldry stood vivid against the grisly backdrop. His hand lingered on his sword hilt out of habit, though the danger had passed. The work of his men had been swift—a knight's charge left little room for defense. Too swift. They had left none alive. No tongue remained to speak answers.

John crouched by a fallen brigand, turning the man's head with a gloved hand. Eyes wide, lips frozen in a snarl. Young. Perhaps no older than twenty summers. He bore no coat of arms, but his mail was of better craft than common cutthroats could afford. Curious.

Hugh, the burly knight at his side, gave a low grunt.

"Some silver, my lord, but their weapons—good steel. Not the sort peasants carry."

John's gaze shifted to the overturned wagon beyond—splintered wood, cargo scattered like entrails. The merchant Edwinson and his young daughter lay discarded to the side.

Aerin.

He forced himself to look. Her small hand rested near her father's—as though she had reached for him in the end.

Too late. Always too late.

A crow landed beside the bodies, black beak probing soft flesh. John rose abruptly, sending the bird flapping skyward. His lip curled in distaste—not for the bird, but for his own failure. Protection promised, yet not given. At least, not on time.

"Shoo, you devils!" another knight barked, waving an arm. The scavengers scattered but would return. They always did.

John exhaled through his nose, steadying the roil within.

14

"Search the bodies. See if anything gives them name or purpose."

The knights fanned out, boots scuffing against dirt and death. John stepped to the wagon. Silver coins glinted in the grass. Untouched. The goods remained largely intact—sifted through but not taken. Not a raid for profit then. Purpose lay elsewhere.

Edwinson's ledger. Always carried on his person—his lifeblood.

Gone.

John removed his helm, revealing dark hair damp with sweat. Thirty-four years had carved lines into his face, tempered by sun and steel. The weight of a barony pressed upon his brow—Breckington, his inheritance, his burden.

A young squire ventured a question, voice tentative.

"My lord, what need would brigands have for a ledger?"

John glanced at him—the boy's eyes still held innocence, unspoiled by war. He envied that.

"It was not loot they sought," John said, voice low. "They wanted something in that ledger. Something worth more than coin."

The large knight named Hugh approached, his helmet removed, expression grim.

"Fresh hoofprints, my lord. Northward."

John's jaw tightened. A rider had fled. With the ledger.

The implications gnawed at him. Coin could be replaced; knowledge could not. Records of trade, debts owed, or secrets better left buried—all contained within that simple book of ink and parchment. What truth had Edwinson carried that was worth slaughtering him and his child?

"We pursue," John decided, though the trail was already fading into the shadows of the forest beyond. "But first, gather what we can. Give it to the merchant's kin. And see to their burial—our coffers will bear the cost."

He crossed himself, lips forming a prayer for the souls departed. Words spoken countless times before, yet each utterance wore his spirit thinner. He felt the land—his land—beneath his boots. Soil nourished by toil, watered by blood. His charge, his duty.

Yet duty alone would not ease his mind.

The ledger was *gone*.

And someone, somewhere, had planned for this day long before.

The wind carried more than the scent of blood. It bore a memory. Memory of a day John de Ontivero could never forget—the day his father returned home, lifeless.

Only sixteen summers he had seen by then, standing at the gates of Breckington as the procession arrived. He was young, but old enough to take the mantle of leadership.

Still, it stung. He was in no hurry to become baron in his father's stead. He remembered the scene like it was yesterday: the sun was low, casting long shadows, and the banners drooped like the hearts of those who carried them. His father, Sir Roland de Ontivero, wrapped in linen, borne on the shoulders of his knights—his men. They had brought him back from the burning sands of Arsuf.

John blinked, as if the sting of that sun still haunted his eyes. He had heard the tale often enough—his father, leading the rearguard under King Richard, the Lionheart himself. Holding the line against the Saracens while the army pressed forward. A Saracen blade had found him, torn deep into his side. For a fortnight he endured his mortal wound, his men refusing to leave him.

He recalled as his father's broken body arrived home on the shoulders of his best men. They told stories—of what happened, what befell his guide, his light.

They spoke of angels guiding their way as they marched through the desert with their dying lord. But it was not the mere wound itself, but the rot that finally claimed him.

John remembered the faces of the knights as they entered Breckington that day—faces carved from grief and endurance—of defeat. Their eyes hollowed by the long

16

journey, their loyalty as if etched into every scar on their bodies.

They had kept their oath: no man left behind.

Roland de Ontivero had returned to his land, though his soul had gone beyond. John had stood there, trying to be strong, trying to fill the void already opening within him. He had failed. He had wept like a child because he *was* one.

Three days of mourning followed. The town stopped. Work ceased. The people grieved because the baron had earned their love. Roland had been more than lord; he had been protector, judge, and kin to all in his realm.

Beneath the stone of his sepulcher, the words carved into the cold surface spoke of *faith* and *honor*, but they could never capture his laughter, or the way his hand rested on John's shoulder when he spoke of the future—now only existing as memories in John's mind.

John had not been ready, but there was no choice. The weight of Breckington's leadership fell upon him. The Earl of Devon, his liege, and Father Bartholomew, the parish priest, became his guides. They shaped his hand, his tongue, his will.

Yet, it was the land that truly forged him. The fields and forests, the streams winding through fertile valleys—this was Breckington. A place whose name, the old men said, came from "*brucan*"—to use, to enjoy. Saxons named it. Saxon hands had tilled it before Norman swords and spears claimed it.

John's ancestor, Ricardo de Ontivero, had come with William the Conqueror to the shores of England. A man of Iberian blood, exiled from Toledo when Christian and Moor were tearing each other apart.

He had found favor in Normandy, fought at Hastings, and was rewarded with these lands in Devon. Yet, he had not ruled by sword alone. He saw the wisdom in what the Saxons built. He listened, learned their tongue, broke bread with them. Breton, Saxon, Norman; all found a place under his

17

hall. That was the way of Breckington. Peace bought with understanding, not steel.

But the de Ontiveros had never been strangers to war. Ricardo had fought for his king. His son had put down Saxon uprisings. John's grandfather had ridden into Wales to crush rebellion. And Roland—Roland had followed the cross to the Holy Land. Their swords had never rusted, but they wielded them to defend more than pride. They fought so that their fields might remain quiet, so their children might know harvest and not hardship.

But today John looked over the bodies strewn on the road before him. Peace was broken in a violent way—for the first time on his watch.

Brigands or something worse? He should know the difference. The dead whispered truths if a man had the eyes to see. Their weapons, their numbers; this was no rabble of desperate thieves. Steel of that quality was bought with coin, or blood.

He inhaled deeply, the scent of sweat and blood mixing with the faint sweetness of crushed heather. This land had seen peace for generations, but peace was not simply the absence of danger. It was the strength to face it when it came.

He would not fail as protector. He could not. Roland's voice still echoed in his memory:

"Guard them, John. With wisdom and with honor, my son."

He adjusted his grip on the hilt of his sword, the weight of his father's words and legacy weighing heavily upon him—as heavy as the weapon at his side. Heavy as the barony itself.

But he bore it. Because he must.

John's eyes swept across the ground like and eagle's gaze, carefully observing every detail—a skill honed from years of tracking fleeing enemies through sparse clues.

The hoofprints heading north captured his attention, yet his mind wandered with memories that blurred past and present, much like wounds that never fully closed. His hand unconsciously found the hilt of his sword, seeking the steel's reassurance. But these recently slain men were merely pieces in a larger game. The true threat lingered elsewhere, just out of reach. If only he knew where.

The breeze kissed his face, carrying with it the faintest scent of pines from the looming forest. Another smell emerged from the mists of time—salty air weighted with woodsmoke from campaigns along the Mediterranean. Acre. Then a youth of twenty-two, eager yet learning. Still, he recalled donning the heavy chainmail in the punishing sun, and parched lips cracked from thirst as he stood with the men of Breckington below the banner of Christ.

In 1202 the Cross beckoned them, and he answered, hoping to find honor and atonement in equal measure.

But Jerusalem remained a dream—one never fulfilled. Instead, Zara burned under Christian steel against Christian blood. When the host turned toward Constantinople, John led his ten comrades away. Greed glinted in the eyes of so-called "holy" soldiers, and he wanted to take no part in such disgrace.

A fellow lord, Henry of Longchamp had offered another road—a nobler path, John had believed it then. He and his band of knights joined with the Earl of Leicester, Simon de Montfort, and marched onward to Acre, the gateway to the Holy Land. The voyage had tested their resolve; raging storms upon the sea, a sickness that spread amongst the ships. Yet they had prevailed. They had stood upon that antique shore, hearts swollen with pride and purpose.

His boot nudged aside a splintered arrow, splitting it further with a dull crack. The remnants surrounding him merged with recollections from eras past. At Acre, they had defended the ramparts against a ferocious Saracen onslaught, vastly outnumbered and leagues from home. The heathen horde battered them with arrows, stones, and flame. Men perished screaming. The wounded wept for loved ones worlds away. It was a miracle they all survived.

John recalled standing atop the battlements, sword clenched so tight his knuckles blanched. He had felled a man struggling to scale the wall, watching him fall back into the swarm of enemies below. The man had worn a crimson sash—a seemingly trivial detail seared into his mind. He had looked into that man's eyes just before his blade struck true. The eyes had held fear. *Humanity*.

They had seized victory that day, but at dreadful cost. Triumph in Acre brought not peace. Only exhaustion. His knights had grown gaunt with yearning for homeland. And John had felt the weight of their hopes heavy upon him. He opted to lead them home.

The journey itself proved a trial. The Blitheful Ten—as they were called in those days, though little blitheness lingered—found themselves harassed by Saracen cavalry. Forty riders had descended upon them one morn like heavenly wrath made flesh. Dust choked the air; hooves thundered like the sky tearing apart.

John's hand unconsciously flexed as the memories overwhelmed him—the shock of falling from his horse, the panic of blades flashing all around. That day, necessity fueled each blow he dealt, three men met their end by his own hand as he fought only for him and his men to survive. Hugh had carved a path to him through their attackers, his war axe swinging with deadly precision. Together, they drove the Saracens away from the battlefield and they fled a hasty retreat.

Again, it was only by a miracle that all ten of the Blithefuls, John, his two knights and their seven squires, returned home to Devon. Their laughter now came less easily; smiles did not come as freely. Yet their loyalty to one another, that remained unchanged.

The ancient forest was thick around them as they continued their investigation. The daylight lingered on but dusk descended beneath the canopy, and John de Ontivero felt a weight settling upon his weary shoulders.

A hare's sudden scurry through the brush startled his mount briefly. He soothed the animal with a gentle word, though his thoughts drifted back to other sounds long past: the clang of steel on steel, grunts of straining effort, laughter shared among battle-brothers.

The devoted Blitheful Ten, their names he knew by heart. He bore them as a man bears his sword, ever ready at hand. His second-in-command and loyal vassal Sir Hugh Philip rode ahead still, ever the watchful sentinel. Broad as an ox and loud as thunder, Hugh had stood by John's side since first he claimed the title of Breckington's Baron.

Across stormy seas and under burning suns they'd ridden together, from gazing through Acre's gates to Italy's cold shores. It was Hugh who hauled John up when fallen in fray. Hugh who mocked his lord's height in mirth yet would rend any who spoke ill of his friend.

The forest stirred with an ominous creak as a tree branch snapped in the distance. John's hand drifted instinctively to the hilt of his sword, though no threat was apparent. Not yet. His wary eyes flickered to George de Wymondham, ever vigilant as expected.

Sir George, the steady vassal and mentor of men, who tempered hot blood with wisdom as keenly as any blade. Third in the chain, his lordship over Baymundon mattered little when united under one cause. For years he had schooled squires and knights alike, sculpting them into the warriors they had become.

John's thoughts turned to those under his charge, especially his younger squires. Thomas Dalton, his fiery spirit matched only by freckled complexion, loyal as the day is long. James Nugent, wiry and watchful, always observing with keen interest. And Peter Marshall, soft-spoken yet resolute, his attention commanded when steel was drawn. Each had stood guard over him more times than memory could hold. Each had spilled blood in his name.

Hugh's own squires were no less formidable. Hubert Roche, the sharp and loyal retainer, whose keen eyes missed nothing. And Robert "Bobbeye" Le Grand, strong and eager, with a heart as expansive as his brawn.

George also guided his own. Robert Tobias, whose humor and levity buoyed spirits even in darkness' deepest throes. And Reginald de Saint-Clair, known simply as "Reggeye," quietly tenacious, a warrior to have at your side in strife. Their nicknames, borne of camaraderie, had become badges of brotherhood cemented in strife and gore.

Another gust rustled the trees, and John squinted down the narrowing path heading north. The wood seemed oppressive and closing in. He reminded himself this was not Acre, that no Saracen archers lurked here. Yet his heart still quickened. Old wounds of war never fully healed.

He had watched his squires grow from callow youths to hardened warriors over many years of grueling training within Breckington Manor's courtyard. Together, they had endured agonizing drills that left their bodies aching and their spirits worn down to the bone. They had faced the merciless lash of torrential rain and the unrelenting burn of the punishing sun as they honed their martial skills. Every clashing of steel against steel in practice had been more than mere preparation; it had been making ready for the grim day when their prowess would mean the difference between life and death on the battlefield.

John had stood beside Hugh and George, overseeing their formidable forces, the Breckington Levy—a hundred spearmen drawn from across the barony, forged into a cohesive unit through rigorous drilling. The levies of Breckington, sharpened to a standard that elicited laudation from neighboring lords. Their frequent joint maneuvers with the soldiers of neighboring Plympton had validated their status as one of the most elite feudal formations in the kingdom. Weapons burnished to perfection in the bustling armory; armor crafted with exquisite care to withstand even the most brutal strikes. Each piece bore the distinctive mark of their skilled smiths—and of the immense pride they took in their work.

His gaze shifted restlessly to the path once more, but his thoughts lingered upon the stout walls of Breckington Manor, looming upon the hill behind them. It was his birthplace, his home. The towering keep had resounded with the clashing of steel in combat and the lively debates of scholars. All under his ever-watchful eye.

"Order is the bedrock upon which our strength is built," he had counselled his men time and again. He believed it still.

William Lancey, the industrious sheriff of his town ensured that order extended far beyond the courtyard—into the bustling villages, into the fertile fields. Together, they had constructed something enduring. A place where peace stemmed not from weakness but from strength, where various tongues and cultures thrived.

Yet now, that harmony lay shattered. John's jaw tightened as he mulled over the wreckage—*again*—to ensure no stone was left unturned. With Peter and Hubert by his side, he had carefully examined the fabrics, trinkets, and goods strewn about, but found no clues as to what the attackers sought—save that precious book, conspicuously absent. Their rummaging seemed perfunctory; the items held no value to such marauders. He sensed they had come for some prize far greater.

He was motivated, not only by duty but by debts that could not be left unpaid. By justice.

With pursed lips, he gazed once again upon the bodies of his subjects—no, his *friends*.

For you, Edwinson, a loyal friend. To you gentle Aerin, whose memory kept my spirits bright.

And most of all to his people, who depended on leaders such as he to stem the rising tide of danger and disorder. And of course, to the steadfast brothers-in-arms at his flanks—

his beloved Blitheful Ten, without whom this forest would seem all the darker and more foreboding.

As John remounted his steed, a rustle in the brush disturbed the deep quiet of the wood. Sharp and fleeting, the sound drew his attention at once. Was it a bird or hare or something more ominous stalking them through these cursed trees?

His hand drifted automatically to the pommel of his sword as his sense stirred with alarm—they had dealt death quickly upon their foes, cloaked by the noises of nature, and he remained ever wary should more bandits appear. Moments passed without further disturbance, yet unease lingered in his tightened muscles.

Emerging from the trees where two bandits had succumbed to their wounds, James interrupted John's thoughts, boots snapping dry leaves with each weary step. In his freckled hand, something small and stained with blackened blood.

"Milord," James called, voice lowered with unease. He offered the object for inspection, revealing a ring crusted over with blood but for the design now discernible beneath the grime. John wiped it clean against his cloak, sure even before the red wiped away what insignia he would find engraved there. The rose, its knight mid-blow upon his horn against a cross—the token of Simon de Montfort himself, given only to those who had stood bloodied at his side in Outremer.

Memories stirred at the sight, years passing by in his mind.

Some good, others tinged with the trauma of battle and violence.

John's thumb traced the contours of the metal rose as he recalled being in the presence of the man. He was a leader and brother in arms John had come to know and respect.

But what does all this mean? His mind swirled as he sought clarity amid the growing fog of uncertainty.

24

"We make no assumptions," John replied, though his conviction wavered in his tone. "Perhaps the man looted it from one of Simon's fallen. Or found it among the spoils of a prior clash."

James nodded slowly, but restless unease lingered in his gaze. He returned to the grim work of searching among the dead, his internal quest for answers visibly apparent in his demeanor.

John turned the ring between his fingers, cold metal biting into skin. As Hugh neared, his blond facial stubble caught the sunlight, and a pale scar became visible across his cheek—a Saracen blade's parting gift—stood stark against his other weathered features.

"My lord," Hugh murmured, ensuring others heard not, "this reeks of deceit. Reggeye discovered another ring bearing the same symbol upon a different corpse. No coincidence could explain such circumstances."

John tensed at the implication. De Montfort's men, or imposters posing as such? Both prospects heralded dread.

"They were well-equipped for battle," Hugh continued somberly. "Far beyond what mere brigands might carry. Their objective was no mere plunder."

John gazed upon the ruined remnants of Edwinson's wagon; trinkets discarded, bolts of cloth untouched. His intuition now became an inner shout, had prior expressed the truth in but a whisper; the ledger containing accounts and insights was now definitively the sole object of their endeavor.

He turned once again to the fresh tracks which led north, where a lone rider had fled clutching the prize.

John drew a steadying breath, duty's weight constricting upon his chest.

"George," he called.

The lord of Baymundon stood tall, visor lowered yet voice clear.

"My lord?"

"Accompany Bobbeye and Reggeye. Track the rider. Discover what they transport."

John watched as George nodded sharply, swiftly mounting. The three men rode into the forest on their mounts, soon disappearing amidst the dense trees.

Thomas' voice cut through the stillness once the riders faded from view.

"Milord, over here."

The young squire knelt beside the lifeless form of Aerin. The merchant's daughter lay pale and still, her dress torn and throat slit. But it was not just the violence that chilled John—it was the brand upon her chest.

A circled fox was burned into her skin. John's breath caught at the sight, fingers instinctively forming a cross over his pounding heart. Tales were whispered of this symbol, a mark left upon heretics across the channel. French sects hunted relentlessly by the Church, called foxes for how cunningly they crept into God's flock to corrupt believers.

Hugh saw it too, a look of recognition flickering across his face. A somber prayer rumbled from his lips. John knelt beside the girl, pressing his knee into the damp earth. She deserved more than this desecration—her soul deserved peace. With trembling fingers, he closed Aerin's lifeless eyes.

He would get to the bottom of this. Kings bowed before popes, nobles wavered between crown and cloth. Lingering still was the papal interdict upon England, a curse left by King John's defiance of Rome that seeded doubt and disillusion among England's lords.

Now a child bore the mark of heresy on English soil. Truth, not coin, was the prize to uncover. Who was the rider? What did this ledger hold? John would find the answers and expose the rot that dared seep into Breckington's lands.

The forest seemed darker now. John knew they were not alone in the shadows.

A faint crack—twigs snapping underfoot. John halted

again, held his breath. His eyes searched the shadowed undergrowth. Nothing stirred beneath the forest canopy filtering sunlight in mottled patches. Perhaps a fox lurked unseen. Perhaps not.

"A fox indeed", John mumbled under his breath. But he wasn't referring to the creature, rather he contemplated the vile mutilation he had witnessed.

Another rustle parted brush. John turned, his gaze sharp, but this time Hugh emerged, his large frame head and shoulders above the undergrowth.

"No sign yet. But their trail remains clear," Hugh murmured.

John nodded, thoughts settling briefly on Hugh. Three years John's senior, Hugh served Roland since John's first sword days. Their bond was further battle-forged in Acre, fire-tempered by war. The pious Hugh, stalwart armor of faith, never questioned Church or the fated path. To Hugh, doubt was weakness, devotion was strength.

George, though—he was another matter entirely. John continued musing as he glanced back toward the other men with concern. Ever skeptical of priestly words, George had an uncanny ability to cut through hypocrisy and see to the heart of matters, whether theological or political, with cynical wit. His faith was not in invisible deities or the church. His loyalty to John, however, was beyond question. This loyalty served as his faith.

John knew he could always rely on his two vassals, loyal and devoted to him. Together they had built Breckington into a formidable force and thriving center of commerce, yet maintaining order required constant vigilance against those who would exploit mercy for their own gains.

Faith and honor.

John had carried those words with him from youth, knowing that strength was derived not from might alone, but from the shared purpose and conviction of one's people. Yet the brand seared into Aerin's flesh hinted at menacing

27

forces. Could sincerely held faith be turned toward malicious ends? What twist of fate or malice of men could so corrupt the spirit? He was determined to get to the bottom of this mystery.

Something glinted amid the damp leaves and loam. Kneeling to uncover it revealed an engraved buckle with an insignia of a boar signaling his liege, William de Redvers, Earl of Devon. It was a reminder of the lessons learned in his youth, when the Earl had raised him from grief to leadership.

"Mercy is a virtue but threatens you if not wielded with care and cunning," the Red Boar had advised. "Wolves will exploit the door left open by kindness if vigilance does not stand guard."

De Redvers had detected the compassion within him, the drive to lead with equity. Experience had balanced it with caution. Hugh had served as his safeguard, counteracting John's idealism with realism. When John expressed mercy, Hugh made sure it was not mistaken for weakness.

A sharp crow's shriek suddenly pulled John back to the present. He clenched the buckle in hand while rising to his feet. His gaze met Hugh's.

"The Earl of Devon has ties along this road," John said softly. "His mark lingers here."

Hugh frowned pensively.

"Do you suspect he knows of this attack?"

John shook his head.

"No. But we must tread carefully. This is no petty brigandage. It touches on faith. It touches on power. And it reaches past our borders."

The men stirred behind them. James adjusted his saddle. Peter wiped his brow fatigued. Sir George, Bobbeye and Reggeye had already been gone for half an hour, the shadows of the trees indicating the time of day it was.

John squinted into the distance to the northern hills. These were his lands, but they now seem foreign, its soil now

28

drenched with foreign blood. This land was his keep, his responsibility. His sister, Isabella, had long since left for Aragon with their mother after Roland's death. He had not seen her for years. He had few blood kin remaining, but these men—Hugh, George, the Blitheful Ten—were his family now. They look to his strength. His clarity. His faith.

But today, faith wavered. And honor felt fragile. He had failed to protect his most innocent subjects in time.

John's eyes drifted over the trail ahead, waiting for any sign of the return of Sir George and his men, but his thoughts fell backward—to his liege, his mentor, Earl William de Redvers. The Red Boar of Devon. The man who had shaped him, raised him up from grief and youth into the mantle of command.

He had been too young to witness the full breadth of his lord's rise. He knew it instead through stories told beneath Tiverton's vaulted ceilings; tales recounted by old knights nursing cups of wine, their eyes far away, gazing into battles long past.

The reign of King Henry II—a realm not merely English, but sprawling into the lands of the Angevin Empire. A kingdom bound together by the will of a king feared by all. It was under Henry's banner that De Redvers had earned his place. He had fought not only against the French across the Channel, but against his own countrymen—discontented barons who bristled under Plantagenet rule. The kingdom's borders were lines drawn in blood, and within those borders, loyalty was tested as fiercely as swords in battle.

John nudged his horse forward as a squirrel darted across the path—a quick, fleeting thing. He followed it briefly with his gaze, then looked down. A boot print in the mud, faint but fresh. Only one brigand had escaped their swords. Sir George would be near in finding him, if he had not already. The air of Devonshire was filled with the scent of herb and leaf, tranquil, as if nature had not known of the loss of life in its midst. But it was how the earl intended it to be.

Earl William had been more than a soldier. In the great hall of Tiverton Castle, among stone walls warmed by tapestries and firelight, he had crafted something rare. A place of learning. Minstrels had sung there; poets recited their verses beneath the watchful gaze of mailed guards. Latin prayers blended with the clink of goblets, and the Earl himself had listened to philosophers speak of virtue and justice.

John had seen it; he had heard those echoes when he was brought to Tiverton as a grieving boy. The Earl had raised him in that court, molded him with both sword and book. The balance of courtly intrigue and wisdom—it had become John's creed.

A memory he had was of the earl, gray-bearded, with eyes like a hawk, standing before him on his sixteenth birthday.

"No more will you call me guardian," William had said. "I am your liege now. You are a man. And you will lead."

The words had been as a seal upon his youth. A reminder that childhood had passed, and duty had taken its place.

John scanned the treeline. Birds scattered, startled by something unseen. His hand found the hilt of his sword once more.

De Redvers had taught him more than command. He had warned him of the wolves—those who lurked with smiles and honeyed words, seeking to take what was not theirs. Mercy was good, but too much bred weakness. One had to rule with might to ensure justice prevailed.

Justice was not merely law—it was protection. The dead merchant, Edwinson, and his child, Aerin—their deaths now stained this land John had sworn to keep safe. This hunt was not only for the ledger. It was also intended as proof to his people that their baron had not been neglectful in his duty. That those who broke the peace would face swift reckoning.

Faith and Honor.

That was what the legacy the de Ontivero barons had left

him. That was what he would uphold.

The smell of blood still clung heavy in his nostrils. Even now, as they pushed deeper into the dense wood to search for more evidence, it stuck to him like a spectral shadow. Sweat mixed with the metallic scent of death coated his skin, and the faint brush of leaves overhead stirred with the ghostly echoes of the brief but brutal clash.

John had always led the charge; he was not about to let his men go into danger without him. His blade had been first to fall in fealty to duty—a baron did not merely order men from afar. He intended to bleed alongside them, just as his sires before had done before him. The men of Breckington deserved no less.

He replayed the encounter over and over again in his head, hoping to find conclusive answers. The bandits had grown careless, their jeers carrying over Edwinson's body and that of his daughter. It was that sound—that vile and taunting chorus—which had snapped something within him. It was that sound which spurred them into frenzied battle once they realized innocents had been cut down in cold blood.

His sword struck true this day. Four lives were taken by his hand alone, though in the heat of battle he'd no chance to really count. But their faces lingered now in his mind, twisted with shock and agony as his steel felled them. Sixteen men-at-arms, slain by him and his knights. No guilt took hold—only cold satisfaction that justice had been served. They had slaughtered the innocent and mocked their victims. Their fate was earned.

The breeze shifted, and with it came a distant crow's call mingling with the echo of that final scream. John blinked the memory away, wrenching his focus back to the present trail.

Retribution had come swift, but it could not undo what had passed. Edwinson and Aerin gone because he had failed. He would lay them to rest with dignity. Their kin would find what small comfort his efforts could offer. Breckington's soil would not keep the innocent as carrion. This he owed them.

Justice had been served by steel; now honor would see it fulfilled.

The forest pressed closer, dark and hushed. He tightened his grip on the reins and pressed onward. There was still work to be done.

A faint breeze stirred the trees that lined the clearing, carrying with it the scent of damp soil mixed with the faint remnants of death still clinging to the scene. The squires on foot began to remove armor and weapons from the deceased. John's gaze swept once more across the scattered forms, pondering their origins as his mount shifted restlessly beneath him. Above, crows cawed in chorus, beginning to glut themselves on the fallen. The weight of his helm pressed against his arm—a grim reminder of obligations as yet unfinished.

"Jamey, gather some villagers to assist in interring these souls. The father and daughter we shall bear to town, allowing their kin to identify them and claim their worldly possessions."

John spoke firmly, though the dead father and daughter weighed heavy on his heart. Ever obedient, James Nugent nodded and swiftly mounted his horse in one lithe motion, sending up small puffs of dirt as he turned his horse toward Breckington. John watched him depart, the squire soon lost to the forest's depths.

Incoming hoofbeats snapped John from his thoughts. He faced north, hand instinctively finding the hilt of his sword. A rider approached at top speed: Bobbeye, breathless, eyes wide with urgency.

"My lord, hasten! For we've apprehended the fugitive, but more has come to pass!"

John felt his chest constrict, knowing peril still gripped these lands. Without delay he donned his helm, its chill metal settling upon his brow. Purpose filled his arms he grasped his reins firmly.

"Thomas, keep watch here until Jamey returns!"

The freckled man nodded crisply.

"Aye, milord."

John pulled hard on his reins and dug his boots into his charger's flanks.

"Bobbeye, lead the way!"

As the two riders thundered across the terrain, John sought to understand the situation amid the clattering hooves. In all his years of governance, he had not experienced such a calamity as this in his lands.

"Bobbeye, what peril has befallen?" John's voice cut above the din; his earnest inquiry accompanied by grave concern.

"It's Reggeye, milord! We successfully cornered the fugitive after questioning the people living around Fitzsimon's farm. Owen and Baruch, two laborers, directed us to the Purcell's abode."

"The dwelling on Caden Ridge?" John sought confirmation.

"Aye, sir!"

"And then?"

"At the Purcell's house, we spotted a tethered horse, sir, and..."

The duo rounded a bend, emerging into a clearing adorned with sprawling fields and rolling hills. In the distance, a house perched on a ridge came into view—the residence of the Purcells. As kin to Reginald de Saint-Clair, the Purcell family motto expressed "*loyalty and tranquility*", yet, in a twist of cruel irony their humble estate was now robbed of its tranquility with this disturbing development.

"Speak freely, lad," Lord Breckington commanded over the din. They were coming upon the estate fast.

"Yes, milord. Reggeye's kin, they were set upon by this miscreant, who did menace them grievously. He bound them quickly and inflicted harm!"

"The Lord preserve us! What did he do, lad, did he take their virtue?"

"Nay, milord. But he brought along a dire tool, glowing with heat, some sort of branding iron which he wielded to mark the poor girls! Poor Reggeye lost his mind."

John, keen for more details, pressed on.

"And then, what unfolded?" John had to shout out of his helmet for Bobbeye to hear.

"Upon arriving, Reggeye, Sir George and I ran upon the shrieking lot—Almerah and Sarah, Reggeye's young cousins, wailing as the scoundrel pressed the heated brand upon their flesh. The knight brandished a wooden cross, chanting in the Latin tongue. He bore noble colors, clad in a maroon and gray-hued tunic."

"A perverse madness! I wonder what dark purpose drives this rogue, invoking the Church?"

"Reggeye, unable to bear the sight in silence, lord, threw himself immediately at the intruder. Sir George and I stood witness as the two engaged in fierce combat."

"Reggeye is a skilled warrior, and you, formidable in your own right."

"Grateful for your words, milord. Yet, the fugitive overcame Reggeye, dealing a blow to his side. By the grace of God, not a mortal wound. Sir George then intervened, confronting the assailant. In a hard-fought duel, Sir George emerged victorious. The miscreant sought mercy, but then, Reggeye, his strength renewed, impaled him with his blade!"

"Dark news you bring indeed, lad!"

"Indeed, milord. That is why I sought you with all haste."

The clamor of pounding hooves resounded through the air as John and Bobbeye charged into the Purcell homestead courtyard. An unsettling stillness hung heavy in the air—the kind that follows in violence's wake. John leapt swiftly from his mount, boots sinking into the damp soil as his hand instinctively found the groves on his sword's pommel. Sweeping his gaze across the scene, details caught his sharp eyes—shattered pottery strewn across the ground, a chicken aimlessly wandering by an upended bench, a solitary crimson smear leading inward.

Soft cries echoed plaintively from within the dwelling. The kind of weeping that clenched one's chest. Achingly familiar. The sounds of those left to carry sorrow's burden and pain.

John strode through the splintered doorway, boots brushing broken furniture remnants. The atmosphere was oppressive—the faint scents of singed flesh intermingled with the sharp tinge of blood. His vision adjusted to the dim light. Chaos. Pots and plates in ruin. Wooden chairs reduced to shards. An upturned table, its leg fractured.

Near the hearth, Sir George knelt beside a man in maroon and gray heraldry, chainmail stained dark with blood. The knight—middle-aged, dark-haired, face pale yet proud—lay on his back, hand pressed to his side where his armor had failed. The wound was grave; his lifeblood pooled and seeped into the stone floor.

Reggeye stood at the room's edge, sword still in hand, drying blood along its edge. His chest rose and fell in short, wrathful breaths. Fury still possessed him, his face flushed with crimson.

The intruder knight gurgled, coughed—a thin spray of red mist escaping his lips. Even in demise, his eyes blazed with defiance.

John removed his ornate helmet, the polished metal catching the light of the hearthfire as he tucked it under a gauntleted arm with care. His gaze softened as it drifted to one shadowed corner of the great hall, where two small figures huddled close together, young faces stained with tears that glittered faintly. The elder, Almerah, enfolded her younger sister Sarah protectively within trembling arms, as if to shield her from further harm. Upon Almerah's neck, a raw fresh brand still smoldered in the flickering half-light, the emblem of some foul injustice.

Turning to his aggrieved subjects the lord rose and approached them, his tone gentle yet authoritative.

"My ladies, what grievous wrong has been done to you here?"

Almerah met his eyes reluctantly.

"My lord..."

With a sigh, she drew back fabric to reveal upon her throat an angry welt, the same mocking sigil he had seen burned into the Aerin's skin. A mark meant not only to claim property of body, but to desecrate the spirit.

Within John, a flare of wrath ignited—searing, consuming—but he quenched the flames of rage, focusing instead upon his sworn duty of protection.

He turned next to the dying knight, surrounded now by a gathering pool of his own blood, his stained lips parted in a grimace. Yet the man's defiance had not wavered, not even at death's door. John addressed him, summoning the authority of his station so that it resonated through every word.

"Sir, you have forced your way into my barony with malice in your heart. You have shattered our peace, and brought death and injury upon innocents under my care. You have trespassed upon this, my lands and home. As Lord Baron of Breckington, I demand you explain yourself before these witnesses."

The knight laughed then, a broken, rasping sound that dissolved into wet coughs as crimson flecked his chin.

John leaned close.

"Your vile actions have scarred souls within these walls," he warned softly. "You have defiled my domain with brutality and cannot escape judgement, whether by law of man or law of God."

The knight's breath came quickly. He struggled to clear his throat, his words rasping raw.

"In the same way I spoke to your vassal, lord baron... hear this decree..."

A cough wracked his body, blood bubbling past his lips.

"The home of Purcell is condemned. Heresy dwells within... I have branded them enemies of the Church. And you, Lord Breckington, now stand as protector of heretics."

John's pulse quickened at the grim pronouncement.

"Are you an emissary of the Pope himself?"

The knight's chest heaved with each laborious breath. "I am Sir Renhard Galt... appointed Lead Inquisitor... for His Holiness in England. And you, sir... are... denounced... as anathema..."

His fading strength carried the final word as a whisper.

John's jaw clenched tightly. He had sought answers, but now faced a name—*Renhard Galt*. The inquisitor that lurked in the shadows of England. The dying knight began to murmur a Latin prayer under his breath. John recognized the words well.

"*Pater noster, qui es in caelis...*"

As the Lord's Prayer weakened on his lips until dissolving into a gurgling choke, a few shallow gasps followed before silence fell.

For the longest time, it seemed that the world was as silent as it was mysterious. The intrigue had only grown more sinister, and John knew not what to think. He simply stared at the now dead man, dumbfounded, wishing the shadows could answer the questions that now flooded his mind.

Finally, George exhaled heavily.

"The wretch meets a kinder end than what he deserved."

John gave a slow nod, eyes lingering on the still form. Though death had stolen the knight's pride, his last words carved a wound deeper than any blade.

Mystery.

A shuffle emerged from the shadows as Reggeye stepped forward, his sword dripping with the dead knight's lifeblood.

"S-sorry, my lord!" His voice cracked. "It was too much. My cousins... that monster..."

John raised a weary hand, signaling for silence, his face flush with frustration.

"Reggeye, there were other avenues we could have explored. We required him alive to face interrogation."

Reggeye clenched his blade tighter, knuckles white with fury.

"Alive, my lord? That devil would have danced out of our grasp before a fortnight had passed. Some church official would have shielded this inquisitor from justice. He would have returned to inflict further torment!"

"And what do you think will happen now?" John snapped back, infuriated. "They will have your head, man!"

George stepped beside John, exuding calm.

"While he speaks harshly, the lord makes a fair point. The Church will now come at us with fury. But the lad Reggeye also speaks fair milord...If we had bound the inquisitor, he would have escaped justice. And the Church would have moved the heavens to retrieve one of their own. They care little for others."

John inhaled deeply, then released a long, steadying breath. The iron grip of responsibility squeezed upon his heart unrelentingly. Fair judgement demanded answers to troubling questions. Yet the dead reveal no truths, no matter how vigorously one persists.

"What signs have you uncovered on the inquisitor's body?" John asked wearily.

George produced the ledger.

"This, milord. And perhaps there are further clues within to be gleaned."

John sighed as he took the ledger. Crossing himself, he surveyed the chaotic scene with a solemn prayer.

Faith and honor. But here, in this place of chaos, intrigue and death, faith felt twisted and honor stained.

John removed his greaves and quickly flipped through the pages. *Names*. This was not a list of merchant transactions. It was a list of people. He flipped a page and out fell a letter with a wax seal. He picked it up and opened it.

My dear brother in Christ, these are the few in your area that hold to our sympathies in the Lord. We believe God wants this truth accepted by many, and we give our lives willingly for spreading it. There are not many now in England with this truth. We face hard tribulations in the Midi for our beliefs, and we pray you will find us refuge there in England, for we fear our cause will die here. However, we leave our fates to the hands of God, the Almighty and Merciful, and pray you help us find reprieve.

The letter was left nameless. Both the addressed and addressee remained anonymous.

A security precaution, no doubt, John thought.

But what escaped him is that if the correspondents were so concerned for security, why the names in the ledger itself were so exposed. Sure enough, the Purcell's were among the listed.

A list of what?

A list of *heretics*. It was the only explanation to why an inquisitor would be so obsessed with such a ledger.

Heretics?

The thought pressed on his chest like a millstone. So, this was what Sir Galt had sought. Not gold. Not goods. *Names*. Men and women who lived within John's lands, under his protection. People he knew.

The implications struck him hard. He was a baron of England, a son of the Church. His father had bled for the Cross at Arsuf. His duty was clear: root out heresy, safeguard the faith. But John knew the truth in his heart was far less simple.

He had harbored doubts for years, though he had dared speak them only to George and, in the subtlest terms, to

Hugh. The priests taught that heretics defied God and subverted order—that doubt led to rebellion and blasphemy bred chaos. Yet what John had seen in his barony told another tale.

The Purcell's were named in this ledger, and yet, they were the kindest souls he knew. Generous to their neighbors, faithful in their work. Respectful to his rule. If they whispered prayers different from those chanted in the church, what of it? He had seen more villainy from men who crossed themselves daily than from the so-called heretics.

John rubbed his thumb over the corner of the ledger, feeling the rough edge of parchment beneath his calloused fingers. He glanced toward Almerah and Sarah, still trembling, their red-rimmed eyes fixed downward. The brands on their necks would heal, but the scars would not fade. Society would see those marks before their faces. They would be whispers of shame in every market, unwelcome eyes upon them whenever they walked the streets.

The scent of scorched flesh lingered faintly in the air, mixing with the cold stone beneath John's boots. The embers within the iron kettle once borne by the now deceased Sir Galt still faintly glowed, a sinister heart beating in the ashes. There it lay on the floor, next to its dead owner. He stared at it—the branding iron resting beside it—its wicked tip stained with burnt skin and soot. An instrument forged not for justice, but for suffering. For control.

His stomach knotted with anger—not just for the suffering of these girls, but for the perversion of what he had been taught was holy work. If this was God's justice, it was a justice he struggled to recognize.

He took a breath as he examined the device, steadying himself. The smoke from the still-burning embers bit at his throat.

"Ladies," John said gently, his voice softened beneath the weight of his authority, "you will be brought to Breckington Manor. Bobbeye will bring you both and you will be safe there. I will see that you are tended to. No harm will come to you under my roof."

Sarah wiped her tears with the corner of her sleeve, her voice faint.

"Thank you, milord. We are most grateful."

They curtsied with what dignity they could muster, though their internal and external wounds twisted the gesture into something fragile and forced.

"Bobbeye, kindly escort the ladies to the manor."

"Yes, milord."

Bobbeye placed a hand on Sarah's shoulder as they stepped out into the fading light beyond the ruined doorway. He would see them safe.

"Reggeye, you stay with us."

Reggeye remained silent, his head bowed. His shame, John knew, was a burden he would carry longer than the stain of Galt's blood on his sword.

The door creaked shut as Bobbeye and the ladies exited the abode. The house grew eerily quiet save for the faint crackling from the kettle.

John turned back to George, who knelt over Galt's corpse, rifling through pouches and inspecting the man's garments with practiced scrutiny. The maroon and gray tunic bore fine embroidery, though dulled now with blood and dirt.

"George," John asked, his voice low, "could this have been some personal quarrel made to look like Church business?"

George did not glance up, his fingers tracing along the hilt of the fallen inquisitor's dagger.

"Improbable, my lord. This man was no mere brigand posing as a holy servant. He truly was one. Look here."

He held up the branding iron. Despite its vile purpose, the craftsmanship was undeniable. The handle was finely wrought, with intricate carvings of vines wrapping around it—no crude tool fashioned in haste or poverty.

"This work is costly. Commissioned, perhaps. Not the mark of any commoner seeking revenge against his neighbor."

John nodded slowly, his eyes falling upon the embroidered cross on Sir Galt's tunic, and then to the kettle again. The heat radiated faintly onto his boots, warming his calves. He could almost feel it on his own flesh, the hiss of iron searing into skin.

He gritted his teeth.

"What depravity," John muttered with tightened lips. "To bear such a thing with pride—and to wield it as if doing God's work."

George stood as he brushed debris and dirt from his knees.

"Aye. This is not the first time I've seen zeal twisted into cruelty, my lord. You know as well as I."

John did. The so-called "Holy War" had taught him that. He had seen "men of the Cross" butcher innocents with the same fervor as they raised their voices in prayer.

Faith and Honor.

The words felt even more distant now.

John ran his hand over his jaw, rough with stubble. He looked back to Galt's lifeless form—the man who had died unrepentant, proud of his work even as his life drained into the earth.

John stepped away from the body. He would carry this burden. He would uncover the truth. But he knew one thing already: if the Church believed this to be God's justice, then perhaps the Church had been misled.

He would defend his people. He would defend his land.

But was he willing to bear the cost?

"Gentlemen let's proceed to the castle at haste. Then, we shall decide on what to do next."

The men emerged from the chaotic scene to the outdoors, greeted by a gust of wind. Mounting their chargers, they advanced from the Purcell's at a modest trot, as Reggeye favored his wounded side and struggled to keep up.

"You'll be alright, lad," George smiled, as the squire cringed with pain.

"Well, George, your keen sense of observation remains unparalleled," John expressed, determined to make sense out of all that had transpired. "You make a fair point. Galt and his cohorts pose a mystery that demands solving. How does a renegade like him rally such a force? Their armor and weaponry suggest deep pockets, though where the funds came from remains unclear."

George pondered this with a raised brow.

"The Church has long meddled where they've no business. Might they truly play a large role in this? Might this truly be the work of the Inquisition? And what of our acquaintance De Montfort? Rumor holds Galt once rode with his lot while we were out in the Outremer."

John nodded slowly. "Both are lines worth pursuing. For now, we must keep our eyes and ears open for further clues. The truth is out there, we need only uncover it."

George held out Galt's ring, bearing the unmistakable de Montfort insignia and a Holy Warrior cross—a testament to Galt's participation in de Montfort's campaign in '04. John sighed with recognition. Reggeye remained silent, as if he knew his guilt could only grow with every word he might utter.

The forest itself was still.

The kind of stillness that bred unease. Not the peace of a gentle dusk, but the breath held before a storm.

Lord John tightened his grip on the reins. His eyes flicked toward George, who rode beside him. They had left the Purcell house behind, but the weight of what happened within those walls rode with them.

A man lay dead. A knight. Possibly an inquisitor. Killed not in the heat of battle, but on his knees, surrendering. Murder, in the eyes of the Church.

Reggeye had done it. The lad's sword had been sure, but

43

his hand had trembled after.

John glanced back. The squire rode a few paces behind. His face was pale, eyes forward, jaw tight. He had escorted his cousins home and now rejoined them on the path. The boy's shoulders were stiff—bearing the invisible yoke of what he had done.

The trees above them whispered with the evening wind.

John's mind whispered louder.

Sir Galt's blood would not dry quietly on those stones. The Church would see to that. A knight slain under their banner—by one of John's own. That would reach ears in cloisters and courts alike.

Penance. Excommunication. Worse.

He cursed under his breath.

A month ago, he had worried about the harvest. Now, it was his men's souls—and their heads.

His gaze turned forward again. The road wound toward Breckington. Home. But for how long?

Simon de Montfort.

The name continued to circle like a carrion bird. Once an ally at Acre. Now possibly tied to a hunter of heretics. Lord of Montfort-l'Amaury, and Earl of Leicester—at least in name. King John had stripped him of his lands in England. Montfort did not press his claim; he had what he wanted in France.

Yet his men had come here. To Breckington.

Why?

The Inquisition had stretched its hand far—across Languedoc, into the hearths of humble folk accused of believing differently from the common faith. But here? This was not the south of France. This was England. And still, they had come.

Had they verified this "heresy" in his lands? Or was it something else?

John rubbed his temple, feeling the ache creep in.

He needed answers. And he needed to survive long

enough to get them.

The path opened into a clearing. The manor's stone walls loomed in the distance ahead, comforting but fragile. Bobbeye, who had accomplished his task of escorting the Purcell girls to the manor, had ridden out to meet them.

"Bobbeye," John called out, his voice low. The squire halted his mount once he was within earshot.

"Milord?"

"Take James, Thomas, and Peter. Fetch Sir Galt's body. Treat him as a knight, whatever his end."

Bobbeye gave a slow nod. He understood. They all did. This was not merely about honor—it was to cool the blood of the Church.

"Yes, milord."

He spurred his horse back toward the Purcell home.

John exhaled. A small step. But the path was longer still.

Father Bartholomew.

The old priest had guided him since boyhood. The man knew both the ways of heaven and the weight of a sword. He would need him now.

Not just for counsel—but to stand before the Church when the questions came.

A crow cawed above. A harsh sound. Ominous.

John's knuckles whitened on the reins.

He had kept his land safe from bandits. From rival lords. Even from the crown's greed. But this—this was different.

The Church's reach was long.

And its grip was final.

The wind stirred again, carrying with it the faint, distant toll of the village chapel's bell.

A warning. Or a prayer?

John did not know.

But he pressed his heels to his horse and rode toward home.

Toward whatever came next.

The path grew darker, reflecting the dim uncertainty

which shrouded John's thoughts. A large critter jumped out of the bushes in front of his horse and scurried hastily across their path.

"Good heavens!" John exclaimed as the creature startled his horse. He half expected more of Galt's men coming out of the brush to ambush them. But the forest otherwise remained silent.

As soon as they could reach the safety of his castle's fortified walls, John intended to convene a meeting of his trusted knights and squires. For now, silence had become their companion, as even the trees seemed to have ears, waiting as if to hear more about the plight of Breckington's nobles.

John returned to his contemplation. He needed to know what to do next. Hugh and George rode beside him silently, understanding that their lord was in deep thought.

So, what can be done next? John thought.

Ignoring the situation as if nothing had happened would mean awaiting a Church inquiry, an unwanted situation wherein papal representatives would crawl over his lands, combing every nook and cranny for heretics and evidence of heretical teachings…all this after the inquiry would purge the nobles responsible for Galt's death.

Alternatively, the path of humility seemed more practical—an admission of responsibility, a groveling confession at the feet of the pope and his envoys. There was the chance, however, that penance could be refused, and the justice required would be Reggeye's life. The potential outcomes and consequences of the most recent sequence of events weighed heavily on the thoughts of the men, especially on the young squire, Reginald de Saint-Clair.

As they advanced the dense forest closed in around them, and Reggeye pondered his uncertain future, gazing upon the darkening trail ahead as if wondering whether the shadows would hold mercy or condemnation. The forest seemed to be filled with voices mocking him and his predicament.

Lord John, sensing the weight of the situation bearing heavily on the young squire, knew that immediate discussions with his vassals and his liege Lord de Redvers were imperative—he needed counsel and direction.

"George."

"Yes, milord John?"

"Follow up with Bobbeye and the men to ensure that Sir Galt is brought to Breckington and readied for burial. I'll make sure Father Bartholomew is informed he is to be given the proper rites as a priest and nobleman."

"Yes, milord."

"Afterward, I would like you gentlemen to meet me at my manor after dark. We must discuss this situation as soon as practicable."

George spurred his faithful steed, a sharp "*Hyah!*" leaving his lips as hooves tore at the earth in urgent flight toward Breckington's town. The galloping departure faded swiftly into silence, abandoned woods sighing lightly in the lull while the two men remaining found quiet breath.

John watched as his vassal rode off, his hand settling heavy upon the pommel of his blade, tightening with each thunderous heartbeat. He eyed Reggeye, the squire caught in the middle, who remained quiet and contemplative, as if pondering his ultimate fate.

John instantly felt for the lad. In fact, he felt for all his men and his subjects. The realization of what had occurred on this day bore down upon him, heavier still than plate and mail. In days past he had known only peace in his dominion. Now that calm hung by fraying threads, threatened by a coming storm.

The name of Pope Innocent III drifted like a dark omen across his thoughts. The Holy Father, whose wrath had toppled thrones and launched holy wars would now have him scrutinized.

And his sovereign King John - impulsive, perilous, ever grasping to fill depleted coffers with the lands of ruined vassals would be no help. Excommunication still lingered like a looming cloud above England, and Breckington now stood near the tempest's eye, vulnerable to the gale.

John felt his jaw clench fast. He had been content to rule as a lowly baron - distant from the intrigues of kings and prelates. His work had been here, among his folk - his people. Those who tilled his fields, who sought his judgment in disputes, who called on him for sheltering aid. He had granted them security; they had granted him their trust. That bond had built Breckington mightier than any wall of stone.

But now, the branding of innocent flesh threatened to break it all asunder.

The forest trail now slid into open fields. The breeze greeted them, bearing faint scents of damp grass and woodsmoke from a distant hamlet. Ahead, Breckington Manor rose atop a rocky crag, defiant against the encroaching dusk. Its stout walls caught the fading sunlight, a bastion of authority—or so it had always seemed. Today, John saw it differently. A refuge. A prize of hope.

He paused his mount at the clearing's edge.

"Go onward, Reggeye. I'll meet you at the castle."

The squire nodded.

"Yes, milord."

As his final companion rode off into the distance, John lingered beneath the boughs shadows, his breast tight. Counsel he required, though not from Redvers, or Bartholomew—nor even Hugh or George. Only the divine could direct his course.

Dismounting alone within the wood, damp earth cushioned his knees beside an elder tree's knotted roots. Bare palms pressed the soil that had been soaked by the blood of Sir Galt and his men, and the Purcell girls' tears, shaping the future of his precious land.

"Father, Son, and Holy Spirit..." his prayer but a whisper, trembling for strength, wisdom, and souls lost—with scars outlasting this day, for the living trusting his lead, and for a

48

strengthening of his faith borne hidden in his heart.

The leaves' rustling soothed his soul as Heaven seemed to hearken to the baron's appeal beneath the darkening green canopy. The peace he had desperately sought now eased him, and he buried his face in the ground, submitting to Divine fate.

::

The dying embers of the sun slid beyond the horizon, enveloping the landscape in dusk's cool veil. A faint chill crept amongst the trees and across the grassy slopes of Breckington. The forest whispered in the fading glow, a chorus of rustling leaves and birds calling from afar before roosting for the night. Hugh Philip, Hubert Roche, and George de Wymondham were returning from their grim errand of securing Sir Galt's body, their horses kicking up soft clumps of earth as they slowed at Breckington Manor's gates.

John observed their approach from the stone parapet above, his gaze fixed on their silhouettes against the darkening ground. Though modest compared to other great fortresses found throughout the realm, the castle stood like a sentinel atop its hill, a legacy of William the Conqueror who bequeathed it to John's ancestors—its walls withstanding rebellions in the early days of Norman rule, safeguarding the town below and surrounding barony. Today, however, it felt as though those walls would be powerless to stop the growing storm that approached.

As the men dismounted, John descended into the courtyard to greet them. The clink of stirrups, snorting of weary horses, crunch of boots on gravel—familiar sounds that usually brought comfort.

Tonight, however, they bore the weight of the day's grim deeds. Hubert led the horses to the stable, his usual jovial muttering absent. Hugh and George crossed the courtyard toward the main hall, their steps measured, shoulders heavy with the toll of their duties.

Deep within the fortress, the glow from torches danced upon cold stone walls. The scent of roasted meats and fresh breads wafted through the air, though faint against the lingering stench of blood upon their armor.

John removed his gloves slowly, stiff fingers struggling as his thoughts filled with tension. He took his seat at the head of the long table. Dishes clattered softly as a page delivered plates of food and wine—the dark red liquid resembling the stains under their nails.

Together the three men raised their goblets, voices low but resolute.

"Faith and Honor!"

The wine provided little relief from John's weariness. He set down his cup, eyes falling to the intricate designs carved into the wooden table. The squires ate at the far end of the table. Silence lingered, interrupted only by the crackling hearth. He breathed deeply as he summoned the energy to speak.

"Good men, brothers," John began, voice steady yet strained. "Today, we fought well and true."

George nodded solemnly.

"Aye, my lord, that we did."

"Indeed," Hugh added.

John exhaled softly, tracing the patterns on his cup's rim.

"Yet those we felled were no mere bandits. Sir Renhard Galt led them, an Inquisitor of the Church."

His words hung heavy in the air, foreboding as a curse.

John continued, brow furrowed.

"His purpose here remains unclear, except that it may have had something to do with heretics. Bailiff Lacey knew nothing of his arrival. No messenger came before to give warning. 'Tis as though he intended to pass through this land unseen—until Edwinson and his daughter crossed his dark path, their ledger his object of obsession."

The memory of their broken bodies flashed in his mind as he closed his eyes—Aerin's branded flesh, eyes frozen wide with terror. John attempted to push it away, but still it lingered at the edges of his thoughts.

"Justice had to be served for trespassing on our lands. Yet the Church sees their rules as above our own," said John with a solemn sigh. "They may view this differently than we do."

He turned to George with an inquisitive look.

"You bore witness to the end. Pray tell what more you saw than I."

George leaned back wearily, pouring himself more wine. He drank deeply before speaking, wiping his mouth on his sleeve.

"We tracked the fugitive north, following clues past Fitzsimon's farm. The family pointed him to the Purcells, oblivious to his motives. We hurried on."

George tapped restless fingers, reliving each moment.

"When we arrived...screams pierced the air. Reggeye rushed in first, I close behind. Sir Galt was binding the Purcell sisters, the hot iron already scarring their skin. Their cries..." His voice caught in his throat.

John clenched the armrest tight, envisioning the brand's glow and recalling the smell of burning flesh.

George steadied himself.

"Reggeye lost control. He charged without thought. Galt met his fury blade for blade, he was no novice with a sword. I called strategies to Reggeye through his rage..."

A faint smile crossed George's face as he paused to take another gulp. The fire crackled low in the hearth, casting long shadows that danced across the stone walls with each flicker and pop. The lingering scent of roasted hog mingled heavily in the air with the rich damp earth carried in on the evening breeze drifting in from the courtyard.

"In the end, Reggeye pushed too eagerly forward, overextended beyond recovery. Galt seized the opening without hesitation, caught him unprepared along the side,"

George recalled, voice steady but underlaid with lingering remorse. "Reggeye fell. I interceded promptly, challenged Galt directly to single combat then. Bobbeye remained behind to attend to the lad before running off to summon Lord John."

Hugh refilled his cup before emitting a short bark of mirthful laughter.

"I see you've trained your man well, George. He'll learn in time. Future Galts would do well to be wary."

George smiled grimly but his eyes remained grave.

"The lad has heart, Hugh, if yet inexperienced. Anyway, Galt sought to delay me by tossing a table across my path. I leapt over it cleanly and closed the distance between us without pause. We clashed fiercely. Though skilled—measured and precise—Galt stumbled where I did not. Yield he did in the end."

John leaned back pensively, fingers tented under his chin as if hearing the ring of steel in George's voice, feeling the mounting tension of that scene, the Purcell girls' screams fading but not yet forgotten in his mind.

George's tone darkened further.

"He was surrendering to me his weapon, my lord, when Reggeye... came from nowhere suddenly. Before I could stop him, he drove his blade deep into Galt's unprotected side."

John exhaled slowly, his eyes dropping down to the crackling fireplace.

"I arrived soon after Bobbeye's summons. Galt was fading fast, but he spoke enough. His mission here was apparent. He was hunting heretics," he said grimly.

The word hung heavy in the air, as foreboding as a curse.

Hugh's brow furrowed deeply as he set his goblet down with force.

"Heretics? Do we harbor such deviants within our walls, my lord? Should the village priest, Father Bartholomew, be alerted?"

John's gaze hardened like steel.

"Not a word of this leaves these grounds. Whether by design or carelessness, Galt acted without informing the local clergy. We took them for simple brigands as they gave us no cause to assume otherwise."

George scowled darkly.

"They brought this fate upon themselves. What authority have they to meddle in our domain?"

Hugh shot him a piercing look. "They operate under God's mandate, George. They have authority that grants them dominion over all men."

John sensed the rising discord and raised a hand for calm.

"Regardless, we have a quandary, my brothers. Rumors will spread of our killing an Inquisitor. King John cares little for the pope, but the local lords revere the Church. Our lands, our titles—all could be at stake if this is discovered," he warned gravely.

Silence fell upon the room, broken only by the soft crackle of the fireplace. Servants brought more platters of pork and fresh bread. The aroma stirred hunger within, but the gravity of their discussion tempered their appetites.

Hugh leaned forward, his brow creased in thought.

"We should seek counsel from Father Bartholomew. He is measured in his judgments, my lord. He may help us navigate this without inviting the full wrath of the Church upon our heads."

George, pacing restlessly, paused.

"Bartholomew? He lives robed as a priest. He answers to his superiors. You believe he won't report this?"

Hugh met his gaze steadily, calm but resolute.

"It has to be reported, George. Word of what happened will spread anyway. Besides, Father Barth knows this land. He knows these people. He knows our lord. He would pursue peace, not ruin."

John studied their words with care, seeking wisdom from both men.

"George, what counsel would you offer?"

George halted and turned to John directly.

"De Redvers, my lord. As your liege, his voice carries influence in court and with our clergy. If any can shelter us, it is he."

Hugh leaned forward.

"Yet what if he deems us a liability? What if he sacrifices us to safeguard his standing?"

George rebutted, "And what if Bartholomew betrays us the moment he is told?"

John raised his hand once more.

"Enough. Each route holds risk. But we will not sit idle while danger circles around us."

He rose, his voice filled with the authority of leadership.

"We will confer with Bartholomew initially. He is near, and his guidance may shape our next step. We will also inform my liege De Redvers. He will need to be apprised of this matter."

George nodded, though his lips were tight.

"As you command, my lord."

Hugh inclined his head respectfully.

"A prudent plan, my lord."

John rested his palms on the table, leaning in slightly.

"George, dispatch for Father Bartholomew. He will meet us here come the morrow. And Hugh, draft a letter to the earl."

George met his eyes, the weight of responsibility settling upon him.

"As you wish, my lord. Let us hope this path leads us to safety, not ruin."

He paused for a moment.

John gazed into the fire once more, its embers flickering faintly—like the fragile peace of Breckington.

"If it leads to ruin, George, it will not be for lack of trying," John replied as he ascended from his seat, a tone of resolute determination resonating in his voice. "As it has been decided, we shall now get our rest. At the break of dawn, Hugh shall ride to Tiverton to bring our letter and convene with Sir William."

Turning his gaze towards George, John continued, "You, my stalwart companion, will summon Father Barth to me and then arrange for Sir Galt's interment and delegate the burial of the other unfortunate souls to Bailiff Lacey's men. Enough death has befallen upon our lands this day. Gentlemen?"

Until this moment, the squires ate in silence, listening intently to their overlords discuss the day's event. It was not that they were prohibited from speaking, but that they were all exhausted from all that had recently transpired. Along with Hugh and George they stood in unison, and together they elevated their goblets, uttering in harmonious accord, "Faith and Honor!" before savoring the final remnants of the libation. The lateness of the hour had signaled the cessation of their day's endeavors. John, weary and prepared to conclude the day's affairs, was eager to retire.

Moments later, after seeing his vassals and servants off, he finally found solace within the confines of his chambers. His personal page, Benjamin, had departed with his armor and vestments for cleansing and refurbishment come the morning. A tumultuous day had transpired, and exhaustion had set in. He wished to resolve the dilemma he faced, yet fatigue won over his concerns as he slumped upon his bed, yearning for rest. With eyelids closing, he succumbed to the embrace of a deep slumber, leaving the trials of the day behind in favor of the realm of dreams.

Confession

May 3rd, 1209 AD

Shire of Devon, England

raucous crow's cry shattered the dawn's stillness. John stirred awake as pale light probed through the narrow window. Cool morning air washed over his hastily roused form. Though the hour was early, he found no peace in slumber's embrace. Duty called, and with it, the ghosts of yesterday.

Recollections clung to his restless mind—shaking voices, pleading eyes filled with fear. The Purcell girls, clutching each other. The memories of the event gripped his pounding heart as tightly as the frigid stones clutched last night's chill. No fire could thaw the ice in his veins nor the weight in his weary bones. Reality set in—calamity was at the door. He needed to act.

Time dragged its feet, each moment an eternity. John stood, steadying himself with a trembling hand. The moment of reckoning was nigh, however much he wished to flee its call.

Confession. *Absolution.*

He wanted to seek solace in a familiar presence, one who had comforted him through loss and guided him through growth. But could even he lift the burden he now bore? Doubt seeped into once sturdy trust as shadows lengthened in a world grown darker than he knew.

Father Barth.

If only he could stay in bed forever. Still, duty drove him from his bed with practiced purpose. Though his blade now felt as a bitter comfort, its weight could not steel his wavering resolve nor still the turbulence within. One task remained before facing his fate—a summons to the sole soul who knew not the tempest raging within his composed mind.

"Ben."

The name tumbled from chapped lips in a rasp, calling the eager page to ready for the task ahead, so he could gain counsel for whatever the future may hold.

"Send for Father Bartholomew. Tell him I require his presence urgently."

The boy lingered a moment but offered no reply, only a nod.

"Inform him he will find me in prayer within the chapel."

Silent acknowledgment, then soft steps faded into morning halls.

Alone again with his turbulent thoughts, John exhaled slowly. Unburdening his soul to God, perhaps salvation might be found.

But would confession restore what was lost? Ease aching memories? Would penance be granted for such a great misfortune?

Outside, life proceeded as usual—voices and footfalls in corridors, the manor awakening to routine.

Not for Aerin, her mortal days now stilled.

Not for Edwinson, the merchant whose jovial presence would no longer grace these halls.

They had not been strangers passing through—they had been part of Breckington's pulse.

Edwinson, with his wine-laden stories and laughter that disarmed even dour knights. His trade kept the barony fed through lean winters, yes—but more than that, he was trusted. Valued. John remembered long evenings by the hearth, charting safe roads through turbulent lands.

And Aerin...

A life too brief. All of fourteen years, it was not long ago she once ran across the courtyard barefoot as a young girl six springs ago, arms full of wildflowers for her lord.

Her joy was disarming, pure. She'd tug on John's glove and ask if he truly wore a sword to dinner, eyes wide as the sky.

He had sworn to keep them safe.

Now they were gone.

Not in the clamor of war, but in the silence of a road where help came too late.

What is the worth of a sword, if it comes too late...

Leaving his chambers heavy with the memories and regret, John walked the familiar path toward solace—or at least, some semblance of it.

Brisk air sharper than expected greeted the courtyard. Damp grass and moss between cobblestone softened footsteps. Smoke from the forge mingled with lingering woodsmoke on the breeze. In the stable, horses stirred as dogs barked beyond the walls.

So much existence surrounded him, yet he never felt so alone. So helpless.

Entering the chapel, shadows shifted as candles flickered in the dim stillness. The mingled scents of wax and damp stone soothed as much as stirred.

John moved quietly over stone polished by centuries of

prayer, his gaze finding Christ's visage upon the altar.

That placid expression had long forced upon him an unsettled quiet contemplation. This Christ on the crucifix, serene even in torment, at peace though His flesh was rent? Or was there some deeper meaning that eluded his understanding?

Through narrow openings, a flowing draft sighed like faraway voices, rippling candle flames and altering shadows across the walls. John shivered, crossing himself to seek solace on his knees as stone leached warmth from him.

The expression sculpted upon the crucifix unsettled him even deeper than before. It shouldn't have, for he had studied that divine face for years in contemplation. But something seemed changed this dawn, stirring sentiments unfamiliar.

The suffering depicted was plain—wounds wept crimson down the emaciated flesh, thorns tore into the skin above those eyes. Yet within those painted eyes dwelt not agony but peace, and upon those lips not a grimace but calm acceptance. John's breathing slowed as understanding blossomed.

No person smiles in the face of demise or embraces implements of torment. No one welcomes the executioner's tool so willingly—at least, not logically.

And yet the Son of Man did so, not in joy or derangement, but in resolute purpose. The priests' sermons of sacrifice and salvation through suffering, the burdens shouldered so others may walk unfettered, echoed in John's thoughts.

Often did Father Barth discuss how a man must know his calling and tread the path set before him, however steep, as Christ had with His mission. Until now John had never questioned.

But his ruminations turned instead to another—not the Son but a daughter named *Aerin*. A father named *Edwinson*. The horror in the girl's open eyes and blood upon her throat haunted him.

She had accepted no fate, simply been taken against her

will.

Faith, honor, duty—these words felt hollow against the image of a girl who had asked no martyrdom. Christ chose His cross while Aerin had not choice at all.

A prayer or plea—he knew not which as questions churned without answer.

"Give me strength to forgive, Lord..."

Aerin's pale, open-eyed face intruded once more, her throat slit, chest branded. Edwinson's broken body, frail in age, yet ravaged by sword.

He squeezed his eyes closed, yet the image lingered still. The scent of blood, clinging within his nostrils. The cries of his men as they charged, seeking to exact justice. The crackling flames from Galt's branding iron. The piercing screams of young girls. The Purcell girls.

He forced himself to calm his breathing.

Faith and honor.

Words which had guided his entire life. Yet where was the honor in this?

The Church preached love and mercy. Still men like Galt bore the cross while burning human flesh.

His father Sir Roland had once knelt here on this very spot as well. Had he, too, wrestled with similar doubts? Had he the same contemplations as he gazed upon the solemn sight of a crucified Christ?

John imagined Arsuf. The Saracen blades. The Crusader's banner waving high over blood-soaked sand.

Faith and honor.

Did Roland ever wonder if it had all been worthwhile? Or had he merely accepted it as his duty?

John pressed his palms into his thighs.

The stone below seemed to pulse—as if the earth remembered the dead buried within its soil.

He opened his eyes once more. The sculpture stared back, unchanged. Christ's smile remained.

A soft set of footsteps at the entryway took his attention.

John sharply turned his head.

Father Bartholomew's silhouette, stooped and cloaked with staff in hand. He stepped inside.

Warm eyes peered out from under heavy brows, lines deeply etched into his face—years spent listening to sins heavier than his frail shoulders could bear.

"My son," Barth's voice was gentle yet worn. "You called for me."

John stood slowly, muscles stiff from kneeling for so long.

He met the old man's gaze. Words fought to escape—like stones lodged in his throat.

He wished to tell him everything. About Galt. The ledger. Aerin's branded corpse. Edwinson's broken body. The tortuous ordeal of the Purcell girls. The stain on his lands. The Church which he had served, and the fear gnawing at his gut.

Yet when his lips parted—Only four words came out.

"I need your counsel."

The priest nodded, understanding more than the words. He always did.

Bartholomew stepped further into the candlelight. Their shadows joined on the stone wall.

And John realized—He was not sure if he sought forgiveness…Or permission.

John knelt. A gesture of deep respect.

The old priest sighed.

"Stand up, son." Barth's voice carried the weight of years, steady, firm. "These gestures are meaningless. Haven't I taught you anything?"

John hesitated, then pushed himself to his feet.

"I bow before the king, Father. I surely should be able to bow before you."

Barth scoffed, shaking his head. "Yes, but the king commands your feudal allegiance. You owe nothing to me, as you go straight to God."

A hand on John's shoulder. Light. Reassuring.

"I am but God's humble servant, to serve others and not to be served." A pause. "Come, let us walk."

John exhaled. The old man always knew when a chamber felt too confining.

They stepped outside. The air had warmed since dawn, but the chill of morning still clung to the earth. Dew lingered on the grass, glistening in thin patches of sunlight breaking through the courtyard trees. A soft breeze stirred the branches.

The sounds of the manor carried in the distance—clattering pots from the kitchens, the rhythmic hammering of the blacksmith, the murmuring voices of servants going about their duties. But here, beneath the trees, it was quiet.

Barth walked slow, staff tapping against the earth.

"I perceive that troubled brow, young man," his voice was gentle, yet knowing. "A great and heavy trouble has settled upon your shoulders."

John hesitated. Then spoke.

"You may have already heard whispers, Father," he took a measured breath, "that yesterday, we encountered a group we believed to be common brigands—assailants of a merchant caravan. We fought. We won."

He paused.

"But they were not brigands."

Barth's steps slowed.

"They were the retinue of an inquisitor," John continued, his voice tight.

"A man named Sir Renhard Galt."

The priest frowned. A deep frown, one that carved lines further into his weathered face. His hands clasped around his prayer beads, fingers moving idly over them.

"Renhard Galt…" he murmured. "The name does not stir familiarity in my ears. Yet there are many such men these days, rising to prominence, each eager to wield the sword of righteousness."

John exhaled, jaw tightening.

"He bore no noble standard, but his colors were regal—purple and somber gray. His emblem was peculiar. A dragon, pierced by a sword."

Barth halted. His expression darkened.

"The dragon pierced by a sword," he repeated, voice lower now, weighted with meaning. "That is not an idle emblem, my son. It evokes the iconography of Saint George, the patron saint of soldiers, and the eternal triumph of virtue over evil."

John studied him.

"St. George?"

"The knight who slew the dragon," Barth nodded. "You know the tale. A beast terrorizing a town, demanding human sacrifice. A hero who vanquishes it, delivering the people from fear. His victory became a symbol of Christian valor, the triumph of good over evil, the defense of the innocent."

John's voice became mournful as he spoke.

"And yet, in this case, the emblem is borne by a man who slaughtered innocents, claiming them as heretics."

Barth's expression grew grim.

"Such is the danger of zeal untempered by wisdom."

He sighed.

"For an inquisitor to adopt this symbol… it suggests he sees himself as a modern-day St. George, slaying the 'dragons' of heresy."

His eyes flicked to John.

"It is both fitting… and troubling."

John's fingers twitched at his side.

"Galt was no mere knight. He once served alongside Sir Simon de Montfort."

A flicker of recognition passed over Barth's face.

"Simon de Montfort? The erstwhile Earl of Leicester? Renowned for his loyalty to the Church?"

John nodded.

"The very same. But while de Montfort wields his fervor

with precision, Galt wields his like a hammer. His every action betrays arrogance and pride."

Barth's lips pressed together, the lines on his face deepening.

"The emblem of St. George carries deeper significance than mere external victory over evil, my son."

John furrowed his brow as Barth continued.

"It is a reminder of the darkness within each soul. In our quest to vanquish external evils, we risk becoming the dragons we fight."

John pondered this as Barth explained how Galt saw himself as righteousness incarnate:

"With unflinching certainty, he uses faith to excuse any action, no matter how cruel. But to truly follow God is to first confront one's demons."

Barth met John's troubled gaze as he continued.

"Men of Galt's ilk believe themselves hands of providence. Yet more often than not, it is pride and hubris that guides their hands."

John looked away into the trees, deep in thought. Sunlight danced upon the forest floor. After a long silence, he spoke quietly:

"For all his brutality, Galt's eternal fate will be no different than any man's."

Barth smiled sadly.

"Perhaps. But tread carefully, my son. Those who share Galt's conviction seldom walk alone. There are forces you will face that will cause you to tremble."

The austere cleric's eyes scanned the horizon, his expression inscrutable.

"The shadow of the dragon stretches far. And those who cloak ambition as principle are most dangerous of all. This, I fear, drives his campaign against heresy."

More quiet followed before John asked the question weighing on them both.

"Where do you stand on this, Father? Should such

heretics face persecution?"

The priest's expression became contemplative as he looked up at a high window, his eyes searching the sky.

"In all my years," he said softly, "immersed in prayer and Scripture... I've never found cause for believers in Christ to hold others to the flame for their convictions."

His gaze met John's.

John's eyes froze in recollection. He could still remember the smell of burning flesh—impossible to forget as it lingered, even many moments after the fact. He did not witness the event, but he could imagine the hiss of searing iron. The girls' screams. His jaw tightened. He forced himself to meet Barth's eyes.

The old priest's gaze was steady. Kind. But there was a steely resolve beneath it.

"Men can burn bodies, John. But only God judges souls."

The words landed like a stone on John's chest. He opened his mouth, then paused. He licked his dry lips.

"Then why burn bodies at all, Father?" His voice was quieter than he intended.

Barth sighed, his hand brushing across the beads at his waist.

"For crimes against man—murder, theft—there must be punishment. Justice," his eyes softened. "But I reckon God is able to handle crimes against Himself."

John inhaled slowly. Relief. Like a cool stream washing over fevered skin. He nodded, once. The tension in his shoulders eased—slightly.

This was why he came to Barth. Always.

The old man was more than his confessor. He was his anchor. His guide through the tangle of faith and duty.

"I've gleaned much wisdom from you, Father," John's voice was low, sincere. "Thank you. I'm grateful I confess to you... rather than the rector at Plympton. I might be chained in the tower by now—branded as a heretic's ally."

Barth chuckled, the sound warm, like the crackle of

hearth fire.

"Indeed, that would be likely."

A pause as Barth's eyes softened.

"But recite the scripture, John. From the Gospel."

The words were already forming on John's tongue. Together, their voices rose—low, steady, familiar:

"*Non enim misit Deus Filium suum in mundum ut judicet mundum, sed ut salvetur mundus per ipsum*...For God sent not his Son into the world to condemn the world, but that the world through him might be saved."

The Latin rolled over his tongue—eased by practiced memory. The cadence of Mass. They were part of the whispered prayers of his youth. Familiar. Comforting. Unchanging.

John closed his eyes for a heartbeat. Relief. As though those ancient words themselves carried enough weight to lift his burden.

The weight on John's chest loosened. Like stepping into sunlight after days beneath storm clouds. *This* was faith.

Not the brands. Not the blood. Not the terror.

This.

"I presume not all of de Montfort's retinue survived?" the priest asked, moving out in the courtyard toward the shade of a tree.

The sun had risen now—its heat creeping into the courtyard. The grass smelled fresh, damp with morning dew, but already drying under the light.

John followed, boots pressing lightly onto the cobblestone.

"None, Father," he answered. "They bore no identifiable banner. We believed them brigands. We dealt with them… summarily."

He hesitated. Then—

"Only later did we learn who they were."

Barth made the sign of the cross. His lips moved—silent words. A prayer. When he raised his head, there was no judgment. Only weariness.

"Such is the nature of your duty, my son."

Barth paused. Then he continued.

"And this Inquisitor… Sir Galt? What of him?"

John's fingers curled at his side.

"Deceased, Father. Slain by de Saint-Clair. An outburst of rage."

Barth's brow lifted, faintly.

"Your men are disciplined. Why such violence from this young man?"

John's throat tightened.

"He saw his young cousins… suffering at Galt's hands," the words came slowly. "Bound. Branded as heretics."

Barth's breath caught. His face darkened with sorrow—then, concern.

"This is concerning, John."

There was a pause.

"That we harbor supposed heretics, Father?" John's brow curled.

The priest stepped closer. His voice dropped to a near whisper.

"No," His eyes searched the courtyard—checking for ears, "but that papal agents seek out heresy in our land without informing the local lord. You. Without informing me, the parish priest."

John stiffened. Barth's eyes were sharp now.

"It means they do not trust us."

The words hit harder than John expected.

Suspicion. From the Church. Against Breckington. He hadn't thought of that. He should have. He swallowed.

"I pray you do not misconstrue my words," Barth raised a hand. "You know my loyalty lies with God and His Church."

His voice was firm but heavy as he continued.

"Yet… I cannot help but ponder if His Holiness concerns himself too much with earthly borders. With land. With power."

The wind stirred the leaves overhead. A branch creaked. Barth's eyes softened again and he continued.

"These matters yield more bloodshed... not less."

John let the words settle. The doubt in his own heart—spoken aloud now by his priest.

"What course of action should we pursue then, Father?" His voice was low. "When this reaches Rome, the threat of excommunication will loom over me. Over Breckington."

Barth's hand closed around his beads.

"Fret not about that, my son." His smile was faint, but sure. "I shall handle it. A miscommunication. A tragedy. There will be penance, perhaps... but I will plead for mercy."

John exhaled—another wave of relief.

Barth gestured toward a servant standing at the edge of the courtyard, head bowed, waiting.

"Breakfast awaits," The old man smiled, but his eyes remained shadowed. "Let us speak of lighter things while we still can."

John nodded. No more words. At least, for a while.

Together, they stepped into the manor hall.

Warmth met them. The kind that softened the edges of a hard day—firelight licking across stone walls, torches sputtering gently, their glow casting restless shadows that danced across the timber beams overhead.

Thin rays of sunlight sliced through narrow slits in the stone, catching the dust that hung like faint mist in the air.

The scent of roasted pork—fat sizzling, crackling skin—mingled with the yeasty sweetness of fresh bread. Apples, sliced, resting in bowls alongside wildberries, their juices staining the wood beneath them. Mead. The sharp tang of cider.

A feast. A comfort.

But John's gut was still tight.

The weight of the day clung to him still—the blood, the

brands, Aerin's lifeless eyes. Wouldn't go away.

Barth's robe brushed against his arm as they sat.

The old priest sighed, folding his hands, eyes flicking over John like a physician reading the lines of a wound. He would try.

The silence stretched.

Then Barth smiled—soft, knowing.

"Do you remember, my lord," his tone lighter now, playful, "when old Tom Fletcher tried his hand at brewing cider for last year's harvest festival?"

John gazed into the hearth, brow furrowed in thought.

Barth's grin widened as he spoke.

"They said his brew was so fiercely potent that even the hardiest men feared a second sip!"

The memory surfaced in John's mind—a small flame amidst the chill.

"I recall it well," he murmured. "The poor man was so embarrassed he vowed to never brew again, claiming he'd leave it to the inn's ale."

Barth chuckled heartily, like sparks crackling to life on the fire.

"A prudent choice, I'd say. Though some insisted it was the finest night of rest they'd had in years."

The tightness in John's chest loosened—if only slightly.

Barth leaned in closer, eyes gleaming with amusement.

"Then there was young Maud's sheep! Her sheep became the talk of town. Did you catch wind of that tale?"

John shook his head, curiousity fighting against his gloomy mood.

"No, I have not heard of the tale. What of the sheep, Father?"

Barth's voice dropped, low and conspiratorial for theatrical effect.

"Her prized ewe wandered into the churchyard... during morning prayers. Just as I read from the Gospel, the beast let out a bleat—loud enough to wake the dead. Sent the choirboys into a fit of laughter."

John let out a breath—a chuckle, unbidden.

"And what did you do?"

Barth raised his hands, mock defeat.

"What could I do? Sent the boys after it, of course. Though, I suspect they took their time… enjoying the chase. Poor Maud was beside herself later—claimed the ewe had a devil's will. I was inclined to agree."

John laughed. A proper laugh this time. Short, but real. The shadows seemed to shrink back from the hall's edges. Barth pressed on—sensing the small victory.

"The bountiful barley harvest this season, Humphrey claims, surpasses any yield in the past two decades. Meanwhile, young Alan from the bordering village boasts that his orchard has borne fruit twice over. A prosperous gathering, to be sure—a divine blessing seldom seen."

John exhaled slowly and smiled, though its comfort wavered as he spoke.

"If only peace could flourish as freely as golden grain and crimson apples. Alas, such tranquility feels tenuous as morning mist, ever drifting beyond our grasp."

Barth's visage softened as he leaned near, his hand—steady and comforting—enveloping John's broad shoulder.

"Take solace that for this moment, at least, our thoughts drift freely, unhindered by strife. Let joy, however transient, buoy our spirits on the winds of time."

The words sank deep into silence. Hope, though fragile, began to blossom anew.

John held his gaze. Then, he nodded. The tension in his chest loosened—though it did not leave. The meal continued—laughter woven through talk of harvests, weddings, and quarrels over grazing lands. Familiar names. Familiar troubles. The hum of ordinary life.

For a while, it drowned out the screams that echoed in his mind. But beneath the warmth—beneath the bread, the cider, and the stories—John knew. The fire had not gone out. It smoldered. Beyond these walls. Beyond this meal. The shadow of yesterday stretched long into tomorrow.

::

The shadow of Tiverton Castle fell away rapidly behind him. Sir Hugh rode hard. Warm air clung to his skin—thick with the scent of wildflowers, sweet and heavy, tangled with the damp musk of freshly tilled earth. Life waking. Blooming.

But his chest was tight. *Cold.*

The earl's words still rang in his ears—sharp, like steel scraping stone.

It had not gone well.

He swung into the saddle with the ease of habit, but his hand trembled against the reins. His bay snorted—ears flicking back, sensing the weight in his rider's body. Hugh glanced once over his shoulder.

The earl's castle loomed in his view—stone walls kissed by the late afternoon sun, golden and proud.

But beauty was no comfort.

Not now.

He dug his heels in.

"*Hyah!*"

Hooves struck the dirt—hard and sure. The wind bit his face as they surged forward at a gallop. Fields stretched out ahead—green spilling into yellow, gentle slopes dotted with grazing sheep, and smoke rising from distant cottages. Hedgerows lined the road, their leaves whispering as the breeze stirred them.

Birdsong flitted above. The low hum of bees drifted from the blossoms. The faint call of farmhands, laughter carried over the fields. All of it—life, ordinary and good.

But Hugh heard none of it. Felt none of it.

His eyes stayed focused on the road—narrow, winding. Every hoofbeat felt too long.

Sweat traced down his temple—salt on his lips. Not from the heat. The chill in his chest only deepened.

Time is running out.

It was slipping. Slipping fast.

Whatever followed him from Tiverton would not wait. His grip tightened on the reins. He pressed his mount harder, hooves pounding, rhythm quickening.

Breckington. I need to reach Breckington.

He had to reach Breckington—before it was too late.

::

The sun crept toward its zenith. Heat thickened in the air, settling over the manor courtyard like a heavy cloak. The faint hum of insects drifted on the breeze, mixing with the distant clatter of hooves from the stables.

John and Father Barth walked slowly beneath the shade of an elm in the courtyard, their pace unhurried, their talk wandering.

Old stories. Old laughter.

Fragments of youth—when John had been no more than a stripling under his father's roof, learning duty, learning swordsmanship. And learning from Barth… the gentler lessons. Lessons of faith. Lessons of compassion.

The world had been simpler then. Or so it seemed now.

Barth smiled, eyes crinkling at the corners, the warmth of familiarity softening his words.

"My lord, it brings joy to converse about those times. You were but a stripling then—and behold how you've flourished in both stature and wisdom."

He sighed, his voice lowering as he continued, "Regrettably, the demands of our roles seldom afford us such leisure as times like this."

John nodded, the corner of his mouth lifting faintly.

"Indeed, Father. Despite our frequent crossings, meaningful conversations elude us. I appreciate your swift

72

response to my summons."

"Naturally, my lord," Barth said, his hand brushing across the beads at his waist. "Uncommon are the instances when a grave matter such as this beckons. I am honored to lend my assistance in any way possible."

John felt the weight of gratitude pressing behind his ribs.

"Thank you, Father."

The old priest's eyes glimmered—mirth flickering behind them.

"Recall when you were sixteen, and Lord Devon convened that assembly of local nobles?"

Barth's tone shifted, playful now as he continued.

"I urged you to engage with the young ladies, and your reluctance was quite amusing," He chuckled softly. "yet there was one damsel who caught your eye. I often pondered why it never developed further than it did. I think you remember her? Adelinda was her name."

John's step slowed.

Adelinda.

The name struck like a pebble rippling across still water—disturbing what had long settled.

She appeared to him—like in a sudden vision—sunlight on auburn hair, eyes bright with mischief, a laugh that had made his chest ache even then, though he had not known why.

He forced a smile as he looked longingly into the distance. Of course he remembered her. He had never forgotten, only set her aside as she seemed forever lost, yet his heart could never totally let go.

"She was a delightful maiden, Father. However, I was… unprepared for romantic entanglements, and so our paths diverged."

His gaze shifted downward, to the dirt beneath his boots.

"I held an extreme fondness for her."

He paused.

"It was an unfortunate loss for me when she left."

And then… *Mary*. John felt his jaw tighten.

"The following year, I found myself betrothed to Mary," he continued, voice harder now. "Swiftly wed. Earl Devon deemed the familial alliance advantageous."

He exhaled sharply through his nose.

"Alas… she proved to be a most wretched woman."

Barth gave a knowing nod, his face darkening with shared memory.

"Ah, Mary de Dustanville," he said softly in response. "That union was ill-fated. She lacked piety and brought turmoil into your life." His voice dropped lower. "The annulment—granted upon the revelation of her infidelity—was a providential relief. I was pleased to facilitate it."

John said nothing.

But his mind wandered—despite himself.

Dustanville. That name. That house.

He saw it—Dustanville Manor, proud atop rolling hills, surrounded by meadows and hedgerows. Built with stone and pride. A symbol of new wealth, new power, clawing its place among older names like his own.

Sir Reginald de Dustanville—Mary's grandsire—had earned his knighthood at Acre and Arsuf, standing with King Richard's vanguard, shoulder to shoulder with John's own father. Warriors baptized in blood under the Lionheart's banner.

John had admired the old knight. Respected him.

But the son—Sir William—had inherited more ambition than wisdom. Under King John's reign, William had maneuvered well, expanding lands, strengthening his grip through marriages and gold.

Then came Mary. The daughter. The alliance. The union that should have strengthened both houses.

But she had been like a poison wrapped in silk.

Her beauty had turned heads at court, but behind closed doors—venom. Sharp-tongued. Deceitful. Her eyes always sought something beyond him. Some other conquest. Some other advantage.

The whispers had come quickly.

Adulteress. Schemer.

The scorn of other nobles. John's name dragged through it all. He clenched his teeth.

Henry de Dustanville—her brother—had taken it as a personal affront. Blamed John for the rumors.

Trial by combat. That had been his demand.

John still remembered the heat in Henry's eyes—that thirst for blood masked as honor. They were close to clashing swords.

But the Earl of Devon had intervened. Ordered peace. Reconciliation. Smothering the feud before it could spark into fire.

Still… the bitterness lingered.

For Henry. For John. For everyone.

And "Wretched Mary"—that name had followed her. Lingered in the mouths of servants. A jest in the market. A cautionary tale for young men.

A curse.

Barth's voice brought him back.

"You ponder, my son," the priest said gently, reading his silence.

John exhaled, the air heavy with the scents of hay and smoke drifting from the nearby kitchens.

"I was not made for vengeance, Father," he murmured. "But I wasted too many years with that woman. And too many more carrying the weight of her sins."

Barth nodded, understanding in his eyes.

"Some burdens we choose," he said quietly. "Others… are placed upon us."

John glanced toward the horizon—where Breckington fields met the sky, golden under the sun's height.

Adelinda.

Mary de Dustanville.

All woven like a tenacious thread deep into the fabric of

his life.

Threads that still pulled—some with warmth, others with pain. He looked back at Barth, forcing a small smile.

"But I am here. And I endure."

The priest returned the smile, faint but proud.

"That you do, John. That you do."

He was lost to thought, however, reaching into the recesses of his mind, to the past, to a love that he once thought would last forever.

Adelinda.

The name lingered—like the faint trace of lavender after a woman leaves a room.

She had always carried that scent. Or so he thought. Or perhaps he had imagined it—woven it into memory because he needed something to hold onto after she was gone.

John's fingers traced the rim of his cup. The warmth of mead had long faded, but he held it still.

"I often ponder what became of Adelinda, Father," his voice was low, almost cautious—as though speaking her name aloud might stir the past from its grave. "She possessed the loveliest eyes, and her smile was akin to the morning dew after a cold, arid night."

The words came unbidden, but once they were spoken, he felt them settle. Real. Tangible.

That smile—soft, uncertain at first—had bloomed into laughter. He had thought he would spend his life chasing that sound.

But she had vanished. Leaving only silence. Barth said nothing.

But John felt the priest watching—measuring the weight of his words, the ache beneath them. Barth had seen it all. Had blessed their courtship. Had nearly bound them together before fate had taken her from him.

She had been his future once. Before Mary. Before war. Before blood and brands. John had buried that future beneath duty. Beneath the years.

But now…now he wondered. Where had she gone? Did she think of him still?

Barth shifted in his seat. His knuckles brushed the beads at his waist. A hesitation. A deep breath.

Then—

"My son… If it is Adelinda you seek, I happen to know where she is. In fact, she's living in—"

The words stopped. Interrupted.

There was a shout.

Sharp. Cutting through the quiet like a blade.

John's head snapped up. His heart leapt—trained to react before thought.

Boots thundered across stone. Metal clanged—men moving fast. Voices overlapping. *Urgent.*

John pushed back from the table, the bench scraping against the floor. His hand found his sword belt as he strode toward the hall's open door.

Barth followed, robes catching on the threshold.

The manor's great hall opened eastward into the inner yard, a sun-drenched rectangle framed by barracks to the west and the chapel to the south. A stable clung to the wall near the gate. Stone steps rose to the north wall—where the tower overlooked the valley like a sentry of old memory.

Sunlight struck hard—blinding, after the dim hall.

John squinted. The courtyard buzzed with activity—guards moving swiftly, hands on weapons, faces taut with readiness.

The heat was stronger now. The air thick with the scent of dust and sweat.

Above them, a figure on the northern wall—outlined against the sky—waved his arm frantically.

"My lord!"

The voice rang out—sharp, clear over the commotion.

"A company approaches from the north! Three banners. Spearmen and men-at-arms!"

John's chest tightened.

The warmth of Adelinda's memory evaporated—like dew under the sun. For now.

He crossed the courtyard quickly, past a row of younger squires struggling into mail beside the well. The oval footprint of the manor, designed long ago to cradle the hilltop like a helm, funneled sound upward as he climbed.

His hand gripped the cold hilt as he scrambled up the stone steps—each fall of his foot a reminder not only of the urgency to meet his fate but of the grim tally awaiting him below. At the pinnacle, the panoramic sweep of Devon's rolling hills offered no comfort today—only a stark panorama of what he had sworn to defend. His eyes roamed over the vast expanse and then fell on the approaching host, still quite a distance, yet starkly visible in the clear day: a swirling mass in a familiar yellow, their banners dancing like wild omens in the wind.

As the army crested a barren hill in the distance, an azure lion on a golden field caught his gaze on their largest banner, confirming his dread. Three banners in total. Three hundred warriors—mostly spearmen—charging as though the very earth had split. John's pulse thundered in his ears as he recalled the meager strength of his own garrison: barely thirty armed men, perhaps twenty more if the servants joined in defense. Should the Earl of Devon choose to besiege, Breckington's walls would be assailed by forces nearly tenfold his number.

A rider approached. Familiar. Friendly. Perhaps a good hour ahead of the incoming formation of footmen in the far distance, who marched slowly.

With a steadying breath, John bellowed, "Unbar the gates!" and the guards moved with disciplined haste.

Moments later, Sir Hugh Philip burst into the courtyard, his steed's hooves drumming the earth in a rapid cadence, his eyes carrying the hard lessons of many battles.

"Bar the gates!" John commanded, and within seconds, the lofty gates closed shut.

Sir Hugh scaled the steps to the parapet and bowed low before John and Father Barth.

"My lord. Father," came his measured greeting.

John's voice, firm yet laced with worry, cut through the tension as recognized whose army approached.

"Sir Hugh, tell me—what are the Earl's intentions? Is he poised to strike, or is this merely a grand display?"

Hugh's reply was calm but edged with urgency:

"I delivered our account, my lord, every detail laid bare. Sir William soon mustered his men. As you already know, they are a league behind me, marching on our humble castle. I know not their intentions."

Father Barth, his tone soft as a murmur amid the storm, interjected, "I suspect it is but a show of strength—a display of unwavering loyalty to the church, not an all-out assault against a vassal."

It was both a prayer and a hope. Perhaps driven by wild desperation. But hope could be a powerful thing.

The approaching army was formidable, no doubt comprised of Tiverton's finest. What they intended to do, however, was unclear.

John watched as the Devonshire footmen marched in formation to form a perfect semi-circle at the base of the castle hill. John's thoughts raced: if war broke out, his scant numbers would be overwhelmed by the tidal force of three hundred men. Every heartbeat hammered home the reality of his fragile defense, a burden he carried with both dread and determination.

However, he knew that he could still mount a formidable resistance with the handful of men he had, and since the Earl had no siege equipment, even ladders, they could hold out for days, even weeks until they brought some in.

But he would prefer that it did not come to that.

Then, like a clarion call from destiny, four knights clad in resplendent Devon armor burst through the formation, their visors raised in heraldic salute.

"Lord Breckington! Your liege lord demands your immediate audience for a matter grave beyond words!" their booming voices declared.

"John, open your gates!"

A jolt of recognition and old memories surged through John as that familiar, commanding tone echoed—a voice from his mentor's past. With a nod, he signaled the gates to swing open. Gesturing to the gate guards, John signaled for them to swing the gates open. Four knights adorned in the heraldic hues of yellow with a red boar symbol traversed the threshold, dismounting in the courtyard. John instructed his pages to aid them, and with measured steps, he and his companions descended the stone steps.

De Redvers, a graying man of fifty-seven, removed his helmet and greaves, relinquishing them along with his weapons belt to an attending page. Possessing an aura of commanding authority, the earl stood tall and formidable as John approached. His hair and beard were a silvery white hue which spoke to his wisdom as an aged and experienced nobleman.

"My Lord Devon," John spoke, dipping his head with a humble bow. "Your presence brings honor to Breckington Manor."

"Sir John. Father Bartholomew," de Redvers acknowledged with a nod. "Shall we delve into matters within your hall?"

"Aye, milord," John responded, lifting his gaze. "Follow me."

Pages scurried, chairs were hastily cleared, and John led de Redvers—an elder with silvered hair and the weight of history in his gaze—into the hall. On one side sat Baldwin de Morain and Owain Fitzroy, Norman Knights of rapport, and then Peter Drake, a scion of an ancient Saxon noble house, seated themselves on one side of the table. On the other, John was accompanied by Father Barth and Sir Hugh, while his squires, Tom and Jamey, stood sentinel on either side of the hallway entrance.

John's thoughts, fragile as a dropped apple blossom in frost, swayed—diplomacy's tender hope against the cold, iron truth of his uncertain future. His heartbeat, soft and insistent, echoed like a foretelling wind. Breckington's fate—held in each bated breath—hung, trembling on the edge of destiny.

A heavy sigh.

The creak of old armor, a low groan as De Redvers sank back into his seat. His face bore the weight of irritation—or was it irritation? He didn't look furious. Simply *annoyed*.

John sat composed, drawing solace from the steady presence of Hugh and Father Barth, the murmur of their quiet support like a gentle breeze in a storm. Minutes stretched, thick as dusk, until De Redvers inhaled deeply, breaking the silence.

"This news is dire, John. Dire indeed," the earl declared, his voice rough with vexation.

"I understand, my lord."

A pause—a measured break—before the earl continued, turning to John.

"I do not blame you, my son. My own men could have done the same thing. Yet, this incident places me in a precarious position. Father Godwin, our rector at Tiverton was present when your messenger, Sir Hugh, informed me of yesterday's events, and he demanded I take immediate action against you."

The sound of his hand ruffling his trimmed beard echoed like leaves in a restless wind.

"Having known Sir Renhard Galt personally, Godwin insisted upon accompanying me here today. Only upon the sight of me assembling my men did he desist, trusting me to resolve this matter with you—by force if necessary."

Or perhaps the plump priest did not want to be bothered to travel, John laughed internally.

"My lord, with your indulgence," interjected Father

81

Barth, his tone soft yet firm. De Redvers motioned for the priest to speak further.

"Lord Breckington sought my counsel with utmost haste. His men knew not that the company they waylaid was a mission sanctioned by the Church. This was merely a lamentable lack of communication—a circumstance oft encountered in the course of such events."

A skeptical sigh, then a forward lean as the earl addressed the gathered assembly.

"I was but ten winters, Father, when I became aware of the slaying of Thomas Becket, the Archbishop of Canterbury. Though youthful, I grasped that the ensuing political tumult could have plunged the English monarchy into ruin. I am well acquainted with the dire consequences of secular potentates meddling in ecclesiastical affairs. Once tidings of Sir Galt's death reach the ears of Pope Innocent, we shall fall under an interdict, perhaps even the dread of excommunication," he pronounced, concern etched on every line of his face.

"Indeed, my lord, such dire prospects loom on the horizon. Yet, allow me to dispatch a missive to the emissaries of His Holiness to temper the brewing tempest," Bartholomew proposed, his words falling like measured drops in a vast, unsettled sea. "Assuredly, they shall seek a visible act of contrition, and, in our deliberations, Sir John has unequivocally expressed his willingness, along with his men, to humbly acquiesce and submit themselves to penance here."

A sudden firmness gripped the earl, as a ripple of discontent flashed across his face.

"No, that shan't suffice. Not to contradict your counsel, Father. But the rector Godwin will not be appeased with such gestures. Nothing short of Lord Breckington's personal appearance before His Holiness or one of his legates will satisfy him. You may accompany him if you wish, but a personal appearance is imperative."

"My lord, I am bound to my pastoral duties," Bartholomew contended, his voice low and resolute. "To abandon my flock for an extended sojourn is beyond contemplation."

A still, heavy moment, then the earl's voice cut through with finality.

"In that case, John shall go. Swiftly. Those are my terms, and I shall withdraw my forces from these walls. What say you, John?"

John pursed his lips—a brief, hard silence—then spoke with quiet determination.

"I shall embark on the journey and prostrate myself before His Holiness or one of his representatives," he declared. "Hugh will oversee the governance of Breckington during my absence. Father Bartholomew shall remain to shepherd his flock. George will accompany me, alongside Reggeye, who must undergo a penance of due humility for his deeds."

Father Bartholomew cleared his throat, leaning forward once more.

"If I may, my Lord Devon—before Sir John embarks, it would be wise to consult with His Grace Bishop Raymond of Brest. He is of considerable stature among the Gallican clergy and maintains cordial ties with the Roman Curia."

De Redvers raised an eyebrow, intrigued.

"The Breton bishop?"

"Aye," the priest replied. "He may offer counsel—or at the least, a formal letter of passage and instruction to gain favor before an audience can be secured."

John nodded, understanding the weight of ecclesiastical intermediaries.

"I shall make for Brest, then," he said. "And from there… to Rome, or as Providence directs."

Silence fell, deep and brooding, until the earl's laughter burst forth like a sudden summer storm, his palm slamming upon the table with force.

"By the saints, that's my young lad! Have I not imparted wisdom unto you? Diplomacy, you wield it with care. Yet, reserve it, for strength's visage must adorn you, especially 'gainst a foe as indomitable as the Church, my son. In such encounters, victory is a prospect that is ever elusive, slipping through fingers like grains of sand."

"The Church seeks not victory in a contest, my lord," Father Barth protested, his tone ringing with fervor.

"Ha! Speak such sentiments to your superiors, priest. The Church's grip on state matters is firm, yet it leans on the arm of the state to enforce its bidding," retorted his Grace, a scowl carving deep lines upon his face. "And due to these intricate maneuvers, my vassal John here, shall embark on penance for this...unfortunate mishap. Now that accord is reached, shall we?"

A rustle, then a murmured agreement as Sir William rose, and the others followed. The earl downed the rest of his wine, then slammed his goblet with a final, echoing thud.

"Oh, and John, my men crave sustenance. Provisions for fifteen-score men, I presume?" he inquired, a wry smile playing on his lips. "Consider it a penance...towards your liege lord."

"We shall procure them at once, my Lord Earl."

"Well said. Now, at first light, set forth to Rome. A two fortnight's journey at speed. Once this lamentable affair is behind us, we shall all draw breaths more tranquil."

John bowed deeply, his heart a mixture of duty and resignation.

"Yes, my Lord Devon. May God speed your homeward journey."

And as the company filed out of the hall, the heavy air shifted—tension giving way to a fragile relief. The matter, as dire as it was, found a temporary reprieve in the soft glow of shared understanding.

Much worse, so much worse, could have been.

A cringe. A shudder.

Especially if that fat rector Godwin were there—John's thoughts churned bitterly. The sound of his own heartbeat, heavy with dread. *No doubt that clumsy priest would have goaded the earl to attack me.* His breathing slowed as relief began to rush over him.

But the attack never came.

Oh, the relief.

A slow, exhaled release. Lord John felt it—the weight lifted, if only slightly—as Sir William's once stern gaze softened, exchanging an expression that believed in his fealty.

Father Bartholomew, Breckington's steadfast pillar of wisdom, remained unmoved outwardly—a mask of serene composure. Yet beneath his priestly veneer, a subtle tremor of concern was discernable. It was still far from over. Around him, the Breckington nobles—tired eyes and cautious smiles—exchanged relieved glances as they began the mundane rituals of preparing to feed the earl's entourage; the clatter of cutlery, the murmured rustle of busy servants. But the stores of the castle would not be enough for the men outside.

Then out of the hall Sir Hugh approached his lord, as if stepping out of a veil of uncertainty with quiet clarity in his eyes, his voice but a silent whisper.

"You navigated those treacherous waters well, my lord. The earl may be hard-nosed, but he admires reason. You have spared us from a direct conflict with the earldom."

John nodded more out of reflex, as both relief and anxiety flooded him—making every breath a combination of hope and dread. One difficulty overcome, yet so many more to face. The road to Rome stretched out long before him, filled with the unknown and the uncertainty of the penance that the Church would undoubtably require. The weight of his barony, of duty, bore down on his chest, heavy, stifling. Uncomfortable. Yet, it was not an impossible burden. He only needed to tread wisely.

Sir William nodded in silent salute, his eyes coming to rest on the huddled Breckington faces, staring somberly before them. With a subtle gesture, he signaled his Devon knights to follow him; the procession wound its way back near the gate, where John's pages—swift as whispered gossip—returned the knights' gear, readying the horses.

Outside, loyal Breckington men stood sentinel as their liege lord, the Earl of Devon and his retinue, rode through the castle gates. The figures receded down the hill, shrinking into the distance like fading echoes and disappearing into the mass of the earl's golden-clad soldiers below.

"Hugh," John called, relief clear in his tone, "Ride into town and instruct the food market to ready provisions for fifteen-score men. Ensure the merchants are duly compensated from our coffers."

"As you command, my lord," came Hugh's prompt reply as he mounted his horse with practiced ease. In a blink, he galloped through the gate, down the hill, his hooves drumming a fervent beat—drawing cheers from the Devon spearmen as he sped toward the town of Breckington, a league away.

Father Barth approached then, standing quietly beside Lord John, arms folded, eyes following Sir Hugh's retreating figure. In the hushed atmosphere, Barth's wry tone broke the stillness:

"Well, that's one way to feed an army. Do it at the expense of your vassal."

John turned, a fragile smile playing on his lips, and murmured, "Would you care to trade places, Father? You be the baron, and I'll be the cleric."

"Not a chance, my son," Barth laughed softly, turning toward the chapel as if preferring to return to the warmth of familiar prayers and lit candles.

::

A hush fell over the dew damp meadows as the ink black night eased quietly into a subtle dawn.

Unusually cold. Yet the crispness of the air was satisfying.

A cool breath wisped softly through the tall grass, stirring secrets in its wake. Behind a gauzy veil, the ancient verdant hills of Devon stirred from slumber, every blade of grass and sigh of wind whispering tales from times past.

George de Wymondham stood steadfast at his post, eyes like dark still pools taking in the growing light. His keen gaze scanned the mist shrouded horizon, as he stood to fulfill his loyal duty as the first rays of light breached the eastern sky.

He gently coaxed his steed into readiness—a beast both patient and sure, its flanks heavy with humble treasures.

Three loaves of coarse bread, a water-filled leather pouch, spare garments neatly bundled—a motley offering for the long road ahead.

Reginald, the faithful squire, clutched his own burden: Additional supplies—tents for shelter, extra rations to stave off hunger, and tools that promised the prospect of survival. Yet beneath the surface, wounds old and new still gnawed at Reginald, his battered shield bearing scars from arrows near Acre in his youth. Though those battles steeled his arm, his heart still quaked from the fear and guilt of slaying Renhard Galt in cold blood. After all, it was that momentous decision that embarked them on this path to seek redemption.

What perils would they meet upon the road? Would any of them live to see home again? Such thoughts preoccupied the young squire and troubled him deeply.

Meanwhile, John meticulously readied himself, but no preparation could calm his nerves. Hopes and doubts warred against each other in his mind. His being skilled in stratagem and combat would not be of help in his desire to foresee what fate was held in store for them beyond his castle's walls. He had packed for a sojourn of four weeks, yet a secret yearning pulsed within him for a swifter journey—two weeks, if fortune permitted passage by sea.

In his simple, unadorned attire—a dark blue Breckington gambeson paired with sturdy leather boots—he wore his heraldry proudly.

On his tunic were thirteen azure roundels, arranged like scattered droplets of a long-forgotten rain, gracing upon a bright yellow field.

Above them, a yellow lion rampant as if it were roaring without sound, a dramatic herald of the de Ontivero legacy that bound him to both faith and honor.

The early morn was a canvas of fragmented moments of both joy and anxiety.

It is time.

A nod from John, and the sentry understood his assignment.

A slow creak of the monumental gates at Breckington Manor. And then, the gates swung open and the trio—baron, knight, and squire—unshackled from the familiar, galloping down the hill.

Their descent exploded into a burst of rhythm: the pounding of hooves, the rustle of wind flowing through tattered cloaks, and the murmur of anxious countenances.

They were bound for Sutton, known to the locals as "Plym Mouth," where the river Plym, in a lover's embrace with the sea, promised passage to lands not so familiar.

After the journey of an hour, the ocean awaited—a vast, shimmering promise, blue and infinite, stretching to the horizon.

There, upon a barge, they would leave behind the green embrace of Devon towards the port of Brest to gather provisions and then venturing further inland, toward an unknown fate, not unlike a moth fluttering against the looming light of Rome and as the morning brightened to full daylight, the road they galloped upon became a pathway to hopes and hidden terrors.

The path through town and into the southern woods was worn by many feet, but each step was laden with more uncertainty.

A heavy tension hung in the air—a silent companion that tightened their chests and whispered of dangers lurking beyond every bend.

Inside each rider beat a heart heavy with trepidation. There was no guarantee of a happy outcome. The prospect of presenting themselves before Pope Innocent—the highest authority in the Church—loomed like an increasingly darkening storm.

They had never trodden as uncertain a pilgrimage such as this before, and though hardened veterans of the Holy Wars, the anxiety could not be quenched.

A fear of the divine judgment lingered, of the depth penance that might be required, a fear that made Reginald's pulse race and made even the storied George de Wymondham, a doubter, buckle at the knees. This was the effect of the terrifying power of the Church.

Reginald's shield, bearing battle scars unrepaired, became more than a mark of past strife—it was a mirror of his inner turmoil, the battle within to still his soul.

Every indentation, every scratch left by arrows years ago, spoke to his angst and begged the pressing question:

What do they think of me at the Vatican? Was I considered a fugitive fleeing justice? A heretic worthy of condemnation? Undoubtedly a slayer of inquisitors.

Merely the consideration of facing the pontiff or his legates to admit to such a vile act was so overwhelming that it churned his stomach. Indeed, there upon his mount he did retch, violently, startling his horse mid-gallop and causing it to buck for an instant. Elsewhere life and peril remained relentlessly busy. Travelers crowded the road to Sutton more than they did in the secluded trails of their own fiefdom, many with stony faces that seemed to know the knights had committed some unspeakable sin and were riding headlong toward an inescapable fate.

Or perhaps it was simply an unrelenting yet unfounded distrust of anything, a sentiment borne of the recent events.

Sutton, a bustling port of trade, now became the crossroad of hope and uncertainty. What lay beyond they could only guess. They were no strangers to travel, having campaigned all the way to the Outremer. But it was not simply an unfamiliarity of the land that was so disconcerting and concerning, but rather the oppressive pall of the tightening grip of ecclesiastical authority. At any moment they could be identified as fugitives. George knew the French lands more than the other two, and he knew of the rumors that swirled like autumn leaves—whispers of bandits lurking in the woods, rogue knights who roamed the shadows and soldiers of fortune, looking to make coin from a sudden thrust of a dagger.

Yet, amid their dread, there remained a fierce, defiant determination that preserved their spirits.

Each breath became a vow to seek redemption, to brave the perilous unknowns ahead of them. Even as the world around them bristled with the murmur of danger, the trio clung to that single, steadfast flame of resolve. It was all they had left.

Will it be enough?

John's eyes, though clouded with uncertainly, burnt with the fierce desire for absolution. Every mile they rode was a step toward a future yet uncharted—a future where perhaps the weight of sin might be lifted, where the promise of penance offers a balm for their weary souls.

The journey to Rome was not merely a passage through lands but a pilgrimage of penance into the depths of their faith—a test of loyalty and of the strength of their convictions. George, of course, was exempt in terms of faith; John knew his loyalty was reserved solely for his brothers, for John—his lord—and for his men, especially for the young Reggeye, whom he would never abandon.

The horses, their steadfast companions, carried them over fields where the dew still clung like ships to the sea. The air, crisp and saturated with the scent of wildflowers and fresh earth, brushed against their faces, sometimes soothing, other times a stark reminder of the transient beauties—and dangers—of life.

Every gust of wind, every flicker of a shadow beneath the ancient trees, spoke to them with cheer and mystery, reminding them that the uncertainties were simply a part of living—but this realization gave only a slight relief. In those moments, the landscape shifted—a sudden rustle—a branch snapping underfoot—made them grip their reins tighter.

Jumpy.

Even the horses knew the danger that would be ever near, even this close to home. Who knew of their quandary? How many papal agents were on this road? How many were trained in inquisition? In assassination?

As the day marched on, they reduced their speed to give relief to their horses. The sun climbed higher in the sky, and the gentle warmth began to banish the early chill, and their thoughts turn inward.

What if the papal judgment was too harsh? What if their sins, both old and new, demanded a penance too heavy for them to bear?

They knew the answers to such questions would be given none too soon. John just hated the feeling of helplessness. Yet he knew that patience was the key—to their survival, if nothing else.

::

A hush.

A shudder of cold as Hugh Philip clung to the ramparts of Breckington Manor, his eyes wandering over endless, dew-dappled fields. Then the sound of heavy wood—a thud, then a slam—echoed from the gates where his lord and his two attendants had vanished into the morning mist.

Silence.

His heartbeat slowed. In that quiet, a weight fell—the somber mantle of responsibility pressed against Hugh's mind, as the felt the burden of leadership seeping deep into his bones. His world was once confined, his own lands were all he knew. The occasional patrols with Lord John broke the monotony.

Now before him unraveled the vast barony sprawled in all its wildness. Untamed fields and forests teemed with dangers, also with possibilities. The scent of challenge hung heavy on the crisp morning air. The possibilities abounded though fear and uncertainty lurked near. He breathed in deep the mingled scents of the fields, of nature's bounty yet untapped. This vast untamed realm called to his adventurous spirit. Perhaps he would use this as an opportunity to visit every yard of the barony, a task he had once challenged himself with but never attained.

The challenges looming before him were as numerous as the leaves on the trees that surrounded the keep. He worried for his friend and lord. For now, he was the man in charge. Yet this opportunity felt hollow and even distasteful with the absence of his liege.

Yet all was not doom and gloom. A bright future could still lay ahead.

He was determined to stay positive and commit himself fully to his task. It would not be easy.

There were many forces working against him. The earl? His spies were everywhere. Perhaps waiting for the slightest mishap as an excuse to descend upon the barony and eliminate it altogether.

King John, whose eyes were like that of a bird-of-prey, looking to confiscate lands of disloyal lords. Perhaps he had agents watching him as well.

The memories of the previous day lingered: the charge, the cries of men as they were cut down, Edwinson's and

Aerin's lifeless bodies...

Then the sting—learning of Sir Galt's identity had cut through him like an unexpected chill. Then there was the fallout...he could imagine the subtle murmur of scheming nobles and prelates. There was Godwin—the steadfast cleric of Tiverton, his voice clanging like steel on the anvil of inquisition and heresy—reminding him that the earl's retribution would be fierce.

Devon's finest were sent as a show of force against his lord, and now, Breckington's future hung in the balance.

John had set off for Rome. Now, under de Redvers' unblinking gaze, every misstep might ignite a chain reaction. The fragile peace of Breckington dangled by a mere thread, ready to crumble like dry earth if the pope, in a twist of fate, denied an audience—or worse, excommunicated his lord.

True loyalty burned inside Hugh. He would never consider being in a plot to unseat his friend. Yet the thought flickered in his mind: if John's mission failed, the Earl of Devon might seize the barony or even offer it to Hugh. Tempting. He was not one to deny it. Yet he discarded that prospect with a firm shake of his head.

The next task was clear. He must ride into town. The scent of damp stone and cold earth urged him onward as he prepared to meet Father Barth. Lord John had decreed that the fallen inquisitor be laid to rest in the crypt of Barth's church, dedicated to St. Michael—a delicate, symbolic act to soothe both de Redvers and Rector Godwin. Hugh was to oversee the burial. Later, Fathers Godwin and Barth would join him. John had arranged for no extra witnesses. Even Godwin had agreed, though his tone had been edged with reluctance.

The dawn broke pale and uncertain, matching the heaviness in Hugh's heart as he descended into the courtyard. He continued his contemplation of the recent situation.

There was a careful avoidance of scandal, deliberate and

cool. De Redvers—the earl wanted order. A calm, fragile order, its mechanisms kept hidden from the public eye.

It was a duty to be fulfilled. The earl had marched on his vassal—silent, reserved. The message came across loud and clear. John understood the assignment. Sir Galt's death? A travesty kept secret until John could meet the pope—or a legate.

Danger. There was always danger. Public revelation could shatter realms. Lands would tremble on the edge of chaos.

Hugh felt a heavy knot growing in his chest. Complexity crawled like damp ivy over everything.

His decision was simple: keep one step ahead. One thing at a time. Ride to the town church. Seek solace in prayer. Find his clarity in whispered words. And a conversation with Father Barth, before rector Godwin's arrival. Then, perhaps Sir Galt's soul could have rest.

A diligent page arrived. Hugh's mount was readied in moments. The ground split under the hooves of his charger as he galloped out the manor gates, his duty beckoning.

Then—a pause. A lone monk emerged on the dusty road. Younger than Barth, leaner than Godwin.

A distinctive tonsure. Sunken cheeks. A mystery walking closer.

Hugh reined in. His horse neighed loudly as it reared up before settling down before the traveler.

"Greetings, brother monk. How may I be of service unto you?" inquired the knight.

"Good morrow, sir! I seek Lord John Breckington. Are you him?" responded the monk.

"Nay, but I am his envoy and vassal, Hugh Phillip. At this moment, my lord baron is distant from the barony due to an urgent matter and shall not return perchance for at least four fortnights."

"Ah, I see. Then I have matters to discuss with you, good sir."

"Very well, shall we journey together to the town and deliberate at the local inn?"

"I prefer the sanctity of God's abode, Sir Hugh."

"Of course, brother—"

"Peter. Peter of Vaux-de-Cernay."

The monk turned to change direction towards town.

"Brother Peter, then. You seem far from your home. I have heard tell of your Abbey in France. Perhaps on our way into town, you can enlighten me about why you are here?" inquired Hugh, urging his steed forward at a slow trot to match his guest's paces.

"I shall, good sir, once we find ourselves within the sacred walls. For now, I wish to offer my prayers."

Hugh nodded, though his eyes narrowed ever so slightly—annoyance simmering beneath calm. His mount trotted steadily beside the newcomer as they quietly slid into Breckington—buzzing, alive, quaint.

Stalls and markets were bustling with vendors pushing fresh produce, butchers' meat glistening under the morning light. The laugher of children, familiar and melodious, flowed over the noise of business. Business as usual, even though their lord had left them. Hugh's large stature always brought a commanding presence when he entered town. Respectful nods from the townsfolk. Faces, fleeting yet kind.

St. Michael's Church loomed ahead—simple stone, weathered gray. A lone bell in a humble belfry. A steeple stretching high, modest yet proud.

Once, opulence reigned here—tapestries, gilded splendor, a glow too bright. But Father Barth had it all stripped away. All that excess gold and ostentatious display of jewels, given to the needy. He taugh true worship, pure and simple, a rarity amongst the clergy of the day.

The previous baron Sir Roland once craved grandeur. Yet over time he softened his views on the matter. Barth's teachings, which had influenced Sir Roland had also seeped into young John's heart—service and modesty over wealth.

Integrity and honor over opulence.

And the young Hugh?

Devout as ever, never missing Sunday mass, even when a fever burned, he went, accompanied by his loyal squires.

Sir George, though... his faith was a quieter murmur, spoken only rarely, perhaps even non-existent.

Approaching the church grounds, Brother Peter bowed deeply, crossed himself before stepping into the empty sanctuary. Latin prayers he whispered on his lips, the words soft and steady. Hugh dismounted and entered. He knelt. The two souls in quiet devotion, the silence facilitating a deeper contemplation on things divine.

Time stretched for what seemed like an eternity—a long, hushed hour of prayer. Then, Brother Peter arose, a disquieting concern etched on his face. Sunlight filtered through stained glass, scattering a flutter of colors across the cold stone floor. Hugh caught the monk's look—it was an expression of worry and he had a hunch that something was amiss.

The tension thickened as the two men faced each other in the hallowed quiet. In that stillness, Brother Peter cleared his throat, ready at last to reveal his quest.

A breath—sharp, desperate.

"Sir Hugh, I pray you be of urgent help to me," Peter's voice trembled, pulling the air tight. A flash—a realization too late. Hugh's face betrayed him, an involuntary twitch. So, this was what Peter meant.

"So, you do know of this knight? He traveled with a troop of footmen. Sir Renhard Galt is his name. He is my kin, a cousin of mine," the monk continued, his voice laden with concern. Galt's name clung to the air, overburdening Hugh with sudden unease. The monk's worry deepened at his expression.

"He was supposed to meet me in Sutton yesterday," Peter murmured. "But he never arrived. Not him. Not any of them. It's…unusual. Not like him."

Sweat beaded, cold against Hugh's skin. The truth was there—strained, and Hugh knew that the monk knew it was ready to spill. But not here. Not yet. He swallowed, clearing his throat, buying time to think.

Breathe.

Breathe. Delay.

He just needed time. Just enough to think of something. Anything. Then—footsteps. Drawing near. Two figures, rising from the crypt stairs—a murmur became audible, a conversation confined. Fathers Barth and Godwin—unaware of their presence, lost in their talk as they emerged, oblivious to the confrontation above. Father Barth saw him first.

"Ah, Sir Hugh," Barth began, "We've prepared the body of the Inquisitor for burial, and..." His voice trailed off as he detected something amiss.

Hugh's wide-eyed panic met Barth's eyes too late. A slip. A crack. The secret had been spilled into the open, the floodgates opened wide.

Peter's jaw dropped—agape, shocked at what he had just heard.

"The body—of the—Inquisitor?" Peter's voice quivered, his fear blossoming.

"Yes, well... the knight..." Barth's words tangled, still unsure, his hand gestures chaotic.

Hugh's breath hitched, as he panicked internally. Peter's face grew pale in horror. Inquisitor? To be buried?

Godwin smirked—eyes lighting up with sick amusement as he realized what was transpiring. Peter's feet moved, slow, deliberate as he backed up. His lips were trembling.

"Who—who is this Inquisitor?" he demanded. His body continued to move, drawn toward the crypt, dread creeping in.

"Father Barth! Get him to stop!" Hugh's whisper—frenzied, hushed, but frantic.

Barth looked at him, confused.

"Who is he?"

The words sputtered out the priest's mouth as he stared at Hugh, eyebrows furrowed.

"He's from Vaux-de-Cernay! Galt's kin! He's been searching for him!"

Barth's realization came late—much too late.

"Not good," Barth muttered.

"Not good at all!" Hugh spat.

But the monk was already halfway down the stairs, dreading what he was about to find. Father Barth was a beat too slow, his feet scrambling after him.

Thump. Thump.

Godwin and Sir Hugh followed, hearts pounding in the silence, uncertain of what would come next.

A flicker.

It was dim. But not much more could be expected with only two torches and a dozen candles lighting the crypt, the reflections of the flames dancing on the cold stone walls. The crypt opened—a silent gallery of tombs. Two were for the old priests of St. Michael's. Simple, austere wooden caskets with engraved symbols of piety.

Towards the western wall elaborate stone sarcophagi held generations of Breckington's nobility.

At the north end, quiet and solemn, lay the grandparents of Lord John—Gerald and Joan de Ontivero, side by side, their rest separated by only two years. Nearby, their son, Sir Roland II de Ontivero, John's own father, found his eternal repose within stone.

Closer now, Hugh saw the monk, Peter, standing near the body of Sir Renhard Galt—shocked, trembling. His body was racked with sobs as he shook with grief.

Hugh stopped. He felt for the grieving man.

Peter's hands shook; his eyes brimmed with tears. Godwin had descended casually, standing beside the grieving monk, his face continuing to sport that irritating smirk.

His harsh whisper cut through the silence.

"Good brother, he is with the Lord now," Godwin declared, his high-pitched tone aggravating every bone in Hugh's body.

Silence.

Then, a heart-wrenching cry pierced through the quiet.

"My dear cousin! My God, what has befallen him?" Peter moaned, his gaze shifting, pleading for answers, "sickness? Accident? Murder?"

A single word from the calculating rector. Cold, cutting. Godwin's answer, whispered like a chill wind: "murder."

Hugh stood frozen, his mouth agape in disbelief at Godwin's candid revelation. The abrupt and forthright reply caught him off guard. While he didn't expect a cleric to lie, he anticipated a more tactful, perhaps more nuanced response, especially in light of the earl's desire to maintain secrecy. Glancing at Father Barth, he saw a similar incredulity in his expression.

Cramped and dim.

It felt even more so at this moment. Especially so if one was of his height and build.

Sir Hugh Phillip stood as if carved from the stone itself—unyielding on the surface, while inside his heart trembled with desperate restraint. The cold air, heavy with the scent of wet stone and mildew, seemed to press in on him. This would be a critical moment. One that could shape the entire future of these lands.

Across from him in the shadowed vault, Peter of Vaux-de-Cernay advanced, wild-eyed and burning with a grief which had now twisted into a rage. His voice, hewn with grief and anger, shattered the stillness:

"Who… who did this?"

Godwin, seeing his chance, revealed the truth in a low, sinister voice:

"It was one of Lord Breckington's men, brother."

So, the fat rector is eager to win favor with his betters,

Hugh simmered within as he gritted his teeth in silent frustration.

Peter exploded in fury as he spun toward Hugh, his tone a mighty thunderclap that one could imagine it awakening the dead within.

"Who!? You and your men did this? For what reason? He was hunting heretics!"

Hugh's mind raced with thoughts: duty, honor, and the desperation to calm the situation. As much as they had tried, the secret was now out in the open. The Church would know of this deed much sooner than they had hoped. Worse, the aggrieved monk was now in a violent mood.

Atop Sir Galt's body lay his sword in a knightly pose. With one swift move Peter had it in hand, approaching Hugh with murderous intent.

Hugh shook his head in disbelief. Would a man of the cloth dare to challenge a veteran knight in combat?

He raised his blade in an attempt to intercept the attack. The monk would not be trained. The sword should have been heavy in his hand.

"Hold," Hugh pleaded, his voice strained with desperation, "it is not as you presume, brother."

Hugh feared not for himself, but for the greater scandal that would occur should he slay the young priest. Peter, consumed by a torrent of grief and wrath, continued to advance with relentless anger.

"No! Justice demands retribution!" he roared, swinging his sword with terrible determination.

A desperate voice then cut through the melee—Father Barth's strained interjection:

"Woah, woah, there, brother! Let us parley—no need for further bloodshed!"

Yet Peter's eyes, aflame with loss, fixed on Hugh with accusing intensity.

"You and your men!" he spat, every word dripping with bitterness, "How could you have robbed him of his life?"

The clang of steel against steel became a dissonant chorus of violence that echoed within the crypt. Hugh's heart pounded like a war drum, his internal faculties screaming for him to restrain. Amid the violent exchange of parries and thrusts, his mind fragmented: *I must hold this line—if I fail to restrain, all honor will be lost.*

"Brother, listen to reason!" Hugh called out again, voice echoing desperately against the ancient walls. "Let us talk!"

But Peter's grief-fueled assault did not waver.

"No! I will avenge my kin!" he bellowed, his voice raw with fury as his sword sliced through the cold, damp air.

In that crucial moment, every sensory detail—each spark of clashing steel, each breath of exertion—seemed to etch out the inevitability of disaster into the very walls of the crypt. Hugh's gaze darted from the furious monk to the indifferent, ancient stone, feeling as though the scandal was a living thing, ready to shatter the fragile peace. He sprung from stone pillar to stone pillar, skillfully using them as bulwarks against Peter's furious strikes.

One thing was for sure, this monk was more trained that he thought. Did they train their monks in combat at Vaux-de-Cernay? Peter seemed too young to have had a prior life as a soldier.

"Hold! It is not as you presume, brother!" Hugh tried one more time, his plea echoing, a final, desperate bid for sanity amid the growing chaos. Yet the storm of Peter's wrath surged on, threatening to engulf them both in its irreversible tide. Sir Hugh Phillip was left caught between the duty to defend the barony from further scandal and his moral obligation to leave the monk unharmed.

In the dim crypt, Sir Hugh was incredulous at the scene before him—a cleric, a man of the cloth, apparently well-trained in the art of war. It was more than an unsettling sight, this was a perverse twist in what he once believed to be the gentle, pious character of the Church.

No, he was no stranger to politics. The Church often

involved itself in matters of civil affairs.

Perhaps he was used to the martial clerics under chainmail and iron helmets. The Templars. The Hospitallers.

But this was a Cistercian monk, still clothed in his habit, his head adorned with the distinct tonsure of his monastic vows. This man was given to fury not from mere grief, but by a warrior ethos—and a thirst for earthly combat.

Fragments of fury and grief collided as Peter's uncontrolled wrath sparked with every swing of his sword. Hugh was both astonished and dismayed by the monk's unbridled fury—a stark departure from the restrained dignity he had expected from a man of the cloth.

With each clash of their steel Hugh's disillusionment grew deeper, the sacred image of peaceful clerical virtue was now marred by the brutal martial spirit he was witnessing in the young warrior-monk. He stood, both bewildered and burdened, as the echoes of the battle revealed a troubling new order—a new scandal he feared would shatter all he held dear.

What is this? Hugh mourned internally.

The Church had grown in its lust for temporal dominion.

A brief pause—Peter's attacks slackened, his eyes dimming momentarily as if giving up were his only escape. Perhaps he understood that he had not a chance against such a well-trained and experienced opponent. For a heartbeat, it seemed he would yield; yet the glimmer of madness returned. His brief capitulation revealed as a deception as he lunged anew, the sudden assault nearly catching Hugh off guard. The experienced knight side-stepped to avoid the blow.

Hugh raised his hands as he retreated backwards up the steps into the church, a silent plea for the clash to end—an appeal that his own heart, heavy with disillusion, could scarcely heed. But Peter would not be tamed; he surged forward, chasing him up the narrow steps into the hushed sanctuary of the church above.

A cry erupted from the depths of the crypt. Pleading. Desperate.

"No! No—Not in my church!" Father Barth's voice rang across the stone walls, laced with panic.

"Oh, dear brother monk, you know better than that! There is to be no bloodshed in God's house!"

The plea fell on deaf ears. The clanging of steel—and resolves—drowned it out. The struggle surged from the crypt into the open sanctuary above—where light streamed through stained glass and cast trembling shadows upon the altar. Barth grimaced, his heart hammering in dread. Sacred ground, soon to be defiled by violence.

Peter fought on. A monk, yet nothing about him was meek. He moved with purpose, rage sharpening each strike. The open space of the sanctuary gave him freedom. No pillars, no obstacles. Nowhere for Hugh to evade. No shields, no barriers.

A miscalculation. Peter had swung too hard. Overextended his movement. Typical of those who had little to no experience in actual combat.

Hugh saw it—felt it before it happened. With a pivot, swift and precise, he caught Peter's hilt, twisted sharply.

A cry of frustration echoed in the church, then the loud clatter of steel against stone. The monk's sword slid across the floor, spinning in the candlelight.

Hugh stepped forward. One swift kick—and out of reach went the monk's sword. His own sword he returned to its sheath. Hands raised, Hugh signaled he wanted no more violence. Peter lunged for the blade. Hugh blocked his path. Defeated, the monk sucked in his breath, his hands flailing in frustrated rage.

Then his hand shot out, pointing an accusing finger toward Sir Hugh. His words, now raw and flustered, tripped over each other in his French tongue.

"Hearken well, knight of Breckington, House John de Ontivero is now under a curse! The Most High be witness

103

that revenge will be sought by the House of Galt and vengeance carried out by the House of de Montfort. I will pursue you, Sir Hugh—and your lord to the very death. I shall ensure that justice be done!"

His words beat against the church's venerable silence like the crack of a whip. Hugh stood firm, watching the young monk boil over with anger. It was a sight to behold.

Is he frothing at the mouth?

Peter's burning gaze then turned to Barth.

"And you, Father! You are the parish priest here! Tell me—do you stand with these murderers?"

Barth raised his hands, open-palmed, an attempted gesture of neutrality. Lips pressed tight. No words.

Peter turned, seeking validation elsewhere. To Godwin.

"Father Rector," his tone softened as he pleaded in his French tongue, "please arrange for men to return my kin's body. He will not be buried here. He shall rest in France."

A sympathetic nod. The rector placed a hand on his shoulder.

"You may call me Father Godwin," the plump rector murmured. "Rector of Tiverton. And yes—we will ensure Sir Galt is returned to his family."

Peter inhaled sharply. Bit his lower lip. His shoulders sagged. He crossed himself, whispered a quiet prayer, and turned toward the exit.

"I shall take my leave."

A moment later, he was gone. Vanished into the throng outside.

Hugh exhaled. A weight lay on his chest, heavy and suffocating. His eyes flicked to Barth, who stared in the direction the young monk took, the furrowing in his brow deepening. This was probably not over. It had only begun. The scandal would now be out there.

Godwin's voice pierced the silence.

"Breckington finds itself ensnared in dire straits, gentlemen."

The rector stepped forward. His steps slow and measured. His gaze knowing, his words curling like smoke.

"I'd advise you both to forsake Sir John. Sir Hugh—you know well that the Lord de Redvers has need of men like you. I can clear your name of this travesty. A single word, and all of this—debacle—disappears. But you must first renounce your liege. You can be the new baron of Breckington."

An awkward silence followed.

Hugh's stomach twisted. The weight of it all was crashing down upon him. And he did not know how to react to it.

The enticement was calculated, designed to unbalance Hugh. Pit him against his friend and lord. Godwin was portraying John's fate as an unraveling thread, with the entire realm poised to unravel with it—tempting Hugh with the possibility of ascending to the station of baron, should John be deposed.

He said nothing. Not yet. He was loyal to his baron and friend—indeed, his brother, but his silence was designed to buy time. Without affirmation, the rector would have no clear course of action to pursue—whether to initiate the plot of unseating John in favor of Hugh or to include Hugh in his condemnation.

Godwin sighed. Shook his head. Hugh was not about to give him the satisfaction. Then, without another word, the plump cleric turned and left, his robes sweeping the stone as he followed Peter's path out into the streets.

Hugh and Barth stood still. The air was so thick, one could cut it with a sharp dagger.

Then, at last, Hugh spoke.

"Tell me, Father. Does the flame of vengeance burn hot in all young clerics?"

There was a long pause, then a laugh.

"Only the French ones," Barth chuckled.

Penitence

May 7th, 1209 AD

Port of Brest, Duchy of Brittany

he Port of Brest bustled with life, the vitality of the waterfront abounded with sweat and sea salt, raw fish and the aroma of freshly baked bread. Crowds moved through the port like ants, conversions spoken in a dozen different languages filled the air. Merchants darted across the docks, shifting through passers-by, looking to find customers.

Towering above it all were the remnants of a Roman fortress—ancient stone, worn but unyielding. The walls that had seen empires rise and fall were now standing watch beneath the castle of Viscount of Leon, Guihomar V. A citadel looming over the foaming tide, its presence was a silent warning to those who might come unwelcome.

John, George, and Reggeye stepped onto solid ground,

their horses in tow. A breath. The sway of the ship still clung to their bones, but the thrill of foreign soil beneath their boots banished the discomfort.

Eyes wide. Awe crept into their expressions.

A world so unlike Breckington. Colors and cloth unknown to them, men and women draped in silks, wool, and rough linen. Accents curled in strange ways, the melody of languages they only half understood filling the air.

They had glimpsed the world before—they had to rendezvous with Henry of Longchamp on their way to the Levant. But then, the journey had gone sour, swallowed by warfare between Christian kingdoms, the sights were fleeting between battles and endless sea. Now, they were pilgrims seeking redemption, not soldiers on campaign. A different kind of adventure lay ahead.

The smell of bread curled through the musty port, warm and inviting. A sharp contrast to the rot of fish and brine on the journey over the channel.

John felt the eyes on them. Curiosity. Scrutiny. It was a traveler's burden—to be questioned, to be measured. So, he did what his father once did. He told tales. Tales of his legendary father.

The name Roland de Ontivero drifted into his casual conversation, wrapped in glory. Wrapped in pride. A knight of the Third Holy War of the Cross. He was a warrior who rode with Richard the Lionheart, whose blade swung true at Acre and Arsuf before death took him. And John—his own accomplishments he shared, shaped by war, tempered by holy fire.

George and Reggeye played their part, retelling their own battles and adventures, their own stories of steel and dust. Of survival.

It worked to gain friends. Allies. A sympathetic gesture. It always did.

Still, something gnawed at George's senses. A shadow had been trailing them.

"Milord," he murmured, eyes flicking to a scrawny young woman keeping pace just behind. "Might I suggest a brief reprieve to get a meal?"

It was but a test. A move to break their tail.

John reined in his horse. "An excellent notion, George."

A sign swayed ahead—*Fourn*.

A bakery. Breton words, familiar enough. Their lands had seen many Bretons come and go; their tongue not entirely foreign to them.

With hunger settling in and warm food calling, they eased their mounts forward, pressing through the living sea of Brest.

A tap on the shoulder. A hand, outstretched.

George turned, scowled. A beggar. A scrawny slip of a girl.

"Shoo!" he huffed, swatting at the air between them. But she lingered, trailing them toward the bakery. Her persistence gnawed at him. He ignored her. She did not leave.

The vaunted Sir George de Wymondham stopped as he caught a glimpse of her tender eyes...she was no ordinary girl...there was something about her.

Then—

"Ach, Ysabeau, be gone!"

A bark in Breton.

The men turned. A burly figure stood near the bakery's side, arms crossed, face twisted in annoyance. The girl squealed, then lunged towards them—grasping George's arm with a desperate grip.

Something wasn't right. George stiffened, startled, but did not try to push her away.

John watched, intrigued. The girl—disheveled, ragged. Hair dark, wavy, tangled with dirt. No older than eighteen. Thin, like a starved cat.

The man stepped forward.

"You men are English, non?"

109

John gave a nod.

"Yes. From Devon."

"I am Jacques. I own this bakery," the man replied with a sharp, annoyed tone. "Believe me, this woman, Ysabeau, is trouble. She stole from me! I employed her for a month before chasing her away—just yesterday."

George's eyes narrowed with suspicion. He reached for the girl, gently parting the mess of hair over her temple with his hands, now shed of his leather gloves. A pattern of fresh bruises appeared. Cuts.

"Milord," he murmured. "It seems that this Jacques has a habit of mistreating this lady."

John stepped closer. A scent—yeast, liquor. Certainly, it was a type of fermentation. The baker reeked of both. Jacques shrank back at George's suggestion, the first glimmer of fear now appearing in his beady eyes.

"Gentlemen, you must know..." Jacques stammered, "this girl robbed me."

It was a lie. John knew it instantly.

"I don't believe you," George growled, his fists curled.

John raised a hand, a silent order to stand down.

"Leave him be, George. He is not worth it."

A sigh, then a reluctant retreat. George stepped back, shielding Ysabeau beneath an arm.

"Just give us some bread."

Jacques' demeanor changed, his voice oily and tinged with fear, his lips curling into an uneasy grin.

"*Mignoned ma c'hoari!* My friends! Here, have fresh loaves! On the house!"

George spat at the ground.

"We don't want your charity. How much did Ysabeau steal from you?"

Jacques hesitated, tried to offer a grin.

"T'was a misunderstanding—"

"Did she really steal from you?" George pressed forward, eyes flashing, his hand now resting on the pommel of his sword.

A gulp. A shift of weight.

"She—she did not. I chased her away because I could not afford to pay her."

"So, you accused her of theft," John said flatly. "You did not beat her, did you?"

The baker wilted. His head drooped. A slow nod.

"The guards did it," Reggeye muttered with observation, his voice thick with disgust. "Because they thought she really did steal from you."

John exhaled sharply.

"You, man, are despicable." His voice rang sharp with authority. "You will clear this young woman's name. And you will pay her what she is owed."

There was a pause. A beat of hesitation. A struggle within. But the man knew he had no other choice.

"*Ya Aotrou.*"

A whispered concession.

Ysabeau trembled, continuing to cling to George's arm. John studied the way she held herself—frightened, yet unbroken. There was something about her. She had an air of importance, but he could not explain why.

Jacques disappeared briefly, slinking back into his bakery. Moments later, he emerged with two fresh loaves, still steaming from his oven. George, Reggeye, and Ysabeau took them without thanks, famished as they were. John pulled a silver coin from his pouch and dropped it into the baker's waiting palm.

Jacques vanished, eager to escape their presence.

They shared a hearty laughter as they tore the bread apart. A sidelong glance and John caught George grinning as Ysabeau whispered something in his ear.

A bond was already formed.

John pursed his lips. Contemplative. This could complicate things. He knew Ysabeau was not going anywhere.

"Milord," George said, his voice firm between eager bites, "this poor lass needs our protection. She's been wrongly accused and mistreated. We cannot let such an injustice stand. I will take her under my protection."

John sighed. He couldn't deny it was a noble cause. But a dangerous one, one that could jeopardize their mission.

"George," he began, measured, "our path is already fraught with peril. This girl—Ysabeau—it might not be safe for her."

He knew that look. It was a flustered look. A barely restrained protest was forthcoming.

"Milord, this justice is *our* cause," George argued, his voice low, careful. "If we turn a blind eye to the suffering of the innocent, what honor do we bring to our quest for redemption?"

A pause.

Ysabeau met John's gaze. Her eyes—pleading, yet intelligent.

"I beg you, kind sir," she whispered, her Middle English smooth, practiced. "Help me clear my name by taking me with you. You know that I did not steal. I have nowhere else to turn, nowhere else to go."

Her knowledge and intelligence impressed them. George softened visibly, but John remained wary, aware of the dangers ahead.

A sigh. There was a decision to be made.

"We are in a hurry," John said, voice firm. "But you may travel with us."

He then pointed to his vassal knight.

"Under your protection, George. She is *your* responsibility."

George grinned.

"Thank you, milord!"

Ysabeau bowed deeply as her eyes lightened up.

"Thank you, kind sirs. I owe you all my life. One day, I promise that I will repay you for your kindness."

John studied her very carefully. There was something about her that was off. She was no simple peasant girl. She was too sharp.

Observant. Intelligent.

But he also sensed that she had no nefarious intent. And now, she was theirs to protect.

A hush settled over the group. The last of the bread vanished, the crumbs clinging to their tunics, their fingers dusted with flour. A quiet nudge—John's elbow into George's ribs.

"Ahem."

A cue. If George wanted to formally take Ysabeau with him as his charge, she would have to take an oath.

Sir George swallowed the last bite, wiped his mouth with the back of his hand, then gave a sharp tilt of his head. It was time to move to another place and set expectations with the girl out of the prying ears of passers-by.

The streets of Brest churned with life—voices, wagons, the sharp tang of salt and livestock.

They felt the stares of strangers on their backs as they navigated through the busy grounds. A secluded area could offer the needed respite from watching gazes and over-eager ears. Among the throng of cottages and stone buildings, one structure stood near-empty: a pigpen where a wooden frame once held firm now sagged with age.

Within, the dry earth and pottery bore records of its past inhabitants. Though far from luxurious, its walls granted that which they sought: much needed privacy. There, George clasped Ysabeau's shoulders gentle yet insistent, turning her to face him fully. Through touch he hoped to anchor her attention and calm her spirits, if only for a time.

The young woman, though shaken from her encounter with Jacques, gave her full trust to the noblemen, whom she saw as her protectors.

"Ysabeau," George's voice was low, measured as he looked into her gentle eyes, "we ride on urgent business. If you stay with us, you must swear to abide by our rules. No foolishness. No recklessness. We cannot afford complications or any delays. If we ask you to leave, you must comply for your safety and well-being."

A nod. Small, eager, nearly trembling.

"I understand and I swear, milord," she murmured, her voice barely more discernable than a breath, "I will be as silent as the wind. I bring no harm to your quest. I only seek protection… and if fate allows, a chance to clear my name."

John studied her responses, his arms crossed. Still wary. A woman among them—trouble. Uncertainty. Perhaps even bad luck.

"You must understand the risks, Ysabeau," John's tone was firm, edged with warning. "Our road is perilous. Any distraction could cost us dearly. Maybe even our lives. I pray you do not become a burden."

A bow of the head, as Ysabeau made her pledge.

"I swear on my life, milord. I will be no burden."

George held out his hand. A solemn moment of promise—by both parties.

"Then by your oath, you are one of us now. And I, your protector."

She took his hand, fingers small, cold. A glint in her eye—determined, unshaken.

The four of them turned from the shadows of the alley, stepping back into the world. The path stretched before them, uncertain, treacherous. But at least, they had some direction.

Brest's cathedral loomed ahead—a sanctuary of stone, its steeple clawing at the sky, crowned by a brooding belfry.

They did not enter blindly. It was Father Bartholomew who had urged them—before their departure from England—that they first seek His Grace, Bishop Raymond of Brest, a man known in ecclesiastical circles as a trusted intermediary with the Roman Curia.

Within the cathedral, the scent of old parchment and

melted tallow filled the air. They were received not by an usher or a monastic underling, but by Raymond himself—a man of some sixty years, shrouded in a black mantle, with intelligent eyes beneath a furrowed brow. His ring bore the seal of episcopal authority, and his voice, when he greeted them, carried both gentleness and fatigue.

He listened as John recounted their tale. The bishop nodded slowly, absorbing the account with careful silence.

"The pope?" he echoed, when John finished. A slow shake of the head followed. "No man walks into His Holiness's presence unbidden."

John stiffened. He had expected as much.

"Then how?" he asked.

Raymond steepled his fingers.

"Through the legate. His Holiness has entrusted certain matters to the Abbot of Cîteaux—Amalric, a man of harsh judgment and rigorous orthodoxy. He is in Burgundy now. If your cause holds merit, he will judge it."

John's heart sank. *Cîteaux.* The very heart of the Cistercian order.

"So far inland?" he murmured. "We had thought Rome our aim."

"If you cannot endure Amalric," Raymond said grimly, "you would not survive Rome."

He turned and summoned a scribe with a sharp gesture.

"A messenger shall ride ahead with your names and intent. The abbot's men will meet you. Whether they receive you with grace or condemnation... that is not mine to say."

John exchanged a glance with George and then Bartholomew's scroll—sealed and tucked into his belt—felt suddenly heavier.

The path to penance—and perhaps redemption—now lay before them. They prayed they could live and endure through it.

It was not the most convenient of routes. To land at Brest only to ride southeast across kingdoms, fractured lands, and hostile eyes toward a fortress of orthodoxy... but the journey to Cîteaux was now their burden.

It was not the most convenient of journeys, having to land at Brest, then overland to Orleans. It would be a long road to the renowned Abbey of Cîteaux near Dijon, nestled in the Duchy of Burgundy. Possibly a fortnight and a half of a travel. And at the end of it stood this Amalric.

Political uncertainties only added to the complications they would face ahead. Brittany was no friendly land. Otto III, Duke of Brittany, stood firm in alliance with Philip II of France—a king with no love for England. Any traveler bearing ties to John's liege, King John of England, would be met with suspicion, perhaps worse.

King John—bitter, restless, ever seething over the loss of Normandy—watched for any excuse to break the fragile peace with France. With one misstep, one wrong encounter, this journey could turn from pilgrimage to a political disaster.

John of Breckington knew this. He knew the delicate game of diplomacy, the need to be mindful of his words, the need to smooth out his apprehensions and ensure safe passage for himself and his men—and the woman under his vassal's care. His name would carry little favor here. His title, though significant, would not guarantee him safety—in fact, it may even bring them peril.

So, as they moved further inland, deeper into the town leaving the bustling port behind, unease would cling to them like a second shadow.

Brittany—a land of shifting allegiances, a melting pot of tongues, faiths, feudal rivalries. Lords and dukes, counts and abbots, each ruling their own carved-out piece of dominion, each balancing between loyalty and defiance. The scars of war still fresh—castles that bore the marks of siege, abbeys that once housed Norman lords, now sworn to France.

The people—watchful. Wearied by the endless tides of conquest and crusade. The Third Holy War had come and gone, and so had English rule. Strangers were met with caution. And caution could too easily turn to hostility.

De Redvers had foreseen it. Had warned him of it.

As he promised, the priest of the church in Brest had sent a herald ahead, a single voice to ease their passage. The abbot of Cîteaux would be expecting them, warned of their approach. The emissary would be traveling beyond, to the Burgundian court, securing safe conduct for them through both French and Burgundian lands.

A relief for their small band. No need for disguises. No need for secrecy. They would ride openly. They could bear their colors, the crest of Breckington displayed without fear. They were Englishmen, after all.

The road stretched long beneath them, winding past fields and scattered villages, still connected to the vast metropolis of Brest. Then—a palisade now rose before them, wooden stakes looming in the afternoon light.

A checkpoint.

A line of weary travelers and merchants, stopped beneath the watchful eyes of armed men. Soldiers in chain and surcoats, shields painted with a black lion rampant over orange. The crest of Léon.

One among them stepped forward.

A commander, clad in chainmail and greaves, his great helm gleaming dull in the sun. He reached for his visor, flipped it up, revealing a face lined with the weight of duty, with the fatigue of long days spent watching the road.

His gaze settled on them. Studied. Measured. Heavy.

John held his breath. They were about to enter deeper into a foreign land. Would they be granted passage?

A loud voice rang out, firm and assessing.

"Hail, men of England! What venture brings you to our humble county?"

The commander stood tall, eyes observing them with a quiet scrutiny.

John nudged his horse a few steps forward so he could be

recognized. He inclined his head slightly, a gesture of respect. A master of many tongues, he responded in the local Breton.

"Passage through, my good sir, onward to the Duchy of Burgundy. I am John de Ontivero, Baron of Breckington."

He paused with measured breath before continuing.

"These are my comrades—Sir George de Wymondham, my loyal vassal, and his squire, Reginald de Saint-Clair. And this lady, Ysabeau of Brest, now under Sir George's protection."

The knight studied them intently. A flicker of light in his eyes as he recognized the heraldic crest of Breckington.

"I am Sir Harvey, brother to the Viscount."

The commander shifted in stance. Less formal, more relaxed.

"You may have our leave to pass, Lord Baron, but I should caution you—highwaymen prowl these roads, preying on travelers, especially those who look foreign. They are also very adept at combat, and we have lost several a man."

John's jaw tightened. Expected, perhaps, yet unwelcome news.

"We can spare you no escort," Harvey continued. "You will have to ride alone and assume all the risks."

A moment's pause. A flicker of something concerning in the knight's tone. Indeed, the countryside was dangerous with all the menaces roaming the forests and fields.

John could only give a slow nod.

"We thank you for your warning, Sir Harvey. We shall proceed on with due caution. May God keep you."

A grunt of approval and a wave of the hand. Then a sharp command in Breton set the guards moving.

The gates groaned open. As the two guards pulled them apart, the road beyond was revealed—a dusty, stony dirt path surrounded by a vast sprawl of plains, stitched together by patches of dark forest. The unknown was waiting for them. Beckoning. Enticing, yet filled with potential terrors.

John nodded with respect and motioned his group to advance.

Then—forward they trotted.

Their horses' hooves clattered against the dirt and rock. Soon, the last of Brest disappeared behind them, swallowed by distance.

The road ahead seemed endless, a spattering of travelers littered the way, seeking the refuge of the port city, while others were heading away from it. All were armed, except the women who were always accompanied by a male companion. These were not safe roads.

John knew their path. East. Always east.

To Rennes—where rest and supplies awaited. Then onward to Orléans, and finally Dijon, near to where the Abbey of Cîteaux loomed at journey's end.

It would take several fortnights of hard riding. There were to be no delays. No unnecessary stops. Their horses would be pushed to their limits.

Speed was their ally. But the road was going to be long. And danger—all but inevitable.

::

A pounding. A dull, relentless throb behind his temples.

What is this perversity?

Hugh Phillip groaned, shifting in his bed, his body protesting every movement. His head felt like it had been split in two, a painful reminder of the previous night's indulgence. While excess had never been his custom, he felt that the recent trials demanded more than what an able mind and strong will could provide.

He was wrong.

In a rare slip of resolve, he drank heavily from the burden of relentless demands of his newfound duties. Alas, the drink brought no relief, only a headache that was one of the strongest he ever had. He felt the urge to vomit, to cast out the malady.

A deep breath. Then, a slow, painful rise from the mattress.

He staggered to his water basin, gripping the edge of the table for support. The cool splash against his face sent a fleeting shock through his system, a brief relief before the burden of duty returned, even heavier than before.

Cursed drink.

What was it that Father Barth had taught? Something about Saint Paul's second letter to the Corinthians of his day. Drunkards would not be welcomed into the Kingdom of Heaven.

That's it, I'm done with wine, Hugh thought, his head in pain so bad he'd rather that pesky young monk had run him through with his sword.

Peter of Vaux-de-Cernay.

The name alone twisted in his mind, a reminder of the confrontation, the look of grief turned to rage, the whispered word by the plump rector—*murder.*

Drip. Drip.

Water fell from his face back into the basin, each drop echoing in his ears.

John.

Hugh exhaled sharply, pushing himself upright. Whatever troubles plagued him, they were nothing compared to those weighing upon his lord.

John had set out for Rome, carrying the fate of them all upon his shoulders. If he failed—if he could not sway the Pope—everything would unravel. The barony, their homes, their people. And here, in his absence, Hugh had been entrusted to hold Breckington together.

Two months, at least. Or more. Who knew? Months of walking on the thin line between order and chaos.

He was not alone, however. His squires remained steadfast, and the sheriff Lacey and his men kept the peace in the barony as best they could. But he knew unrest simmered beneath the calm surface.

The townsfolk would murmur in hushed voices. The whispers would grow daily—rumors of the waylaid caravan, of the murdered inquisitor, of the Purcells and their plight, of Lord Devon's march on Castle Breckington. Fear would spread like wildfire, and fear that would breed chaos.

Only yesterday, Lacey had been forced to break up a brawl—men throwing fists over words half-heard, speculation turning to anger. It would not be long before all this confusion hardened into resentment. Before discontent turned to something far worse. Agents of the crown and the Church would be hovering over the barony like carrion birds around a corpse.

Hugh pressed a damp hand to his forehead before burying his face in a drying cloth.

This was no time for weakness.

A storm was gathering, and he stood alone at the gate. At least, on this side of the sea.

A knock interrupted his contemplation, and his page, Henry, entered with fresh linens and a pitcher of water.

"Good morning, Sir Hugh. I brought some fresh linens and some water."

"Good lad, thank you."

"Is there anything else I can do for you, sir?"

A weight now settled in his limbs. A haze kept clinging to his mind. Never again would he seek solace in drink. Too much was hanging on his shoulders.

He slogged forward, arms hanging loose at his sides, his body still sluggish from sleep and the hangover. A hunch gnawed at him, relentless. Something was wrong. The forces that set this whole predicament in motion would not rest. He needed to face them, head-on.

The wooden beams groaned under his step as he dragged himself through the open oaken doors, blinking against the harsh stab of sunlight. Too bright. Too sudden. It was a sharp shock to his system.

He took a breath. Deep. Steadying.

Focus.

He needed focus.

His gaze cut across the landscape, the familiar sprawl of the town of Breckington nestled in a clearing beyond the trees. Too far to see details, but something—something was amiss. He had a hunch, and he needed to act upon it. Immediately.

He shifted slightly as he made his decision.

"Yes, Henry, please prepare my mount—now."

No hesitation.

Minutes later, armor strapped, sword at his side, Hugh swung into the saddle. The beast beneath him tensed considerably, its hooves kicking up dust as he drove it into a full gallop, first past gates held ajar, then down the hill leading from the castle.

Fields blurred past. The rolling expanse of Dartmoor flowed by, familiar yet fleeting beneath the pounding rhythm of his horse's gallop.

Then—the belltower.

St. Michael's steeple pierced the sky above the trees ahead. The town lay just beyond.

Faster.

"*Hyah!*"

He pushed his mount harder, breath coming fast, gripping the reins as the wooden gates loomed. Already congested—carts, people, animals clogging the entrance.

No time.

He dismounted in one fluid motion, boots hitting the packed earth. The helmet came off, sweat from the heat slick on his forehead, perspiration trickling down his temple.

Then he heard it—the noise.

Actually, a swarm of voices. A town in chaos. A large gathering, not normal unless there was a festival. But this was no festival.

He forced his way forward through the crowd, pressing toward the square, a sense of dread tightening in his gut.

His fears, his hunch, were now confirmed.

A crowd had gathered. Two hundred strong, maybe even more.

Hugh forced himself through the mass of people, his skull pounding with every heartbeat as he was still recovering from his stupor. The remnants of last night's indulgence still gnawed at his senses, turning the morning air thick, the noise sharper than it should be. But at least the need to vomit had now vanished.

Head and shoulders above the townsfolk around him, he pushed his way near the front of the crowd. They had surrounded the town square, a hobbled wooden platform that had served them for generations.

And at the center of it all—*him*.

Peter of Vaux-de-Cernay.

The warrior monk stood at the center of the square, a figure cloaked in his religious habit and a vengeful fury. His voice, deep and unwavering, rolled over the town square like thunder. He spoke of a vision.

A vision of *hell*.

Hugh blinked hard, trying to focus. The effects of drink were flushing from his system, but he needed to concentrate harder to discern the full picture of what was taking place.

Peter's words lashed the air, painting images of damnation and divine wrath, twisting the fears of the gathered townsfolk into something relatable. And it seemed as though he was becoming successful. Whispers turned to hushed prayers, uneasy glances darting between neighbors and fellow townsfolk. Fear, real and tangible, spread like ink in water.

Hugh swallowed against the dryness in his throat. The crowd had started to shift, a restless energy was spreading like wildfire through it. The whispers had changed, no longer quiet—murmurs of unease bleeding into something sharper. Suspicion. Agitation. Fear. No, not fear—panic.

Damn it all.

Peter was a stranger to Breckington, but his habit, the weight of the crucifix at his chest, his bearing—it all spoke to his authority. He was no wandering hermit, no mad zealot on the fringes of faith. He was a monk of the Church. And that, above all else, meant the people would listen.

And they *were* listening.

Breckington was no den of heretics. Its people— hardworking, devout, humble—held fast to Rome, as had their fathers before them. Saxon blood ran through most of their veins, though the Norman conquest had carved its mark here, too. The Bretons, the few among them, had carried their own fire for the faith. The Church bound them all together, despite their differences, despite the wars and kings and endless tides of power shifting hands.

Rome had long ceased to rule as an empire, but its grasp remained firm in the matters of the soul. The townsfolk understood their place, their duty to the Holy See. In matters of faith, they yielded. They followed.

And Peter, foreign though he was, wore the weight of Rome upon his shoulders.

Had it been another man—some wandering knight, a merchant, even a noble—he would have been met with skepticism, even outright resistance. But a monk? A preacher of the Word?

They would listen.

Hugh gritted his teeth.

His hands twitched at his sides, instinct screaming at him to act, to step forward, to cut through Peter's sermon with the voice of reason before this fervor turned to something more dangerous. But no—he knew better.

To interrupt would be folly.

So, he waited, swallowing the bile in his throat, the lingering ache behind his eyes, and watched.

Had Peter noticed him? It would have been hard not to;

Sir Hugh was easily the largest man in town, and with his armor and heraldic colors donned, only a blind man could have missed him.

Whether he had or not, Peter continued his speech, unfazed.

His voice rang sharp, slicing through the morning air, rising above the shifting sea of onlookers.

"Lo, I beheld a river, burning with fire, twisting towards a vast lake of flames where souls of all kinds thrashed in anguish," he proclaimed, "their tormented wails renting the fiery air!"

Very theatrical. Dramatic. But it worked.

A gasp rippled through the crowd, as many frantically whispered amongst one another, eyes wide with horror. The scheming monk had them in his grasp now, their minds filled with the image of fire and brimstone of his conjured vision.

"And furthermore," Peter's voice lowered, thick with grim authority, "I witnessed your lord, Sir John, immersed in torment as the flames consumed him."

Shock. Confusion. Faces turned toward one another, seeking answers in the unspoken. It was the first that they had heard of this. I woman broke into tears.

"Your lord," Peter pressed on, "in his folly, committed a grievous sin."

A murmur. A nervous energy creeping into the gathering, unsettling as a distant storm.

John de Ontivero had ruled Breckington for years, and he was beloved like his father. Respected. His character impeccable. A warrior. A noble. Protector of his people. Yet now, here stood this monk, this foreigner, daring to condemn him in the name of Rome itself.

Hugh knew too well to dismiss the effect of a so-called man of God could have, however, even if he were a stranger.

"Sir John and his company have transgressed the laws of our Holy Church!" Peter's tone sharpened. "They assaulted and slew the Lord Inquisitor, Sir Renhard Galt—my kinsman!"

The revelation struck the crowd like a hammer.

Gasps. Faces filled with shock and disbelief. The crowd's murmurs grew louder. An inquisitor? Killed by Lord Breckington?

"Sir Galt," Peter continued, voice quivering, first with indignation—then with emotion, "was on a divine mission from His Holiness himself! He endeavored to purge England of heresy! And yet, your noble lord slew him!"

A woman, her expression conveyed her incredulity, broke through the whispers with a high-pitched voice.

"Heretics? Here? In Devonshire?"

More whispers, the speculation spreading like embers caught in dry thatch.

"Yes," Peter declared. "It is difficult to fathom, but it is the truth that your rulers have betrayed you! Breckington and its nobles shall face judgment! Cast out your lords or share in their impending fate!"

"Lord John would do this?" asked an old man.

"That can't be," piped up a young woman.

"We can't go against the will of the Church!" cried an older woman.

A beat. A shift in tone. Chaos would soon erupt.

Peter's lips curled into a knowing smile as he gazed right at Sir Hugh.

"Look! Here comes one of your lords now!"

A finger shot outward, accusing, commanding all eyes to turn.

Right at Hugh.

His presence alone was enough to still the crowd. A giant among men—six feet, two inches of solid, armored bulk. The metallic clank of his approach sent a shiver through the tense air.

"Do not listen to the lies he speaks," Peter sneered. "Let us see what devilish tripe he will come up with now."

Silence.

There was not a sound as Hugh moved slowly, deliberately, his breath steady despite the thick fog in his skull. The throbbing from his wretched hangover continued to claw at his temples, but the importance of this moment demanded clarity.

He mounted the platform, helm tucked beneath his arm, eyes scanning the faces before him. He saw suspicion.

But also confusion. Fear. Anger. Townfolk were more intelligent than most nobles would give them credit; they would grumble should they feel that their lords kept secrets from them. Therefore, he would speak with the utmost care.

Father Barth stood at the edge of the throng, his gaze steady, silent encouragement in his expression.

Hugh exhaled, regretting—for the first time—how distant he had always remained from these people.

John had felt it before, the rift between noble and commoner. Hugh had mocked his concerns, goaded by the Earl of Devon.

"*A noble's place is above his people, not among them,*" de Redvers had once insisted. "*Power must be preserved, protected.*"

But here, now, with eyes filled with doubt locked upon him, Hugh found himself wondering.

Perhaps Father Barth had been right all along. Perhaps Lord John's approach was best.

The King of Heaven, Christ Himself, had left His throne to walk among men. Should not a noble at least know the names of those under his care?

Indeed. But now there was no time for reflection. The silence stretched as he cast his gaze upon the silent throng.

Then—finally—a breath. A soft sigh.

And Hugh spoke.

"Good people of Breckington," his voice carried, measured, firm. "I see you have encountered Brother Peter of Vaux-de-Cernay. He has traveled a great distance—from France, no less—to visit our humble dwelling in

Devonshire."

A ripple of murmurs and whispers swept through the crowd. Hugh continued on.

"What our esteemed brother in Christ has shared is accurate. We confronted a band of armed men who attacked a caravan—"

"A caravan led by a *heretic!*"

Peter's voice cut through Hugh's, sharp, biting, accusing. Gasps followed. A shudder of unease moved through the gathered townsfolk.

Hugh's fists clenched in silent irritation. He raised his voice slightly, but reminded himself he would show no frustration or the monk would best him in this clash of wits. He spoke gently.

"A caravan led by a Breckington resident—our dear merchant, Edwinson."

There was a pause. A shift in tone, sentimental, familiar.

"You all knew him, we supplied the linen market each day. And his poor daughter, Aerin. May her soul rest in peace."

He lifted a hand, pointing to their home, a quiet mark in the town's landscape. He did not have to say more. They knew. The home now empty, its inhabitants laid to rest. Two of their own. Faces turned. Recognition flickered in their eyes. Understanding. He had struck a chord.

Peter scoffed but held his tongue. He was waiting. Calculating. He had something up his sleeve.

"When we came upon the caravan," Hugh continued, "we did not pause to question the motives of those who attacked. We saw our own—two citizens of Breckington—struck down, defenseless," Hugh's voice hardened, "so we acted."

A slight murmur. A sudden rift of expression in the crowd.

Hugh looked down. Regret edged around his next words. His voice choked with emotion.

128

"We arrived too late to save them. But we ensured the assailants would harm no one else," he took a measured breath. "They bore no banners. No markings. We did not know then who they served, we did not know they were sent by the pope."

It was the truth.

The crowd whispered among themselves, excitement across their faces.

Peter's stance changed—tightened. The monk felt the ground shifting beneath him; he had loss the momentum. He stepped forward, his voice rising, desperate to reclaim command.

"You see?" He turned to the people, hands lifted in proclamation. "Your Sir Hugh himself *admits* to attacking a Papal representative. Surely, you see this for what it is! A crime against the Church! Against God! Your lord must face justice—*divine* justice!"

Silence.

Hugh could feel the tension thickening, twisting in the air.

Peter's voice thundered.

"The Inquisition will have your Lord Baron burned at the stake! Rise, Breckington! Cast out your overlords and His Holiness shall spare you from the wrath to come!"

Hugh exhaled slowly. He needed to move carefully. One wrong word, one misstep, and this could tip into disaster.

There was another pause. Then, a revelation.

"People of Breckington," he said, voice steady, unshaken, "your lord, Sir John de Ontivero, even now, rides to see His Holiness the Pope—to seek penance for this... *misadventure*."

A play of transparency. Of reason. An assurance that the predicament was being attended to.

Peter sneered.

"Don't believe that for a second!" His voice was venom. "Your Lord Baron is a *heretic*! He will burn at the pyre. And

do not think—*not for a moment!*—that the soldiers of God will not come for *you* next. Your homes. Your villages. Razed to the ground."

Silence.

Thick. Heavy.

A single coin could have clattered to the dirt and all would have heard it.

Hugh let the stillness settle. Let it weigh upon the people.

Then, with deliberate calm, he spoke.

"As your noble protectors, it is our duty to safeguard Breckington and its people."

He turned, his eyes sweeping the gathering, searching their faces, meeting them where they stood.

"We acted against an immediate threat to *our town. Our people*."

The townsfolk began to nod at his words. Hugh continued.

"Only later did we learn who those men were, that they were agents of the inquisition."

His voice did not waver.

"The blame does not lie in our ignorance. It lies with those who sowed confusion and chaos by entering our lands without warning."

It was a gamble to speak sharply against agents of the Church.

Hugh gazed over the crowd. The anxiety was still there, as was the looming uncertainty. But the doubt—a lingering doubt that Hugh had exposed had now clung to Peter's prior words, the monk's credibility now in question. For all their loyalty to ecclesiastical authority, they were even more loyal to one other. To their families. To their neighbors. To their friends. Now, even Peter's priestly status could not help him save face.

Peter glared, but remained silent. He had no rebuttal, and he could only simmer with frustration.

Hugh pressed on.

"Citizens of Breckington. My fellow citizens! Yes, I am one of you. This is my home," his voice softened, even if ever only so slightly. "Let us not be divided by this misinformation. I respect the Church, as God is my witness. But only He can judge us, not this outsider! We have faced challenges, yes, but together, we *overcame* them. Let's not allow *fear* to be the architect of our discord."

He took a breath. A much-needed reprieve. Then, he raised a fist.

"We are stronger when we are *united!*"

There it was. A turn of the tide.

The murmurs swelled, no longer uncertain but angry—fury simmering just beneath the surface. Faces twisted, eyes narrowing, fists clenching, punching the air. The crowd had come seeking answers, and now, with clarity settling in, their wrath found their proper target.

The monk.

A head of cabbage hurtled through the air, striking Peter of Vaux-de-Cernay square on the shoulder with a dull *thud.* He gasped in pain. Then—another projectile. A turnip. A rock. A crust of stale bread. The dam had broken, the floodgates were open.

"Your kin *killed* Edwinson!" a voice spat.

"And Aerin! Murderers!"

Peter flinched, raising an arm to shield himself as the jeers turned to outright condemnation. The town was no longer his audience; it was his jury, and the verdict had been passed. Unless an intervention occurred, the crowd would become his executioner as well.

Hugh's heart pounded as he watched the chaos unfold.

Damnation. This had gone too far.

"*Enough!*"

His large voice boomed through the din, sharp and commanding.

The crowd stilled, arms half-raised, projectiles clenched in tense grips. Hugh stepped forward, his helm now back in

131

place, steel catching the light, his presence looming over them all. He spread his arms, a barrier between them and the discredited monk.

"Citizens of Breckington, *we are better than this!*" His voice boomed, his breath steady despite the pounding in his skull.

"Outsiders may doubt our loyalty, but let our *actions* prove them wrong! Breckington shall show its devotion—to our barony, to our King, and to His Holiness."

The crowd shifted. Nods. Low murmurs of agreement. Then—a roar of approval.

"Let him show the Pope our loyalty!" someone cried.

"Let him through!" another yelled.

A cheer rose as the mob stepped back, the energy of their anger redirected into unity, into purpose. A number of the townsfolk stepped aside to make a path for the monk to escape.

For a moment, Peter stood frozen, his face twisted in shock and fury.

"This isn't the end," he hissed, eyes burning with resentment at Sir Hugh. "You and your *lord* shall pay. The Church never forgets who has slighted her."

Hugh flinched not an inch. He met the monk's gaze with an unwavering stare of his own. He raised his voice again.

"My friends, let us not be swayed by fear and false prophets," he addressed the people, voice measured, more gentle. "We stand together in loyalty—to our barony, to our King, and to the Holy Father. *Breckington's honor remains untarnished.*"

A cry of agreement erupted. More nods, more cheers.

He pressed on.

"We shall not bow to such baseless accusations. Let our *actions* define us! I pledge—*I pledge*—to investigate this matter fully, to see justice done. But we shall not allow anyone to turn us against one another. That—that is what those who wish us harm desire."

132

The people rallied behind their knight protector; their doubts now buried beneath his words.

Peter scowled as he began to back away from the platform. The tide had now fully turned against him, and there was no reason for him to stay.

Defying logic, he refused to accept defeat.

The crowd left him a pathway to walk through unmolested, save from their glares of disdain, but instead of leaving, he clambered onto a table at the far end of the square, his voice rising once more, desperate, clinging to what little ground he had left.

"Judgment is coming upon you all!" he bellowed. "This isn't the end! I will return, riding upon the vengeance of the Lord!"

His words landed flat, the only responses were antagonistic jeers as the crowd—once rapt with fear—had already begun to disperse.

Ordered by their knight protector to leave him untouched, the people chose to simply ignore him, aside from glances of contempt.

In truth, Peter was nothing but an outsider, a foreign monk whose threats rang hollow in the ears of a town that was loyal to its own.

Hugh approached the monk, whose voice had become raspy from exertion. He removed his helmet to look at the agitating cleric in the eye.

"I am counting on it, brother monk, that you will return, riding upon the vengeance of the Lord."

His voice was quiet, amused, carrying just enough weight to tease Peter's ears. He watched the monk sneer, watched the rage flush his face red before he turned sharply, pushing through the dispersing crowd.

No one stopped him as he left. No one molested him further.

Instead, townsfolk clapped their Sir Hugh on the back, voices rising in approval, fists raised high in victory as Peter of Vaux-de-Cernay disappeared from sight. The knight had won—*Breckington*—had won.

The monk was vanquished, he was gone. Vanished into the distance, swallowed by the winding roads beyond Breckington, heading into the unknown. No one grieved his departure.

Relief settled over Hugh like a heavy breeze, but he knew better than to savor the victory in public. It wasn't *his* charisma that had turned the people—it was Father Barth's wisdom, the steady guidance that had kept them from tipping into true madness, and ultimately it was Divine guidance—he believed—that assisted his actions—his words.

Still, the ordeal was far from over. In fact, it may have even been made far more complicated.

The Church would not let this stand. The Inquisition would not forget. Soon, pressure would bear down upon the King, upon the realm, to *discipline* a barony who dared to defy a papal envoy.

Hugh exhaled slowly, his mind already racing ahead.

My Lord John, he thought, *you had better succeed.*

A final sigh escaped his lips as he turned away from the dispersing crowd.

Life would be simpler if the Church refrained from meddling in the affairs of the realm. But that, he knew, was a fool's hope.

::

The heavy doors of St. Michael's groaned shut behind Father Barth, muffling the lingering echoes of the town square. Within the sanctuary's still air hung the mingled scents of incense and candle wax as the silence pressed upon his ears. He strode through the nave, sandals scuffing upon worn stone, callused fingers tracing along polished altar rails as his solemn steps advanced with purpose.

Not here within the open sanctuary, he reminded himself.

This was not the place.

His path led him to a narrow corridor behind the altar, his pace never faltering as he reached the sacristy. Beyond it, tucked away behind an aging tapestry, was a door known only to him, opened with a key only he possessed. A forgotten chamber—small, unremarkable, built for a purpose long lost to time.

The turn of a key. The latch clicked.

Barth stepped inside, striking a flint. Indeed, it was he who taught Sir George his skill. The flame flared to life, wavering as he touched it to a candle's wick. Shadows twisted against the stone walls, the space danced alive with flickering light.

His gaze fell to the table.

The merchant's *ledger* lay where he had left it, its presence a secret only to himself and the Almighty. Poor Edwinson and Aerin lost their lives over it.

Sir George had pressed it into his hands before his departure with Lord John. No explanation. No request. Only a look—one that carried a message, that told him everything and nothing at once.

He knew what it contained.

Names.

The names of men and women in Breckington, written in ink, recorded in silence. Not criminals. Not thieves. Not rebels.

But *others*. Some would say, heretics.

Those who spoke in hushed voices, who questioned in ways the Church did not tolerate. Those whose beliefs did not align with Rome's will.

In Toulouse, in Albi, in Carcassonne, they called them *Bons Hommes*. Even some others they called the *Valdois*. They preached virtue, simplicity, rejection of Rome's authority. And Rome had taken notice.

It was 1209. The world had changed, and if challenges to ecclesiastical power were tolerated in the past, they were no longer.

Pope Innocent had declared them a corruption, a sickness spreading through Christendom, and the Inquisition—though still young, still without the full machinery of ecclesiastical and secular power—had been tasked with their eradication. But this was no grand, organized tribunal. No singular hand guiding justice. It was a patchwork of authority—local bishops, fervent noblemen, the occasional papal legate. Each enforcing doctrine in their own way. Some sought conversion. Others sought fire.

Barth knew which hand had touched England. Personally knew its influence. It was the *Valdois*. Their doctrines were starkly different from the *Bons Hommes*, yet they shared a solidarity in decrying the temporal power of the supreme pontiff. His Holiness.

Barth turned a page. A name stared back at him, black ink against yellowed parchment. He gasped.

If this ledger fell into the wrong hands, he knew there would be no inquiries. No confessions. No mercy. Simply flames.

His jaw tightened as he stiffened at the thought.

The candle sputtered, its flame dancing against the dark. He reached for the ledger, rolling it tight, wrapping it in a swath of cloth before moving to the far end of the chamber. His fingers traced the grooves of the stone wall, searching, feeling for the flaw.

There.

A gap—thin, deliberate. A hollow carved into the wall, concealed behind loose mortar. He pressed the ledger into the space, tucking it deep, before covering it once more.

His hands lingered, pressing the stone back into place.

With a slow breath, Barth turned, eyes darting to the candle as it burned lower.

The ledger was safe. Secure. Hidden. The walls of St. Michael's would keep its secrets.

For now.

136

::

A crackle. A shifting ember.

John de Ontivero, Lord Baron of Breckington, sat near the fire, its flickering light casting long shadows across the damp earth. The night was still, save for the occasional rustle of leaves in the wind. Two weeks into their journey, and they had yet to leave Normandy.

Too slow.

They had purposed not to stop unnecessarily, but their horses were exhausted from the journey.

The road still stretched long before them. The goal—to meet the Papal Legate at his headquarters in Cîteaux, deep in Burgundy, secure a rite of passage, and press on to Rome—should the legate deem it necessary.

So far, the messenger who was sent before them had not returned to meet them. They remained close enough to the road to be seen, with Reggeye hoisting up their blue and yellow banner.

John sighed. He shifted restlessly.

George sat across from him, tending the fire. Flint and steel in his hands, working with ease, as always—a skill he was known for. John could manage, of course, but he took longer. A skill worth having, but one he was glad to leave to his vassal.

The night smelled of roasting meat. A familiar comfort.

Ysabeau, their unlikely companion, stood watch over the spit, turning the skewered fowl with practiced care. She had refused to sit idle, insisted on pulling her own weight. She would not be a guest, not merely a charge to be protected. John had already given her his tent—a gesture of chivalry, a man's duty to a lady—but she had repaid it in kind, proving her usefulness tenfold.

However, she still remained an enigma.

Ysabeau Le Merchand—nineteen, she had told them.

137

Young, yet hardened by the world. Beneath the grime of her former life, her features were striking, but not in the ostentatious way of noblewomen nor in the pretentiousness of some common women. Hers was a quiet beauty, subdued but undeniable.

But she was no ordinary beggar. John suspected she was more than who she claimed to be. As a gentleman he would not push her on the issue; perhaps she had some reason to keep her full history to herself. Whatever her past, she was under Sir George's care, and he trusted him with his life. Still, he could not but remain curious as to who the young woman truly was.

She spoke *Lingua Anglica*, Anglo-Norman, Breton, French, and even Occitan with ease. More astonishingly, she could *read*.

George, ever the romantic, was enthralled.

He prodded her for details—where she had learned, who had taught her. But at the mention of family, she fell silent, her jaw setting, her eyes darkening, probing the ground.

She had secrets. That much was clear.

They did not press her further. She would speak when she was ready.

In the meantime, she had become one of them. A traveler, a companion. They had bonded, laughed and ate together.

Reggeye had taken to her fastest. They were closest in age, their conversations easy, filled with quiet laughter as they shared stories in the firelight.

John noticed George watching her.

Not with the guarded suspicion he had first worn when they found her, but with something softer, something thoughtful.

Cleaned up, free from the dirt of the road after a wash, Ysabeau was a beauty who held herself with a dignity that rivaled any noblewoman. There was grace in the way she moved, an effortless confidence that betrayed a past she refused to share. Perhaps she had some noble blood? The mystery deepened in John's mind. Yet he knew she was not ready to reveal her old life. Another time.

The night deepened.

The wind shifted, carrying with it the scent of distant fields, the open expanse of northern France stretching for miles around them. No sign of civilization. No flicker of distant fires. They were alone.

They had chosen to stay close to the roads, unfamiliar as they were with this land. It was a risk, but a necessary one. It would also keep them visible, should their messenger come looking for them.

Ysabeau, however, knew these lands well.

She had guided them carefully, avoiding paths known to be prowled by highwaymen. John knew that no mere band of thieves could match the steel of trained knights, but with greater numbers they were always a danger. Even the strongest warrior could be overwhelmed.

The land was familiar in name, but John's feet had never trod this deep into this part of France. And yet, it was here— two centuries ago—that his ancestor, Ricardo de Ontivero, had carved his name into history, serving the Duke William before the Bastard became the Conqueror and King of England. Normandy was where his lineage had passed through, before the Conqueror's grant had settled them in Devon.

But that was long ago. Now, the land bore the banners of Philip Augustus, and King John of England fumed over its loss.

A smirk from across the fire. Ysabeau teased the men.

"Your King John still wants these lands back," she said, green eyes alight with mischief. "He will fail, of course."

John scoffed, shaking his head.

George, leaning back on his elbows, huffed.

"You know a lot about politics, do you?"

"Only the parts that matter."

Ysabeau turned the spit, the meat sizzling over the

embers. "You'll find I know many things, Sir George."

George grinned, stretching his legs out toward the fire, savoring its heat.

"Then I hope to learn a great deal more about you in the days to come, Ysa. We've a long road ahead."

The playful tension was interrupted by Reggeye's voice.

"My uncle, Roy Purcell, joined the king's campaign here in Normandy," he said. "He was at Mirebeau."

John raised a brow.

"I wasn't aware of that, lad."

"Aye," Reggeye nodded. "Rank and file. Given a spear. He told me the stories. He saw the young duke—Arthur, I believe it was—taken prisoner. The rumors were that the king had him killed."

George scoffed, shaking his head.

"T'was a mere rumor, lad."

Reggeye's gaze darkened.

"My uncle Roy was there when it happened."

"Is that so?" George mused incredulously. "Perhaps it is true."

"It is. It is what he said. He was there."

A silence settled over them, only the crackle of the fire filling the space between words.

John exhaled, shifting slightly, his gaze settling upon George.

Unlike John, George knew these lands well. He had spent many years here in his youth, riding through the countryside, learning its roads, its rivers, its people.

"You think you know Normandy, do you?" Ysabeau teased, eyes catching the firelight, lips curled at the edges.

George smirked, brushing ash from his sleeve.

"Better than most."

"That so?" She leaned forward, her voice soft but dangerous. "Then tell me—where does the Yvette River run?"

He blinked. A pause.

"The Yvette?" he repeated, his brow furrowing. "That's… southwest of Paris. Cuts through the Vallée de Chevreuse."

She grinned, pleased. But not quite satisfied.

"And what does that have to do with Normandy?" he asked, again narrowing his eyes.

"Nothing," she said, flashing teeth. "I'm just testing you, good sir. Of course, the Yvette does not run through Normandy!"

George exhaled, shaking his head.

"Saints preserve me," he muttered, "a woman with riddles and no map."

Reggeye snorted, enjoying the exchange. John simply shook his head. It was strange—comforting, even—how easily she had settled among them.

She was still a mystery. She spoke of Normandy as if she had walked every inch of it, but her origins remained cloaked in shadow. She was no common beggar—that much was clear.

But he did not ask. Not yet.

The war between Philip and John had ended, but the peace was fragile and could shatter at any moment. If hostilities resumed, men like them—English-born, Norman-blooded, flying the banner of an English barony—would be seen as enemies, imprisoned or ransomed.

John had chosen to camp openly, but he was no fool. His ears were attuned to every sound beyond the fire's glow, his fingers never far from his sword. He, George and Reggeye would take turns at watch, ensuring at least one sentry was awake at all times. War could break out again, at any time. The key was to maintain their vigilance.

Ecclesiastical influence over politics cast its shadow over all the realms. It was Rome that whispered in the ears of kings and nobles, shaping the course of empires.

John had always obeyed.

But the road they were taking was too uncertain.

And for the first time, he questioned God as to where it would lead him.

The fire burned low now, casting restless shadows across the cold earth. Smoke curled into the night sky, its tendrils reaching for the heavens as if in silent supplication. They would need supplication.

John sat still, staring into the embers, his thoughts remained heavy, tangled in the complexity of it all. The road, the mission, the uncertain judgment that awaited them. He could not rest. This journey was not merely about securing absolution—it was about survival. His own. Reggeye's. Breckington's.

It was in these troubled times he sought to cling to the faith Barth had instilled in him—one of mercy, of humility, of a Christ who walked among the lowly. But the contrast gnawed at him, sharper with each passing mile. A contradiction, a contrarium.

The meek and suffering Son of God.

And then there was the Bishop of Rome, who sent his hounds hunting after alleged heretics across kingdoms and countryside's.

The flames flickered, a mesmerizing, untamed force. John almost wished fire alone could purge these burdens from his mind.

A voice cut through his thoughts.

"Lord John, a piece of bread for you?"

Reggeye, offering what little they had.

"Thanks, lad."

Silence settled again. Then, a quiet voice, laced with uncertainty.

"I've been pondering, milord," Reggeye's gaze was lost in the flames. "Would the pope show mercy to me?"

John hesitated, but before he could answer, George scoffed from across the fire.

"The real question, lad, is whether God—if there even *is* a God—would extend His mercy to you," George said, his tone edged with skepticism in a rare open admission of his doubt. "The pope claims to be God's voice on earth, but he is not the Almighty."

Reggeye tensed.

"But the pope wields the power of the Church. He is basically God on earth. From the mightiest king to the lowliest peasant, all listen to him. And if he refuses to grant me pardon..."

He swallowed hard at the thought.

"I could bear my own death, but I cannot bear the thought of Breckington bearing the weight of my sins."

John exhaled deeply as he listened. He could feel the weight in Reggeye's words—the fear, the doubt. The boy was not afraid of his own fate, but of what his sins would cost others. It was this unselfishness that John envisioned all followers of Christ would have. Instead, he witnessed only lust for power and lucre among those who claimed to be operating under the name of God. Still, he wanted to remain loyal to God's Church.

"What can we do," George expressed frustration, picking up a rock and throwing it into the embers, shooting glowing ashes into the air.

"We must trust in His Holiness' mercy, George," John said, eyeing his vassal. "As he serves as God's earthly representative."

George smirked, the flickering firelight catching in his knowing eyes. He said nothing, only prodded at the embers with a stick.

John pressed on.

"But that is not the real matter at hand. It is not only Reggeye's fate that is in question. It is Breckington itself that will be judged alongside him."

Reggeye buried his face in his hands as he wept softly. Ysabeau sat next to him and placed a comforting arm around him.

"Then I am condemned either way. I only pray they spare

our people," he mourned.

John sighed as he got up and walked over, patting the boy on the head.

George exhaled, shaking his head.

"Unlikely that we would be forgiven without some form of restitution," he muttered. "But at least we can say we made the effort. Our honor will remain intact either way."

John leaned back, his mind restless, frustrated. The Church no longer confined itself to the realm of souls—it had entangled itself in the affairs of kings, of lords, of war. Did Rome's reach know no bounds? It judged not only men's faith but their swords, their allegiances, their lands. And now, it sought to judge him, his men—and Breckington itself.

Faith and obedience had long been taught as being one and the same. But when had obedience become unquestionable submission?

He thought of Barth, of his gentle but unyielding teaching of a Christ unburdened by politics, a King who did not sit on earthly thrones nor command earthly armies. Indeed, Barth's Christ was only interested in the hearts of men, not land or lucre.

What would Barth say of this trial?

John did not know.

What he did know was that the Church did not concern itself with the struggles of one small barony on the edge of England. To the pope, to his legates, to the men who wielded the law of God like a sword, they were but a name on a parchment, an offense to be corrected.

John straightened. "Enough talk of doom. We will not bow before fate." He rose, stretching out his limbs. "Get some rest. I will take the first watch."

Reggeye hesitated. "Are you certain, milord?"

John nodded. "Yes. And do not let your mind wander too far into despair. Have faith that all will be well."

The boy swallowed, nodding, though his expression

144

betrayed no relief.

A soft step behind him.

Ysabeau.

"My lord," she said, dipping into a slight curtsy. "With your leave, I shall retire."

John gestured toward his tent. "It is yours, my lady. I will take my rest after my watch with the others."

She nodded, stepping away into the night, disappearing beyond the canvas folds.

The night air was growing colder. The weight of the journey pressed upon them all, but none more than John, the head, the leader. Upon him lay the responsibility of it all. He was exhausted, yet he could not rest. Too much was at stake.

George slipped into his tent, though John knew sleep would not come easily to him; George was as thoughtful a man there was, and the whole ordeal would weight heavy upon him as well. Reggeye sat in prayer before slumber, the boy clinging to what faith he had left...indeed, what life he may have left.

John remained where he was, staring into the dying fire, listening to the soft symphony of the wildlife around him.

The Church had demanded submission.

John would be giving it.

Now, as the flames curled and faded and the darkness grew, he wondered if there would ever be a line he could not cross. A point where faith and duty would stand at odds.

A moment when he, like George, would begin to doubt. In the Church. In God.

The night stretched long ahead. Yet he kept watch, waiting for the dawn.

A new day.

A new start.

He only wished it were that simple.

::

145

Sir Hugh awoke with a start.

No sound. No cry or footfall stirred the stone chamber. Yet his breath caught short, as though summoned from some dreamless void by a presence unnamed.

He sat up slowly, the weight of sleep still pressing against his shoulders. The room, once cloaked in blackness, now shimmered in silver—moonlight spilling through the arched window like a blessing or a curse. The heavy quilt slid from his chest as he rose, bare feet brushing cold rushes.

He crossed to the window, the tower's height giving him full view of Breckington's slumbering lands. The hills stretched like folded parchment beneath the stars, still and pale beneath the waning moon.

And there—

A flicker.

A blur against the rise. Dark forms, vague and swift—riders, perhaps. Four? Five? He could not say.

They stood—or moved—on the eastern slope. Not torch-lit, not loud, but there. Perhaps half a league from the castle walls. Shadow figures against the still-dark grass, low and lean like wolves sniffing at the edge of a sleeping flock of sheep.

His hand instinctively reached for the hilt of the sword resting on the wall beside the window. Were they infiltrated? Should he alert the garrison?

For a breath, he watched, unmoving. But the shapes did not advance. They did not retreat. They simply… lingered. Flickering, as if unreal. As if they were only the imprint of something that had already passed.

Then—they were gone.

Not with a gallop. Not with fanfare. Simply… *vanished*.

Hugh blinked. Rubbed his eyes with the back of his hand. Looked again.

The hills were empty.

Only the silence remained—deep, whole, untouched.

A long moment passed before he turned away from the

146

window. The night pressed inward, no longer threatening, only vast. He sat once more on the edge of the bed, palms to his brow, his breath slow and even.

He told himself it was nothing. A trick of moonlight and worry. Too much wine the night before. Too many burdens now.

He lay down again. The mattress held the memory of John's weight. Hugh pulled the blanket over his shoulders and closed his eyes, though the image of the figures still lingered behind them.

"You're seeing ghosts now, Hugh," he muttered to himself, half in jest, half in dread.

The silence answered him with stillness.

He attempted to drift back to sleep, but the shadow in his mind became a constant companion, stubborn, insistent.

It would be a long night.

::

The dawn broke cold and golden, the mist retreating from the hills and fields like a specter fleeing the light. The faint glow of embers still smoldered in the firepit, casting a fleeting warmth over the dew-kissed canvas tents.

John de Ontivero pulled his woolen cloak tighter around his shoulders and nodded to George as the knight rose to take the next watch. The night had been quiet, the road remained devoid of activity. That, in itself, was cause for suspicion in George's mind. He would take no chances.

He stood fully armed, the weight of his chainmail a familiar feeling as he adjusted his sword belt. It was second nature to him now. The early morning silence stretched around him as he paced the perimeter of their encampment at a generous distance. He wanted to make sure he got wind of threats well before they got anywhere near the camp.

Then—faint at first, but unmistakable—the steady rhythm of hooves against the hardened dirt. George tightened his grip around the hilt of his sword—someone was coming—actually several men were coming.

Travelers at this hour were rare. The roads lay mostly still at dawn, save for merchants or messengers with urgent business. George moved toward the sound, slipping into the tall grass, concealed in the shadows of the landscape.

Three riders emerged from the mist.

They came at a brisk gallop, their gray and yellow garments unmistakable in the early light. Nasal helms gleamed dull in the morning haze. They bore little in the way of arms—short swords at their belts, no lances, no shields. Couriers, perhaps. Or something more.

George remained perfectly still, observing. The riders rode with purpose. Urgency. Their eyes darting left and right, looking for something.

Satisfied that they posed no significant threat, he stepped into view. His presence alone was enough to halt them.

The lead rider raised a fist, signaling the others to stop. He straightened in his saddle as he trotted his mount near, eyeing George with measured scrutiny.

"Good knight, might you be in the company of Sir John Breckington?" he called out in French, his accent sharp, his tone weighted with authority.

George met his gaze steadily. A sergeant, by his bearing—one in the service of an important man.

"Aye," he replied in English, his tone even. Of course, he knew French and could speak it well. He could have also responded in Anglo-Norman, but he wanted to emphasize his distinct English identity—solidarity with the common people of his land, nobility be damned. "Who queries?"

"I am Aubert Charlot, sergeant in the service of His Eminence Arnaud Amalric, Abbot of Cîteaux."

The sergeant switched to broken English, his words thick with a Northern French accent.

"As papal legate, he requests you join him forthwith at the Abbey of Cîteaux to deliberate upon the fate of Baron

148

John and his men."

George exhaled through his nose, nodding. The summons was no surprise.

"Follow me," he said, motioning toward their camp.

The men urged their horses forward, but George did not miss the way their hands lingered near their hilts, their posture tense, their gazes darting toward the trees.

He smirked.

"Relax. If we intended to ambush you, you'd already be lying by the roadside."

Aubert, unimpressed, held his stern expression.

"I hear it is your *talent of ambushing* that has led you to this plight."

His gaze was sharp, the insult barely veiled.

George chuckled, amused.

"Well struck, my friend."

The sergeant said nothing in response, but his posture eased ever so slightly. He gestured for George to lead the way.

They pressed forward through the brush and over the frost-hardened ground, the road widening into the small clearing where the Breckington men had made their temporary camp.

John and Reggeye were already awake, tending to a breakfast of roasting fowl.

"My lord baron," George called as they entered, "these men come in the service of the papal legate. They ask us to accompany them to their abbey in Cîteaux."

John rose, wiping his hands on his tunic. His expression was warm, his posture welcoming. "Friends, please, join us."

But the Frenchmen remained stiff, unmoving.

John feigned disappointment.

"Ah, I see. No time for socializing."

Aubert shook his head. "We are under strict orders to escort you to our abbey. His Eminence has insisted you come

149

at once. We were dispatched in four groups to find you." His fingers hovered near his sword belt. "When we saw your man in blue and yellow, we knew we had found your retinue."

John's jaw tightened, his body stiffening. They had been *hunted*—hunted like prey in the forest.

"Forgive me, lord," Aubert continued, "if we are not too keen on staying longer than we must."

John folded his arms, lowering his voice for George's ears alone.

"You'd think we were already excommunicated by the way they treat us."

George only gave a knowing smirk.

The Breckington men moved swiftly, breaking camp with the efficiency of seasoned warriors. Their mounts were saddled, their gear carefully distributed, their preparations wordless but precise.

Transient as it was, this encampment had been no different from countless others—a fleeting pause in a march that stretched endlessly into uncertainty.

John pulled the saddle's strap tight, his mind turning to their destination.

The Abbey of Cîteaux.

A place of reverence, of monastic discipline, of reform. Or so it was told to him. Founded over a century ago by men who had sought to return to the purity of Saint Benedict's rule—rejecting the wealth and decadence of places like Cluny, stripping faith down to discipline and toil.

To John, its history was no abstraction, but real and tangible—several of Breckington's priests had been trained by the monastics from that abbey.

Stephen Harding, its famed English abbot, was a name spoken with admiration in Dorset and Devon, a man who had left his homeland to forge something new—a movement that had reshaped monastic life across Christendom.

And now, Cîteaux was no longer merely a house of

worship. It seemed to have become something else. Armed guards who answered to the abbot? He entertained the possibilities in his mind.

A seat of power.

A place where men did not merely seek God, but sought *judgment*—judgment of others, their rivals, their enemies.

The unfortunate encounter with Sir Renhard Galt made it clear that the monks of Cîteaux had abandoned the silence of their cloisters to whisper in the ears of kings and lords, to shape the fates of men. This was no longer about faith—it was about domination. About control. Political power.

John swung into his saddle, the familiar weight of his sword resting at his hip.

He had obeyed the orders of the Church all his life.

But now, he had second thoughts.

Yet, he understood the implications for his barony should he defy.

John adjusted the reins, his fingers tightening against the worn leather. His thoughts thick with concern and uncertainty. About the road ahead. About the weight of history pressing down on them, unseen but certainly felt. The abbey of Cîteaux awaited. He thought of Stephen Harding's legacy—a legacy which had a significant influence on their destination. It was Harding who had authored the *Carta Caritatis*—the Charter of Charity—the document that had bound the Cistercian order under one rule, one vision. Poverty, toil, devotion. A return to the simplicity the older Benedictine houses had forsaken.

Was it the same today? It did not seem quite so.

A century ago, monks had built the abbey. Built a vision. Simplicity, labor, devotion. A rejection of excess. A return to something pure. Yet now, a hundred years later, that purity now held the power to shape empires.

John let out a breath. A shift in the saddle.

"All prepared, milord."

Reggeye, patting his steed, voice light despite the tension

curling at the edges.

John nodded. "Excellent. Sir George?"

A grin.

"Prepared, Lord John. Shall we ride forth to glory?"

The mood did not match the weight in John's chest. But he let it pass. Let it settle.

Then—*Ysabeau*.

A question unspoken, hanging in the morning air.

John turned to Aubert.

"What of her?"

There was a shift. A tightening of the Frenchman's jaw.

"The abbey has strict rules. Women are not permitted."

A blow. Expected. But a blow nonetheless. John knew it would hit his vassal hardest.

George bristled, voice sharp.

"That is absurd. She has been invaluable to us. We cannot simply leave her behind."

A stillness. Just for a moment. Then, he felt her hand on his arm. A soft touch, steady, grounding.

"Sir George," she murmured, "please, do not trouble yourself. I understand how it works."

Her eyes gazed upon John now.

"Lord John, I will not burden you. I will make my way to my father's estate. Perhaps my family will take me in."

John studied her. Searching. He had himself become attached to the lass.

"Are you sure?"

A smile. Warm. Sad. But fully resigned.

"Yes."

She stepped back.

The decision had been made, yet the weight of it pressed against John's chest. *A woman alone. A girl, truly.* The roads were not kind. Not to men. Even less to women.

He studied Ysabeau. She stood firm, chin lifted, hands clasped in quiet resolve. Unshaken. Unafraid. Or perhaps simply resigned.

It did not sit well—not with any of them. But it was George's jaw that clenched.

"This is madness!" His voice was sharp as he turned to their escort, cutting against the silence. "She cannot go alone. My lord?"

John pursed his lips. He could of nothing in response to his friend. He turned to the Frenchman.

Aubert did not flinch.

"The abbey has strict rules."

George's grip tightened on the reins.

"Damn their rules."

Ysabeau exhaled softly. A hand on his arm. It was a quiet consolation, a reassurance.

"Sir George," she murmured, "please."

The knight protector paused. He breathed deeply. Then John turned to his vassal.

"She's right."

George turned to him, eyes burning.

"*She's right?* My lord, she has no mount. No protection. You would send her to fate's mercy?"

Reggeye piped up, voice hesitant.

"Milord, I—I would give her my horse. If she would take it."

John glanced at the boy, surprised by the offer. Reggeye's face was set, determined, though his hands trembled faintly against the saddle.

George did not hesitate. He swung down from his mount, taking the dagger from his belt.

"Take this," he said, pressing it into Ysabeau's hands. "If a man comes too close, use it. If an animal snarls, use it. If you need to gut a hare, use it."

She looked at him, her lips parting as if to protest.

He shook his head, his voice lowered.

"No refusals. You ride, Ysabeau. I detest having to abandon you. With every fiber of my being, I protest having to do this."

"You are not abandoning me, kind sir. You have given me more kindness than I have known in years. And I know these roads. I will be fine."

George was not so willing. He reached for her hand, grasping it tight. A promise in his grip.

"I will find you," he swore. "No matter what, I will come back for you."

A silence. A flicker of something in her gaze.

Then—a whisper.

"It is not you who will find me," she paused. Took a breath. "It is I who will find you."

George kissed her hand gently. The warmth of her skin a balm for his rough lips. He reluctantly let go and mounted his charger.

Reggeye was already unfastening his saddlebags, securing supplies. Tent. Armor. Weapons. These were transferred to John's mount.

But the bread, a flask of water, dried meat, wrapped in cloth—these he held out for his friend.

"Take these."

John exhaled, watching Ysabeau carefully. She hesitated.

"He's right. Take them."

She paused, then nodded.

Gracious. Poised. As if accepting a gift rather than a necessity.

Reggeye climbed onto George's mount, settling behind him. A boy riding double. An inconvenience, but a small one.

Ysabeau took the reins, adjusting to the weight of the saddle. She moved with ease, the sign of someone accustomed to riding.

Good.

George still wasn't satisfied. He had his mount trot closer, his grip firm on her wrist.

"Ysabeau," his voice low, urgent, "Promise me."

A silence.

"Promise me you'll be safe."

A flicker of something behind her eyes. A knowing smile.

"No, Sir George," she whispered. "But I promise I will survive."

She turned, speaking once more in her Breton tongue.

"Kenavo, ma mignoned ker. Ra zougfe an aveloù ac'hanoc'h en surentez, ha ra vefe hon hentoù adwelet. C'hwi a zo bet ma sklêrijenn en deñvalijenn. Ra vezo benniget ha gwarezet."

Then—before anyone could say more—she leaned forward, a brush of warmth against George's cheek. A farewell.

And then she was off. The horse carried her forward, hooves muffled against the damp earth. She did not look back.

Reggeye watched her disappear into the mist.

"What did she say, sir?"

George exhaled as he watched his charge ride off into the distance.

"Farewell, my dear friends. May the winds carry you safely and may our paths cross again. You have been my light in the darkness. Be blessed and protected."

Silence.

Then a signal. They advanced, as one by one, they turned east, following Aubert and his men.

George and Reggeye lingered. Eyes fixed on the path she had taken. The dawn stretched wide before them, and still, he did not move.

Then—a sharp breath.

And he spurred their horse forward. They rode east, towards their fate.

::

A knock. Sharp. Insistent.

155

Father Barth paused, fingers tightening on the edges of his cloak. Late hour. Too late for good tidings.

Another knock. Louder this time. The knock then turned to a loud pounding.

Not the touch of a weary traveler. Not the quiet plea of a penitent looking for confession. No. This was different.

He unlatched the door.

Three dark figures emerged. Cloaked. Faces hidden beneath the shadows formed by the dim glow of the candles. The leader took a step forward. A breath of cold air curling between them.

"The merchant, Father," the figure spoke, voice flat and sinister. "The one called Edwinson. Where did his possessions go?"

Barth held steady.

"His goods were given to his kin, then, to those in need."

A slight shift in movement. A flicker of something beneath their hoods.

"All of them?"

"Yes."

It was the truth. But not the whole truth.

A pause of silence. Then—

"His kin," the second man rasped, a scar cutting across his cheek from an old wound. "Where are they?"

Barth's stomach turned. He knew exactly what they were after.

The ledger. The names. The secrets.

"I do not know."

He told the truth again. Edwinson's kin took off, fearful of persecution. He did not know where they went.

There was another pause. A cold, silent, stretching moment.

Then—laughter. Low. Humorless. Scornful. Malevolence was deep in their tone.

"Perhaps the townsfolk do," the third figure mused, voice thick with menace.

Then they turned. Barth's chest tightened as they stepped past him, moving into the town square like shadows spilling into the streets. They approached a young man, carrying a sack of flour.

A voice, rang out.

"You knew Edwinson. Tell us—who are his kin?"

A murmur of confusion. Other townsfolk stirring from the quiet began to wonder aloud, wary glances exchanging between them.

No answer.

The scarred man moved first. A shove. A dull *thud* as the young man hit the ground. Then another. A fist striking flesh. A gasp.

A woman's cry split the air.

"Stop it! Don't hurt him, please!"

The town stirred. Others had come to witness the commotion. More hands. More violence. A boot driving into a hunched figure. A ragged cough from the dirt.

And then—

"Enough!"

A voice, firm. Steady.

It was the squire, James Nugent. Peter Marshall flanked his left, Harold at his right—Lacey's man, hand on the hilt of his blade. The air shifted with unease. The strangers paused. Their work interrupted.

A slow step back. A glance exchanged between them. The leader's lips curled, a finger held out towards Nugent.

"You should choose your loyalties carefully."

Then—they retreated. Not hurried. Not afraid. Just a step back into the shadows, slipping away like mist in the night. They were gone just as swiftly as they had appeared.

The square was now still. The weight of the event lingering in the air.

Harold exhaled deeply, knuckles white around his sword.

"Who in God's name were they?"

Barth shook his head, though the answer was already

settled in his mind.

Trouble. They would return. And next time, they wouldn't come with just questions and fists.

::

The road stretched long beneath the rising sun, golden light spilling over the rolling fields like an opening scroll. A quiet, fleeting comfort.

George rode in silence, his mind elsewhere—on a girl vanishing into the distant mist.

Where would she go? Had she a place she could call "home"?

He pursed his lips. He would find her. As soon as this was all over, and he had finished his mission to accompany his lord, he would seek her.

Reggeye stirred behind him, eyes scanning the countryside.

"Don't worry, Sir George, she will be alright," the young squire assured, as if able to read his thoughts.

George cleared his throat, but otherwise remained silent.

Aubert, unmoved by the sentimentality, tugged sharply at the reins, urging his mount forward. No hesitation. No sympathy. His orders were to ensure they arrived at the abbey without delay. The column followed him, the steady clatter of hooves filling the still morning air.

The land unraveled before them, familiar to George, yet foreign to Reggeye and John. The hills rolled gently, not unlike those of Southwest England, but the design of the homes were different—steep-roofed cottages, their stone walls whispering of a land that was not their own. Travelers were moving along the road, some giving them wary glances, others too lost in their own burdens to care.

Midday approached, the sun at its zenith and the heat was settling in. John urged his horse forward, falling in alongside their leader, Aubert.

158

"Sergeant Charlot, might we perchance break bread and find respite in Orléans by nightfall?"

"No, my lord," Aubert replied without looking back. "We press on."

John frowned.

"At this pace, our mounts will tire. A brief rest is essential."

"My lord, we cannot. We are under strict orders to present you before His Eminence within a fortnight."

John exhaled, his patience thinning.

"But our horses need reprieve. We need rest!"

Aubert's grip tightened on the reins.

"Once more, my lord, we go on," he said sharply before emitting a huge sigh before continuing—"Very well, we shall rest briefly in Orléans, but then we shall continue on. More rest and sustenance will await you upon your arrival."

A flicker of irritation crossed John's face. He urged his mount onward, but he was visibly annoyed.

George, catching his expression, trotted him and Reggeye up beside him. A firm pat on the back.

"Milord, we're going to be fine. Let's get this over and done with."

John sighed. No use pressing the issue further. He leaned back slightly to let his shoulders relax, if only momentarily.

The road that stretched before them was winding through the heart of the northern French countryside. Fields of gold swayed in the wind, the scent of ripened wheat mixed with the damp musk of the earth. Wildflowers peppered the roadside—reds, yellows, blues—bending and trembling in the breeze, as if nodding to the passing travelers.

A large forest loomed over them on their right, its gnarled trees casting deep shadows, filtering the sunlight into shifting patches of golden ribbons and shadow. There was a rustling beneath the thick canopy, the faint snap of a twig. A fox, perhaps. Or something else. John kept his ears sharp, his eyes ever vigilant.

Then, they heard the sound of flowing water. A brook, glinting in the midday sun, stretched before them, snaking through the woods, its wooden bridge worn smooth by countless crossings. The steady gurgling sound of the stream mixed with the laughter and giggles of women gathered at its banks, their skirts held high as they worked, voices light with teasing and chatter, some bathing in the nude.

Reggeye's head turned, eyes lingering a moment too long.

"Eyes front, lad," George chuckled, nudging his flank with an elbow.

Reggeye's face flushed crimson as George playfully jerked on the reins as their horse hesitated mid-step.

Aubert scoffed at this display.

"Hedonism shall unravel the soul," he intoned, voice heavy with condemnation. "A certain path to the infernal fires of damnation."

George rolled his eyes upward in a dramatic gesture of annoyance, finding himself unable to restrain the impulse to respond.

"Tell me true, sergeant, have you ever known the intimacy of a woman?"

The sergeant grasped the reins until his knuckles paled, steadying himself against the inquiry. "The vows of our order forbid such earthly pleasures, as we renounce all joys of the corporeal realm," he replied tonelessly. George released a peal of mirth that echoed across the open fields, finding amusement where others saw only asceticism.

"Then, you, sir, cannot fathom the struggles of us common men. While you took vows of celibacy, young Reggeye here... did not."

The sergeant's face burned dark red, a shade more crimson than Reggeye's.

John chuckled at the debacle, shaking his head.

"Let it be, Sir George. The good sergeant seems to harbor an envy for that which he has chosen to forsake."

"I assure you, my lord, that no envy dwells within me!" Aubert denied sharply.

But the Breckington men were already laughing in their seats, their mirth rolling over the quiet of the road and into the trees.

Aubert's face darkened. He stiffened in the saddle, urging his mount ahead, back straight as a pike as he sought to increase the distance between himself and his tormentors.

The laughter lingered behind him, but he did not turn.

His silence said enough.

It remained silent for a while, as men continue their travel.

Perhaps it was exhaustion—or perhaps contemplation that drove their silence.

The road stretched long behind them, swallowed by the rolling hills and forests of Normandy. Ahead, the land unfolded, the golden light catching upon swaying fields. Thyme and rosemary crushed beneath the hooves of their horses, their scent rising in the warmth of the afternoon sun. Meadows sprawled like a painter's vision, wildflowers dancing against the riders' boots as they passed.

Bridges, old as the land itself, arched over whispering streams. The stone, worn smooth by centuries, bore the weight of countless crossings—traders, soldiers, pilgrims. The water below shimmered, cool and clear, splashing softly as they leaned to fill their waterskins.

A château loomed in the distance, its towers rising from a hilltop like the broken teeth of some long-dead beast. A falcon circled high above the fields, its cry splitting the air before it vanished into the clouds.

Then—the road dipped, pulling them into the shade of a wooded glen.

The air turned crisp. Leaves rustled overhead, a quiet chorus against the steady clop of their chargers' hooves. Light and shadow played tricks along the forest floor, shifting patterns swallowed by the dark.

Dusk began to creep in, stretching the shadows long across their path.

The only sound was the rhythm of the ride, the clinking of armor, the occasional snort of a tired horse.

Then—he broke the silence.

"Silent as a monastery, isn't he?"

George's voice broke the stillness, his grin barely contained.

Reggeye chuckled.

"Maybe he's counting his prayers." He smirked, glancing at John. "What do you think, milord? Ten for every mile?"

John smirked but kept his tone measured.

"Let the man have his peace. Apparently, not all are so easily amused by your wit, George."

"Oh, I'm certain he's just planning how best to convert us heathens," George quipped, succumbing to an irresistible temptation to grin. "A sermon by the campfire, perhaps?"

Reggeye snorted aloud.

"I'd rather have a jug of wine than a sermon. No offense to the good sergeant, of course."

Aubert stiffened, his silence grew heavier by the moment.

George wasn't finished.

"Careful, Reggeye. He might make you trade your wine for water—holy water at that."

Laughter rippled through trio, their voices carrying through the trees. John caught one of Aubert's men stifling a chuckle from the corner of his eye.

Aubert's grip tightened on the reins, visibly irritated.

John finally shook his head, amusement tugging at the edges of his lips, smirking discreetly, out of sight of their escorts.

"Enough, you two. Save your jokes for the evening after our stomachs are full. I doubt the good sergeant would appreciate a homily on humor, no?"

George flashed a grin.

"A shame. I think we could all learn a thing or two about joy, even in chastity."

Aubert exhaled sharply. He nudged his horse forward, pulling ahead of the group, his back straight. The laughter followed him.

The sun dipped lower, swallowed by the treetops. The road darkened, swallowed by the coming night.

George struck flint, his torch flaring to life. One by one, the riders followed suit, flames bobbing in the darkness like will-o'-the-wisps leading them forward.

Then—the woods fell away.

A vast plain stretched before them, the last breath of twilight giving way to the endless shroud of night. The air shifted. A hum in the distance. Faint at first. Then growing.

A city, full of life.

Orléans.

The fortified spires reached longingly towards the stars, shimmering in the moon-glow. Age-worn walls that withstood wars whispered of battles past. Named after the Roman Emperor Aurelian, its guard towers stood stalwart as sentinels, ever watchful over the city. Ever waiting. They drew closer.

The lanes narrowed as houses crowded together, angling towards one another as if to exchange neighborhood news in hushed tones. Cobblestone clattered beneath iron-shod hooves as voices permeated the alleys—low rumbles, drunken cheer, the sporadic clang of mugs meeting wood.

The aroma of mead wafted towards them sweetly, thick and inviting.

Orléans was a place of commerce, of vice, of shadowy agreements made after dark. The journey had been draining. The road had been relentless. But here, for a moment, they could rest at last—if only briefly.

::

A chill penetrated the chamber's ancient stone wall as blasts of wind played a lament against it. Melted wax pooled in circles on the table, its scent permeating the room.

Sir Hugh pressed the seal into the warm crimson pool, cooling it with a sharp breath. The last of the letters—done. Six in total, rolled tight, bound with twine. The hour was deep, the fire in the hearth reduced to smoldering embers, yet sleep would not come. Not with this weight on his shoulders.

If only he had sent a patrol out that night he saw the four specters in the hills. Perhaps this could have all been prevented.

No time for rest. Not now. The message had to reach John.

Wherever he is.

Hugh sighed, his fingers curling around the parchment. The events of the past few days sat heavily upon his chest. It had to be addressed—and soon.

Shadowy figures had been slipping through the streets. Whispers turning into demands. Questions about Edwinson's possessions—about his kin. About what had been left behind after the attack.

Barth had held firm, but not unscathed.

The townspeople got the worse of the altercation.

A bruised jaw. A shaken town. The threat had come and gone, but the message was clear—they would be back.

Who "they" were was not entirely clear.

And they were looking for something.

The ledger.

Hugh didn't know where Barth had hidden it. Perhaps it was better that way. What he *did* know was that the town was no longer safe. If Lord John was their only chance to set things right, then he needed to know *now*.

He turned to his six messengers, their faces shadowed in the dim candlelight. Young men, hardened by duty. Loyal to Breckington.

"Make haste," Hugh ordered in a low, steady voice low. "No delays. Ride as though hell itself is at your heels. Our survival may depend upon it."

A sharp nod. Then—

"Yes, sir."

No hesitation. No wasted breath.

Their boots scuffed sharply against the cold stone as they strode out into the open courtyard. The creak of leather, the jingle of harnesses—and stirrups.

Then—the thunder of hooves.

They vanished swiftly through the gates, swallowed by the darkness, their silhouettes lost to the midnight void. They knew their assignment.

The silence that followed was deafening.

Hugh remained perfectly still, listening intently until the last echo of the messengers' departure faded into quietness.

Only then did he allow himself to breathe.

Time was slipping through their fingers. Lord John of Breckington had to be informed.

::

The pale glow of dawn stretched long across the land.

It had been ten days since Orléans. Ten days of unbroken travel.

The sun, a golden herald of the morning, clawed its way above the horizon, its warmth doing little to shake the weariness that gripped John's body. The long, unrelenting pace had stripped them down to their limits. He had known grueling marches before—the heat of the Holy Land, the endless push through barren wastes—but knowing it and enduring it anew were two different things.

He was not alone in his exhaustion.

Reggeye slumped in the saddle behind George, his head bobbing with every jolt of their mount. George fared better himself, though lines of fatigue etched themselves on his face, his own weariness apparent in the way he clenched the reins of their horse with determination. Aubert and his men, however, pressed on with the same relentless rhythm, their expressions unreadable, their pace unyielding.

No commands were needed. They all knew the cost of the journey.

As John's destrier sidled up beside them, his gaze fell on Reggeye's chest—where a worn scrap of parchment had worked itself loose from the boy's tunic. With each slow sway of the horse, it slipped further.

John reached out and caught it before the wind could claim it. He expected nothing more than a scribble—a scrap of song or nonsense—but as his eyes moved across the lines, he slowed.

The writing was clumsy but earnest. Charcoal strokes heavy with thought.

Twelve days from Orléans. The road's grown colder, even though the sun's still with us. We've eaten less, spoken less. Even Sir George's jokes have run dry.

Lady Ysabeau gave me her parchment before she was turned away. "You're not much for words," she told me, "but maybe the road will teach you some." I miss her. She rides straighter than me, even after all we've seen. Would've given her my own mount again if it meant she could've stayed.

We passed shrines and gallows. Fields full of poppies, and a monk preaching to no one. A man hanging upside-down from a tree two days back— tongue gone. My Lord John's face didn't change. Just lowered his head and rode on.

Soon we see the abbey. Cold like judgment. The kind of holy that makes your spine itch.

But still—I prayed just now. Not for strength. Not for justice. Just for my Lord John. He carries so much. He shouldn't have to. If they judge him, they'll be judging every man who's tried to do right with blood still on his hands. That's all of us. That's me. I'm the cause of it all.

If I die here, I die loyal to him. I hope he knows that.

— Reginald

A lump formed in John's throat. He tucked the parchment into his own tunic and rode with it pressing heavily upon his chest.

He remembered the first time he'd laid eyes on the boy—*Reginald de Saint-Clair*, he was called then, before soldiers and stable boys had shortened it to "Reggeye".

It was after mass, when spring still wore the scent of ash and thaw, and Lord John had returned from the border dispute with the Earl of Salisbury. He was bone-weary, bleeding from a shallow cut across the ribs, and craving solitude.

Instead, he found a brawl.

Not in the taverns of the town, nor among the rowdy guards in the yard, but *in the training green behind the chapel*, of all places.

Two lads were rolling in the mud, fists flying, sashes torn. One was red-haired and broad, from a minor household in Totnes. The other was smaller, wiry, fast. Muck covered them both, but it was the *flicker* in the smaller boy's eyes that caught John's attention—not rage, but calculation.

John signaled the guards to wait, stepped forward, and barked, "Enough!"

They parted at once. The red-haired boy stumbled back, nose bloodied. The smaller one stood straight despite the welt blooming across his jaw.

He bowed. Sloppy, but genuine.

"Name," John said.

167

"Reginald, my lord," the boy replied. "Of Saint-Clair. My grandsire fought under your father in Brittany, at Nantes."

Saint-Clair. The name was familiar. A fallen house— once respected, now little more than landless blood. Yet the boy did not speak it with shame.

"Why were you fighting?" John asked.

"He mocked my accent," Reginald responded plainly, jerking his thumb toward the other bleeding lad. "Said my Latin was peasant-born and I'd never rise past scut work."

John looked between them. The other boy bristled, but said nothing.

"And?"

"I proved him wrong."

There was no arrogance in it—just a defiant edge. A boy daring to hope the world might make room for him, despite all its rules.

John gave a small nod.

"Clean yourself up. Report to Osric in the yard at dawn tomorrow. If you can stay on your feet through the drills, you'll earn a place among the squires."

Reginald blinked. Bowed again—lower this time.

"Yes, my lord."

John turned to go.

"And Reginald—learn to sheath your pride faster than your sword. There are greater battles to fight than avenging insults."

"Aye, my lord. But some insults cut deeper."

John didn't answer then. But something about the boy had lingered. It still did. He was special, that Reggeye.

Back in the present, the wind shifted.

John's fingers brushed against the parchment again, warm against his heart. He remembered that boy in the mud. And the young man now dozing behind Sir George. A squire soon to be a knight. A brother-in-arms. And perhaps— soon—a sacrifice.

John's jaw set. Not if he could help it. He would fight it, tooth and nail.

Duty. Penance.

The need to answer for his and his men's actions, to shield his men, his lands, from the wrath of Roman pontiff. There would be no room for hesitation, no space for doubt. He pressed forward, through aching limbs and the overwhelming haze of exhaustion.

Sleep took him before he realized it.

Just a brief moment of stolen rest. A lull in the saddle. Then—

A hand on his shoulder.

John jolted awake, George's firm grip bringing him back to the waking world.

"We've arrived, my lord."

John blinked against the dawn's soft light.

Before them, the open field stretched wide, an immense clearing cradled in the arms of dense woodlands. Humble huts clustered near a stone cottage, smoke curling from their chimneys in lazy spirals. And beyond them, rising above the mist, stood the renowned Abbey of Cîteaux.

John allowed himself a deep breath. Relief.

Reggeye, shaking off his fatigue, let out a quiet prayer of thanks.

The horses sagged beneath their riders, their bodies slick with sweat, their steps slow. John hoped—prayed—that within these walls, they would find food, water, rest. That for a moment, the uncertainty would fade, and would be replaced by the quiet, comforting sanctuary of the abbey.

But even as they approached, something stirred just beyond.

Figures in monks' robes moved about the courtyard, their tonsured heads bowed, large crucifixes swaying from their necks. But it was not the sight of praying men that caught John's attention.

It was the sound of steel. A sharp clang. A clash of metal against metal.

Then another.

The rhythmic exchange of blows echoed through the cold morning air.

As they passed the outer huts, the source of the noise came into view. A group of knights sparred within a marked ring, their movements precise, deliberate. The duel ended in a swift strike—the victor standing firm, his fallen opponent rising with his aid.

John and his men drew closer as the triumphant knight removed his helm.

A face—worn, lined with age yet strong. A man in his fifties, his features bearing the trials of decades. His head, shaven save for the tonsure, marked him not only as a warrior but as a man of the cloth.

Aubert dismounted, stepping forward with reverence.

"Your Eminence," he said, bowing deeply. "I present to you the Lord Breckington and his retinue."

The knight-monk—Arnaud Amalric—studied them with sharp, knowing eyes. Then, a nod.

"Thank you, Brother Charlot." His voice was rich, his English marked with the thick cadence of a French tongue. "See that these men find proper repose and sustenance. Their steeds as well."

"Yes, Your Eminence."

Without another word, Aubert remounted and led his men toward the abbey walls, their figures disappearing into the great stone church.

John remained still, watching the abbot. Amalric met his gaze, a slow, deliberate smile curving his lips.

"I am Arnaud Amalric, Abbot of Cîteaux and legate to His Holiness, Pope Innocent." His voice held weight, an authority that did not need to be announced. "Lord John Breckington, I am pleased to finally make your acquaintance."

John inclined his head in respect.

"As am I, Your Eminence." He gestured to his men. "This is my vassal, Sir George de Wymondham, and his squire, Reginald de Saint-Clair. We—" He paused. A steadying breath, then—

"We are at your service."

The abbot's smile lingered.

"We have much to discuss."

His attendant moved to unfasten the rest of his armor, the abbot standing patient, unbothered by the task.

"But for now, find rest. I would have you all refreshed before we begin our deliberations."

A flicker of something beneath his tone.

John nodded.

"*Oïl, vostre* Éminence."

The words felt strange on his tongue, even though they were Anglo-Norman, and the learned abbot could certainly understand them.

Yet, John understood the reason for the tense atmosphere. The abbot knew of what had transpired in Breckington.

The meeting had begun long before he had spoken any words.

Hubris

he sunlight poured into the room, painting the interior with a bright morning auburn. The bed creaked beneath him as he shifted over. John stirred gently, his body slow to remember where it was. He breathed deeply. Then—his eyes opened.

Ah, yes. The abbey.

Not the spartan quarters he had anticipated but a room of unnerving luxury—polished furnishings, rich tapestries, a featherbed softer than any cot in the field. This chamber spoke not of austerity but of the comforts of nobility. He did not know what to make out of it all. Perhaps he just needed to rest a bit more.

A knock.

A quiet, deliberate rap against the heavy door. John

straightened, pushing himself upright.

As the door eased open, a young man entered, his movements precise, reverent. The distinctive tonsure marked him as a brother of the order, his dark habit draping loosely over his frame, a large crucifix hung from his neck, the wood worn smooth from use.

His head remained bowed. Hands clasped, just below the cross. Lips moving in hushed prayer.

A slow, deliberate sign of the cross.

Only then did he look up.

"Lord Breckington," he intoned, voice soft, careful. "Blessed morning. His Eminence requests your presence in the dining hall. Please attend forthwith."

A slight bow. Then, as smoothly as he had entered, he withdrew.

John exhaled, rubbing his hands over his face. Two days. Two days of solitude. Locked in thought. Locked in *this room*.

He had not seen George or Reggeye. Had not even been told where they were. The monks had made that clear. He was to *wait*.

To reflect. To pray.

Meals had been delivered in quiet procession. Fresh linens, clean garments, a wash basin—luxuries that should have eased his mind.

Instead, they unsettled him. A prison. But one gilded in comfort. Now, at last, the summons had come.

John rose, shaking the stiffness from his limbs. He dressed quickly, foregoing his heavier attire for something more practical.

Then—the door. A deep breath. A step forward. Freedom.

The hallway stretched ahead, lined with simple doors, each belonging to a Cistercian brother. The silence pressed in, heavy, expectant.

John walked.

Two monks passed him, their steps measured, their eyes downcast, heads bowed in reverence. One lifted a hand to point, a silent gesture showing the way.

He walked in the direction of the gesture.

The corridor ran long then widened into an inner courtyard. Sunlight spilled across the stone from small portals, dappling the ground with shifting patterns of light and shadow. The air wafted with the scent of damp earth, of old wood, of candle wax.

Then—a figure.

Brother Charlot.

The sergeant—now monk—approached, his gait as rigid as ever. The habit did little to soften him. His back remained ramrod straight, his face expressionless, his movements as precise as they had been in armor.

John slowed, stepping into his path.

A curt nod. Recognition. Not respect.

The unease from before returned. Something *was* off here. John exhaled, steadying himself. He needed answers. And he would not move until he had them.

The air was heavy. *Tense.*

John crossed his arms, ready for verbal combat, the cool morning air doing little to temper the heat in his words.

"So, Aubert," he began, voice smooth, deliberate, "tell me—how does a monastic order reconcile vows of humility and peace with the art of war? The sight of swords and spears in a monastery is hardly what I expected."

Charlot's brows pulled together, the muscles in his jaw tightening. Annoyance flickered in his eyes, though he remained composed. Barely.

"It is *Brother* Charlot to you now, *milord,*" his tone was clipped, each word sharp as a drawn blade. "And you should know that it is not for you to question the ways of this holy order."

John maintained his stare, unshaken by the monk's impudence.

"Indulge me, Brother." A measured pause before he continued, "What caused this order—once devoted to quiet piety—to take up arms like the Templars and Hospitallers?"

Charlot's lips pressed into a thin line. He exhaled sharply, as though wasting breath on the conversation was already a burden.

"A tide of heresy, lord. A plague upon these lands unlike any before it." A flicker of something behind his eyes—zeal, perhaps, or something colder. "The brethren have been called to defend not just the faith but the sanctuaries entrusted to our care. Brother Amalric himself has decreed it."

John arched a brow, feigning ignorance.

"Heresy, you say?" He let the words linger, slow and easy. "And it demands monks become warriors?"

Charlot's patience thinned. His fingers flexed at his sides, itching to do anything but continue this conversation.

"A grave threat to the Holy Church, lord," he bit out. "One cannot sit idle while the enemies of God gather strength. Prayer is no longer enough. We must be prepared to defend with the sword what we hold sacred."

John exhaled, shifting his weight. "And how do you train for such dual roles, Brother? Priest and soldier—an unusual combination, wouldn't you agree?"

Charlot's movements turned sharp, jerking his chin toward the training grounds. The clash of wooden swords echoed in the air, monks locked in controlled combat beneath the watchful eye of their instructors.

"You've already seen, lord. The brethren train daily under the abbot's guidance. What once were hands accustomed to turning pages of scripture now wield blades to strike down heresy."

John followed Charlot's gesture, his gaze settling on the monks moving in tight formations. A contradiction in motion—men of the cloth moving as soldiers, faith and steel intertwined in a way that should have never been.

175

"And do you find it fitting, Brother Charlot, that men of the cloth take to arms?" John asked, voice level, though the weight of unease pressed against his words.

Charlot's jaw clenched. The irritation he had struggled to contain cracked through.

"It is not for us to decide what is fitting, lord. It is for us to *obey*." His words came stiff, unyielding. "His Eminence sees the path of God clearly, even if all others, such as one like yourself, do not."

The tension between them thickened.

Charlot stepped back, hand resting—not casually—on the hilt of his belt knife.

"So, if there is nothing else, milord," he said curtly, disdain dripping with every word, "I suggest you direct your questions to the abbot himself. But I warn you, he will have little patience for this...idle curiosity."

John let the moment stretch. Then, with slow deliberation, he inclined his head.

"Perhaps I will." A pause. A slight smirk. "Thank you for your… insight, *Brother* Charlot."

Charlot remained silent, his eyes with a steely glare. Without another word, the monk turned on his heel, his bare feet slapping against the stone floor, his posture rigid with a disdain he cared to conceal.

John watched him go. Let him go.

The air was still, but his thoughts churned with speculation.

A monastery turned into an armory and training ground. A man of the cloth, bristling at being questioned.

This was no holy sanctuary. This was something else entirely—and he was going to find out exactly what.

John stood near the cloister's edge, his gaze drifting past the great stone walls. Beyond them, the monks trained. Wooden swords clashed in steady rhythm, their movements measured, disciplined. Once, these men had taken up quills and scripture. Now, they took up arms.

The cloisters—once a place of quiet reflection—had become something else. A bastion. A forge, not for the spirit, but for war.

John exhaled. His questions would soon find their answers.

He turned, striding down a long corridor, his boots echoing against the stone. The air was thick, heavy with the scent of wax and damp earth.

Then—the hall.

Vast.

A ceiling high as a cathedral's vaults, stretching toward heaven in towering arches. A great table ran the length of the chamber, twenty meters or more, its broad expanse prepared to seat scores of men. At the head of it, a single chair stood apart—large, unadorned, yet commanding. A throne, in all but name.

No windows. No doors to the outside world. No distractions. No escape.

George and Reggeye were already seated, their armor set aside, their faces eased from the strain of the road. They met his gaze, a nod of acknowledgment passing between them.

John settled beside his squire.

"Good morning, milord," Reggeye greeted, his voice lighter than expected, as if the morning had offered him a brief reprieve from his burdens.

A servant—young, silent—stepped forward, filling their goblets. Still, the abbot had not arrived.

John rolled his shoulders, grateful for the chance to sit unarmored. Across the hall, Cistercian brethren moved with practiced grace, setting plates and arranging the table in quiet reverence. Some knelt in prayer, their heads bowed, lips murmuring in hushed Latin.

No idle chatter. No wasted movement.

The flickering glow of candlelight cast shifting patterns against the stone, the air thick with the scent of incense. The monks' discipline was absolute, each motion deliberate, each ritual precise. It was a world governed by order, by obedience.

John's eyes flicked to the higher-ranking brothers, their faces carved from stone, their devotion unwavering.

A life given wholly to God. Or so they claimed.

A chime. A single bell. A monk at the doorway lifted his voice.

"His Eminence, Arnoldus Amalricus!"

A rustle of robes. A scraping of chairs.

The monks rose as one, and John followed suit, George and Reggeye moving with him.

Then—Amalric appeared.

He strode purposefully across the stone floor, his gait steady and solemn. Though he had been described as having elegant robes adorning him, today plain brown robes hung loosely from his frame. An appearance of modesty, or so it seemed from afar. The steady chorus of Latin litanies intertwined with the savory scents wafting from the kitchen. Voices melodic yet rote lifted and dipped in harmony, prayers on repeat yet different each time.

John stood, hands resting against the table's edge, watching.

Of course. A ritual. He understood how it worked.

Holy words spoken over earthly sustenance.

George and Reggeye, though largely unfamiliar with monastic customs, remained still, respectful, reverent.

Then—the final blessing.

Amalric lowered himself into his seat. A ripple of movement followed, each monk taking his place in turn.

The room shifted.

The solemnity of prayer now gave way to the motions of the meal, the sacred blending with the mundane of the meal. Other monks moved about with quiet efficiency, placing platters of bread, mutton, and cheese before the gathered men.

John sat, though his thoughts stirred heavily beneath the

calm of the hall.

This was no simple monastery, his thoughts repeated. This was something else entirely, and his suspicions were being confirmed.

Amalric's voice cut through the noise, smooth, measured.

"Messieurs, my English friends."

The words rolled off his tongue, deliberate, calculated as he spread his arms in an amicable gesture.

"I trust your accommodations here have been to your liking?"

John bowed his head in reverence.

"Yes, your Eminence. We are grateful for your hospitality."

A smile—thin, knowing—curled at the edges of Amalric's lips.

"Excellent." He paused. "Tell me, how fares England these days?"

A simple question. Yet not so simple at all.

John kept his voice even.

"Faring as well as she can, Your Eminence."

A careful answer. Amalric's eyes glimmered knowingly as his fingers continued their steady rhythm against the polished wood of the table. Though relations between their lands had seen better days, some bonds could not be so easily broken by ambition or anger alone.

John met the abbot's gaze evenly, feeling the current run deeper than mere shared history.

"While my blood may hold echoes of that distant past, it is the present which concerns me most. Our peoples now follow separate paths, as is their right."

Amalric smiled, unsurprised yet pleased by the steady reply.

"Rightly spoken. And it is in addressing such present truths that understanding may yet be found. If I understand correctly, you are of Iberian descent?"

"My father's lineage traces to both Toledo and Normandy. His ancestor, Ricardo de Ontivero, fought alongside Duke William during his conquest of England."

A flicker of intrigue in Amalric's gaze.

"Ah, *Ricardo de Ontivero*. A fine Iberian name. How did he find his way to Normandy?"

John allowed a trace of pride to enter his voice.

"My ancestors served the Christian kings of Iberia, defending Toledo from the Moors during the early struggles to restore Christendom in the south. But ambition carried him north, where he entered the service of Duke Robert of Normandy, William's father. Ricardo proved himself loyal and capable, rising through the ranks. When William rode to England, Ricardo rode at his side."

Amalric leaned forward, nodding slowly as if encouraging him to articulate some more.

"A knight who turned his sword from one front of Christendom's defense to another," John smiled with pride.

Amalric leaned back against his seat, studying him intently.

"A remarkable journey. Toledo's fields and England's shores are a far cry from one another."

"Indeed they are, Your Eminence," John replied. "Ricardo was then granted lands in England for his service to the king. It was there that our family name made a home. Though my father would always remind me of our heritage in Toledo, England is our home."

A glint of something unreadable flickered in Amalric's eyes.

"A legendary lineage, Baron John," he mused. "You carry the blood of men who helped to shape Christendom's borders. Perhaps it is ironic, then, that you now find yourself here."

John swallowed hard as he gazed penitently at the abbot.

"I am but a lowly servant of my lord and of God, Your Eminence," he answered, voice firm. "I am open to the leading of the Holy Church."

His hearted pounded.

"And your father," Amalric continued, "Roland de Ontivero—he fought the infidel alongside your King Richard at Arsuf, did he not?" The abbot paused for a moment. "And did he not lose his life in the process?"

John's grip on his goblet tightened.

"Indeed, Your Eminence."

The hall, which was moments ago steeped in ritual chanting, now resounded with the clinking of goblets and the low murmur of voices. It seemed as the blend of sacred and divine.

Amalric lifted his knife, cutting into a piece of bread, before chewing thoughtfully, then speaking again.

"Then your father is to be considered a protector of Christendom," he intoned, pausing to savor his meal. "A true *Defender of the Faith.* A dedicated soldier of Christ."

Then—a not-so-subtle shift. A sharp turn of phrase. Deliberately cutting, deliberately raised.

"The question now, my friend, is whether *you* are a dedicated soldier of Christ."

John felt the insult beneath the words.

The challenge. The judgment. A silence fell upon the hall, the clattering of silverware stopped, all eyes turned to him.

His jaw tightened.

His hands remained steady, but the weight of the room pressed against him. Too many eyes. Too many ears.

He leaned in slightly, lowering his voice.

A hush. A breath of tension thick in the air.

John leaned in, voice low. "Your Eminence, must we do this here?"

A slow smile crept across Amalric's lips.

"Of course, my Lord Baron," he said, his voice rising, filling the hall. "We are all servants of Christ here. Every one of the Cistercian brothers present is able to take confession."

A pause followed. A deliberate gesture—arms spreading wide, welcoming, commanding.

"This—this is your tribunal of penance. So, Baron Breckington, *please*, make confession."

The clatter of silverware faded. The hum of quiet conversations died.

All eyes turned to John.

His fingers curled around the edge of the table. Appetite gone. A lump of something bitter sat in his throat. He dabbed at his mouth with the cloth napkin, buying himself a breath, a moment.

To protest further would be folly. Dangerous, even.

A slow inhale. A measured exhale. Then—

"Father Abbot, Cistercian brothers in Christ." John's voice carried, though his chest felt tight. "I have a very grave confession to make."

A silence. Waiting. Expecting.

"Not too long ago, my men and I waylaid a band of soldiers under the employ of Sir Renhard Galt, Inquisitor to England."

A ripple through the hall. Low whispers. Gasps.

Amalric lifted a hand.

"We will hear the confession of the Baron," he ordered. "*Silence!*"

The monks stilled.

John pressed on, his voice steady despite the tightening in his gut.

"On my orders, my men attacked the band, unaware of their true identity. We assumed they were bandits and did not stop to ascertain their purpose, nor did they reveal their nature to us, for we did not give them the opportunity."

An uncomfortable shift beside him.

George's jaw tensed. Reggeye stared down at the table, pale, his knuckles white where they gripped the edge of his seat—like a man trying to hold fast against a tide.

John stepped forward, eyes filled with defiance.

"Also, on my orders," he said, his voice even, "my men pursued the Inquisitor northward. We found him branding two of our citizens with a hot iron. At that time, we still did not know who he was. We believed him to be an outlaw."

A hush swept the hall—then came the murmur. A flicker of movement through the assembly. The tension was shifting. Whispers curling like smoke in corners.

Amalric let the unrest spread, allowed the moment to fester. Then, lazily, he raised his hand.

"Brothers—order," he said with the softness of a man who relished disorder.

He chuckled quietly, leaning back in his chair. The firelight caught the edge of his smile—thin and curling like a blade.

"Branding," he mused, almost fondly. "A hallmark of the Vaux-de-Cernay Inquisitors. Abbot Guy is a clever man. Elegant, in his way."

The smirk remained. There was no sorrow in his eyes, no gravity. Only the glint of pleasure, like a butcher admiring his cleaver.

John's stomach turned. He pressed on, throat tight.

"We attacked the Inquisitor… and caused his death."

Amalric's grin widened—hungry, expectant.

John paused. Looked once—only once—at Reggeye. Then squared his shoulders.

"It was I who delivered the final blow. I personally ended the life of Sir Renhard Galt."

The silence that followed was absolute. A breath held by the room itself.

George stiffened like iron beside him. Reggeye's head jerked up as though struck. His eyes searched John's face—wide, stunned, pleading for something unspoken. His lips parted.

Don't, John's gaze cut to him, his thoughts inaudible, but

183

its meaning plain to the young squire. A warning, clean and swift as a drawn blade.

Reggeye froze. His mouth closed. He looked down again, jaw tight, eyes glassed with disbelief. The blow had landed—not in his body, but in his heart.

Amalric's fingers tapped once against the rim of his goblet. His brows lifted—not with surprise, but calculation. Disappointment flickered in his expression like a snuffed candle.

He had expected another name. A lesser man. A disposable scapegoat—no, the true culprit, as was reported to him by reliable sources.

Reggeye.

That was the plan, wasn't it?

A squire. A vassal's son. Young, fervent, loyal to a fault. The kind of boy no one would weep long for if the flames claimed him.

But John would not give him that. Not after what he read in that parchment. Not after what Reggeye had offered in silence, while asleep on the road, wrapped in loyalty, dust and aching devotion. It was all the boy had, and he gave it willingly.

He would not let this boy burn.

John stood tall, jaw set. He'd spoken the words that might doom him. But he would not flinch. He knew the cost, and he was willing to pay.

Amalric had no interest in truth—only in pageantry, in the theater of justice cloaked in so-called "holy" fire. A baron's confession was inconvenient, too noble a neck for the noose. But a *squire*? A servant? That was clean. That was safe. Reggeye could be cast as a cautionary tale: a young lad corrupted by misguided loyalty, his ashes a sermon to all who dared question Rome's reach. To burn a lord was to stir revolt. To burn a boy was to silence a barony. A display to the world that none should dare challenge their might.

John upended all of it.

The abbot sighed, but nodded knowingly. Then, leaning forward, his voice came out, cool, measured, collected.

"I was under the impression," Amalric said slowly, "that it was one of your men who struck Sir Galt after he had parleyed, *non*?"

A final chance. A chance to correct. To shift the weight.

John's hands curled into fists beneath the table.

"It was *I*, Your Eminence," he said, voice unwavering, unyielding. "Frustrated by the knight's behavior, I sought to put an end to him before he could cause more damage."

There was a lengthy pause.

Silence.

"I humbly submit myself to this tribunal for my punishment and fate."

Then—John took two steps back. Then another.

And then, before all assembled, he *knelt*. Then, he prostrated himself on the ground before the Cistercian brothers present.

Then came silence. A stillness. Only the soft whisper of the valley wind through the stone halls was heard.

Then, at last, Amalric sighed once more.

A breath, drawn out, as if he alone bore the weight of this upcoming decision.

"Your loyalty to your men does you credit, Lord Breckington," the abbot finally declared. "But whatever the truth may be on this matter, your men share responsibility for this act as much as you. They, too, shall need to conduct penance."

A murmur of agreement. A ripple of whispers.

Amalric let them talk. Let them *stew* in the implications.

Then—he straightened.

"Lord John, please return to your seat," he commanded.

John stood, his expression stoic. He moved slowly back to his place, his hands steady despite the fire burning low in his gut.

Amalric rose to his feet.

"Now is the time, *brothers!*" His voice rang through the hall.

The monks rose in unison, their movements precise, obedient, reverent.

George and Reggeye attempted to stand, but Amalric extended a hand, motioning for them to remain seated.

Latin incantations filled the air. Rhythmic. Chanting. The voices of the monks rising and falling in unison, their words wrapping around the room like an iron chain.

A sign of the cross. A bow of heads. A moment of stillness.

Then—Amalric turned to his gathered men.

"Now is the time to determine the penance for Lord Breckington, as his guilt is certain, and he is penitent."

A pause. A deliberate, theatrical sweep of his gaze.

"Has anyone come to an idea of what penance our dear Baron must pay?"

A teaching moment. That much was clear.

A low murmur passed between the monks. Discussion. Deliberation.

Then—a voice, young, barely past adolescence.

It was of a young monk at the far end of the table, his face pale, his eyes sharp.

"Your Eminence," he said, "we have concluded that since Lord Breckington, albeit inadvertently, has allowed the spread of heresy by causing the death of our Inquisitor, he must pay penance by helping to suppress heresy."

A silence, save some whispers, before the abbot straightened.

"Then it is settled!" Amalric declared, his voice rich with satisfaction.

"The Lord of Breckington, along with his knights and levy, will *join the Holy War against the heretics in the Languedoc!*"

The hall erupted in cheers.

John's stomach turned to stone. A game. That's all this

was.

He saw it now—Amalric's disappointment wasn't in the crime itself, but in how the confession had unfolded. The abbot had expected him to give up Reggeye, to do what any practical noble would do—sacrifice the lesser man, protect the greater. A squire was expendable. A baron was not.

Killing John would be inconvenient—who would govern Breckington? Who would provide knights and levies for the war in the Languedoc?

No, Amalric needed him alive, indebted, broken—not *dead*.

The abbot had wanted him to betray the boy, to buckle under the weight of duty, to trade honor for survival. And if John had done so, if he had spoken Reggeye's name instead of his own, then this trial would have ended swiftly.

A clean execution, a lesson in obedience, a public display of the Church's power over even the lowest of warriors. But now—*now*—John had upset the game. He had forced Amalric to rethink his next move, because instead of a broken lord, he had a defiant one. And that, more than the death of an inquisitor, was the true problem.

John had thought himself clever—thought that by taking the blame, by confessing with humility, he could bear the punishment alone. Shield his men.

Spare Reggeye. Control the outcome.

But Amalric had seen it coming. Disappointed that it unraveled the way it did, but he had expected it.

John cursed himself inwardly.

He had walked willingly into the snare, believing it to be a noose meant for one. But instead of tightening around his own neck, Amalric had spread the sentence wide, casting it over Breckington itself. The abbot had not been satisfied with a single soul in chains—no, he had taken an entire barony under his yoke.

Had John given up Reggeye? Perhaps there would have been an execution of one. Then, he would get a trial before the king. A slow, political dance that he could have navigated, given John Lackland's disdain of the Church.

But now? Now, the Church had everything.

Not just his confession, not just his submission, but his men, his lands, his people. He had given them everything without realizing it, and Amalric had turned that offering into a command—*march to war*. Atone through blood. Lead Breckington's sons to fight in a crusade that was never supposed to be theirs.

John had wanted to protect them. And instead, he had damned them all.

Across the table, George and Reggeye met his gaze, the weight of their fate pressing down upon them all.

Amalric spread his hands as if bestowing a great honor.

"Prepare yourselves," he intoned. "For the path of penance is seldom an easy one. The Languedoc awaits."

John's chest tightened. *Not just any war.*

The War of the Cross. A holy campaign. The monks cheered, but he heard only silence. The Blitheful Ten were going to war. *Again.*

::

A storm was brewing. No signs of relief could be found.

Sir Hugh paced in the chambers, his mind a tangle of worry. The riders should have reached John by now. There should have been word—some sign, some message. Instead, silence. And with it, the unease in Breckington deepened.

Murmurs spread through the town like rot. John was gone. The people whispered of it in hushed tones, glancing over their shoulders, wondering how long before trouble came knocking—again.

Peter of Vaux-de-Cernay had already stirred the pot, poisoning minds with his fiery sermons. The strange men who had assaulted Barth and the townsfolk? Still at large. Still watching, perhaps.

Then—Hubert Roche's report. Hugh had barely had time to process it. Armored riders.

Gray and purple banners. The same colors borne by Sir Renhard Galt. Spotted near the town's edge, moving deliberately, scouting, waiting.

Papal agents? Mercenaries? Something worse? Unknown.

Hugh had no orders, no certainty—only instinct. To watch them. To not move unless they made the first strike.

And then—another disturbing report. An envoy.

De Redvers had sent men.

The Earl of Devon was asking questions, prying, waiting for an opportunity. John's absence, his unknown fate, was a gaping wound that was not only open, but was festering, and the Earl was circling like a vulture. If John was excommunicated—if he was deemed unfit—Devon would make his move.

The king might intervene. Or he might not. Either way, Breckington would not remain unmolested.

No heir. No certainty. No protection. Time was running out. Breckington needed its lord.

Now.

::

John stood firm, his voice steady despite the weight pressing down on his shoulders.

"Ride with haste, Sir George. Return to Breckington. Muster the levy. Ensure provisions for two fortnights."

George, already adjusting his saddle, nodded without hesitation.

"Aye, milord."

"The abbot has directed us to lead the campaign to Lyon by next month. March in haste to meet us there. Can you manage this charge, George?"

A smirk.

189

"You can rely upon me, milord."

John exhaled, gripping George's forearm in silent gratitude.

"Reggeye will remain under my care, I presume?"

"He is a guardian for the Lord of Breckington," George quipped, smiling as he mounting his steed.

"Very, well. My friend, may you journey with faith and honor!" John spoke softly as George gripped the reins. A reassuring hand found the horse's flank. "Godspeed to you."

George met his lord's eyes and nodded.

"Faith and honor will guide me, as they do you, milord. I shall see you again in Lyon."

With a sharp breath and pull of the reins, the steed leapt forward. Its rider crouched low against the mounting speed, hooves beating in a wild rhythm. George and his mount grew smaller in view then disappeared into the countryside.

John's gaze lingered on the direction where his friend and vassal had vanished.

Then—figures on the horizon.

Two riders. Fast. Urgent. Their mounts panting, foam-flecked from the journey.

Messengers.

They saw him in his heraldic blue and yellow, reined in hard, dust curling around their boots as they dismounted.

"Praise be to God, our Lord Baron! We have sought you diligently! We found word that you had journeyed here," one gasped, his voice strained from exhaustion.

John stepped toward him, already reaching for the letter extended to him.

"Men of Breckington!" His voice rang sharp and urgent. "Quickly—what news do you bring?"

His heart pounded as he broke the seal, eager to read the contents of the parchment, unrolling the scrolled letter. He scanned each line with diligent determination to unravel the news.

My Noble Lord John,

I dispatch this message with utmost haste. A sennight past, six riders were sighted within our borders. They were clad in gray and purple, the colors of the late Inquisitor. They have kept their distance for now, but their presence alone is an ill omen.

Days before their arrival, a certain Peter of Vaux-de-Cernay came to Breckington. He is a monk, a Cistercian, and, kin to the late Sir Galt. Through a mishap, he had deduced the fate of his kinsman and a confrontation followed, and though blood was not spilled, he sought to drive fear and confusion into the hearts of our people, wielding the threat of Papal interdict like a sword.

Through God's mercy, I was able to temper the flames before they spread. The people did not rise in panic, nor did they turn against you. But Peter left with a promise of divine retribution. That is not all. The Earl of Devon has sent an emissary. He inquires about your absence, your standing, and whether you have successfully conducted your penance. I suspect he does not come in goodwill. If the Church will brand you a heretic, if Rome determines you excommunicated, Devon will make his move. He seeks full control of your lands, your title, and the very existence of Breckington itself.

Canon law dictates that a Christian vassal is no longer bound to a lord deemed a heretic, and it is this law that was quoted to me to get me to turn against you. It is a law that men like Devon will seize upon without hesitation.

But I do not bend to such laws. Not as your vassal. Not as your friend. You have my loyalty, Lord John, regardless of what judgment may come.

Yet, I will not hide the truth—your enemies circle you like vultures over a dying beast, waiting for it to fall. But you are no dying beast. You must return. Now.

Breckington cannot endure your absence any longer.

Yours in friendship and servitude,
Hugh Philip

John lowered the parchment, the words burning into his mind.

Six riders. Colors of the late Lord Inquisitor, Sir Galt. This Peter of Vaux-de-Cernay, stirring confusion. Devon, preparing a claim on his lands.

A proverbial noose was tightening around his neck. Around all of Breckington. He curled his hand into a fist.

George had just left for Breckington. He had to ride harder. There was no time. John breathed heavily as the events of the day overwhelmed his senses.

He had fallen into a trap with no escape. Things seemed to get worse by the moment. He tightened his lip as his eyes scanned the words again. Hugh's message was clear—return now, or risk losing his barony. The people needed him.

But it wasn't that simple. Nothing was ever that simple.

Refusing Amalric's crusade? Unthinkable. A denial would mean instant excommunication, a papal decree branding him an enemy of the Church. Devon or the Crown would immediately seize his lands legally. John had no choice but to see this through, trust Hugh to hold the barony together, and pray that when he returned it would not be too late.

At least George was enroute to Breckington. While his purpose was to raise the levy and lead them to Lyon, where Amalric's forces were assembling, George would have the wisdom to spread the word that the penance of this duty meant his reconciliation to the Church. Therefore, it was a duty that could not be ignored.

John exhaled sharply, calling for Reggeye.

"Reprovision the messengers, Reggeye. They ride at first light."

By the hour's turn, the letter was written—a response to Hugh, an explanation of their penance and a promise that John would return, though when, he could not say. Each messenger took a copy, mounting their exhausted steeds and disappearing down the same road George had taken homeward.

Then—the waiting.

A day stretched long, with each hour an eternity, each day that passed filled with frustration, with desperation. The urge to return home was unbearable.

John chafed at the boredom. Powerlessness. The confinement. The abbey was comfortable, but such luxuries brought him no comfort from the situation.

Prayer, they told him, was good for his soul. Reflection. The cornerstone of his penance. A means to cleanse the soul before marching to war.

At least Reggeye was permitted to accompany him, a welcome companion in the endless hours of ritual and stillness. The monks allowed them to roam the abbey grounds freely, yet the openness of the lands around them only increased the weight that bore upon John's chest.

Meanwhile, Amalric moved around with purpose.

The abbot strode across the grounds, his energy unrelenting, his presence towering despite the simplicity of his robes. He was no ordinary priest—that much had been obvious from the start. His eyes were too sharp, his posture too measured, his nature to conniving, his very being woven with a discipline that belonged to a man who had seen more than just scripture.

He was a scholar of both faith and war—but to what reason, John was at a loss. He would attempt to uncover the matter.

The next morning, as John stood watching monks train with wooden swords near the abbey walls, Amalric approached.

He smiled warmly as his voice cut through the crisp dawn

air.

"Tell me, my dear baron," he mused, tone thoughtful yet direct, "when preparing a fortress to withstand siege, how would you best distribute your archers along the parapets? Concentrated at critical points, or spaced evenly to cover the walls?"

John blinked.

This was a question he had half expected. The abbot spoke more of warfare than of spiritual matters. He turned, studying the abbot's face.

"I would think a man of the cloth would concern himself with peace rather than fortifications."

A smirk. A faint glint in Amalric's eyes.

"Peace, indeed, is our end," he replied smoothly, "but war is often the means. A shepherd must know how to defend his flock from the wolf." A pause. A slow inhale. "Now, answer me."

John exhaled, bemused but intrigued.

He outlined what he knew. The defenses he had seen, the strategies he had employed in the Holy Land. Walls could hold, but only if the men defending them knew their purpose.

Amalric listened, nodding, absorbing every word.

"Your experience serves you well," the abbot said at last, clasping his hands behind his back. Measured. Calculated. "The art of defense, like the salvation of souls, demands precision and forethought."

John studied him, unsettled.

It was one thing for a knight to speak of war.

It was another thing entirely to hear such tactical deliberation from a man of God.

He found himself wondering—what trials had shaped Amalric into both a priest and a student of battle?

All of it seemed like a contradiction. A monastery forged into a fortress.

John stood in silence, watching as monks trained in the yard—swords clashing where there should have been silence, formations drilled where there should have been prayer.

This was not the Cîteaux of legends and tales spread in his domain. Perhaps it was so at some point. But now, it was not.

The Cistercians, once known for their asceticism, their devotion to simplicity and spiritual purity, had taken an extraordinary shift back in 1157. They had founded a brotherhood not just of monks, but of warriors. The Military Order of Calatrava—knights bound by both martial and monastic vows were born.

They were not the Templars. Not the Hospitallers, whose banners John had once fought beside in Acre. No—these knights were Iberian-born, their blades sworn to the Christian kings of the south, their charge was to defend against the rising tide of the Moor.

Yet even their steel had faltered in battle.

Alarcos.

In the year of our Lord, 1195.

A slaughter.

The Castilian army lay shattered. The knights of Calatrava, once stalwart defenders, lay broken and butchered among them. Their fortresses, their strongholds—gone. Overwhelmed by the Almohad banners.

For a time, it had seemed their end. But they endured.

From the wreckage of their defeat, they rebuilt. Regathered. Regrouped. Their Cistercian brethren took them in, steeled their faith, financed them and reforged their discipline. Monasteries across Spain became not just places of prayer, but of preparation—for war. Not spiritual war, but temporal, physical war. Training. Drills. Readiness.

Now—their banners flew once more. The crimson cross with each end tapered with the Fleur-de-lis.

They were not dead. They were not broken. They had been reforged—revitalized.

And here, in Cîteaux, John saw that this is what he was

truly witnessing.

Here, finally, his suspicions were now confirmed beyond a doubt. This was not simply a monastery. It was a proving ground. A crucible. A war machine hidden beneath the trappings of devotion.

Amalric had seen what the knights of Calatrava had done in Spain and brought their methods to Burgundy. He had now summoned them here. Under his orders, Cîteaux had been reshaped, reborn.

The cloisters now housed stables, an armory, barracks. The practice yards hummed with activity. The very monks who once copied scripture by candlelight were now constructing miniature siege engines, perfecting the methods of war as though preparing to storm castles of their own.

All in the name of God.

John's gut twisted with disgust.

Pope Innocent had called for a Holy War against heretics. And the Cistercians had answered—not with prayer, but with the sword.

It unsettled him. He had fought the Saracens before. Waged war where war was expected, against those who stood against Christendom with the sword. But this?

This was different. This war would not be fought in heathen lands.

This war would be fought against fellow Christians. What would be the difference from the sacking of Zara—of Constantinople?

And now John would be expected to march in it. A monastery turned war camp. A faith turned to steel and iron. And God's will decided by the sword.

"Deus lo vult!"

A shout emanated from the far corner of the training ground. John stood at the edge, both horrified and fascinated as he watched armored monks thundering past him on horseback, their lances poised, their movements disciplined. They maneuvered just as knights would, drilling with

196

precision, their habits tucked beneath layers of steel.

His unease grew at the sight. Men of God wielding swords, training for war.

Yet he knew better than to question the workings of the Church. It was not his place. Yet, the unease would not leave him.

"Regnum meum non est de hoc mundo."

Father Barth's voice echoed in his mind. The words of Barth's Bible, the Vulgate in its splendor. From the words of Christ Himself.

My Kingdom is not of this world.

Barth had always spoken those words with quiet conviction, a lone voice among the zealous cries of his fellow priests. In his eyes, Christ's kingdom had nothing to do with any earthly conquest. The sword had no place in matters of faith.

John exhaled, shifting his weight against a wooden railing.

The sword belonged to the law. That, he understood. It was his duty as a lord—to uphold order, to protect his people, to see justice done. Murder, theft, treason—such crimes demanded swift reckoning.

But faith?

Could convictions of a spiritual matter be carved into a man with cold steel? Could belief be forced at the edge of a blade?

The thought unsettled him. Perhaps some men may be convinced thus, but not in their innermost souls; their true convictions would only be hidden inwardly.

His mind drifted—back to the Holy Land. The days where they tread upon the same dirt as their Savior had.

Five summers past, he had spent months in that scorching, unforgiving land, where men killed one another in God's name. Yet even there, in the heart of war, he had seen something unexpected, something that had shifted his mind on such matters.

Honor.

Between enemies, between men sworn to destroy one another in the name of their God.

He had witnessed truces born of necessity, Christian and Saracen kneeling side by side, drinking from the same waters, sharing the same sun. And more than once, he had watched Muslim warriors halt battle to pray—prostrating themselves with a devotion that rivaled any monk's.

The image clung to him. Did they not, in their own way, seek God? Were they not, however misguided, souls to be won, not slain? And if that were true of the Saracen, then what of these heretics in the Midi?

These *Bon Hommes*, these *Bons Chrétiens*—they did not even take up the sword.

They did not raid or sack, nor did they ride into battle in violence. Rather, they spoke of nonviolence, of purity, of rejecting worldly corruption—or so it was told to him by the monks of the abbey. Were they truly so dangerous that the only answer to quell them was fire and steel? His eyes flicked back to the training grounds.

The sight of clerics preparing for war gave him no answers. Only deeper confusion.

Then—another memory hit him like a vision.

Near Acre.

A young Saracen, no older than sixteen, dropping his weapon, falling to his knees, whispering a prayer with closed eyes, awaiting the death blow.

John had lowered his sword.

Some of de Montfort's men had called him weak. Had sneered. Had jeered.

But John had felt something deeper stir within him that day—a quiet certainty that mercy, not slaughter, was what truly honored Christ.

And now?

Now, he was expected to march into war against fellow Christians. Against these *Bons Chrétiens*.

His throat tightened.

He told himself to trust the Church. To trust the wisdom of men like Amalric. But did the Church still remember its own purpose? Had it begun to believe that saving souls and destroying them were one and the same?

John closed his eyes for a moment, contemplating what he was witnessing. He was disturbed to his core, yet he knew that to protest was futile—and thus, folly.

The men continued their drill; their number was modest—three dozen in all.

There were ten heavily armored cavalrymen, a dozen spearmen in full kit, and an equal number of archers training in the courtyard. Among the armed retainers were the two distinguished soldiers of the Order of Calatrava, easily identified by their heraldic colors of black and crimson.

They were the chivalrous Sir Enrique Lopez and the venerable Sir Alfonso Nuñez.

Upon the abbey grounds, John engaged the knights in conversation. Their exchange inevitably turned to their common lineage as he brought up his Iberian ancestry, tracing his bloodline back through the generations to the noble Visigothic house of Ontivero. The mention of this storied family sharpened the interest of the weathered warriors who honored its heritage.

"Visigoth blood, eh?" Lopez's wiry frame tensed with excitement, his sharp features lighting with recognition. "Tell me, my lord, are you familiar with the tale of Covadonga? Pelayo and his men, holding the mountain passes against an army ten times their size? 'Twas no less than a miracle of Santiago himself!"

"A miracle indeed," Nuñez agreed, voice reverent. "My *abuelo* told it like a romance—the stones raining down upon the Moors as though God Himself cast them. They say Pelayo's men were angels in flesh that day."

John allowed himself a faint smile.

"It's a tale I know well. My ancestors were among those

who stood with Pelayo that day. It was a long fought victory, but on that day I believe it was more than miracles—it was grit, strategy, and perhaps Umayyad arrogance."

Lopez nodded approvingly.

"Grit, yes. Of course, it is about grit. But now tell me, my lord. The Saracens in the Levant. Is it true that their shield walls and formations differ from the Moorish ones we are familiar with?"

John's gaze drifted. The memories began to return.

"They do," he said, voice steady. "The Saracens move as one body. The Moors are more flexible, fluid. Their infantry does not form walls like ours—rigid and unmoving. They rely on speed, precision. Their shields vary—round for skirmishers, light and maneuverable. But their cavalry? They favor longer, curved shields, not unlike our kite shields—made to protect both horse and rider."

Nuñez leaned in.

"And their tactics?"

John exhaled.

"Clever."

A word he did not use lightly.

"Their infantry holds just long enough for their archers or cavalry to strike. When they form a shielded line, it is tight, effective—but temporary. They fight to disorient, to break a formation, not to withstand one."

Nuñez grinned broadly, thumping his chest.

"*Dios quiera*, I'd relish breaking one of their lines! Straight to the heart, eh?"

John's voice darkened.

"Do not be so eager to meet their spears."

The other Calatravan's grin widened as he broke out in poetry.

"Their shields may lack our strength in make, but in skill their warriors do not quake. I've seen them kneel with heads bowed low as monks in prayer before the solemn show. Their lives they give without a second thought, as if by fighting valor could be bought," Lopez gazed off in a jolly mood as he continued his contrived poetic rhyme, "To see in foes devotion thus imbued, what strange phenomenon, this attitude. Strange truth you speak, this twisted pair of fates," Lopez said. "But war and faith join as unholy mates. 'Tis not the fervor of the war they wage, but the rightness of their aim that should engage."

John chuckled at the knight's talent as he applauded— spoken in the English tongue at that!

"Impressive, my friend," he laughed.

Lopez bowed mockingly as they laughed together. The moment lingered as thoughts flowed.

Then—Nuñez spoke, his tone shifting. Pride creeping into his words.

"We've been summoned here to Cîteaux," he shared, chin lifting slightly. "Abbot Amalric himself seeks our counsel and expertise. He is having us train this formation of warrior monks, my lord."

John's frown deepened.

"Monks with armor and swords," he expressed aloud at last, his unease evident. "That is not entirely without precedent, but it still gives me pause. As I told the Brother Charlot, the Templars, your own Calatrava—they were founded as warriors from the start. Your vows and arms are intertwined. The Cistercians? They were meant for prayer and study. For labor."

His voice hardened as he stiffened with discomfort.

"What has driven them to seek the sword?"

Lopez exhaled.

"A fair question, my lord," Lopez admitted in a rare admission.

"It is true," he continued, his tone reflective, "we Calatravans began with the sword in hand. Born of necessity, defending Calatrava la Nueva against the Moors. But the Cistercians? Their roots are in simplicity. In the silence of cloisters. In the toil of fields. This new path…" He hesitated. "It is a departure."

Nuñez, however, was unmoved. His voice rang with conviction.

"Necessity changes many things."

A pause.

"The faith is under siege, my lord. With the Moors at our southern gates, and heresy spreading within, even monks cannot afford to remain behind walls of parchment and prayer. They must take to arms, for the hour demands it."

John studied him.

A man who believed every word.

"And yet," John said, voice low, "it is that departure from their calling that unsettles me."

He took a breath. A slow, careful exhale.

"A monk with a sword must not only wield it, but bear the weight of the blood its sheds upon his soul. Have they considered what it means to take life, even for a just cause? To spill blood is no light burden, even when it is the blood of an enemy."

Lopez pursed his lips and nodded, slowly.

"You speak truth, my lord. There are certainly many among the Cistercians who struggle with this change of focus. However, the Abbot Amalric believes it is our duty to protect Christendom by all means necessary. Some still wonder if such means might stray too far. For us, it is our life."

Nuñez leaned closer, his tone conspiratorial—but tinged with pride.

"And yet, my lord, you should see them train. For men who once toiled in silence, they have taken to the sword with fervor. They are not like the Templars, seeking glory, nor even us, who defend our own lands. No, their zeal is different—pure, untempered by ambition. They fight not for themselves, but wholly for God."

A chill ran through John.

He had seen where unchecked zeal could lead. He had

seen men burn cities to the ground in the name of righteousness. He had seen devotion twisted into cruelty, faith hardened into fanaticism. And this seemed to be heading in that same direction.

His voice was quiet, but firm.

"A man who fights for God must tread carefully," he said at last. "The line between righteous defense and blind fanaticism is thinner than a blade's edge."

He swept his gaze across the training yard, where monks drilled as knights beneath the watchful eyes of their masters.

"I pray these men understand the weight of what they take on."

The contradiction continued to bother him, but he understood the Church did not always do what seemed logical. These monks had shattered all preconceived notions he may have had in the past.

Once, they had built not fortresses, but communities. Their order had given the world great abbeys, water mills, mechanized tools, efficient farming practices— transformations that had fed the hungry, strengthened villages, and drawn admiration from lords and scholars alike. Now, those same hands that had tilled fields and copied scripture were learning to hold swords. Plows traded for steel. Benedictions replaced with battle cries.

And at the heart of it stood Amalric. The abbot. The pope's legate and representative. The head Cistercian.

John recalled stories told to him of the famed Saint Bernard of Clairvaux, whose name was spoken in reverence throughout the abbey halls. Bernard was the embodiment of Cistercian values. He was a mystic, a thinker, a preacher whose words had moved armies.

It was Bernard who had stirred Europe to take up the cross for the Second Holy War of the Cross. During his day his voice carried through cathedrals and courtrooms alike, calling knights and commoners to form in columns and march east in defense of Christendom.

But Bernard's holy war had ended in failure—his armies destroyed, villages razed, the moral gravity of the resulting bloodshed crushing even the noblest of intentions. Had it been Bernard's zeal that led them to ruin, or the ambition of others who twisted his words?

The answer was unclear.

And now, Amalric sought to follow in Bernard's footsteps—but this time with a sword in hand. No longer adequate was the preaching and exhorting from pulpits and platforms—the sword that would cut asunder had to be wielded.

In the preceding days Amalric invoked the saint's name with a fervor bordering on idolatry, but where Bernard had wielded his voice, Amalric wielded his will—and an army of knights. He was not merely stirring hearts—he was sharpening swords. His war was not one of distant deserts and heathen kings, but of Christian against Christian, in the rich lands of southern France.

"Heretics," he called them. "Foxes in the fold."

John inhaled sharply, the word cutting through him like a blade.

Foxes.

He visualized Aerin's scarred body in the dirt. The merchant's daughter, her pale skin branded with a fox, seared into her flesh by Galt's iron.

The mark of the Inquisition. The same mark Amalric now spoke of so easily, so righteously branded upon the damned.

John's stomach turned.

This was not the Cistercian Order he had heard of. That he admired. Their greatness had always lain in their quiet, transformative work—building, feeding, healing. Now, under Amalric, they were being reforged into something else entirely—a force bent on unleashing fire, sword and brimstone.

Faith, wielded as a weapon. Fatal. Unforgiving.

Invoking Bernard's name offered no comfort. If a man as

wise and revered as he could rally men to war, only to watch it unravel into disaster, what hope was there that Amalric's war would be any different? Even if it were to succeed, would the cost be too great? Would the soul of Christianity be forever tainted?

John did not need to wonder long. A shadow moved in his periphery. Amalric himself approached.

"My noble baron," the abbot called to him, his voice rich with satisfaction. "We shall bear the cross to the farthest reaches of the Earth, and our swords shall triumph in the name of Christ. Your duty of penance will help us conquer in Christ's name!"

John's mouth was dry as a bone. This was certainly not the Christ he knew. Not the Christ of Father Barth's teachings, not the Christ he himself read of in the scriptures, the Christ who spoke of love and mercy, whose kingdom was not of this world. If Amalric's doctrine had any root in the Scriptures, John had not seen it.

No, this was not faith—at least not a faith grounded upon a loving, merciful, self-less God manifested in Jesus Christ of Nazareth. This was zeal made into steel, righteousness reforged into conquest.

And where did that leave men like him—men who wielded the sword to protect their people?

What use is a noble when the clergy makes war?

At the next meal, Amalric's fervor bled into every conversation.

"The Lord's work is not always gentle," he declared, gesturing with his knife like a weapon. "Sometimes it requires the cleansing fire of righteousness."

John, seated among monks and knights, said nothing. But the unease clawed deeper. This was no mere preacher rallying men simply to a cause. This was a general shaping an army. An army itching to kill in the name of the Lord.

::

The road stretched long into the distance beneath the setting sun to the west.

George rode hard, the rhythm of his gallop reminding him of his mission. Breckington lay ahead. The levy awaited. The legate's war was to begin, and they were to participate. Sir John had entrusted him with the charge—muster the men, prepare for battle, lead them to Lyon.

Yet even as his duty pulled him forward, his thoughts slowed him down.

Ysabeau.

She had walked away, as propriety demanded. When the road had turned toward Cîteaux, she had turned away, cast adrift by rules neither of them had been allowed to break. Women were not permitted beyond those sacred walls. Aubert had made it clear.

She had accepted it. She had chosen to leave.

"I can manage," she had told him. Brave words, spoken too quickly.

And he had let her go.

Now, as the miles wore on, so did his guilt.

What if some danger had befallen her? The road was long, the world unkind. She was strong—he knew that. But even strength had limits. The thought of her walking alone, exposed to the dangers lurking in the shadows, gnawed at him like a blade pressed too close to the skin.

Then—a shape ahead.

A lone traveler among the thinning crowd on the road. A woman. Cloaked against the chill of evening.

His breath caught for a moment.

The slope of her shoulders. The way she moved. Familiar. His heart skipped a beat; could it be?

He nudged his horse forward, trot turning to a brisk canter. The woman glanced back, her hood casting her face in shadow, and his pulse kicked hard against his ribs.

"Ysabeau!"

206

The name escaped before he could stop himself.

She stopped. Turned. His heart plummeted.

Not her.

The woman standing before him was older, harder, her eyes wary rather than fierce, her hands clutching her cloak tightly against her frame.

George exhaled, forcing down the bitter knot in his throat. A fool. He had been a fool.

"Pardonnez-moi," he said quickly, the words tumbling from his lips. "I mistook you for another. A thousand apologies."

She gave a slow nod, suspicion easing into mild understanding, though she said nothing.

George inclined his head in respect and pulled the reins, urging his horse forward, leaving her behind.

But the weight in his chest did not lift.

Of course, it hadn't been her. It was never going to be her. Yet he had hoped all the same.

The wind carried the scent of wildflowers from the fields, soft and fleeting, but it brought no comfort. He had done his duty. He had upheld his vows to John, to the cause before them.

But in doing so, had he failed her? She had left, yes. But what choice had she been given?

The road stretched ahead, but his thoughts remained behind. If ever their paths crossed again, he would not let her walk away so easily. With a sharp kick, he spurred his horse to a gallop, the sun dipping lower in the horizon.

Breckington awaited. The levy awaited.

But so did the vision of Ysabeau, her presence in his mind as inescapable as his duty.

::

A steady rain was falling.

Droplets tapped against the wooden shutters, rousing

207

John from sleep.

Not yet.

He wanted just a few more moments in the quiet, before duty called him forward. But the voice of his squire, armored and ready, would not wait.

"My lord, the time has come."

John exhaled.

"So soon?"

"Yes, my lord. His Eminence has decreed that we leave forthwith."

The words settled over him like a weight. His penance. His holy duty. The war that was no longer a distant echo, but here.

John rose, bracing himself against the chill of morning, and stepped to the wash basin. The cold water burned against his skin, forcing the last remnants of sleep from his body. Resolve. He would need it now.

Reggeye helped him into his armor, the chainmail settling over his shoulders like old burdens returned. The colors of de Ontivero—blue and yellow, the lion rampant—stood in stark contrast against the monks who watched them pass. Black robes. White habits. Simple. Humble. But no longer set apart from war.

They stepped into the open, boots sinking slightly into the mud, the sky above still heavy with storm clouds. Ahead, the ranks stood ready. Cistercian warriors, Calatravan knights. Swords where once there had been scrolls.

John and Reggeye took their place in the formation, standing among men who prayed as fervently as they prepared for battle. The rain fell lightly upon them, soaking into the damp earth beneath their feet. A fitting scene for their departure. A march not just to war, but to something darker—something John could not yet name.

From the ranks, a voice arose.

"I am glad to see you prepared, Lord Breckington."

John turned.

Amalric.

The abbot sat astride a white destrier, clad in polished armor that gleamed despite the overcast sky. The man had shed his priestly robes in favor of war steel, his helmet hanging at his side. He was a monk no longer, but a general.

The warriors of Cîteaux mirrored his transformation. Black armor lined with purple. Scarlet crosses emblazoned across their chests. The knights of Calatrava, mounted and ready, bore similar insignias—only theirs carried the *fleur-de-lis*, a mark of their Spanish order.

John gave a nod, mounting his own horse, Reggeye doing the same. A horn sounded.

The march began.

Southward. Toward Lyon. Toward war.

John kept his gaze ahead, but his thoughts lingered behind. George. Had he reached Breckington? Had he mustered the levy? Ninety men, that was the expectation. The Blitheful Ten would accompany them. If Breckington still stood.

Hugh's letter gnawed at him. Enemies encircling. Devon watching. Riders bearing Galt's colors lurking at the edges.

He had left his barony vulnerable. And now, he rode away from it.

A voice cut through his thoughts.

"What troubles your spirit, my son?"

John turned slightly. Amalric had drawn beside him.

"My barony, your Eminence," John admitted.

"Leave such worldly worries to the Lord," the abbot said, voice smooth. "Your divine calling here transcends earthly concerns."

John nodded, because it was expected. But the weight of his anxieties did not lift.

Amalric's gaze sharpened. "Very soon, the hand of God shall be manifested in the eradication of these heretics," he declared. "Blessed are we, by the Holy Mother, His Holiness the Pope, and our sacred mission. We shall prevail."

John's fingers tightened around the reins.

"But why, then," he said carefully, "did we not prevail in the Levant? Why does Jerusalem elude our grasp?"

The abbot stiffened slightly.

"Que dites-vous?"

John kept his voice level.

"In the Holy Land," he said. "We did not reclaim Jerusalem. When I embarked on the Holy War with my men, including young Reggeye here, our fervor led us to aspire to recapture the Holy City." An intentional pause followed. "But instead, we found ourselves in conflict with fellow Christians, besieging Constantinople and our Greek brethren."

A flicker of something in Amalric's expression. Annoyance. Displeasure.

"Ah," he said at last. "But were you complicit in that tragedy?"

"No, your Eminence. We marched with de Montfort to Acre."

Amalric's features smoothed.

"So, despite the distractions, you fulfilled your duty and journeyed to the Levant. His Holiness rightly condemned the tumult at Constantinople."

"And yet," John pressed, "are we not engaging in a similar conflict now? Against fellow Christians?"

An uncomfortable shift. Then the abbot's eyes darkened. His jaw set.

"These *heretici* are not true Christians," he snapped, voice taut with fury. "Such have been ensnared by the Devil himself. Or did you not know? These fiends burn their children in sacrilege to their pagan god."

John inhaled sharply.

Lies.

The people in his barony listed as "heretics" were nothing but law-abiding citizens. There were no reports of child sacrifice or any other type of debauchery. He would have known of them. He would never say it aloud. Especially not here. He knew lies when he saw them.

But Amalric believed them. Whether he created the lies himself, it didn't matter—he probably told them so often he believed them himself.

John felt the words rise to his lips, he wanted to object, to challenge—but he swallowed them down. There would be no reasoning with the abbot. Not now. Not ever.

Amalric crossed himself, lips curling in barely contained disdain.

"These animals—foxes—are an infestation," he said, his voice lowering into a seething whisper, as if merely speaking of them tainted the air. "Such heresy cannot be allowed to fester in our lands."

John's hands clenched, but he kept his silence. He knew better than to speak out.

This was the war he had bound himself to.

And it had only just begun.

It was a slow, relentless march. The rain had eased, but the weight in the air remained, thick as oil, prompting men to remove their helmets in the humidity.

"These... heretics," Amalric continued, his voice low but brimming with contempt. "Wolves in sheep's clothing. Their doctrines—a poison, a corruption—a twisted blend of half-truths and blasphemies that lead souls to damnation."

John's fingers tightened around the reins. The same words. The same certainties and absolutes. He had heard them before—on other roads, in other wars.

"But surely," he countered, keeping his tone measured and respectful, "would not burning them only seal their damnation?"

The abbot scoffed, gesturing with his hand.

"At least they won't get to spread it!"

A chill ran through John's spine. Such words came so easily to this man. Amalric truly believed them. John exhaled slowly as he reminded himself:

I have to tread carefully, or I will be trampled.

John tried to bite down the words, but he could no longer restrain.

"But in truth, Your Eminence—does not Christ advocate for reconciliation through love?"

The silence that followed was as tight as a taut rope, stretched to its breaking point. Amalric's head snapped toward him, eyes dark with warning.

"Know your place, my son." His voice was quiet, but it carried the weight of hubris. "My knowledge of scripture runs deep. My monks are well-versed in theology and church teachings. You should know you place."

"Of course, your Eminence. Forgive me."

"We have labored long," the abbot went on, his voice gaining momentum. "But we have labored in vain. The methods you suggest have already been tried."

The Cistercian's gaze burned with righteous fire, eager to consume all that would stand in its way.

"His Holiness sent emissaries—pious men, wise men—to call these lost sheep back into the fold. And what was the fruit of our efforts?"

His jaw clenched. He paused. Perhaps for dramatic effect. A slow inhale. A fire rising, barely contained.

"The murder of my predecessor," he said, voice taut and somber. "A righteous servant of God. His Holiness' legate. And now—the Blessed Saint Pierre de Castelnau."

A moment of grief softened the edges of his rage.

"He was a holy man, a man touched by God," the abbot murmured, "then struck down by treachery! He was a martyr, fulfilling only his sacred duty."

John responded with a careful nod.

"A most tragic affair, indeed, Your Eminence."

But the fire was far from doused. Amalric's eyes sharpened, his fury redoubling, his tone forming the edges of a sneer.

"And Count Raymond of Toulouse—that fox—that

deceiver—harbored these vipers within his lands. He abetted their wickedness. He orchestrated Pierre's death."

John stilled.

Toulouse.

Raymond's excommunication had been a near certainty—his alignment with the heretics undeniable. And yet—

John measured his voice, hiding his surprise.

"His excommunication has been rescinded?"

"Indeed," Amalric's disdain was thick as tar. "And he has even been permitted to join the Holy War. But mark my words, Sir John—his penitence is as fleeting as morning dew. It will not last."

The abbot's voice dropped, dark with contempt. He continued.

"The Count of Toulouse has crawled back to the Church like a whipped cur, but do not be fooled, milord. His so-called penitence is a hollow shell. I suspect his loyalty will falter the moment it serves him."

John nodded, acknowledging but not digesting the abbot's words.

"His situation is not unlike your own," Amalric mused, his tone light, almost casual—too casual. "A nobleman responsible for the death of an agent of the Church, seeking absolution through service in the Holy War."

The words slithered through the air, curling around John like a noose. Amalric turned his head slightly, studying him.

"In your case," he added, voice silk and steely, "I pray your penitence is genuine."

John said nothing. Held his breath. Did not let his shoulders tense, did not let his fingers tighten around the reins. Did not let the words find its intended target.

A test. That was what this was all about.

The abbot's gaze lingered a moment longer, waiting for something—a flinch, a sign, a slip.

John gave him nothing. Only silence. Only the steady

rhythm of his horse's gait.

John exhaled through his nose.

The abbot sighed, resigned in his defeat. But he would go on. It wasn't like him to remain defeated.

"These heretics," Amalric continued, voice like iron, "these foxes amidst the Lord's vineyard—they have been given every mercy. Every opportunity to repent. And yet they persist. In their sorcery. In their devilry. There is no salvation for them. Only fire."

John said nothing. He had no words left. So, it was not about justice—it was a purge.

"Now, you see, my son," Amalric pressed, his voice thick with conviction, "there is no parleying with these demons. The world must be purged of them by the hand of God. And we shall be His instruments."

A slow breath. The abbot's voice then rose as he turned to the men marching behind them.

"And we, in unison, decree that these heretics must be purged from the face of the land!"

A roar erupted from the ranks.

"DEUS LO VULT!"

The chant thundered into the morning mist, voices rising like a battle cry.

"DEUS LO VULT!"

John's hands tightened around the reins as the column passed through a small hamlet.

Villagers lined up along the road, watching with curiosity as the Holy Warriors marched past, their eyes wide with fascination.

A lone priest stood at their vanguard, raising a wooden cross, making the sign of benediction. The men cheered and roared, their voices redoubling, rising, emboldened by the zealous display.

The shouts faded away in John's ears. Something else stirred in the depths of his mind. A different road. A different army. A different war.

214

The world around him dissolved. His vision blurred into the past.

Dust—thick and choking.

The sound of the hot wind kicking sand in the air. His horse, moving fast beneath him, muscles taut, straining. An arrow, whistling past his ear.

A Saracen warrior—charging forward, eyes blazing, sabre gleaming in the merciless sun. War cries tore through the air.

The Holy Land.

John did not want to remember. But the past did not care for what he wanted. It was coming for him.

Like the enemy at his gates.

He took a desperate breath. A brief moment to assess—to calculate.

John's knuckles whitened under his greaves as he gripped the reins tightly, his stallion's hooves shuffling nervously under the weight of its armored rider. Coiled like a serpent, man and horse awaited the impending clash, poised to strike. Infidels swarmed the scrubland on foot while he had the advantage of position, protection, and swift motion from his mounted perch.

The Saracen charged, scimitar lifted as he sprinted toward him. Time slowed as the distance between them lessened with each pounding step, the world fading away until only opponent and steed remained.

With a practiced flick of his wrist, John guided the stallion aside, the brute dancing out of reach with uncanny elegance. A ruse to bait the foe nearer their demise. It seemed like it was all in slow-motion—as if time had been slowed.

John pulled sharply, the horse sidestepping with practiced ease. A feint. A deception. And it worked.

The enemy swung—too soon. The curved blade sliced through empty air, grazing just inches from John's leg.

A fatal mistake by his foe.

John's sword arced downward, a ruthless, final stroke. A cry rang out as chainmail split, bones severing. The Saracen crumpled beneath his horse, his spine cleaved by John's blade, body collapsing onto the dusty ground.

Then—a shout. An unmistakable call for aid. This was distinct, rising over the din of battle.

"Au secours! Venez vite!"

John's gaze snapped to the distance. There. In the haze of dust. A lone rider. Surrounded.

No hesitation.

"Hyah!"

His mount surged forward, hooves churning sand, momentum crushing as he bashed through the fray. A battering ram of war. Saracens scattered, their cohesion breaking as John and his warhorse barreled through, sending men sprawling in his wake.

A flash of steel. *Swing. Parry. Strike.*

One down. Then another. The air thick with the scent of blood, sweat, and hot metal.

The embattled rider—red and white, a lion rampant on his shield—broke free, wheeling to John's side. But the enemy regrouped. Scimitars raised. A tightening ring of death around the duo.

Then—a chorus.

A harmony of voices that cut through the chaos of violence, rising over the din of battle.

A chant.

Louder. Louder still.

"Deus lo vult! Deus lo vult! Deus lo vult!"

The Saracens stepped back, demoralized. Then, a charge. John and the stranger pressed forward towards them. Lord Breckington's blade became an extension of his will, his strikes relentless. Beside him, the rider—now emboldened, steadied by the presence of an ally—fought with renewed vigor. Together, they drove straight into the retreating enemy column, scattering bodies, shields, and swords.

The chants swelled. A thunderous march. Then—from beyond the crest of the hill, they came. Spearmen in blue and yellow.

Their voices echoed across the battlefield, their steps measured as they marched, disciplined, and righteous. The ground trembled on their approach.

The Saracens turned. Hesitated. Broke.

Defeat set in. They fled, vanishing into the distant hills, their lines shattered, their retreat scattering like dust in the wind.

John took a breath. Respite. The battle was won.

The rider turned to him, breath still heavy, but steadied. Alive. Thankful.

"I believe we have yet to be formally introduced, my friend," he said, sheathing his bloodied sword and removing his helm, revealing a battle-worn face.

John wiped the blood from his own blade, his pulse still steady, eyes lingering on the battlefield. The Saracens were gone. Their war cries now only leaving an echo.

"John de Ontivero," he replied. "Baron of Breckington, in the Earldom of Devon. At your service, sir—"

"Simon de Montfort, Earl of Leicester," the knight interjected, his expression shifting into something between gratitude and pride. "Though I prefer Lord of Montfort-l'Amaury. I am in your debt, and one day, I wish to repay it."

The chanting continued, growing louder, swelling, enveloping him.

"*Deus lo vult! Deus lo vult! Deus lo vult!*"

John inhaled sharply.

Something had changed. His vision cleared. The dust, the heat, the battlefield faded. The sun was no longer searing overhead. The scent of blood and bitter sand was gone.

He blinked.

A different light bathed the present. A kinder sun. The drizzle had ceased. The sky was clearing.

No Saracen host. No Levantine war.

The cries of "*Deus lo vult*" were not from Acre.

They were under the clouds of Burgundy. Cistercian and Calatravan voices. Marching in step behind him.

John exhaled, fingers flexing against the reins, the last vestiges of the memory still clinging to him.

The past was never far. And neither was war.

"Are you alright, my dear baron?" Amalric inquired, his expression one of concern. "You seemed distracted."

"I am alright, your Eminence," John reassured, the echoes of his past merging with the present march towards an uncertain future.

Amalric's gaze stretched across the rolling plains, his expression serene, untouched by the burden of their march. The road ahead wound through low, gently sloping hills, disappearing into the misty horizon.

Then—movement coming out of the distant fog.

A slow-moving column, single file, no banners, no armor. A hundred, perhaps more. A procession of the marked. As they drew closer, John heard it—a murmur, soft and low, rising from their ranks. A chant.

Then he saw them.

Men and women, their garments worn by the elements, their shriveled faces hollowed by hunger and submission. And across each chest, sewn in crude, unmistakable stitching—the yellow cross. A symbol of penance—or rather, a symbol of abject defeat and humiliation.

John's stomach twisted in horror.

"Penitents," Amalric declared, his voice flowing with satisfaction. "These are former *heretici* who have returned to the True Faith."

John's eyes lingered on them, their heads bowed, hands clasped, feet dragging through the mud as they made way for the holy warriors. No cries, no protests—only silence.

"How long," John asked, his voice careful, "must they wear that?"

"For as long as they draw breath, my son."

Amalric did not even glance at them as he spoke.

"Their lives have been spared, though should they stray again…"

His voice turned colder as he finished.

"The flames await."

John's lips pressed into a thin line. He recoiled inwardly but forced his face to remain still.

The penitents bore their shame in silence. Others did not.

The two Calatravan knights sneered as they passed, spitting curses, hurling words sharp as daggers.

"Wretched vermin."

"Look at them. As if they can ever be cleansed."

The armed Cistercians did not mock. They chanted.

"*Deus lo vult!*"

Again and again, each repetition like a hammer striking an anvil. And still, the penitents said nothing.

John watched them endure. Silent. Stoic. Waiting.

Perhaps it was their refusal to react, their refusal to beg, that only hardened the soldiers' contempt. A shift in the chant—no longer presuming God's will, but now a declaration of victory over these infidels-turned-penitents.

A single voice rose—rough, commanding, unwavering.

"Te Deum laudámus: te Dominum confitémur."

A hymn.

It rippled through the ranks, spreading like fire in dry grass.

Voices joined. Some deep and steady, trained in the discipline of monastic song. Others faltered, stumbling over the Latin, their tongues unused to such reverence. No matter. The hymn did not stop.

John rode on in silence, listening as the earth itself seemed to vibrate beneath the weight of devotion.

"Te ætérnum Patrem omnis terra venerátur."

All the earth worships Thee, the eternal Father.

A chill crept down his spine.

All the earth.

But only under the compulsion of the sword?

His gaze flicked over the armed men around him—fingers curled around hilts, eyes alight with fervor.

Is this worship?

Or fear, cloaked in obedience?

"Tibi omnes Angeli; tibi cæli et univérsae potestátes."

The voices wavered in places. Some fell out of rhythm, others surged ahead, dragging the rest forward. But the melody endured. The beauty of it was undeniable. And yet—to John, it carried something else.

Something twisted. Something wrong. His mind drifted—to the Languedoc. He could see it. Vineyards and fields. Lands untouched by war. Not yet.

But they would burn. John had seen it before. Fields leveled by soldiers of the cross. Walls crumbled to dust. A torch to a thatched roof. A family screaming inside. One house at first. Then a village. Then an entire countryside, swallowed in fire.

And all in the name of God.

"Sanctus, Sanctus, Sanctus, Dóminus Deus Sábaoth."

Holy, holy, holy, Lord God of hosts.

The soldiers sang louder, triumphant.

John's grip tightened on the reins. What of those they would soon make martyrs, not by their own faith, but by force?

Would their voices, too, cry out to God—in the silence of death?

Triumphant. Absolute.

John listened, but he did not join. He knew Amalric would notice, but he did not care.

The voices around him carried certainty, unwavering and bold. Not the song of men marching to battle, but of men who believed the victory was already won. Fanaticism had made them blind.

As the final refrain of the *Te Deum* faded into mist, the

220

road still stretched long before them. A path carved by countless boots, hooves, and cart wheels. The silence left in its wake was not one of peace. It was one of suffocation.

The penitents continued to trudge on slowly past them.

John watched them—backs bent, feet dragging, bodies wrapped in rags that clung to them like burial shrouds. No chains, yet still bound.

The image of their emaciated and broken bodies burned against the dull gray morning, a pathetic sight to behold. They bore no arms. No banners. No defiance. Only submission.

These were not the warriors he had faced in the Levant—no Saracen sabers, no battle cries tearing through the heat of the desert.

No shields to meet his own. Only silence.

Farmers. Mothers. Old men. People.

Their only crime? They dared to express a different conviction.

Amalric sensed his troubled thoughts by his expression.

"You are troubled, my son."

A statement, not a question. A probe, not a concern. He knew it. John kept his eyes forward, his jaw tightening, fighting the temptation to speak in haste.

"This is not the Levant," Amalric continued, his tone a measured blade, sliding as if between gaps in his armor. "Where your English sense of chivalry found its test in noble combat with Saracens."

John said nothing as a smirk flashed across the abbot's lips.

"Here," Amalric went on, in an almost hissing tone, "the battle is deeper. It is not a fight against flesh, but for the soul of Christendom itself."

John knew better than to answer aloud, although he had so much to say. Silence was the only defense against men like Amalric. The abbot let the thought hang, then pressed further in a voice too casual, too calculated.

"You English are peculiar creatures," he mused. "Always clinging to your sense of independence. Much like your king—John the Lackland. A man who dares to oppose the Holy Father's will over something as trivial as an archbishop."

His tone curled with contempt.

"Such insolence. Such arrogance," he paused. "It seems to run in the blood of your people."

John felt the insult land like a thrown gauntlet. Still, he did not react. He knew the price of saying too much.

His lips pressed into a thin line, his gaze locked on the mist ahead. Again, he would not give Amalric the satisfaction. The abbot studied him, as though inspecting a tool he had yet to determine the use for.

"But even the unruliest creatures," he mused, voice softening into a tone almost benevolent, "can serve the Church's purpose."

His gaze swept over the penitents, wading through the mud beneath the weight of their scorn.

"Redemption is a powerful thing, my son."

The words came slow. Measured. A lesson. John continued to keep his tongue. Amalric continued.

"You, like these penitents, walk a path of penance."

John's grip on the reins tightened as he stiffened in his saddle. He nodded compliantly.

"Spare your pity for them," Amalric sneered, "for they have erred but now find grace in suffering. Perhaps you will find the same."

It was the final stroke of the knife. Yet he was determined to bear the indignity, at least, for now. The leather beneath John's fingers groaned. Amalric was testing him. Waiting for him to slip. To fall.

And John could not fail. He understood the price. So, he nodded—somber, distant. A knight conceding to his superior. He knew his place.

Amalric held his gaze a moment longer, then, satisfied,

fell back into the chanting ranks of Cistercians.

John exhaled. However, the weight did not lift. Behind them, the penitents stumbled on. John's thoughts drifted.

The Levant had been different.

There, the enemy had met him as an equal. Swords drawn. Shields locked. Their faith as fierce as his own. Where they marched now, the enemy had no weapons.

Only conviction.

Was it justice to wield the sword against such people? To burn their homes? Destroy their lives? And call it the will of God?

The mist thickened.

John exhaled, watching his breath disappear into the cold. The road ahead would offer no answers. Only more questions. And each one felt weightier than the last. He knew this. But he had no choice. He people depended upon him for it. He would endure so that they could endure.

A stumble. Several gasps—A penitent had collapsed. A soldier barked. Dragged the man up.

John turned and stared.

Felt the blow of it. But he did not move. Did not react. Did not let the scene affect him. Although deep within, he held hidden sympathy. He adjusted his cloak, spurred his horse forward. He was determined to see the journey through.

Yet behind his steady gaze, beneath the mask of resolve—the storm of doubts and regrets raged on.

The Crusade

July 5th, 1209 AD
Lyons, Kingdom of Arles

he ground trembled, cobblestones rattling beneath the iron-clad charge of a hundred horses. Across the bridge they came—banners snapping, colors twisting in the wind. A tide of men, armored and armed, flooding into the sprawl of tents that blanketed the outskirts of Lyons.

John scanned the standards, searching for something familiar. Nothing. The banners bore the sigils of France, Burgundy, Castile, the Empire. But none from England, none from Devon, none that told him his men had arrived.

Reggeye worked swiftly, driving stakes into the damp soil, pitching their tent among the endless sea of canvas. The air pulsed with voices—French, Germanic, Castillan—a dozen tongues weaving into one cacophony of laughter, boasts, and prayers.

224

But no English.

A tap on his shoulder. Reggeye, pointing westward. No banners there. No noble crests. Only men in mismatched armor, their gear piecemeal, their mail rusted and ill-kept. No unity in color or cause.

John's stomach turned.

"*Routiers*," he muttered, eyes narrowing.

Mercenaries.

Reggeye frowned.

"I thought the Church condemned them, my lord?"

"They did," John said, voice clipped. "At the Third Lateran Council."

A slight pause ensued. Reggeye waited, brow furrowed.

John exhaled. A bitter smile.

"It seems the Church has found a use for them now."

The words dripped of irony. The men in the western camp did not march in ranks, did not carry the air of soldiers sworn to duty. They lounged, drank, laughed with a recklessness unfitting for a holy campaign. Their only allegiance was to the coin that had hired them, and now, it seemed, the Holy War paid well.

John's mind darkened.

The Church, so quick to damn them, now called upon them.

Routiers. Mercenaries—but much worse. The fought for more than just coin—they fought for plunder, and for the thrill.

Once reviled. Now God's chosen sword. What had changed? Faith? Or necessity? The answer was obvious.

Necessity.

Perhaps that is why the lives of heathen mercenaries were valued over heretics. Heretics were nothing but fodder for the fires.

It made no difference that *routiers* behaved like the scum of the earth, plundering and murdering at will. They served their purpose for the so-called glory of God.

John watched them a moment longer, unease settling deep in his bones. These were not men bound by oaths. No cause held them. No loyalty anchored them. When the blood began to flow, would they stop?

He doubted it.

Doubt. It was becoming a familiar companion. As the sun dipped low, the first fires of camp crackled to life.

Still, no sign of his men.

John paced near the entrance of his tent, scanning the throng of soldiers moving in and out of the city. Too many faces, too much movement. Any inquiry would be fruitless. He resigned himself to the wait.

Then—hoofbeats. Rhythmic. Purposeful.

John turned.

Emerging from the dusk, three riders appeared. Familiar. *Amalric.*

And behind him, Lopez and Nuñez, their Calatravan cloaks draped over steel armor. John straightened. Stepped forward. Bowed his head.

"Ah, my noble baron!" Amalric greeted with unrestrained enthusiasm.

John lifted his gaze, his expression measured.

"Your Eminence."

The abbot's smile widened.

"I extend my gratitude for your unwavering loyalty and dedication to the Faith."

Something in his tone shifted. *Amusement? Anticipation?*

"You have brought forth substantial reinforcements to our holy cause."

John stiffened.

His reinforcements? A puzzled look flickered across his face. Amalric saw it, smirked, and gestured westward. Over the rise of a hill, movement.

Men—marching. A column. Blue and yellow.

Breckington.

226

The chant rose, clear and strong.

"Faith and Honor! Faith and Honor!"

John caught his breath. Breckington had arrived.

Hugh.

George.

Leading the column, the knights of Breckington pressed forward, steel catching the last light of the sun. Behind them, the levy—one hundred spearmen strong—moved in disciplined ranks, banners snapping sharp in the evening breeze.

Reggeye burst from the tent, his face breaking into a rare grin.

"Ey!" he shouted, arms raised. He ran to meet them.

John exhaled.

Relief. Pride. But also a heavy weight settled deep in his chest. These men. His men. Pulled from their homes. Torn from their fields. Bound now to a war in a foreign land. The sight filled him with pride, but not joy. The chanting grew louder. The column drew closer.

John stepped forward, watching as his knights dismounted.

Hugh, then George. Their expressions weary, but their eyes gleamed with commitment.

John met them halfway, clasping their arms in greeting. Behind them, the levy halted. A command rang out. The men turned in unison, facing the tents bearing Breckington's colors.

Amalric, watching from horseback, nodded with approval.

"Your men display admirable discipline, young baron," the abbot remarked. "They shall prove a most formidable force on the field. Perhaps, some of our best!"

John straightened.

"Indeed, Your Eminence," he lifted his chin. "They rank among the finest in England."

"They shall serve steadfastly."

227

Amalric's smile lingered.

"Lo! The Lord's host stands prepared."

The abbot's tone changed.

"This brings me to the purpose of my visit, my son."

John braced himself.

"I am at thy service, Your Eminence."

Amalric's expression turned somber, as if he were to share some unwelcome news.

"Good," he said smoothly. "For as you know, I am bestowed with the honor of leading our Lord's forces by His Holiness."

A brief pause.

"I desire you to join my command staff as my *aide-de-camp*."

John blinked, incredulously.

"Me, Your Eminence?"

Amalric's smile widened.

"*Oui*, my English comrade. You shall serve as a counselor in matters of war."

Another pause. The abbot continued.

"Did not your father perish while in service on the staff of King Richard—*Cœur de Lion*—battling Saladin and defending the Faith?"

John inhaled sharply.

"Indeed."

"Then t'will be an honor for me," Amalric declared, "to have the son of Sir Roland de Ontivero by my side."

The words felt like shackles.

"We shall convene tomorrow at noon," the abbot continued, as though it were already decided.

"To discuss our campaign."

John bowed his head, but because he had no other choice.

Amalric wheeled his steed, nodding once before riding off, Lopez and Nuñez at his flanks. Behind them, Breckington's levy stood at attention, the sun now lost beyond the trees.

Fires flickered to life across the encampment. A sea of men, waiting for war.

Then—a horn. Low. Echoing.

Summoning a council of war.

John turned his head, watching the dark swallow the road behind them.

No turning back now.

::

"Non!"

The word crashed through the war tent like a war drum, sharp and final.

A moment of stunned silence. Then—uproar.

A thunder of curses in French, Occitan, German— profanities rolling from Amalric's lips with a fury so raw, so venomous, it stilled even the most hardened men. The papal legate—a man of the cloth—spitting expletives like a mercenary in a losing fight.

John and his knights had barely stepped inside when Amalric's fist slammed onto the wooden table.

"Your *routiers*, Lord Harfleur, will not lead this army."

The words rang out like a falling gavel.

A murmur. Shuffling. Lords shifted in their seats. The tension was thick as iron.

Across the table, Harfleur bristled.

"We are not criminals, Your Eminence," the mercenary leader bit out. His voice was rough, tinged with barely restrained fury. "We are soldiers—paid by the Church, no less."

He turned, sweeping a broad hand toward the gathered noblemen.

"Have we not the same right as these—fine Christian men—to take our place at the head of a Holy War?"

Amalric's eyes darkened.

"You are only concerned about the loot," he spat, "like

229

rabid dogs."

Harfleur's nostrils flared with intensity, his arms flailing in frustration.

"Your Eminence—"

"Silence!"

The force of the command cut the air like a blade.

Harfleur clenched his jaw, his fists twitching at his sides. He held his ground for a moment longer, muscles coiled— then turned sharply, storming from the tent.

A brief quiet.

John scanned the room, eyes flitting over the banners and sigils around the table.

Toulouse. Burgundy. Nevers. Lords who had warred against each other now bound together under a single cause.

He caught sight of a newcomer.

Tall. Robed. A priest's habit, the tonsure marking him. He moved with calm precision, his presence at once commanding and unshaken.

Amalric straightened, his armor clinking under his robes as he gestured grandly.

"Attention!"

The room fell silent.

"My good lords and faithful nobles," the abbot proclaimed, "may I introduce my brother legate, Master Milo, notary of His Holiness."

Milo stepped forward, lifting his hand in blessing. The men present in the tent began to shift where they stood.

The moment was a pause—the calm before the storm. Then Amalric's voice rose again. Authoritative.

"Christian brothers, defenders of the Faith!"

His words rang with an oratory fire, each syllable meant to ignite.

"As commander of His Holiness' armies, we have been called to defend the very existence of the True Faith!"

He lifted a parchment—a letter sealed with the Pope's mark.

His voice boomed, reading aloud:

"Attack the followers of heresy more fearlessly even than the Saracens—since they are more evil—with a strong hand and a stretched-out arm."

A murmur of approval rippled through the room. Lords began tapping on their breastplates.

"Forward then, soldiers of Christ! Forward, brave recruits to the Christian army!"

The air crackled with activity.

"Let the universal cry of grief of the Holy Church arouse you, let pious zeal inspire you to avenge this monstrous crime against your God!"

A shiver ran down John's spine.

The tent erupted.

Nobles and monks rose to their feet, goblets lifted, swords unsheathed, crucifixes raised. The roar of *"Deus lo vult!"* thundered through the canvas walls.

John turned—Hugh was chanting along. His usually measured friend swept up in the fervor, his clash with the monk of Vaux-de-Cernay all but forgotten.

George, by contrast, stood stone-faced.

John knew that look.

Knew the man behind it. George had never believed. But here, before the abbot, before God's chosen army, he kept his doubts buried beneath the appearance of loyalty.

John made no move to expose him. Amalric raised his hands. The chants faltered. His gaze settled on John.

A slow smile crept onto his lips.

"I have appointed the stalwart Baron of Breckington to my command staff."

John's breath stilled.

The abbot's voice rang out:

"Son of the valiant defender of the Faith, Sir Roland de Ontivero, who perished at Arsuf, alongside the Lionheart, battling the infidel!"

A resounding "Hear, hear!" echoed throughout the large

tent as dozens of lords cheered his name.

John forced himself to breathe.

Amalric draped an arm across his shoulder. Heavy. Binding. Obligating. Intimidating.

"Lord Breckington," he declared, "and his levy shall lead our vanguard as we embark into the Languedoc."

A second cheer. Louder than the first.

John stood still, his face expressionless. Yet, inside, he was drowning. His father's name praised. His lineage exalted. But the weight of what he had just been given— what he had just been bound to—settled like a cold iron around his throat.

Pride burned in his chest. And beneath it—a deep, gnawing dread. This was war. Not against Saracens on the open field. Not against warriors who met steel with steel. This was war against the defenseless.

And he—John de Ontivero, Baron of Breckington— would be the one to lead their formations.

A dagger slammed into the table, piercing the parchment map with a force that rattled the goblets nearby.

John's eyes followed the blade's hilt, its steel buried deep in a spot on the map marked "Béziers".

"This," Amalric declared, his voice brimming with certainty, "is the first major fortified town that we may need to besiege. Montpellier remains loyal to the true faith, as we shall see. But Béziers…"

He let the moment hang with a slight pause. A smirk. Then, he laughed—a sharp, almost amused scoff.

"The citizens there must surrender their heretics."

A ripple of approval spread through the gathered lords, the heavy presence of knights, clerics, and war-hardened men nodding, murmuring, agreeing.

An elderly man in bishop's robes raised a gloved hand.

"The locusts of the Albi shall be crushed!" he cried.

"DEUS LO VULT! DEUS LO VULT!" the gathered throng chanted.

Amalric's gauntleted finger traced a path from Lyon to Montpellier, dragging across the inked rivers and towns sprawled before him.

"At the break of dawn, we march south," he continued. "Through the lands of Viscount Trencavel, who—according to reliable sources—grants freedoms to the *heretici*." His smirk widened.

"Freedoms."

He said the word like a curse. Then—a chuckle.

"Ha! Can you fathom it?"

Laughter.

John's jaw tightened, as the discomfort rippled through his body. It was then that a figure stepped forward from the shadows of the tent.

Not a warrior. A politician.

His cloak was gray and red. His stature unremarkable—neither tall nor broad—but the presence he carried was undeniable. Dark hair. A beard streaked with silver. A face worn by years of intrigue, of regret, of something far heavier than either.

Count Raymond of Toulouse.

John's gaze narrowed, his breathing shallowed.

He had expected to see him. But even so, the sight still stirred something bitter in his chest.

A man excommunicated. Condemned. Yet here he stood. Among them. A participant in the very campaign that declared against him. How quickly sins were forgiven when they served a greater cause.

John's thoughts stirred bitterly.

He remembered Amalric's words from nights past, spoken over shared wine, laced with contempt.

"The Count of Toulouse has crawled back to the Church like a whipped cur, but do not be fooled, milord. His so-called penitence is a hollow shell. I suspect his loyalty will falter the moment it serves him."

And yet—there Raymond stood. Moving through the

room with quiet purpose.

He exchanged words with a knight, a small nod here, a murmured response there. Occasionally, his gaze flickered over his surroundings, calculating, measuring.

His demeanor was submissive.

But what lay beneath?

A southern lord, once hunted as a protector of heretics, accused of complicity in the murder of the papal legate Pierre de Castelnau.

Now—he walked among them.

John clenched his jaw.

The war had been called to destroy men like him. Now, he marched beneath its banner. But John had heard the whispers. Raymond's penance had been no simple affair.

He had been paraded in sackcloth, barefoot, forced to endure the jeers of clerics and commoners alike. A public spectacle of submission.

He had been made to swear allegiance, to renounce any ties to heresy, to kneel before the very men who had condemned him.

Humiliating.

John's own penance had been private. A few words. A bow of the head. A promise of service. His pride had been wounded, but not broken.

Raymond, however—he had been laid bare before all of Christendom.

And now?

Now he walked among them, smiling where necessary, silent where needed. A man reformed. Or a man who had learned to survive.

John watched as Raymond clasped forearms with a knight, exchanging cordial words. The movements were smooth, easy—too easy.

Had he truly found absolution?

Or had he simply mastered the art of wearing the Church's leash?

234

John shifted where he stood, his fingers curling into fists.

The contradictions of this campaign pressed down on him like a poorly fitted cuirass.

At first, he had suspected this Holy War was little more than a conquest of the north over the south, cloaked in the language of faith.

Now, seeing Raymond of Toulouse standing here—a man once condemned, now tolerated, even accepted—only deepened his unease.

Faith.

Politics.

Power.

Which of the three truly steered the course of this campaign? He already knew Amalric's answer. He would say:

"The Count is like a viper. He slithers where the Church allows him, but mark my words, Baron, his fangs remain sharp. God's wrath will fall upon him yet—if only through our hands."

John's stomach twisted.

Raymond clasped hands with another knight, his expression calm, unbothered. No visible scars from his humiliation.

But John knew.

Some wounds do not show. Was this penitence? Or was it something else entirely?

John exhaled slowly, his unease growing.

The Holy Land had been different. There, he had faced men who fought with steel in hand. Men who met their fate on the battlefield. Not like this. Not against the unarmed. Not against those who wielded nothing but conviction.

And now—seeing Raymond standing among them—a man stripped of dignity, then reforged in submission—only confirmed his worst fears.

This was not simply a war of faith. It was a war of control.

The realization of it all pressed down on him like a heavy weight. This Holy War, he realized, was not simply about the subjugation of the south. At first, it seemed like material greed, disguised as a religious campaign

It was bigger than that. *Much* bigger.

A campaign for papal supremacy over all Christendom—control over all consciences. A war not just for land, for fortresses, or for coin—but for the minds and souls of every ruler, every people, binding them under the *absolute* unquestionable authority of Rome.

John exhaled slowly, his unease growing like the darkness permeating the land after dusk. Had the Church's power become more insidious than that of any king?

To him it was clear. Money, land, titles, wealth, an abundance of which one could purchase desirable things to one's content—but not absolute control. What had once felt like a spiritual endeavor now reeked of something far more dangerous—ambition—not the kind wielded by lords in courtly intrigue or battle, but a different ambition. A colder, more calculated one—an ambition to dominate and subjugate. No, this was a war to crush dissent, to ensure that no ruler, no people, no belief could stand unchallenged by the papacy.

And what unsettled John most was the realization that he was part of it. A pawn in a game far larger than himself.

Like Count Raymond.

The thought sent a bitter taste to his tongue.

It was true that Toulouse and he both stood to gain pardon and grace from the Church. But Breckington? A forgotten barony in a distant land. Not coveted by Rome. Not a threat to its dominion.

Yet Pope Innocent wanted more than just lands.

He wanted the entire continent to kneel. And Raymond's very presence at this council was proof enough.

The Count wasn't just *surviving*.

He was helping them tighten the noose on his kin because

he knew it was the path to thriving. A growing murmur of voices pulled John back into the present.

"Yes, it is true, Your Eminence," Raymond finally answered Amalric's inquiry, his voice smooth, practiced.

"My nephew, Raymond-Roger Trencavel, will seek to negotiate with us."

John's jaw clenched tight as he listened. Toulouse took a measured breath.

"He will offer platitudes of goodwill, but the truth of the matter is, he will not bring the people back into the True Faith."

Silence.

Then—Amalric sighed. A deep, theatrical thing. The performance of a man feigning sorrow.

"So, you see, my dear brothers…" His voice oozed regret, but his smirk betrayed him. "The man who knows this heretic lover so well shows us how the evils of heretical doctrine can poison even such a youthful mind."

The abbot paused. Then—a shake of the head.

"So much promise… lost."

It was a feigned expression, one that John had seen time and time again during his time with the legate. And then— the final condemnation was pronounced.

"Now, Viscount Trencavel and his precious heretics will die accursed."

The direction of the war was now decided.

John felt his stomach turn. Not at Amalric's words. Not even at the lords cheering for Trencavel's doom.

But at *Toulouse*.

At the ease with which he spoke. With which he condemned his own kin. Toulouse and Trencavel had been rivals, yes. Their houses had fought over borders, quarreled over land.

But *this*?

This was not feudal war. This was full betrayal. And for what? For the same men who had once damned him? The same Church that had stripped him, humiliated him, forced him to his knees?

John had fought wars. He had seen men change allegiances, turn their backs on former allies.

But even in that world of shifting loyalties, there were rules. Toulouse had bent the knee not just to save himself—but to destroy another. His own nephew.

A *boy*.

John's contempt burned slow. *Honor*. *Chivalry*. The code of knights.

Toulouse had spat upon it all.

A lord was bound to his kin, even in rivalry. A true knight, a true liege lord, would have stood with Trencavel against the foreign invaders. If they wished to burn the south, then let them burn both houses together; they had a much better chance standing beside one another.

But Toulouse had chosen another path.

A path that John would never have taken. And for the first time, John saw the truth of it.

This "Holy" campaign had never been about heresy.

Not really. It was about ultimate control.

And Raymond VI had chosen the side that would win. John's contempt was absolute.

The cheering continued. Lords toasting to Trencavel's destruction. Monks raising their crucifixes, speaking words of God's will with bloodlust in their voices.

John turned. Left the tent. He needed the air. His thoughts swirled in circles, heavy and sharp. Weeks ago, he would have felt pride standing in this command staff. Pride in being chosen for this Holy War. His father would have been proud. Roland de Ontivero had died for the Church. For a cause that had seemed righteous.

But John's conscience would not rest. Not after this. The war had come too quickly. The justifications too thin. The violence too eager.

He walked somberly back to his tent, the sounds of

chanting warriors ringing in his ears. He barely noticed George and Hugh—Locked in argument. George, his voice sharp with doubt. Hugh, his words heated with defense.

John didn't stop. Didn't listen to the rest. He slumped into a chair, staring at the table before him. For all his rank, for all his position, he had said nothing at the council. He had been present. But he had been silent. And now, the weight of it crushed him.

Then, the council was over. A relief to John's exhausted soul. He wanted to escape from there as quick as he could. Perhaps the further he went from that forsaken tent, the lighter his demeanor would become. The flap of the council tent snapped closed behind him, but the stench lingered—sweat, incense, and self-righteousness.

John exhaled sharply, the cool evening air of Lyon cutting into his lungs like truth. He stood still for a moment, watching the steam of his breath drift skyward. The lords inside were still speaking of absolution as if it were currency, of sieges as if they were pageantry. God's war, they called it. But God seemed curiously absent—except as a bludgeon.

The crunch of boots on frosted grass drew his attention.

"Hell of a sermon in there, *non*?" came a voice, dry and unhurried.

John turned. A tall, broad-shouldered noble approached, crimson cloak trailing behind him, the white cross of Nevers stitched into its trim. His dark beard was neatly trimmed, his tone relaxed—but the eyes beneath his hooded brow were sharp.

"I take it you weren't inspired either," John said, gaze returning to the field where soldiers trained in tight squares.

Count Nevers gave a short laugh.

"Inspired? No. Entertained? Slightly. Did you catch the part where the Bishop of Auxerre compared the Albigensians to locusts?"

"I did," John replied. "I was half expecting him to quote the Book of Apocalypse and call fire from heaven."

Nevers smirked.

"Give him another day. He might."

They stood in silence for a beat, watching the movements on the field below. The Breckington levy was drilling under Sergeant Owain. Shields rose in unison, suddenly their spears struck forward, then reset—tight, clean, without wasting a single motion.

"Yours?" Nevers asked, nodding toward the blue and yellow formation.

John nodded.

Nevers let out a low whistle.

"*Mon Dieu*, they actually listen. Mine barely form a straight line unless I threaten to confiscate their wine."

"They're English," John replied. "They respond well to dry bread, clear orders, and the promise of survival."

Nevers chuckled.

"And yet the council lords think victory comes from shining one's armor."

As if on cue, the Duke of Burgundy emerged from his pavilion, plumed helm tucked beneath his arm, a retinue of heralds flanking him like painted ducks. His tabard sparkled with golden thread, and his boots looked as though they'd never touched mud. He looked towards the men, then marched off in pompous fashion without saying a word.

Nevers raised an eyebrow.

"Ah, Burgundy. The man enters a campaign as though he were attending a coronation."

John's lips twitched.

"Shame that his plumes can't swing a sword."

"No," Nevers said dryly. "But they do distract from the fact that his men are busy gambling and groping stable girls while the rest of us prepare for war."

John gave a rare, low laugh.

"The Church certainly loves its bright colors."

Nevers glanced sideways at him.

"And what do you love, Lord Breckington?"

John's smile faded.

"Justice. Clarity. The kind you don't find in tents filled with bishops who've never seen a battlefield."

Nevers nodded slowly.

"Then we may yet get along, *monsieur*."

A minute passed as they watched in silence. The clang of training resumed in the distance. The Breckington levy rotated ranks, shields locking, spears rising in a forest of resolve.

"Will they stand when it matters?" Nevers asked.

"They'll stand," John agreed quietly. "Whether they'll be thanked for it is another question."

Nevers extended a hand.

"Count of Nevers. Hervé."

"John de Ontivero, Baron Breckington," he replied, clasping it. "I suspect we'll be seeing a lot more of each other. I hope you will count upon me as a friend."

"I am at your service, my lord," John inclined his head.

Nevers turned toward the edge of the hill, where a pair of camp stools had been planted near a cart stacked with javelins and salted meat. He motioned toward it with the flick of his gloved hand.

"Walk with me. I've no more taste for incense and papal thunder."

John followed, his boots crunching over the brittle grass. They sat in silence for a moment, watching a troop of mounted knights gallop a lazy circuit across the lower field—plumes flying, cloaks trailing, laughter echoing far too loudly for men preparing for holy war.

Nevers handed over a small pewter flask.

"Don't worry. It's not Burgundy's. You'd taste more silk than spirits from the casks in his cellar."

John took a swig. *Armagnac*. Rough, honest. It burned just enough to remind him he was alive.

"You've fought before," Nevers said, more statement than question.

John nodded. "Indeed, my lord. I was in the Levant, near Acre in the last Holy War."

Nevers snorted.

"Saracens. And now you're here, being asked to kill Occitan farmers and herders for the salvation of your soul. God does have a sense of humor."

John didn't smile.

"I don't know that God has anything to do with it, my lord. But I know what men want. Titles. Penance. Land."

Nevers sighed.

"I'll admit, the Pope's offer of indulgence caught my steward's attention more than my own."

"I came for penance. My penance—which may cost the lives of some of my men."

The response was a soft, knowing grunt.

They sat in companionable silence again. Down in the valley, Nevers' own men were attempting a staggered shield drill. It went poorly. A young knight tripped over his own sabaton and toppled backward into a water trough, drawing hoots of laughter.

Nevers winced.

"They've got heart. But no cohesion. Not like yours."

John glanced at him.

"You could train them, my lord. Constant drilling could do wonders."

"I could. But to make them stand like yours?" He shook his head. "You didn't just train yours. You built them, with care, with passion."

John said nothing. The words struck deeper than expected.

Nevers continued, his tone quieter now.

"You've got something rare here, *mon ami*. Men who follow you not because you threaten them or dazzle them, but because they know you would die for them."

John's gaze returned to the Breckington levy. *His* levy. The men were now resting—some seated, others cleaning weapons, still alert even in pause. Sir George stood among them, speaking to a group of squires, his shield balanced over one knee. Familiar. Steady.

"They trust you," Nevers said. "I hope to God you're not wasted on this war."

John turned the flask in his hands, the dregs sloshing gently.

"I came because I believed it mattered. Now I think it matters only who survives it."

Nevers glanced sideways.

"You don't think the cause is just?"

John stood slowly, his gaze fixed on the city of Lyons beyond, where smoke curled faintly from merchant chimneys and church spires.

"I think men with swords shouldn't be the ones deciding what heresy looks like, my lord."

Nevers remained seated, watching him with an expressionless face.

"They say we're marching for the soul of Christendom," John added. "But every road I walk feels more like marching for the devil."

A gust of wind stirred the banners below. He had to be careful. His standing with the abbot could be placed at risk, should the reports of his discontentment reach the legate's ears.

Nevers rose too, brushing dust from his cloak.

"Well then. I hope it eases your conscience to know that I, too, march with unease. For now, look to your men, Lord Breckington."

"My lord."

John nodded once, then turned toward his camp. They would be marching soon, and he would need all the rest he could get.

The March

 he ground trembled beneath the weight of thousands of marching feet. Steel clattered. Horses snorted, their riders scanning the horizon with restless anticipation. The "Army of the Cross", as Amalric so fervently called it, stretched out over the road like a river of iron and fluttering banners. Montpellier lay ahead.

John's hands tightened on the reins. Nearly a fortnight had passed since Lyon. Tensions had festered in that time— worse than before.

The Frisians and Germans chafed at being pushed to the rear, their resentment growing toward the Frankish lords who claimed precedence near the vanguard.

And the *routiers*?

They were always a problem. Mercenaries drawn from all corners of Christendom, they owed allegiance to no

245

banner but coin. Most hailed from Germanic lands, and when the Frisians began pushing for a greater share of glory, they found themselves gravitating toward the *routiers*.

What followed? Disputes. Shouting. Nearly bloodshed.

Amalric had brought the column to a grinding halt outside Montpellier. A week of negotiations followed, while the Holy Army camped in the fields beyond the city.

John found himself dragged into the thick of it, his role as *Aide-de-Camp* forcing him to serve as both mediator and witness to the endless bickering. The army had begun to resemble a den of wolves, each pack fighting to claim its rightful place.

And the war had not even begun.

Montpellier's gates loomed ahead, its white stone walls bathed in the glow of the midday sun. Banners fluttered above the battlements, but no soldiers stood in defiance.

Only a delegation.

John narrowed his eyes as the town's officials approached. At their head, a man of middle years, broad-shouldered despite the weight of his robes. His steps measured, his face carefully composed.

Bertrand of Montpellier.

Beside him, Captain Mateo, clad in armor, his face expressionless.

John felt George nudge him.

"Think they'll bring us wine?" George muttered.

"If they're as clever as they claim," John murmured, "they'd be wise to."

Hugh shot them both a look.

"A bit early to be thinking of wine."

"Never too early for hope," George quipped with a smirk.

But John was already watching Bertrand's expression, his eyes scanning the approaching group. Sweat on his brow. Not fear—but wariness.

A man hoping for the best, preparing for the worst. The delegation halted.

Captain Mateo stepped forward first, bowing low.

"Lords of the Holy Army, I am Captain Mateo, commander of the garrison."

Bertrand followed shortly after, his voice calm, firm.

"Noble lords, I am Bertrand of Montpellier. We come in peace, bearing gifts and assurances of our town's loyalty to the Faith."

John's eyes flickered to Amalric. The abbot's face was unreadable. Then—a scoff.

"Words are wind, Mayor Bertrand."

His voice cut like steel. Deliberate. Intimidating.

"Many claim loyalty until the heretic's shadow is cast. Why should we trust you?"

Bertrand did not flinch. He gestured, and his attendants stepped forward, bearing crates of wine, sacks of grain, bolts of fine cloth.

John exhaled softly and watched as George's lips quirked upward.

"Clever man," he muttered under his breath.

"We offer these as tokens of goodwill," Bertrand said. "More importantly, we open our gates. Send your men— inspect our churches, our homes, our markets."

The mayor's gaze did not waver.

"You will find no heretics within our walls."

Amalric's silence stretched. His gaze swept across the gifts, then turned to Milo. The other legate studied Bertrand. Finally, he stroked his chin, nodding.

"Their offer is bold," he mused. "If they have nothing to hide, it would be prudent to verify their claims."

Another pause. Then—a curt nod by the lead abbot.

"Very well," Amalric said. "I will send my men. If they find any trace of heresy, your gifts will not spare you from the wrath of God."

Bertrand bowed his head.

"Understood, Your Eminence."

The knights rode through the gates. John watched as

Hugh and George led the patrol, their eyes sharp as they observed every street, every face.

The town bustled with life. Merchants haggled. Women carried baskets of fruit, their wary eyes flickering toward the knights.

And yet—

No fear. Not the kind John had expected. The churches were untouched. The homes lined with crosses. A marketplace butcher wiped his hands, watching George with curiosity.

"You seem calm," George remarked.

The butcher shrugged.

"We've nothing to hide, sir."

He paused. Then, he lowered his voice:

"Our priests are devout. Our town has no taste for strange teachings."

George glanced around.

"I don't care either way," he murmured. "I'm just here to do my job."

The butcher nodded knowingly.

"I understand, sir."

By evening, the search was done. Hugh dismounted before Amalric's tent.

"No signs of heresy, Your Eminence."

The abbot's expression did not change.

"Very good," he said at last. "Montpellier shall remain untouched."

Then—a smile.

"Let them send word to other towns: Loyalty is rewarded."

John let out a slow breath. Relief. For now, Montpellier was spared. He hoped the campaign would continue to go this smoothly—for all their sakes.

But the weight of reality loomed ahead. Not every town would be as submissive as this one. He watched as the sun sank lower, casting long shadows across the camp.

Fires crackled. The men settled into their routines. Chants of the "holy" warriors drifted through the night air.

John stared out toward the darkened road ahead. The path wound southward.

To Béziers. To Trencavel's lands. To the place where, soon, there would be no surrender. No negotiation. John saw the look in Amalric's eyes. He was not about to give these heretics mercy.

Only fire.

And death.

But one could still hope. Montpellier itself stood untouched. A rare mercy in any Holy War. John could feel the tension ease from his shoulders, the quiet relief that, for once, they had moved forward without blood.

The city had been wise.

Under the lordship of Peter II of Aragon and his wife, Marie of Montpellier, the town's leaders had navigated the treacherous waters of faith and politics well.

Marie, a devout Catholic, had seen to it that her city harbored no heretics. A concession, perhaps, to her husband, a man of more lenient temperament.

The decree was simple: Merchants would not be persecuted for their dealings, but all who dwelled within Montpellier were required to attend Mass.

A clever compromise. It had worked. John knew that many among them remembered the horrors of Constantinople, only five years past. No city, no matter how loyal, wished to suffer that fate. Montpellier had opened its gates, offered its gifts, and passed the test.

And so, the Army of the Cross moved on.

Southward.

Toward the Viscount Trencavel's lands. Where there would be no gifts. No mercy. Beneath the relentless sun the heat was merciless. The summer sun bore down like a hammer, the air thick with dust and sweat.

Men slogged forward, their steps slow, heavy. The air

reeked of leather, of metallic sweat, of unwashed wool and horseflesh.

By noon, the march had slowed.

Some units faltered, their bodies weighed down by the heat, their pace lagging.

Amalric's patience frayed. He rode ahead, his voice booming over the column.

"Soldiers of the Cross! Quicken your pace!"

His tone cut through the exhaustion, but the men offered little response. Some chuckled under their breath. A mistake.

Amalric's fury ignited.

"I wield the authority to annul any man's absolution!"

The laughter died instantly. John felt the shudder of unease ripple through the ranks. Every man here had come for salvation.

Forty days. Forty days, the Pope had decreed, and all sins would be washed away. Now, with a single outburst, Amalric had reminded them—their souls were at his mercy.

Silence hung heavy in the air as the column pressed forward. As the sun dipped lower, Amalric signaled a halt.

"Let the army pass," he ordered.

"I wish to see the men we march with."

He dismounted, his staff following suit. John hesitated, then fell in line beside them. The crusader host stretched beyond the horizon, a river of banners and steel.

As his own men came into view, John raised a fist in encouragement. The cheer that followed warmed him. These were his levy. His knights. His men. A moment of pride.

Then—gone.

Swallowed by the endless march. John's heart ached to ride among them, but Amalric, keen-eyed, had already noted his body language.

"Your place is here, Baron," the abbot murmured, his voice leaving no room for debate.

John's jaw clenched, but he said nothing. The march continued. Unit after unit passed, their faces marked by weariness, determination, or fervor.

Then—the final ranks came into view. John's stomach turned. The *routiers*—They swaggered. They jeered. They did not march with the reverence of knights or the discipline of trained soldiers.

Their armor mismatched, their weapons worn and bloodstained. These were men who fought for plunder, not piety.

John watched as a mercenary, his teeth crooked and yellow, leaned toward a knight, his grin mocking as he jeered in his French tongue.

"Eh, monk-soldier, how does one pray while holding a sword?"

His comrades snickered. Another swung an invisible blade, chanting *"Deus lo vult! Deus lo vult!"* in mocking piety as they laughed.

John's teeth gritted as he watched. A Calatravan knight turned to the mocker, his glare cold as iron.

"Hold your tongue, brigand, or you'll find it cut out before the day is done."

The *routier* sneered.

"Ah, but who would carry your holy banners when your hands are slick with blood?"

John saw the knight stiffen. The moment stretched. Then—

"Enough!"

The word came sharp, cutting the air. Another knight, his voice edged with steel. The *routiers* fell into silence.

Their mockery did not cease, but now, it was muttered under breath.

John exhaled. These men...

These were the same the Church had once condemned. The same that had been denounced as lawless pillagers. And yet—here they were. Walking beneath the banner of the Holy War. A necessity, Amalric had called them. A blight, John thought. A foreshadowing of things to come.

251

The weight of the march grew heavier with every foot stomp of the soldiers. John's gaze flicked between the two forces—monks and mercenaries.

Both headed toward the same war. And yet, the contrast between them could not have been starker. The *routiers*, bound by greed, cared little for the Church, for the Faith, for righteousness.

The monks and knights, bound by zeal, saw themselves as instruments of divine wrath.

John gritted his teeth. Where did he fit in among them? A baron marching under the Church's banner. A Christian now set against other Christians. His thoughts churned.

This was not like defending Breckington against raiders. This was a war against men and women who knelt in prayer. Men and women who revered the Scriptures as he did—though they may have read them differently.

A bitter taste curled in his throat, like damp ash. His hand drifted to the small cross tucked into his tunic, his thumb tracing the etched lines of the crucifix. The same one given to him by his father, Roland of Breckington, hero of Arsuf.

Father Barth's voice whispered in his mind. *Love. Mercy. The Kingdom of Heaven.*

But those words were being drowned beneath the tide of fire and fear. Amalric's proclamations burned with zeal. Yet they clashed against the gentler teachings of the Gospel John had once cherished.

Could both truly come from the same God?

The rhythmic clink of harnesses. The steady thud of boots against the hardened earth. A faint breeze stirred the dust, carrying with it the stench of sweat, leather, and old iron. Somewhere, in the distance, a lark's song rose.

Clear. *Defiant.*

And then—snuffed out by the sound of marching feet.

John exhaled.

God, are you in the midst of this host?

He waited. And waited. The heavens offered no reply.

The silence pressed down heavier than the dust-laden air. He sighed. The pompousness of Amalric's words. The sight of the *routiers*, grinning like jackals at the back of the host.

It all which tested his resolve. His fingers instinctively found the hidden pocket of his saddle. They brushed against soft fabric. A piece of linen, worn thin by time and memory. Carefully, he drew it out. A lone emblem of sanity in an insane world.

A handkerchief. Faded.

But still embroidered with delicate, intricate patterns. His lips twitched in the ghost of a smile.

Adelinda.

Before Father Barth had spoken her name, she had lain dormant in his heart. A love now lost, but she had never truly left him. He had the cloth to prove it.

They had both been young back then.

Bound by a love that had felt immutable, eternal. He had been on the cusp of knighthood—headstrong, idealistic. She had been his light. He could use a light, especially in this darkness.

Her laughter rang through her father's halls like the chiming of a silver bell. And then—they had parted. He still remembered the night she had pressed the handkerchief into his palm, her fingers lingering in his.

"Carry this with you, and know my heart goes with it."

And he had carried it. Even now. Even after Mary de Dustanville. That wretched marriage—a match arranged for duty rather than love. A match that had dissolved as swiftly as it had been made.

Mary had been a ghost in his life. Adelinda had been his very soul. Through every campaign, every battle, every disappointment, the handkerchief had remained. A permanent part of his armor.

A relic of a purer time. Untouched by war. Untouched by duty.

He heard a chuckle. A voice, playful, edged with

knowing amusement.

"Careful, milord," George's voice cut through the quiet. "You'll wear that cloth thin."

John forced a smile, folding the handkerchief carefully.

"Thank you for the reminder, George," he muttered. "I need to be back to minding my duties."

George chuckled, though his face, too, was lined with weariness as they rode. He lowered his voice, mindful of Amalric's presence only a few meters ahead.

"Aye, I suppose that's fair," he said, his tone casual. "But tell me, milord—doesn't all this marching under holy banners feel more like a show for men than for their God?"

John turned to him, brow lifting slightly.

"What do you mean?"

George shrugged.

His voice remained light, but there was an edge beneath it.

"Look around you, milord John. These *routiers* fight for coin. The knights fight for glory. The monks fight for the Church."

A brief pause.

"And yet all claim to be serving the same God."

John frowned. George let the silence hang for a moment. Then, his tone dropped to a whisper.

"I've stopped trying to make sense of it," George shrugged. "Seems to me, if there is a God, He doesn't much care for our squabbles—holy or otherwise."

John said nothing. Was it criticism? Or honest weariness? George, sensing the question, softened his tone.

"Don't mistake me," he added. "I'll do my duty, as I always have. But faith?"

He gave a small shake of his head as he continued.

"That's something I've left to men like you. The rest of us—well," he sighed. "We live by the sword and die by it. It's simpler that way."

John remained quiet as his thoughts turned. George. The

254

pragmatist. Hugh. The devout. Where did he fall between them? Somewhere in the middle, perhaps. But that middle felt thinner by the day. Elusive. Like grasping at mist.

His gaze drifted.

The *routiers* marched ahead. A sorry lot, armed with little more than clubs and crude spears. John's lip curled. He loathed them. Not just for their lack of discipline. But for what they represented.

This war was supposed to be holy. For his own misgivings about the Church and this campaign, he respected the ecclesiastical order. This campaign could turn out to be a force for good, if it was for the deterrence of infidelity.

And yet—it was filled with men who cared nothing for holiness. Perhaps George was right. Perhaps God did not care for such squabbles.

John spurred his horse forward, pushing past the mercenaries, the monks, the priests. And kept his eyes ahead.

The Army of the Cross pressed on. The summer heat bore down upon them, the midday sun turning dust into a choking haze, clinging to sweat-slicked faces and the dull gleam of armor.

John watched the road unfurl ahead, but his gaze was drawn elsewhere—to the men who marched beside him.

A new formation.

Not the rabble of *routiers* trailing at the rear, but a more disciplined contingent. Their white banner, trimmed in black, swayed in the dry wind. Their weapons sharper, their armor more uniform.

Not simple brigands. These men knew war. Their leader rode at their head—a towering figure clad in black chainmail, helm resting against his saddle, face shadowed beneath the wide brim of his hood.

The mercenary general, the Lord Harfleur.

John narrowed his eyes. A noble name. Yet, the man rode

255

among sellswords. Forced into a mercenary's life, perhaps?

His posture, the way he carried himself—it was not that of a common *routier*. And yet, there he was. During the war council, Harfleur had argued—vehemently—to place his men at the vanguard.

Unusual.

Routiers, by nature, hovered at the rear, waiting for battle to be won before descending upon the corpses to claim their spoils.

But not these men. Not *Harfleur*. What were they after? John's unease deepened. Why were they allowed to march at all? Amalric despised mercenaries.

The Church itself had condemned them. And yet—here they were, marching alongside the soldiers of God. The thought gnawed at him.

The parade of warriors continued. Unit after unit, an endless tide of banners and steel. The sun dipped lower, casting long shadows through the dust-choked air. John and the rest of the command staff watched in review, standing beside the abbot as the men passed.

Amalric's chest swelled with pride.

His voice rang over the march.

"Worthless rabble, transfigured into a formidable force by the Almighty Himself!"

His hand swept over the host, basking in its splendor.

"A fearsome spectacle, do you not agree, *mes amis*?"

Before anyone could answer—Laughter.

Crude. Unruly.

Two drunken routiers stumbled from behind a boulder, fastening their belts, their bodies still shaking with mirth. John saw Amalric stiffen. His face darkened, nostrils flaring in open contempt.

The abbot gestured—a flick of the wrist. A shadow moved. A flash of steel. The Calatravan knight Lopez spurred forward, sword already drawn.

One scream, cut short. Two bodies fell to the dirt. The

256

march halted. Eyes widened. A hushed murmur rippled through the ranks.

The *routiers* stiffened, their posture suddenly rigid. No one moved. John clenched his jaw, his fingers tightening over his reins. The first blood of the campaign had been drawn—not by the heretics of the Languedoc, but by their own hand.

Amalric, his fury momentarily spent, straightened in his saddle. He cleared his throat, masking his embarrassment behind an air of righteousness.

Then, without a backward glance, he rode forward. The retinue followed. John lingered. His eyes drifted to the two corpses lying in the dust. Cut down without trial, without hesitation.

His gut twisted. He turned away, spurred his horse, and rode after his commander, disgusted. What else did the abbot expect? Allowing such rowdy company to march with them. When you allow pigs to come with you, expect them to act as pigs. Almaric had no sense, only hubris. But—there was no point in protesting. He only bit his lip and rode on.

Dust rose in thick clouds as the army pressed south. The shimmering Mediterranean glinted mockingly to their left. The inland terrain to the right—jagged, uneven, thick with bramble—was ripe for ambush. John rode up near to his superior, weary and disgruntled.

Amalric barked orders around him, his patience wearing thin.

The abbot carried himself with the arrogance of divine appointment, but John saw the truth beneath the bravado. The truth was that Amalric was no commander—even with all the hubris and fanaticism peeled away.

His decisions were erratic, his strategies hollow. But the true danger? He knew when to lean on others. When to steal their wisdom and claim it as his own.

John had already seen it—his own counsel repackaged as divine revelation. And he knew it would happen again.

257

"Baron John!"

John's name fell from Amalric's lips, imperious, expectant. John sighed inwardly. Still, he nudged his horse forward, closing the distance. Amalric gestured toward the inland hills, his brow furrowed in concern.

"We are vulnerable on our right flank," the abbot muttered, keeping his voice low. "What would you advise?"

John's lips pressed into a thin line. Hadn't he given this very counsel yesterday? Hadn't he watched Amalric nod solemnly, then pass it off as his own? But John had no choice. His penance, his barony's safety, all of it depended on his compliance.

So, he spoke to give the same advice. Again.

"A column of cavalry should patrol the inland side," his voice was steady, measured, although inwardly he sighed with irritation. "Their mobility will allow them to react swiftly to any ambushes. Scouts should ride ahead. The baggage train should remain light and close to the coast. Supplies ferried by ship will keep us quick and unburdened."

There was a short pause.

"King Richard used these very tactics against Saladin."

Amalric nodded slowly. His expression thoughtful, calculating. Then—a look of satisfaction.

"Yes, yes," he said. "A prudent course. See to it that the orders are carried out."

John inclined his head.

"As you command, Your Eminence."

The words tasted like bile. But he knew he had no choice but to fulfill his role. At least until the end of his penance.

What is forty days? I am already two weeks into that number. I could hold out for a bit more. I'll just grit my teeth.

With a new determination, John gave a command. Shouts rippled through the ranks. Orders were relayed. A column of cavalry was deployed inland, scouts sent ahead.

The baggage train adjusted. The column tightened. The army moved with purpose. John watched it unfold, his own strategy taking shape under another man's name.

He sighed. He thought he could endure it. The sight brought no solace. Only more disillusion. He let his horse fall back, widening the distance between himself and the abbot.

The wind stirred the dust, hot and dry.

To their flank, the Mediterranean sparkled, indifferent to the march of men and their holy war.

John tightened his grip on the reins. The path ahead stretched long. And the road behind was already painted in blood. The march dragged on.

Dust clung to sweat-drenched faces, boots pounding dry earth, hooves kicking up clouds of grit. John rode in silence. His hands steady, his thoughts restless. George, noticing his overlord's furrowed brow, nudged his horse closer.

"I'll give the abbot this," he said, voice light, "he's managed to herd this lot in the same direction. A miracle in itself."

John let out a bitter laugh, shaking his head.

"A miracle? No, George. It's my advice he's parading as divine insight. He pretends at strategy while others do the thinking for him."

George's grin faded. His brow furrowed in concern.

"You've always had the mind for tactics, my lord. Let him take the credit if it spares you trouble. As you would say, your God sees what men cannot."

John's grip tightened on the reins, his jaw clenching as his gaze stayed fixed on the horizon.

"Does He, George? You don't even believe in Him. But I do, and I see less of God in this campaign with every passing day. What I see is hubris—ours, Amalric's, the Church's. This march forebodes darkness, not light."

George said nothing for a moment, then placed a firm hand on John's arm.

"You fight for your barony, for us, for your people. That is reason enough, milord. Leave the rest alone."

John nodded slightly, though his heart remained heavy. The contradictions of this war gnawed at him. In the Levant, he had fought warriors who met him on the field, armed and unyielding. Their faith had been woven into steel, their conviction matched by the fire of his own. But here—

Here, in the Midi, the enemy was not a warrior host, but peasants, craftsmen, mothers. Their crime was not rebellion. It was belief.

The realization came back to him and soured his stomach. *Why am I even here?* He murmured to himself. A voice interrupted his thoughts.

Amalric. Sharp. Commanding.

"Baron Breckington!"

With a weary, clandestine sigh, John glanced ahead of him. The abbot sat rigid in his saddle, eyes locked onto him, impatience creasing his brow.

"Ride closer!"

John exhaled slowly. Spurred his mount forward. As he drew alongside the abbot, Amalric's expression softened, though his tone remained brisk.

"You've been mostly quiet today, Baron," he remarked, lowering his voice. "I trust you haven't been second-guessing the wisdom of our mission?"

John's silence was calculated. Amalric studied him, then leaned in slightly.

"You should know, Baron, your counsel has been invaluable. This campaign has moved as smoothly as it has because of your strategic insights."

John flicked his gaze to the abbot, surprised at the admission.

"Do not look so stunned," Amalric continued, a smirk playing at the edges of his lips as he lowered his voice. "A leader must appear as if he knows what he is doing at all times. The men need confidence in their commander. It is not vanity, but necessity, that compels me to claim the credit. You understand this, I hope?"

John's face tightened. He forced himself to nod, although a bitter taste settled at the back of his throat.

"You are a soldier and a nobleman," Amalric continued. "Surely, you see the value in appearances. Rest assured, Baron, your contributions have not gone unnoticed."

Amalric straightened, his tone turning brisk once more.

"Now, let us press on. There is no time for dallying."

He flicked the reins, urging his mount ahead. John let himself fall behind again. Would Amalric chide him? He didn't care. George rode up beside him once more, his expression unreadable.

"Well, my lord," he muttered, "at least he admitted it."

John gave a faint shake of his head.

The words meant nothing. Whatever satisfaction he might have felt drowned beneath the weight of his growing disillusionment. He had become a shadow advisor to a man he disliked less and less with every passing minute.

But he could not refuse his role. Not while his barony's fate rested on it. John needed a reprieve, however, and finally he urged his mount forward to catch up with the abbot.

"My Lord Eminence, may I ride ahead to check on my levy?"

The abbot, engaged in conversation with Milo, barely turned.

"Of course, my dear Baron," Amalric said with a smile too generous. "Ha! You earned it. Go and see to your men."

John barely waited.

"*Hyah!*"

His horse surged forward, George close behind. The road was flanked by waist-high, golden grass, the host marching ten men abreast. John did not look back. Did not care to see Amalric's pompous grin.

He needed distance. He needed to see his own men, who marched at the vanguard. The sight would ease his heart— even if only slightly. They were his men. They marched not for Rome, but for him. And yet—

The campaign's demands weighed heavy. Supplies dwindled. The wagons, burdened with barrels of grain and salted fish, would not last another fortnight.

They needed resupply.

The fleet of supplies, launched from the ports near Monpellier, laden with the promised provisions, was still miles away, ordered to meet them in Agde. It was much easier to move such supplies over water than on land, and it would prevent them from being harassed by enemy raiding parties from the north—so far, none have attempted to attack.

Each step toward it was a gamble against time and necessity.

Foraging was an option, but in the now-hostile Midi, it was a dangerous one. A wrong step, a misjudgment, a single spark— and the countryside could erupt into rebellion before a single sword had been drawn in battle.

The march was far from over.

Dust clung to sweat-drenched faces. A shuffle of boots. A clank of mail. The dull drag of a pack mule's hooves scuffing against loose stone. A soldier stumbled, his knee buckling. A quiet curse. The mule beside him startled, its load shifting, threatening to tumble. The soldier steadied it with a rough grip, muttering a prayer under his breath.

John watched. Silent.

One slip, one broken wheel, one overturned cart—and the whole host would grind to a halt. Ahead, the wagons groaned against the dry ruts, every lurch sending grains of dust spiraling into the stagnant air. The wheels, overburdened, teetered and rocked—fragile bones beneath the weight of war.

Forty days of service.

The thought clawed at him. A relic of feudal law. Fit for border skirmishes, not this. How could such an arrangement sustain an army marching deep into enemy lands, preparing for siege, confronting a people unwilling to kneel?

It was not heresy that would undo them. It was Amalric's hubris. The lords of the Midi would not sit idle. They were no fools. They saw this crusade for what it was—not a holy war, but an invasion. A northern host riding beneath the Pope's banner, cloaked in righteousness but driven by greed and power.

If it were England—if foreign lords came to claim his barony under the guise of divine authority—would he not fight?

John exhaled slowly, gripping the reins tighter.

Yes. He would.

The *bons hommes.*That was what some called them. The good men. The Cistercians called them something else.

Heretics. Albigensians. Poison.

Their crimes? Rejecting the material world. Rejecting the Church's sacraments. Rejecting Rome's authority. John had heard the sermons. The wrathful speeches. The warnings of contagion, the promise of cleansing by fire. But had they truly done anything to warrant such hatred?

They raised no banners. They wielded no swords. They simply existed.

And for that, they would burn.

The lords of the Midi did not share their beliefs. But they did not betray them either. They would protect them with their swords. Their loyalty was not to Rome. It was to their people.

John understood that. Respected that. A lord was bound to his subjects. Not to some distant power. Yet here he was—marching beneath the papal banner, sword bound to a cause he no longer understood.

How had the Church, the shepherd of souls, become the wielder of the sword? Salvation, they called it. But salvation did not come at the tip of a lance.

John clenched his teeth. The Church was not leading men to heaven. It was forcing them. And those who refused? Not left to their fate. They were slaughtered.

The marching column stretched endlessly behind and before him. John spurred his horse forward. He sought only one thing. One piece of familiarity. Of comfort.

The banner of Breckington.

The blue and yellow. *His* standard. A splash of home in a sea of crimson, white, maroon, purple and black. His men marched with discipline in the distance, their voices strong. He could hear them, even before he could see them.

"Faith and Honor! Faith and Honor!"

At last, something that made sense. He urged his mount faster. There they were. The men of Breckington, stalwart, strong. The cheer that rose at his arrival struck something deep in his chest.

A voice called from the vanguard.

Hugh Philip.

"A cheer for your lord!"

"*Ha Breck! Ha Breck!*"

The shout rang out—not once, but in rolling chorus. It caught the air and bounded off the hills, bounced over the heads of the men, till it filled every empty space on the road ahead.

It had started as a mock-chant, something the lads came up with one night while huddled around a fire outside Valros. Someone had recalled *"Ha Rou!"*—an old Norman war cry used by the dukes of Rouen before battle. That one made sense—Rouen was a city, the ancestral seat. You shouted *"Ha Rou!"*— short for *Rouen*—to summon its strength.

So they gave Breckington its own version. Shortened it. Sharpened it. "*Ha Breck!*" rolled off the tongue with the same punch and had the added charm of being their own. Not French. Not Papal. Not Rome's.

Nobody ordered it. No officer drilled it into them. It just grew legs, as these things tend to do. One lad did it. Then two. Then the column.

Now here it was. Alive.

John rode with them, the reins slack in his hands. The chant—*his* chant—had moved past jest, past ritual. It had become their badge. A thing of meaning, forged in the long marches and the thick bloodshed of the Levantine desert. And what mattered most... it was theirs. Not for Amalric. Not for the Pope. Not for Jerusalem.

They marched for Breckington. For the man who bled with them. Who stayed when others fled. The man who listened. The man who fought.

And just like that—without warning and without effort—the corners of John's mouth curled.

A smile. Unbidden. But not unwelcome.

He would die for his men—and they would die for him. He silently prayed their lives would not be wasted by the pompous prelates at the head of this unholy campaign.

The air smelled of salt and earth, the scent of the sea mingling with the trampled grass and dirt beneath a thousand boots. The march had settled into a steady rhythm—the clang of armor, the creak of leather, the murmur of men recounting old glories to pass the time.

Hugh pulled his horse alongside John's, eyes gleaming.

"Milord, I was just sharing a tale of your father with the men," he said. "They've been reminiscing about Arsuf."

John's grip on the reins tightened, his mind drifting. Arsuf. The clash of steel, the cries of men, the blinding sun over bloodied sand.

"What tale, Hugh?" John asked, his voice quieter than intended.

Hugh gestured to a gray-bearded spearman walking beside them.

"Old Owain here was recalling how we carried Lord Roland from the battlefield."

Owain nodded as he marched, straightening his shoulders despite the exhaustion weighing on him.

"Aye, milord. We bore him for days, even with the

Saracens breathing down our necks. We couldn't leave him," his voice softened. "He was our lord. But more than that—he was one of us."

John swallowed hard.

"I remember the day you all brought him home," he replied mournfully. "I stood by the churchyard, waiting to hear the horns. I didn't think you'd make it, not after the news of the battle."

Another soldier, Alan, younger but just as reverent, spoke up.

"I wasn't there, milord, but my father was. He told me how you all kept him safe, even after he'd… passed. He said it was the proudest moment of his life."

Hugh beamed softly as he turned to the young Alan.

"Pride and grief, both," he admitted. "We mourned him, but we were proud to carry him back. Even when we joined King Richard at Jaffa, our minds were still on Lord Roland."

John exhaled, his gaze fixed on the horizon.

"He would have been proud of all of you," he said, voice steady despite the lump forming in his throat. "Of the sacrifices you made for him—for Breckington, for England. I've tried to follow his example. To protect you all. To ensure no life is wasted needlessly."

Hugh's grip tightened on John's shoulder, who rode beside him.

"And you have, milord," he said. "The men trust you because they know you carry your father's heart with you."

John turned in the saddle, scanning the faces of his men.

"You all stood in formation that day, in full gear, swearing fealty to me," he said, much louder. "I will never forget that moment."

He nodded toward the levy, pride swelling in his chest as he continued.

"Many of you who pledged your swords and spears then now march beside me here."

Owain squared his shoulders.

"And we'd do it again, milord," he said. "We'd march to the ends of the earth for you, just as we did for your father. We know you'd see our families cared for if the worst came to pass."

John met his gaze, solemn.

"And I would. You have my word."

The column pressed on, the rhythmic sound of boots and hooves filling the quiet spaces between them. The blue and yellow banners of Breckington snapped in the wind, the colors bold against the fading light.

Ahead, the sun kissed the horizon, dipping lower, painting the coastline in hues of fire and gold. They were close to Agde, its spires visible just above the trees.

"Hugh," John called.

"Aye, my lord?"

"Let us encamp here for the night," John ordered, eyes scanning the land. He pointed toward a modest hill to the north. "Have the men set camp there."

Hugh nodded. "It shall be done."

The command echoed down the column. A slow halt. The shifting of men and horses. The metallic scrape of armor being loosened, the murmurs of soldiers preparing for the night.

Then, the pounding of hooves. John's stomach clenched. *Amalric.*

The abbot thundered toward them, robes flaring, eyes ablaze with indignation. His command staff flanked him, a storm of black and steel, leaving behind a cloud of dust.

"Lord John!" Amalric's voice was sharp, grating. "What is the meaning of this?"

John exhaled, steadying himself.

"Your Eminence." He inclined his head. "Good evening."

Amalric's nostrils flared.

"*Oui, oui, oui!* Go on! Do not try to placate me," the abbot snapped impatiently. "Why has the army stopped?"

John met his gaze evenly.

"I made the decision to camp here for the night."

"Without consulting your commander?" Amalric's voice dropped to a hiss, barely audible over the conversations of a thousand men. "You forget your place, boy. You are not in command here."

John forced his fists to remain unclenched. He bowed his head slightly.

"Yes, Your Eminence."

Amalric let the moment stretch, savoring his authority. Then, as if realizing the watching eyes of the Breckington men upon him, he straightened, clearing his throat.

"Well," he said, voice louder now, carrying. "It seems you anticipated my strategy, Lord Breckington. Of course, we will camp here and meet with our fleet at Agde in the morning."

John said nothing.

The murmurs among his men were low, tense. George, standing just behind, stiffened, one hand resting on the hilt of his sword.

Amalric smiled. A predator's smile. John saw it for what it was. A reminder. A warning. The abbot turned his horse, addressing the Holy Warrior host.

"We will camp for the night!" he bellowed.

The order rippled through the ranks. A controlled chaos of soldiers breaking formation, carts shifting, torches lighting.

John exhaled slowly, riding away from the command staff. The night stretched over them, thick and heavy. Fire began to burn low, casting long shadows over the weary host.

John dismounted to sit among his men, silent. Their presence steadied him, their loyalty an anchor against the weight of this war. For now, they rested.

Tomorrow, they would march again.

::

The wind tasted of salt and ash.

The night was dark, save for starlight and a sliver of a half-moon, reflecting off of the silent sea. High atop the black flank of *Mont Saint-Loup* overlooking the port of Agde, where twisted brush clung to the lava-strewn soil, a lone rider halted beneath the quivering stars. The horse exhaled, flanks steaming in the cool night air, its hooves crunching softly against old volcanic stone. Far below, the flickering torches of a great host mirrored the stars—the army camped on the plains near Agde, a mass of iron, banners, and restless ambitions.

The figure sat motionless in the saddle, wrapped in a weather-darkened cloak, hood drawn low, a silhouette carved against the sky. No badge of house. No cross or device. Just the outline of a bow slung across the back, and the faint gleam of a steel dagger at the hip.

Below, the soldiers made their fires and sung songs of mirth. From this distance, they were ants bearing torches. But the rider watched with intent—studied their formations, counted their pavilions, marked the standard of the Baron of Breckington by the dull gold and azure finishing that caught the moon.

Mont Saint-Loup had long cast its shadow over this stretch of Occitan coast—a hill born out of fire, as the locals whispered, where the Roman augurs once read smoke to foretell war. It was to be the watcher's perch tonight—lower, yes, but closer to the sea and safer to set unseen eyes.

The hooded figure dismounted in silence and led the horse down to a grove nestled in the mountain's shoulder, where pine and wild olive grew dense enough to mask a small encampment.

The horse snorted.

"Shhhh," the figure patted the horse's neck.

A tiny clearing opened between the gnarled trunks,

269

carpeted in needles and dark moss. There, the stranger pitched a modest camp—no tent, only a bedroll and a cold meal wrapped in oilskin.

No fire. No sound. Just the slow breath of a hidden thing.

The horse was unsaddled and fed in silence. Then the figure knelt, brushing aside a patch of moss to reveal earth, still warm from the day. Fingers traced a small circle in the dirt, and a stone was set atop it. A ritual? A signal?

Or remembrance.

The rider sat back against a tree, cloak pulled close, eyes still facing the camp below.

They come with banners and faith, the shadowy figure thought. But neither of those would protect them from what stirred further inland.

The wind whispered again. And the watcher waited.

::

A flutter of orange and white against the dawn. A banner held high, flapping in the wind, swaying with the rhythm of hooves on damp earth.

John blinked away the haze of sleep, stepping into the crisp morning air. The world felt colder than it should for summer, the dewy fabric of his tunic clinging to his skin. Conversations drifted in the mist—murmured voices, visible breath in the chill.

"Ben," he called to his page, rubbing warmth into his arms. "Fetch my coat."

"Yes, lord," came the page's quick reply. The heavy fabric settled over John's shoulders just as he caught sight of movement at the camp's edge. A gathering. A presence. A tension in the air.

John strode toward the commotion, now joined by the squire James Nugent, their boots sinking into the damp ground. Strangers on horseback. Orange and white surcoats. A flag of truce fluttering in the breeze.

Trencavel.

John's gut twisted. His steps quickened. Where was Amalric? Surely, he would want to handle this himself?

He saw Hugh ahead of him, gesturing animatedly to the viscount's entourage. An argument. A dispute.

John inhaled sharply as he stepped up.

"Good morning, and welcome to our camp, monsieur—"

The lead rider pulled back the hood of his cloak, dark eyes locking onto John's.

"Vicomte Raymond-Roger Trencavel, at your service, *monsieur*," he answered smoothly, voice young but commanding. "I wish to meet with your commander, the honorable Eminence Amaury."

John exhaled slowly, inclining his head.

"The abbot Amalric," he acknowledged. "Allow me to seek him out."

A hand on his shoulder. A firm grip.

John turned.

Hugh.

"My lord," Hugh whispered, pulling him aside. Urgency in his voice. A warning in his eyes.

"His Eminence already knows the lord viscount is here to negotiate. He will not see him. In fact, I've been informed that if he does not depart, he and his men will be attacked."

A flash of heat. A prickle of fury.

"Nonsense, Hugh," John snapped. "This man is under a flag of truce."

Hugh's grip tightened.

"My lord," he said, lower this time. Grave. Unyielding. "His Eminence specifically instructed me that if you intervened, you'd be deemed in league with the enemy and treated accordingly."

A chill that had nothing to do with the morning air. John's mouth went dry.

Why would Amalric anticipate my intervention? He

paused to think. A truth he already knew. *Because I would intervene. Because he knew that my conscience would demand that I must.*

John turned back to Hugh, his voice even. Tested. Resolute. His gaze firm.

"And what would you do, Sir Hugh?" he asked. "Will you report me?"

Hugh hesitated. His jaw clenched.

"No, lord," he said finally. "You are my liege. I swore an oath to you, not to Amalric."

John exhaled through his nose, a quiet relief settling in his chest.

"Good." He clapped a hand on Hugh's arm. "Then allow me to address this."

He turned toward the viscount Trencavel, heart pounding against his ribs. The young viscount sat tall in his saddle, his sharp gaze flickering with curiosity. Caution. Defiance.

"My lord Viscount," John called, voice steady, measured. A façade of control. "I am John de Ontivero, Baron of Breckington, and aide-de-camp to His Eminence, Arnaud Amalric. I regret to inform you that His Eminence is presently indisposed. You will have to return another time."

A silence. The viscount's brow furrowed. A flicker of something—frustration, doubt, understanding, perhaps?

"Indisposed, you say?" Trencavel mused, his voice edged with skepticism.

John urged his horse forward, lowering his voice. A warning only the viscount would hear.

"My lord Trencavel," he murmured quietly, "as one nobleman to another, I implore you—submit to the Holy Church. Amalric's zeal knows no bounds. He will bring ruin upon you and your people."

A flicker of something sharp in Trencavel's eyes.

"Submit?" he echoed. His tone was not angered—it was quiet. Heavy. Knowing. He leaned in, his voice now a whisper between them.

272

"Would you have me betray my subjects, Baron Breckington? Condemn them to slaughter to save my own skin?"

John's throat tightened. A battle waging within him. A fight without steel.

"If not submission, then flight," he pressed in a low, subtle voice. "Evacuate your citizens. Ready your defenses. Amalric's wrath will be swift and without mercy, and I fear for all who remain in his path."

Trencavel considered him. A long pause. A silence that stretched between them like a blade waiting to be drawn. Then, at last, his voice softened.

"You speak as a man burdened by doubt, Lord John." His gaze did not waver. Sharp as a dagger. Piercing as an arrow. "Tell me—do you truly believe this cause is just?"

John's fingers twitched against his reins.

"Belief alone does no harm," he admitted. His voice was quiet now. Weary. Unsure. "But the Church sees it differently. And I…" He faltered. "I am here to fulfill my duty, my lord. That is all."

The viscount studied him. Measured. Thoughtful. Unshaken.

"You are a man torn," Trencavel said, his voice nearly a sigh. Not pitying. Not mocking. Simply seeing. He straightened in his saddle. No fear in his expression. No hesitation.

"I am no heretic," was his emphatic declaration as he continued. It was a truth that burned in the morning air. "But I cannot, in good conscience, abandon my people or yield to this so-called holy wrath."

Trencavel's voice darkened.

"If Amalric desires my lands, he will have to take them by force. And if he slaughters innocents to achieve his aim, let that sin rest upon his soul."

John felt a cold weight settle in his chest.

"Then I beg you, my lord viscount," he said, voice barely

above a whisper, a plea he never imagined making. "Make what preparations you can. I cannot stop what is coming."

Trencavel nodded. Resolved. Unbreakable.

"And I shall pray for you, Sir John of Breckington," he said simply as he tugged on his reins, leading his mount away. "For your conscience. For your soul."

The golden haze of morning swallowed them whole. A blur of orange and white vanishing beyond the horizon.

John sat frozen in his saddle, his pulse drumming against the silence. The faint echo of hoofbeats lingered in the air, the only trace of Viscount Trencavel and his men. *Gone.* Gone to fight a war he could not win.

A breath. Slow. Unsteady.

The boy—no, the man—had courage. No arrogance, no bluster. He had spoken not as a lord defending his inheritance, but as a man standing firm in the storm. Not for conquest. Not for glory. For his people.

John swallowed, his throat dry.

Trencavel did not hesitate in his words. Did not falter. He had no crisis of conscience. No fractured loyalty between faith and duty. No uneasy service to a cause he could not name as righteous. How simple it must be. To look upon the coming storm and meet it head-on, without fear, without doubt.

Without chains.

John longed for this freedom. He hungered for it with all his being. The wind shifted. A whisper of dust and dying embers curling through the air.

A presence beside him.

Hugh.

"The young viscount is a fool, my lord," the vassal knight observed aloud, his voice even, but laced with quiet judgment. "He should have submitted. God does not ask us to resist His will, even when it is difficult."

John turned, staring at him. Did he not see? Did none of them see?

274

"And what would you have him do, Sir Hugh?" he asked, his voice sharper than intended. "Deliver his people to slaughter? Abandon those who trust him to protect their homes?"

Hugh's expression tightened.

"If they are heretics, then their fate is already sealed," he said, unwavering. "Better to surrender and place their souls in God's hands than to resist and suffer greater wrath."

God's hands.

John exhaled slowly. The air felt thick. Suffocating.

"It's not so simple," he muttered. "The Church preaches mercy, yet here we are, marching under banners already stained with blood."

He met Hugh's gaze, his own voice quieter, but firmer.

"Tell me, Sir Hugh, is this truly God's will—or man's zeal?"

Hugh stiffened. The hesitation was brief, but it was there. A flicker. A crack in the armor.

"You question the Church, my lord?"

"I question men who use God's name to justify conquest."

Hugh's silence stretched long. Then—

John pressed, his voice steady now, no longer whispering in the dark.

"Look at this campaign, Hugh. It's a holy war, yes, but not just for faith. It's for power, for land, for wealth. Amalric calls it a divine endeavor, but I see mercenaries ready to pillage farmhouses and knights eyeing southern estates like spoils of war."

Hugh shifted in his saddle. Uncomfortable now. Defensive.

"My lord, the Church has sanctioned this campaign. Are we to doubt the authority of His Holiness?"

John laughed, but there was no joy in it. Only bitterness. Irony.

"Authority is not infallibility," John's fingers curled

around the reins. "Misplaced zeal is a dangerous thing, Hugh. It blinds men. Makes them see what they wish to see. Amalric believes he carries out God's will, but in truth, he carries the ambitions of Rome and the greed of northern lords. And in the midst of it all, men like Trencavel pay the price—not for heresy, but for the land they dare to call their own."

A pause. Hugh's jaw clenched. He said nothing.

Good.

John had no more words left to offer.

A horn sounded, and the host prepared to move again. The banners of the Cistercians fluttered against the dawn, their crimson and grey stark as drying blood.

A whisper of dust curling through the morning air.

And then—a loud thundering as the host moved as one. It was an impressive, yet terrifying sight to behold. Once again, the columns advanced in clear order, even the *routiers* marched in step—the glaring eyes of the Calatravan knights watching their every move.

As they entered Agde, the waters of the Hérault glimmered in the evening light, and the Cathedral of Saint Stephen cast a long shadow over the bustling port. The respite had been brief, John knew, and the path ahead fraught with peril. Béziers waited beyond, its fate hanging by a thread and a prayer. And with it, John's own sense of honor and purpose teetered on the edge of the abyss.

John observed, as Amalric, in solemn silence, passed him astride his mount. If he was informed that the young Trencavel had come under truce, he offered no recognition, no acknowledgement. The abbot signaled to the French lords of the host, instructing them to take their place in the vanguard, and it was implied that John's levy would no longer march in the lead.

In that moment, John sensed the first signs that Amalric was suspecting him of working against the campaign. He knew caution had to be exercised henceforth, if he sought the absolution he so ardently pursued. Amalric was a zealot, but not a fool.

The host of warriors moved as one, their march resolute and determined. In dutiful pursuit, John rode to join Amalric's retinue, mindful of his role's shortcomings thus far. He would play along—for now.

"Deus lo vult!" cried a monk, and the men responded in kind, the chant echoing across the coastal plains.

::

God wills it.

George de Wymondham scoffed under his breath.

Another chant. Another battle cry hollowed out by repetition.

Steel creaked. Hooves plodded. The sea whispered along the coast. His fingers tightened around the reins, the weight of his mail pressing against his shoulders.

His mind wandered.

Not to the dust-choked roads of the Midi. Not to the rising banners of war. But to England. To Breckington. To the past. To the legacy that bound him to this path. A family of fighters. A legacy of service.

The Wymondhams had not always been knights. Not always men of consequence.

Bissel de Wymondham, the Elder, was a farmer. A leader of men before he was ever a lord. Then—the *Anarchy*. A time when the kingdom was divided between a king who wore the crown and a woman who should have. The crowned King Stephen pitted against Matilda. Lords chose sides, swore fealty, spilled blood for thrones that would never seat them.

But the de Ontiveros and Breckington had chosen neutrality. At first. But it hadn't mattered. War came anyway. Lawless men. Soldiers without masters. Raiders in the night. Breckington had been vulnerable, its fields torched, its people prey.

Bissel de Wymondham had not stood idly by.

A pitchfork became a spear. A plowman became a warrior. He rallied the villagers. He stood shoulder to shoulder with Breckington's knights. When the brigands came, they did not find easy plunder. They found men who had learned to defend. To kill.

Roland I de Ontivero noticed. Not John's father, but his ancestor and namesake. The first Roland de Ontivero rewarded loyalty well. Raised Bissel up from his station. Gave him a manor, a title, a place among the landed. Knighthood followed. A name that would serve Breckington forever after.

George carried that name now. The weight of it pressed heavier than his mail. He had spent his youth in France. His mother's land. Her people.

French discipline mingled with English grit.

He trained under the best. Lance. Sword. Spear. Horse.

By sixteen, he was back in England, sworn—as his forefathers were—to Breckington's barons. Baymundon Manor, within the barony of Breckington was the crown jewel of his estate.

His training changed over the years, as was his maturity level.

No longer about raw skill. Now it was about command. Leadership. Strategy.

And John.

John de Ontivero—his liege, his friend, his brother-in-arms.

They had grown together. Bled together. Sparred for hours until bruises bloomed beneath their armor. John learned how to lead. George learned how to fight.

And now?

Now they marched to war under the banner of the Church. A war George did not believe in. John clung to his faith. Hugh, even more so.

But George?

George had seen too much.

Religion. It kept men together. It gave them purpose. It justified everything.

Mercy. Charity. Honor.

But also—

Slaughter. Conquest. Greed.

He had watched priests bless swords meant for killing. Had seen bishops whisper in the ears of nobles and lords, trading indulgences for coin, for power.

And Amalric—*Amalric*.

A man who spoke of God but hungered for dominion.

George certainly could not accept a deity that this religion taught. Nor could he fathom the deity of Saracens. Not when they demanded blood in the name of salvation.

The fleet lay ahead at Agde, fat with supplies. A necessary delay. John had suggested it, framing it as sound strategy. It was. In terms of efficiency, it moved larger stores of supplies. It sacrificed time for volume.

But George saw more.

The delay bought Trencavel time. He knew his lord's strategy, even if his colleague, Sir Hugh, did not see this in his zeal. George glanced toward John, riding ahead, his posture composed but his eyes dark.

Amalric would find out. Not today. Not tomorrow. But soon.

And when he did, George de Wymondham would stand where he had always stood—beside John. Not for God. Not for Rome. For John.

The road stretched ahead, the sea to one side, the army to the other. Boots struck dirt, hooves kicked up dust, and the banners of the Church and its faithful lords snapped in the morning wind as columns of men formed. The ocean, a vast and endless thing, stretched beside them, an expanse seemingly untouched by the ambitions of men. How simple it would be to vanish into it, to leave all of this behind. But that was not his path.

He had come to accept that long ago. He would learn to live in a world that contradicted his ideals.

Years earlier during his youth in France, he had met a man who had changed him.

Étienne de Chartres.

A wandering scholar, sharp-tongued and unafraid to challenge the world. They had sat beneath a chestnut tree, the wind rustling the branches above, while Étienne spoke of the last pagan emperor of Rome—before the institutional mingling of the Christian faith with the civil state.

"Julian did not believe in the gods," Étienne had said, his voice calm but urgent, as though speaking a great truth—one that could cost him his life. "He believed in something greater. A world unchained from dogma, where men were free to seek wisdom without the weight of the Church crushing them beneath it. His revival of the old ways was not out of piety—it was resistance."

George had listened, fascinated. He had never heard anyone speak like this before. He had never heard anyone dare.

"They call him an apostate," Étienne had continued, "because he did not bow to societal pressure. But was he truly worse than those who came after him? Those who wielded the faith not as a guide but as a weapon? He saw what was coming. A world where the Church ruled not by love, but by fear. He tried to stop it by embracing the old pagan gods again. He failed."

George had said nothing then. But now, as he rode through the lands of the Midi, Étienne's words rang louder than ever.

Was this what Julian had foreseen? This war, cloaked in righteousness but dripping with ambition? Amalric spoke of saving souls, but his eyes burned with conquest. The banners of the Crusade bore the Cross, but the men who marched beneath them thought of land, of power, of absolution bought with blood.

George looked to John, riding ahead, blue and yellow flashing against the growing brightness. His friend. His liege. The only man in this war he trusted. Hugh was also his brother, but he was not sure if he would choose them over the Church.

"You're quiet, George," John remarked, without turning.

George smirked. "That's rare, isn't it?"

John exhaled, something like a laugh. "Too rare."

They rode on in silence for a time, the sounds of the army filling the space between them. The creak of leather. The shuffle of weary feet. The distant cries of gulls over the sea.

Then, John spoke again.

"You still don't believe, do you?"

George's grip tightened on the reins. "In the Church? No. In God? I don't know."

John nodded, as if expecting the answer.

"And you?" George asked.

John hesitated. His hand drifted to the cross around his neck, fingers running over its worn edges.

"I believe in what I was taught. In what Father Barth taught me," he paused. "I just don't know if that's what we're fighting for."

George studied him for a moment. "Julian would say we're not."

John glanced at him, brow raised.

George smirked again.

"The Roman emperor. The one I keep talking about. The last pagan to rule. He saw what the Church would become. A kingdom unto itself, no different from any other."

John scoffed, shaking his head.

"You and your wandering clerks and their stories."

George chuckled.

"He made sense, Lord John. Julian wasn't trying to destroy Christianity. He was trying to stop it from becoming this," George gestured at the army, the banners, the chanting monks. "A tool. A means to rule."

John was quiet, his gaze distant. He could not argue against that.

George continued, his voice softer now.

"The Church preaches humility, mercy. But when it wants something—land, obedience—it takes. With fire. With swords. It's no different from any king. Worse, even, because it claims God wills it."

John sighed.

"And here we are."

"Aye," George murmured in response. "Here we are."

For John. Always for John. His loyalty would never waver. Hugh might be the senior vassal, but he knew John could entrust his life to him.

George looked at the men around him—knights, soldiers, mercenaries. Some rode for faith, some for duty, some for plunder. And him? He rode for the only thing that had ever been certain in his life.

The bond of brotherhood.

John's path would take him deeper into this war, deeper into its corruption, its contradictions. And George would follow. Not for the Cross. Not for Rome.

For Breckington. For his lord.

The chant lingered.

George de Wymondham clenched the reins tighter, his horse shifting beneath him. The past had wrapped itself around him, pressing its weight onto his chest, dragging him back to another time, another war.

He blinked.

The port of Agde bustled with activity. Boats lined the shore, their masts swaying with the tide. Men worked quickly, unloading barrels of grain, salted fish, kegs of wine. Cheers erupted among the ranks, voices lifted in the relief of an impending feast as supplies arrived. Even the most devout among them—those who had spent days murmuring prayers between marches—allowed themselves a moment of joy.

282

George barely heard them.

His mind was elsewhere, wandering through the corridors of memory, back to a different battlefield, a different war.

Acre. 1204.

Heat pressed down like a smothering hand. The earth baked beneath the hooves of restless warhorses, dust rising in thick clouds with every movement. The Breckington men stood firm, their shields raised, spears braced. Somewhere in the distance, the shimmer of a banner—red and white, emblazoned with the sigil of Christendom—fluttered above the chaos.

George gritted his teeth. The Saracens rode fast, their bows loosing death into the air. Arrows whistled past, some finding flesh in exposed areas not covered by armor, others clattering harmlessly against shields. The scent of sweat and steel mingled with something darker, the acrid sharp scent of blood soaking into the sand.

To his right, young James Nugent steadied his spear, face set in grim determination. A boy, barely old enough to shave, now a soldier.

John's voice rang out over the din.

"Stand apart! Make them pick their targets!"

George obeyed, shifting with practiced ease. The formation loosened just enough to make them harder to hit, but not so much that they lost cohesion. A Saracen archer drew too close—Nugent struck, his spear finding its mark. The enemy crumpled, his cry lost in the roar of battle.

George did not stop to think. He dismounted, seized the fallen man's bow, notched an arrow. One, two, three riders fell in rapid succession. The fourth caught the shaft in his shield, spurring his mount forward with a cry of fury.

And then—John.

Cutting through the chaos like a force of nature. His blade rose, fell, cleaved through flesh. But he was too far ahead, his horse pushing into the fray, past the line of safety.

A man in distress. A noble, beleaguered, surrounded. John went for him without hesitation.

Too far. He was too far to help.

George leapt onto his horse anyway. Spurred it forward. The formation of Frankish infantry saw his intent, adjusted their line, clearing a path.

The chant had been rising—low at first, then louder.

"Deus lo vult!"

It echoed in his skull, through the ringing in his ears, through the pounding of hooves against sand.

Then—nothing.

The memory shattered, crumbling into the present.

The fires of the Agde encampment flickered in the dying light. George exhaled sharply, dragging himself back.

The campaign in the Levant had been war. A war against men who bore weapons, who fought and died with the same ferocity as their Christian counterparts. There had been no moral dilemmas, no blurred lines between faith and ambition. Only steel meeting steel.

But here, in the Languedoc, the enemy did not march in ranks. They did not bear arms or raise banners against Rome. They prayed. They tilled fields. They lived, quietly, until the Holy War now came knocking at their doors.

George ran a hand over his face.

He had fought for the Church before. He had some semblance of belief then, even as he struggled. Now, he fought for John.

Only for John. And the people of Breckington.

A voice broke his reverie.

"You look lost, George."

John.

George turned, his smirk returning by force of habit.

"Just remembering old wars, milord."

John studied him for a moment, his gaze knowing. Disillusioned. His face weary as he spoke, "And this one? What will we remember of it?"

George chuckled, though there was no mirth in it.

"That depends on who writes it, milord."

John exhaled, a sound caught between a sigh and a bitter laugh.

"So, it does."

The wind carried the scent of sea salt and burning wood from a nearby fire as men prepared to cook their meals. George stared at the flames, the echoes of Acre still lingering in his ears.

The Siege

July 21st, 1209 AD

Béziers, Viscounty of Béziers

he town of Béziers lay quiet. *Too quiet*. John scanned the walls. Not a banner of truce in sight. No sign of negotiations. Just the Trencavel colors fluttering defiantly in the wind.

The city sat perched above the plains, encased in its stone bulwark, the Orb River a natural moat dividing them from the Holy Army. Only a single bridge linked them to the gate—an invitation or a death trap, depending on the next sequence of events.

The siege had not yet begun, but the air was thick with anticipation. When would the violence begin? Days? Weeks?

John's eyes flicked to the troops nearest the walls. *Routiers*. Harfleur's mercenaries. A rabble of ill-disciplined, plundering curs given the best position?

Why?

He clenched his jaw. His own levy—trained, ready— pushed further back. Was it was a deliberate slight, a game played by Amalric, or perhaps something worse?

The *routiers* were unpredictable, dangerous even to their own allies. If an assault was ordered, they would rush forward like starved wolves, unrestrained by discipline or reason. The defenders atop the walls would make short work of them. Their presence at the front was not just foolish—it was a disaster waiting to happen.

John's gaze swept over the ramparts. Two hundred. No, closer to five hundred seasoned warriors. More within, hidden from sight. Then another thousand—militia, armed with whatever weapons they could find, a desperate force fighting for their homes, their families. The soldiers of Béziers were outnumbered by the Army the Cross, vastly so, but numbers alone did not win sieges. The walls was formidable, and protected the defending force behind.

He exhaled slowly.

Tens of thousands of souls were behind those walls— civilians. Catholics, Jews, Mohammedans, *Bon Hommes.* The Church called them all heretics, condemned them without distinction. John was no fool—he knew there could not be more than a few hundred true heretics within those walls. Perhaps even fewer. And yet, the pope's decree had damned them all the same.

A memory rose to the surface of John's mind.

Father Barth, seated by the hearth back home, the firelight flickering in flashes across his lined face.

"Abraham pleaded with Jehovah to spare Sodom," Barth had said, his voice steady, yet filled with quiet sorrow. "Fifty righteous men, then forty-five, then thirty, then twenty… and finally ten. For ten righteous souls, the Lord would have spared the city. And yet, when the fire came, the angels saved Lot and his kin."

John swallowed, the gravity of the tale pressing against his ribs.

But was Béziers *Sodom*?

Could a city with thousands of faithful souls truly be

beyond salvation?

His fingers curled around the reins as he continued to stare at the walls, like he could reinforce them with his glare. If he could stop the slaughter, he would. If he could reason with Amalric, convince him to spare the innocent, he would try.

He thought of Zara. Of Constantinople. Of fire licking the sky, of screams swallowed by the roar of collapsing stone. He had seen the greed, the madness, the way a so-called holy war could spiral into unholy ruin.

It would not happen here. Not if he could do anything about it. If the city surrendered its heretics, perhaps Amalric would be satisfied. A fragile hope, but it was all he had.

He would try. He had to.

The sun blazed overhead, the air thick with the mingling scents of sweat, dust, and roasting meat. The Holy Army sprawled across the dry plains outside Béziers, its encampment alive with the restless energy of men who believed themselves divinely ordained. Laughter, clattering armor, the rhythmic sharpening of blades—it all blended into an atmosphere of careless confidence.

John felt none of it.

A commotion at the edge of the camp. A figure rushing toward him, robes billowing, breath ragged. A monk, sweat streaking down his face, his voice rasping.

"Hail, Lord Breckington! His Eminence summons you forthwith!"

John exhaled through his nose, loosening his belt slightly. The weight of his sword sat heavy at his hip, the hilt warm under his palm.

"Very well."

He placed a hand on the monk's shoulder, then strode toward the command tent.

The camp pulsed with movement. Soldiers sprawled lazily in the shade of their tents, passing waterskins and crude jokes. The smell of charred pork wafted through the

288

air, mixing with the sour tang of unwashed bodies. A mule brayed sharply, wrenching against its tether, its handler cursing as he struggled to calm it.

John barely noticed. His gaze flicked toward a group of young levies tearing apart a stale loaf of bread, their faces hollow with exhaustion. He pressed on.

The command tent loomed ahead, its heavy canvas entrance shifting slightly in the breeze. He stepped inside. The air changed—thicker, heavy with parchment, candle wax, incense. The flickering glow cast deep shadows over the gathered men.

Knights, monks, lords. Faces stern, eyes calculating.

At the head of the table, Amalric reclined in his high-backed chair, the golden crucifix at his throat gleaming in the low light. Beside him, a stranger in the fine vestments of a bishop. His jeweled mitre caught the flickering glow, his sharp eyes assessing John with interest.

"Ah, at last, my aide-de-camp graces us!"

Amalric's voice rang out, laced with mockery.

John met his gaze steadily.

"My esteemed baron, acquaint yourself with His Excellency, the Bishop of Béziers, Renaud de Montpeyroux."

John stepped forward, lowering himself to one knee. The bishop extended his hand, rings glinting, and John pressed his lips to the cool metal.

"Your Excellency," he said, rising. "John de Ontivero, Baron of Breckington, at your service."

Montpeyroux studied him, his expression unreadable.

"I must admit," the bishop said at last, his voice measured, "it is not every day that I meet an English noble in these parts. I have heard much of your homeland's valor and of the steadfast loyalty of its knights."

Loyalty.

John inclined his head, though the word sat uncomfortably on his conscience.

"We serve as we are called, Your Excellency."

Montpeyroux's lips curved slightly, though whether in approval or amusement, John could not tell.

The bishop gestured to the table, where a map of Béziers lay unfurled, its streets and defenses meticulously detailed.

"My people," Montpeyroux began, his voice grave, "have borne the brunt of this heretical scourge for too long. The corruption festers within the walls of Béziers. His Eminence desires to bring it to a swift conclusion. He wishes me to seek your counsel, Lord Breckington. Pray, what course of action do you propose?"

John glanced at Amalric, who watched him with a knowing smirk.

"Your Excellency," John said carefully, "might we extend the city the chance to surrender those named heretics within their walls? Grant them time to act wisely—for the sake of the innocent among them. If we are to act in God's name, should we not also reflect His mercy?"

A beat of silence. Then, to John's surprise, Montpeyroux nodded.

"Indeed, mercy is the mark of the righteous," he said.

John dared to hope.

Then Amalric shifted in his chair in visible discomfort, the air in the tent tightening.

"Time emboldens defiance," the abbot said, his voice clipped. "Delay risks disorder among the host."

Montpeyroux turned, meeting Amalric's gaze without flinching.

"Arnaud, you know these people as I do. Should we rush them, they will resist. Allow them the chance to surrender the heretics peacefully, and you may avoid the need for further bloodshed."

A brief pause. It was a game of wills.

Then, slowly, Amalric sighed with a long, dramatic exhale. He reached for a parchment Montpeyroux had slid across the table. Unrolled it with deliberate slowness. John leaned slightly, scanning the names inked onto the list. Two hundred. Many bore the notation *val.*

Valdensis—Waldensians.

John's breath caught in his throat.

Two hundred names. And yet nearly thirty thousand souls stood behind those walls. The numbers were damning.

Amalric rolled the parchment with practiced ease, his expression unreadable.

"Very well," he said at last, the words carrying reluctant formality. "Inform your city council of this opportunity. But let them know that our patience is finite. If they do not comply swiftly, the consequences will be theirs to bear."

Montpeyroux crossed himself, then exited the tent without another word.

The silence that followed was thick, oppressive. John did not move. He hesitated to even breathe.

Amalric exhaled through his nose, then turned toward John, the flickering candlelight casting jagged shadows across his face.

"You are too sentimental," the abbot murmured, voice laced with disdain.

John held his tongue, the weight of the bishop's departure pressing down on him. He wanted to believe the city would see reason. That they would surrender their heretics to spare the innocent. But Amalric's stance, his barely veiled contempt, told him otherwise.

The ultimatum was simply a formality. A thin veil of civility stretched over an inevitable reckoning. He had no intention of sparing the city. John bit his lip, then finally spoke.

"My I have your leave, your Eminence?"

With a gruff wave of his hand, the abbot dismissed him.

The air was thick with heat and dust as John emerged from the oppressive atmosphere of the tent, the midday sun casting jagged shadows across the sprawling encampment. The Holy Army stirred with purpose, warriors moving like cogs in a great, unrelenting machine.

John's breath was slow, measured, but the pounding in his chest would not ease. He had won them time—however fragile, however fleeting. A city's fate balanced on a parchment scroll and a bishop's measured words. It was not enough.

His gaze followed Montpeyroux's retreating figure, the bishop's robes flowing as he made his way toward the gates of Béziers. John's eyes drifted upward, to the battlements where defenders stood in solemn defiance. The wind caught the crimson-and-gold banner of Lord Trencavel, sending it fluttering against the azure sky.

He exhaled slowly.

Zara. Constantinople.

He had heard the stories of that fiasco, even as he and his men journeyed on to Acre. The jewel of the Byzantine Empire crushed under the weight of zealotry and greed.

Béziers was no Constantinople. But beneath those walls, the fate of thousands teetered on the edge of life and death.

He turned back to the camp, wrestling with his emotions.

The army was moving with methodical efficiency. Pikes sharpened. Helmets strapped. Leather tightened over mail. The *routiers* laughed among themselves, their hunger for plunder unmasked. Pilgrims swarmed like rats, eager to witness the spectacle of divine wrath, some scavenging for weapons they barely knew how to wield.

Then he remembered there was a group of people he detested more than *routiers*.

Pilgrims.

John's lip curled in disgust.

Despicable.

He had seen them before, on the way to the Levant, in Outremer. Wide-eyed zealots who clung to the cause with desperate fingers, eager to spill blood in God's name—until battle came. Then they fled, or they died, their fervor lost in the screaming of the dying.

A band of them jostled past him, their ragged tunics emblazoned with crude crosses, their hands grasping at whatever scraps of armor they could find. They would gorge on rations meant for soldiers, bloat the camp with their stinking prayers, and take what they could when the city fell.

John turned away, his gaze hard.

He moved through the camp, past his men—his *own* soldiers. The Breckington levy stood apart from the restless disorder of the crusader host. They worked in silence, honing weapons, bundling arrows. This was a quiet efficiency born not of zeal, but of duty.

This was his force. *His* men.

They did not fight for indulgences or absolution. They did not raise their weapons for the ambitions of Rome.

They fought because he led them.

And he would not lead them into slaughter. Nor would he lead them to slaughter innocent civilians.

John's hand drifted to the hilt of his sword. Silent, contemplative. He would not stand idle. He would not let Béziers become another Zara. Another stain on the conscience of Christendom. But he was not sure how he would do it.

A stir in the camp arose. A rider was approaching. A banner of truce, became visible through the summer-heated dust.

John's breath caughtfor a moment. He turned, his boots kicking up dust as he strode forward, his pulse quickening. A chance, however slim.

A final chance, perhaps, to stay the violence.

A group emerged from the city gates, banners rippling in the breeze. A delegation. Their pace was slow, deliberate.

John moved to intercept. His heart hammered against his ribs. He wanted to speak to them, to instill a dose of sense in the townsfolk.

Before he could move several steps, however, a voice rang out, sharp with amusement. Familiarly irritating, but perhaps intentionally so.

Amalric.

John's eyes flicked upward. The abbot stood further up the incline, arms folded, a smirk barely concealed. John felt his jaw tighten.

Of course.

The Breckington men had been placed farthest from the walls. A petty move. A calculated jest—and now, John had to run. The heat burned in his lungs as he moved forward, his boots pounding against dry earth.

He could feel Amalric's gaze on him.

Watching. Amused.

John did not slow.

Not now.

The delegates drew closer, crossing the bridge spanning the Orb, the dust of the road swirling at their feet. This was it. The defining moment, where the fate of thousands on both sides of the wall rested upon.

Bishop Montpeyroux's voice rang out, breaking the growing suspense.

"Abbot Amalric," the bishop declared as he approached ahead of the delegation, "the council has cast its decision. Allow them to convey their resolve to you."

John forced himself to blink, to breathe, to think. And to pray. To pray that the people of the town had the sense to give in and surrender their heretics. The burgher stepped forward, his voice ringing with unwavering defiance, as he addressed the Papal Legate by his first name in a gesture of egality.

"Arnaud, we shall not yield our heretics to you or to any other. Every citizen of this town, regardless of belief and origin, finds welcome and protection here."

John did not need to hear the rest. He knew what was coming.

The abbot's face darkened, his fingers twitching at his sides.

"Your fate is thus sealed," he growled, his voice a simmering threat. "If you face death, it will be because of your own hand. Your defiance of God shall be your doom."

He turned sharply, his robes snapping with the movement, and stormed away, his retinue scrambling to follow.

John remained still. Stunned. Unsure as to what to do. The townspeople had likely sealed their fate. Blood was now guaranteed to be spilled. Whether they or the defenders would prevail, violence was all but a certainty.

He expected an anxious desperation to grow within him, but he felt surprisingly calm. He was determined to become resigned to the situation. He had done all he could, yet it was like stopping the wind, or stilling an earthquake, it was a like a terrible force of nature that could not be avoided—so he might as well ride it out.

Montpeyroux climbed into the saddle, his voice carrying quiet sorrow as he bid farewell to the city he could not save.

"*Adieu*. May God show mercy upon you, my children. May we meet in better times."

But John barely registered the response. Something else had caught his attention. The air was too thick for him to be certain. Too heavy with dust, with heat, with the weight of thousands of marching feet pressing into the dry earth. John hardly noticed. His breath, steady and measured mere moments ago, had stilled.

The bishop rode off away from the city, away from the camp. He was trailed by three other individuals, ones who did not want to suffer the fate of a heretic. Three out of perhaps thirty thousand.

Yet John discerned none of it. His breath slowed, almost to a halt. Sweat began to bead on his forehead as he squinted his eyes, turning white as a sheet at the apparition before him. It was as if he had seen a ghost.

It is—is it truly—It couldn't be.

But the evidence of his eyes could not be denied.

He had seen ghosts before—memories flickering in firelight, whispers from a past he had long buried. This ghost, however, was special, a specter of a past he once mourned. He had dreamed of her, of auburn strands catching the sun, of laughter stolen in hidden gardens. But this was not a dream. She was standing before him, in the flesh, part of the delegation that had walked out of the city gates and over the bridge.

Adelinda…

Unmistakably her, the distinctive beauty mark on her right cheek, those eyes that could pierce even the deepest recesses of the soul.

The breath in his chest refused to release. His fingers twitched at his sides, fists clenching and unclenching as if movement might break the spell cast upon him. Was she looking at him? No, she had not noticed him yet—she had been looking at Amalric—stiff, breathless, her body coiling like an animal bracing for the lash.

Revulsion. Fear. It was unmistakable. Observant, John tried to piece together in his mind the possible story.

She *knew* him. And not in the way most knew of Amalric—not as the papal legate, not as the architect of this holy war. This was personal. A recognition carved into her very bones. How had she known the abbot?

But Amalric had not noticed her. Or if he had, the recognition was not shared. His focus remained on the departing bishop and the delegation that had just defied him to his face. He was animated, gesturing to the rest of his staff. Adelinda's gaze remained on the legate, hate filled her expression.

John's stomach twisted. Whatever had passed between them, whatever Amalric had done to her, he had forgotten. And that was the worst of it, wasn't it? The casual erasure of whatever cruelty he had inflicted. The absence of even the faintest flicker of recollection.

John exhaled, sharp and silent. His mind tried to grasp

reason, but reason was slipping, slipping like sand through his fingers. He had steeled himself for this war, prepared his soul for the bloodshed to come, but nothing—nothing—had prepared him for this.

She turned.

And then she saw him.

John felt the ground shift beneath him. A slow, creeping horror and hope twisted together in his gut, a vice around his ribs.

Her lips parted, a sharp intake of breath—or was it a silent scream? Her veil fluttered, catching against the breeze, but she did not lift it. Her eyes—*oh my, those eyes*—locked onto his, wide and stricken, a thousand unsaid things rising in their depths.

A look of shock. Disbelief. Relief.

And something else, something more fragile. A wound that had never quite healed, ripped open anew. It was indeed her.

Alive. Here. In this very place.

His throat worked, but no sound came.

His mind rejected the truth even as it settled into his bones. It couldn't be her. It had been too long, the years had stretched too wide, yet here she stood, close enough that he could reach out and touch her if he dared.

John inhaled sharply, forcing his voice to work, forcing himself to believe the impossible as her graceful figure approached, deliberate. Careful. Unsure.

"Adelinda?"

She flinched as though struck, her shoulders stiffening beneath the fabric of her cloak.

A single breath—quivering, unsure. Then another.

Then—

"John?"

Her mouth remained open. Shocked.

Everything inside John de Ontivero lurched. It was real. She was real. His fingers curled into his palms, nails biting

297

into flesh as he fought for composure.

"I thought you were—" he stopped. He couldn't say it. Couldn't breathe it into existence.

"Gone?" she finished for him, her voice tight, her eyes glistening. "I thought the same of you."

John swallowed, hard. His emotions swirled like the milling of men around them. The weight of Adelinda's gaze pressed into him, heavy, questioning, searching for something.

He wanted to speak, wanted to demand answers, wanted to know where she had been, what had happened, why she had vanished from his world. But the words failed to materialize.

Pilgrims shuffled past, their hollowed eyes fixed on their own burdens. Soldiers muttered prayers or stretched aching limbs, the weight of anticipation thick in the air. No one paid them any mind.

John's hands twitched at his sides, his breath shallow. He forced himself to move slowly, carefully, as though any sudden movement would shatter the fragile reality before him. He wove through the scattered figures, his face carefully set, his steps deliberate. He could not be seen rushing to her. He could not be seen longing.

But, God help him, he *longed.*

John's heart hammered, a dull, aching rhythm against his ribs. How? How could this be? Just weeks ago, he had spoken of her with Father Barth, reminiscing on a love buried beneath years of silence and war. Now here she was. The very woman who had once been his world, lost to time, reappearing in the most wretched of places.

She was older now—not aged, but fuller, stronger, shaped by the years that had hardened them both. The auburn hair, untouched by silver, was woven back with the same effortless grace he had always admired. Her hazel eyes, still deep and knowing, held secrets that had not been there before.

John's mouth felt dry as memories battered against the walls of his mind like a battering ram battering a town's gates. The way she had laughed, the warmth of her presence, the secret glances stolen across the halls of Tiverton Castle.

He had been a youth then, a reckless heir to Breckington, his heart set on her with a firm certainty only young lovers could afford. Then, she had just disappeared. No one could tell him why, no matter who he had asked.

And now, fate had thrown her back into his path.

"How strange," she murmured, a bitter smile forming on her lips. "Of all the places to meet again."

His pulse thundered. He had a hundred questions, a thousand things he needed to say.

Instead, all that came out was, "How?"

Adelinda's lips parted, as if she too did not know where to begin.

"It is a tale long and cruel," she said finally. "One I cannot tell here."

Here, in this place, in this moment, there were things she could not speak of. Yet, he was determined to get his answers—he had to think of something.

His jaw tightened. Gaze darting to the others around them, pilgrims drifting by, soldiers standing idly near their tents. It was too open, too many ears. He had to get her away.

Wordlessly, he reached for her hand, looking around to see if anyone was watching.

She did not pull away. Everyone was too busy to care. The flag of truce ensured their safety until they returned within the city walls. Perhaps Amalric had intended it that way to entice the delegation to simply walk away from the danger now threatening the city.

John led her closer towards the walls—beyond the hum of conversation and the prying eyes of zealots eager to see her city burn. Defenders on the walls would not loose arrows upon him, not when one of their own delegates would be imperiled. Only when they reached the shadowed edge of a cluster of boulders by the riverbank did he turn back to face her.

"Why are you here?" The question spilled from him in a desperate whisper. "Adelinda, of all places in the world—why here?"

She did not answer immediately. Her hands trembled. She clasped them together as if to steady herself.

"These people took me in," she said at last. "When I had no home, no name, no future. Béziers became my refuge, and now it is my duty to protect it. As I could not protect myself."

The words were carefully chosen, but John heard the weight beneath them.

"As I could not protect myself."

Something terrible had happened to her. Something that had left scars too deep to name. A cold realization slithered down his spine.

"Adelinda," he said slowly, "tell me the truth. What happened? How do you know the abbot?"

Her breath hitched. She froze, as if paralyzed by some unseen force. Finally her gaze flicked, just briefly, toward the distant figure of Amalric, his white cloak catching the wind as he disappeared into the command tent.

John followed her gaze.

His blood ran cold.

Amalric.

He turned back to her, but she had already looked away.

"I cannot," she whispered. "Not yet."

John's chest burned, his hands curling into fists at his sides. But he forced the rage down. Now was not the time. He exhaled sharply and reached for her again.

"Come away with me," he pleaded, his voice raw. "This city will not stand. You know it won't. Let me get you out—before it's too late."

Adelinda's eyes shone with unshed tears. For a moment, he thought she might say yes.

Then she shook her head.

"I cannot."

John's grip tightened. "Why?"

She hesitated. Then, voice barely above a breath—

"I have a daughter, John."

The words shattered him. The world tilted. His breath stalled. His body locked in place. His mind reeled.

A daughter.

Her daughter. He searched her face, desperate for clarity, for some sign that he had misunderstood. But the truth was there, plain as day, in her tear-streaked eyes.

"You... have a child?"

The words barely formed, strangled by the storm inside him.

Adelinda nodded.

John swallowed. His throat was dry as dust.

"Do you have a husband?"

She met his gaze. Did not look away. Her answer was succinct.

"No."

Silence stretched between them. Then—her voice broke.

"She was conceived out of wedlock."

John exhaled sharply, running a hand through his hair. His heart thundered in his ears. So many emotions warred within him—joy, sorrow, anger, regret. He wanted to ask— Who? When? How?

But he could not. Not here. Not now. Adelinda straightened, brushing the glistening moisture from her cheeks.

"I will tell you more one day," she whispered after a long deep breath. "But for now, know this—I will not leave her. And I will not leave these people."

John nodded stiffly, forcing air into his lungs.

"Of course," he murmured. "You cannot abandon your flesh and blood."

Adelinda's lips trembled. "Nor can I abandon those who

301

saved us."

John hesitated.

"I serve on the legate's staff now," he muttered.

"I can see that," Adelinda retorted without emotion.

"I had no choice, Adelinda."

A sharp blast of a horn shattered the moment. She flinched, stepping back.

John reached for her. "No. Wait—"

"I must go."

"Adelinda—"

She already turned, walking away.

John stood frozen, watching as she slipped through the rocks to join the delegation retreating back into the city. The gates of Béziers groaned shut behind her.

Sealing her inside a city that would not stand. He did not move. Did not dare to breathe. He could only do one thing. A prayer. A desperate, frantic whisper against the wind. But he believed God was listening.

He wasn't praying for victory. He wasn't even praying for redemption. He prayed for a miracle. Some force, divine or otherwise, to stop what was coming. To halt the siege. To stay the hand of men who would burn a city to the ground for a handful of heretics. So, he would have time to save the love of his life.

He had lost her for so long.

I will not lose her again.

But how cruel fate could be. Now that he knew she was alive and well, a dark cloud of destruction threatened both their lives.

The Orb shimmered under the last gasps of light, the slow-moving current like a barrier between the doomed and the damned. His eyes followed the stone bridge, narrow and exposed. A gauntlet. A death trap. Any attacker crossing it would be met with a hail of arrows from the battlements above. The gates—iron-bound and reinforced—stood unyielding. The walls, old but formidable. Even the most fervent zealot would hesitate at the sight.

John wiped sweat from his brow, though the air had cooled. Not nerves. Calculation. He had to be seen surveying the defenses, not studying them, not searching for a way in. He moved along the perimeter, measuring heights, tracing the depth of the ditches. Every weakness, every strength, he committed to memory.

Not for Amalric. For them. For her.

Adelinda and her daughter must survive this. I will not let them perish with this city.

A distant crow cawed as the wind shifted, carrying the sour stench of tar and tallow from the siege engines being wheeled into place. John's nostrils flared, instinct recoiling at the scent—death had a way of announcing itself before it struck.

He lingered still at the riverbank, boots sunk deep in the muck, heart torn between two prayers that could not be reconciled. If Béziers fell, Adelinda and her daughter would burn with it, along with hundreds of innocents. But if it stood, his own men—his faithful squires, the Blitheful Ten, the levy lads who laughed around evening fires and fought with him at Breckington—might die at the gates trying to tear it down. His mind reeled at the cruelty of it.

The orb of the sun was sinking, and so too was the hope that both prayers could be answered. The gates groaned closed again in his mind, and he could still hear them— Adelinda's laughter, the child's bright voice—now muted behind stone and fire.

He needed to find a way in. Not to help take the city, but to find the quickest way to get to her and get *them* out.

He walked with purpose. On a mission. Counted the archers. Noted the placement of barricades. The defenders were watching. Their sharp glares followed him from the parapets, untrusting. They did not loose their arrows. Not yet. Perhaps they did not see him as a threat. Or maybe they knew. Maybe they saw something in his stance, something

303

that betrayed him, or that he was talking with Adelinda.

Footsteps behind him. Measured. Deliberate. Not a scout, not a threat. John didn't turn. He already knew.

"Lopez," he said, voice even, his hand drifting toward his sword.

The Calatravan knight emerged from the shadows, lowering his hood. Dark eyes, unreadable, without expression.

"Señor John," Lopez said, his tone careful. "The abbot grows impatient. He sent me to find you."

John exhaled slowly, forcing his stance to remain neutral.

"Tell him I'm surveying the defenses. A siege without proper preparation would cost us dearly."

Lopez tilted his head.

"You've been here long enough to see what you need. Do you seek something more, Señor?"

John hesitated.

I have been taking too long. Damnation.

"Amalric wants results," John said, voice firm. "If I am to give him an assessment, I intend it to be thorough. You can tell him as much."

There was a pause. Lopez watched him. Too carefully. Then a slight bow.

"As you wish. But don't keep the abbot waiting too long. You know his temper."

John stayed still, listening to Lopez's fading footsteps. He couldn't afford to linger, but there was still more to learn. He moved closer to the gate. More barricades. More stones piled at the entrance. A breach here would be a bloodbath. And yet—it was also the fastest way inside.

It's possible.

Not for an army. For a few determined souls. Not to expose the city to assault, but to conduct a rescue mission. His chest tightened. This was madness. To defy Amalric was to risk everything—his position, his life, his barony.

But Adelinda. Her child.

If the city fell, there would be no mercy. He knew Amalric. He knew what came next. It happened in Zara. In Constantinople. Would it happen here? Worse, perhaps, as this siege was sanctioned by the Pope. The whole host would be unleashed against the city—this time with the so-called blessing of heaven.

A shout from the walls—mocking, sharp. He ignored it. Turned on his heel, forced himself into a slow, steady walk back to the encampment. Boots on gravel. The smell of burning tallow. The chants of pilgrims rising and falling like the tide.

John was no zealot. No believer in this war. But he had a purpose now.

He would give his report. He would stall for time. And when the moment came, before the walls crumbled, before the killing began—he would act.

He would find a way inside. He would save her.

::

A hush. A tremor in her hands. A storm in her chest.

Adelinda walked blindly through the streets of Béziers, her heart hammering against her ribs, eyes glistening.

John. He is here. John is here.

She had seen him. Spoken to him. Touched him, if only for a moment.

A sob threatened to escape her throat, but she swallowed it, forcing her breath to steady. Not here. Not now. The city stirred around her, the murmur of voices blending into the clatter of hooves and hurried footsteps. Shutters slammed shut. Barrels rolled into place. The air crackled with an unspoken dread. They knew. They all knew.

This was the calm before the storm.

She turned into an alley, pressed her back against the cool stone wall, and let herself break. Her hands curled into fists at her sides, nails digging into her palms. She had prepared

305

for this. For war, for siege, for fire and death.

What she had not prepared for was John. For meeting him. For the way his eyes had locked onto hers, the way his voice had trembled when he whispered her name. A ghost, come back to haunt them both.

She had thought him dead. Or lost. He had gone to the Levant. Or even worse, he could have been indifferent. Could have forgotten their long lost shared love. But now? Now he stood on the other side of the walls, part of the army that would raze her home to the ground. Part of them. Part of him.

Amalric.

Her stomach twisted as she forced herself to remember the other man she had faced today. The abbot. The *butcher.* The man who did not recognize her.

How could he not remember? How could he stand there, so smug, so righteous, so utterly oblivious to the life he had shattered? But of course, men like him never remembered.

They only counted victories—in lives ruined and torn.

Adelinda sucked in a sharp breath under tears, rage cutting through grief like a blade. That such a man would dare call himself a servant of God—that he would lead an army in His name. She should have screamed. Should have torn the smugness from his face. Should have let the whole world hear what he was.

But Béziers needed her.

She had sworn to protect this city. To fight for the people who had taken her in, who had given her shelter when the world had cast her aside. These were her people now. She could not fail them.

She took a slow, deep breath.

Her thoughts wrenched back to John. The cruel joke fate had played on them both. Of all the banners marching on Béziers, why did his have to be one of them? Of all the men standing at Amalric's side, why did it have to be him? Did he even know? Did he understand the kind of man he served?

306

Did he know what Amalric had done to her family—to her?

No. He couldn't have. John was noble, just. He had loved her once. If he knew, if she told him—what then? Could he stop this madness? Could he save her, save the city? Or would it only destroy him too?

The sounds of Béziers rushed back to her. Hammering. Shouts. The shuffle of feet as barricades were raised. Somewhere, a child cried. Somewhere, an old man prayed.

Adelinda wiped her face with trembling fingers. No time for grief. No time for ghosts of the past. There was no turning back time. One could only move forward.

She pushed off the wall and walked forward, steady now, purpose in every step. Amalric might believe himself the instrument of divine justice. But John would know the truth. He needed to.

Heat. Dust. Voices carrying on the wind.

Adelinda walked with purpose, but her mind was tangled, pulled in a thousand directions. The streets of Béziers bustled around her—mothers clutching their children, men reinforcing barricades, merchants sealing their doors as if wooden planks could keep out the storm. Fear clung to the air, thick and suffocating, yet life went on.

For now.

She passed familiar faces—craftsmen, burghers, men who had once tipped their hats in greeting. Some nodded as she passed, others avoided her gaze. Perhaps they sensed it too. The end pressing in. The noose tightening. The Church's wrath had come for Béziers at last.

Her sanctuary. Her refuge.

She had come here with nothing, carrying an infant and a shattered soul. It was a summer's evening in 1199, the memory still vivid—how the people of Béziers had taken her in when the world had turned its back on her. She could still feel the warmth of Berlanda Laborde's hands, the way the *bonne femme* had embraced her, whispered words of kindness when all she had known was fear. Now that kindness was under siege.

Adelinda's fingers gripped the edge of her veil, the fabric damp with sweat despite the midday breeze. The irony of it all. The *bons hommes* and *bonnes femmes* had never lifted a sword, never marched under banners of conquest. Their crime was peace. Of daring to express a differing belief. Their sin was believing in something Rome could not control. And for that, they would burn.

And then there was John.

The name alone sent a fresh ache through her chest as it had for years every time she heard it. Yet, there he was. In the flesh. In front of her. Oh, those eyes—the same piercing gaze that had once set her heart racing in the candlelit halls of Tiverton Castle. He had spoken her name, as though he could not believe she was real. As though she were a ghost.

Maybe she was.

What cruel twist of fate had placed him here, in this army? In Amalric's shadow? How could God—if He even watched over them at all—weave such bitter threads together?

She had wanted to run to John. To throw herself into his arms and weep, to tell him everything—what had happened to her, why she had vanished from England, why the abbot Amalric had such an impact on her.

But she hadn't.

Because war had no room for second chances. And John—*her* John—was on the wrong side of the walls.

Adelinda turned down a narrow alley, pressing her hands against the cool stone. The towers of Béziers loomed above her, dark against the deepening sky. She would not run. She would not flee. She had a daughter to protect. A city to defend.

John was here, and perhaps he still loved her.

But if he raised his sword against Béziers, against the people who had saved her when no one else would—she wouldn't know what to do.

Perhaps he will listen to me.

But she also knew he was simply a spoke in the wheel. She had seen his banner fluttering by the command tent. He was a noble on Amalric's staff—but only one of many voices.

Those voices would drown him out.

She knew it and understood that hope for a peaceful resolution was out of the question. But maybe—just maybe, he could be persuaded to defect to their side. If anything, to be by her side during the worst of the fighting.

Wishful thinking.

But she enjoyed the fleeting fantasy regardless. Oh, how she missed him. She often wondered about him. She had to let him go; after forcibly being taken away from him many years ago, he was now again a world apart, despite just being separated by walls—and holy zeal. Could the world be any more cruel?

The corridor smelled of lavender and drying herbs, a scent that had always clung to the upper levels of the old merchant quarter. Adelinda's feet carried her up the familiar steps, each worn plank creaking beneath her weight. A long day. A harrowing day. But at least now she was home.

She reached the second landing, where a figure stood in the doorway, hands deftly sorting through bundles of dried leaves. Millene. Her scarf, once a deep crimson, had faded with time, but her eyes still held that familiar warmth.

"*Adieu*, Azalaïs," Adelinda said, her voice softer than she intended.

Azalaïs turned, her weathered hands pausing their work. A knowing smile creased her face.

"*Adieu*, my dear. You've carried much on your soul today."

Adelinda exhaled, nodding. Too long.

"The Lord sees us through," she murmured, pressing a kiss to Azalaïs' forehead before continuing down the corridor.

Her door stood ajar. A touch of fresh flowers adorned the frame—Elizabeth's doing, no doubt. Adelinda smiled despite herself. That child, ever thoughtful. Ever eager to welcome her home.

She barely had time to remove her cloak before a flurry of auburn curls came barreling toward her.

"Mother, you're back!"

Small arms wrapped tightly around her waist. Adelinda knelt, drawing her daughter close, breathing in the scent of honey and flour.

"I'm here, my love," she whispered.

Nine-year old Elizabeth pulled back just enough to look up at her, eyes bright with expectation.

"Did you see the flowers?"

"I did," Adelinda murmured, brushing a stray curl from her daughter's face. "You've made our home even lovelier."

Elizabeth beamed but quickly sobered.

"Mother... will those soldiers outside come here?"

The question struck like a blade. Adelinda stilled, smoothing a hand over her daughter's hair.

"We are safe, my darling. Our walls are strong."

"But they have swords," Elizabeth whispered.

A lump formed in Adelinda's throat.

Yes, they have swords. And zeal. And fire.

"They do," she admitted. "But we have faith. And the Lord watches over us."

Elizabeth frowned, unconvinced, but nodded. She kissed her mother's cheek before darting outside, her laughter soon mingling with the other children in the corridor.

Alone now.

Adelinda sank onto the low stool by the hearth, letting her hands rest in her lap. The pot on the fire bubbled softly, the scent of root vegetables and herbs filling the small room. A simple comfort.

But there was no comfort in the truth.

The council had spoken. The gates had closed. There

310

would be no surrender. The army outside would not leave until blood had been spilled.

Her gaze drifted to the window, to the rooftops beyond. Béziers lived on—for now. A baker carried fresh loaves to market. A group of women hung linens to dry. Children weaved between carts, their laughter rising above the clamor of merchants hawking their wares.

Life. Still clinging.

Béziers was different from other towns, different from the world beyond its walls. Here, Catholics and heretics lived side by side, debating, worshiping, sharing the same streets. The *bons hommes* were not feared here. The *Valdois* were not hunted. The burghers, Catholic though they were, refused to turn against their own residents—heretic or not. Not even for the Pope.

Adelinda pressed a hand against her forehead, eyes closing.

Would it matter? Would any of it matter once Amalric gave the command to attack? Would he care who knelt in the cathedral and who prayed in the fields? Or would all be swept away in the tide of fire and steel brought by these so-called "holy" warriors?

And on top of all of that, how could she ever make John see? How could she tell him what kind of man he truly served? Would he even believe her?

The flames flickered. The soup simmered in the pot. The streets outside hummed with life. The scent of fresh bread mingled with the brine of the river, the marketplace still alive with the hum of daily life. Voices called out, bartering over olives and cloth, mothers haggling for the best cuts of lamb, children darting between stalls, laughter bubbling beneath the weight of the siege. Life carried on, stubborn, unwilling to bow.

Adelinda took the pot off the fire, then made her way to the ground floor, the sunlight through the windows streaming in ribbons through the dust. She took a deep breath before exiting into the street.

The light had shifted—softer now, as if the sun itself had grown weary from the events of the day. Harried voices murmured in alleyways, children's laughter echoing faintly between the stonewashed passageways. She pulled her cloak tighter, not for the cold, but to brace against the weight of the impending cataclysm.

The dust of the cobblestone road clung to the hem of her skirt as she passed, each step measured and determined. Faces nodded in greeting, somber yet filled with defiance— old Léon by the well, the young Etienne sweeping his step— but she offered only a small smile in return, her mind already elsewhere.

The scent of crushed thyme drifted on the breeze— someone preparing supper—and for a moment she thought of Elizabeth and whether the child would enjoy the lentils fresh off the pot. Then the hall came into view, tall and solemn. A pigeon fluttered noisily off the eaves as she approached, startling her for a moment.

She lingered at the threshold of the council hall, her fingers grazing the stone, cool against her skin. How long would this fragile peace last? The answer loomed just outside the walls—ten thousand men beneath bloodied banners, chanting of righteousness while sharpening their blades. The thought sent a shudder through her.

A shadow moved in the corner of her vision. Slow steps. Measured. A presence familiar yet always commanding respect.

Father Armand.

The old priest approached with deliberate calm, his robes frayed at the edges, his face lined with more than just the burden of age. A man of faith, but not blind to the world's cruelty. She inclined her head. He took her hands in his, his grip still strong despite his years.

"You wished to see me, Father?"

"The council insists on secrecy, my lady," Armand

whispered, his eyes flicking toward the market square. "The tunnels beneath the hall—our last refuge—must remain unknown to all but a few. Should the city fall, they may be our only salvation."

The words landed like lead.

Our last refuge.

Adelinda's fingers curled against her palms.

"And the defenses?"

She hated how hollow the question sounded.

Armand sighed.

"Our walls are strong, but no defense is unassailable. If they breach the gates, Lady Adelinda, you must be ready."

Her gaze lifted toward the rooftops, the streets winding toward the thick, unyielding walls. They had withstood storms, riots, the weight of time itself. But not an army. Not one like this.

"The tunnels," she murmured. "I remember the viscount saying he explored them as a child. Are they still usable?"

"They are old," Armand admitted. "But strong. The viscounts of old feared a siege like this. They reinforced the passages many years ago, though they have never been tested under such dire circumstances."

The air felt heavier, the sun warmer than it had been moments ago. She looked back into the heart of the city— the mothers clinging to their children, the elders murmuring prayers as they watched the horizon, the boys clutching wooden practice swords as if playacting at war.

"It's a grim thought, Father," she said. "But if it comes to that, I will find the tunnels. I will help as many escape as is possible."

Armand's grip on her shoulder was firm, reassuring.

"You know this city better than most—its streets, its people. When the time comes, you must guide as many of them as you can to safety."

Her throat tightened. She nodded.

"And the tunnels…" she hesitated. "They lead beyond

the walls?"

"To the old vineyards to the north," Armand said. "From there, God willing, escape will be possible. But you must act swiftly when the moment comes."

God willing.

Adelinda clenched her hands, her knuckles pale.

"Let us pray it does not come to that."

The old priest held her gaze, the weight of a thousand unexpressed thoughts behind his eyes.

"Indeed, my child. But if it does, the people will look to you. Do not falter."

He turned, disappearing into the cool darkness of the council hall, leaving her alone in the street. She remained still for a long moment, listening to the sound of life around her.

A city waiting. A city pretending. A city possibly about to fall.

She lifted her chin, inhaled deeply, and stepped back into the square. If the walls did not hold, she would.

Somehow.

Béziers stood apart from the rigid world beyond its walls, a beacon of something rare—*tolerance*. A fragile idea, but bright nonetheless.

Raymond-Roger Trencavel, their young viscount, had won the love of his people not through iron and steel, but through understanding. At twenty-three, his rule bore the wisdom of men twice his age. He did not govern by decree alone; he walked among them, laughed with them, listened. A leader who valued the voices of his subjects as much as the strength of his knights.

He had built something unique here. Something worth saving.

Catholics, Waldensians, and the *Bons Chrétiens* lived side by side, a delicate balance of faiths rarely seen in Christendom. Even the Jews, so often cast aside in other cities, held positions of administration. A town of many tongues, many beliefs, and yet—one people.

Adelinda had been given a place among them, a councilwoman in a world where women had no such station. She had fought for the common good, stood as a voice for the forgotten, woven herself into the very fabric of Béziers itself.

And now, they would come for it, to destroy it all. This so-called "Army of the Lord".

She turned her gaze to the sky.

If the Lord wills anything, let it be mercy.

The streets of Béziers bustled around Adelinda, voices rising with the clatter of carts and hurried steps. Life pressed on, despite the storm gathering outside the walls. Despite the siege at their doorstep. She kept moving, nodding to familiar faces, passing the linen-draped stalls in the marketplace, the scent of baking bread and sun-warmed earth filling the air. But her mind was far away, on a young viscount, a boy who had grown into a ruler, and the promise he had made.

Raymond-Roger Trencavel.

Thrust into rulership before he was old enough to understand its weight. His father's death had placed the burden of the viscounty upon his small shoulders at the age of nine. Too young to wield a sword, yet old enough to be a pawn in the power struggles of kings and lords.

His family had long answered to the King of Aragon, but their lands—their home—had flourished under their own laws, their own customs. A viscounty like no other. A place where Catholics, Jews, Waldensians, and *Bons Chrétiens* walked the same streets without fear of each other.

And for that, Rome had condemned them.

Adelinda passed the towering façade of the council hall, its stones cool against the rising heat of the day. She had stood there, in that very hall, when Trencavel made his vow. He had been barely more than a boy when she first met him, not yet married to Agnes of Montpellier, not yet a father. He had been kind, full of energy, with a mind always turning—

questioning, debating. In another life, he might have been a poet, a scholar. He had charmed her once, his laughter bright, his attentions flattering, but it was never more than a passing infatuation. She had always known where her heart belonged.

John.

But the people of Béziers—of Carcassonne—of Albi—they belonged to him, Raymond-Roger.

She could still hear the tremor in his voice that night in the hall. The way he looked out at his people, hands braced on the table, his young face drawn tight with the weight of his choice.

"I will return and save you."

The words hung in the air long after he had gone. Gone with a handful of his knights and a small retinue of scribes.

Adelinda clenched her hands as she turned down a quieter street, her steps taking her toward the western walls. They needed him now. His banners still flew above the gates, white and orange snapping in the wind. His promise still burned in the hearts of the people. But no one knew if he would—or even could—come in time.

News had trickled back from Montpellier, whispers of Trencavel's envoys being turned away, of negotiations ending in silence. The army outside their walls was not here for diplomacy. They were bent on destruction. No one marches that far to come away without loot and the satisfaction of their lust.

A shadow passed overhead—a falcon, circling high above the city. Adelinda's gaze followed its flight as she approached the steps leading to the ramparts.

Bernard de Servian would be there.

The viscount had left him in command, and if any man could hold Béziers together, it was him. A grizzled veteran, his loyalty to the Trencavels had been forged through years of war. He had fought alongside Roger II, Raymond-Roger's father, against the Count of Foix, earning his place not through birth but through grit, steel, and an unwavering resolve. Now, he was the bulwark between Béziers and full destruction.

Adelinda had watched him from her rooftop many nights, pacing the fortifications, barking orders at the garrison, his presence as steady as the walls themselves. It was said he slept no more than a few hours at a time, always near the gates, always listening, watching. A man who knew that any night could be their last.

As she began to climb the steps up the wall, the air felt heavier, charged with the tension of uncertainty. De Servian stood near the battlements, conferring with a group of soldiers. His shaved head gleamed in the sunlight, his thick gray beard moving slightly as he muttered instructions. Even from a distance, Adelinda could see the exhaustion lining his face, yet his stance remained firm, his voice determined.

She continued to ascend, observing, straightening her posture, composing herself. There was no room for weakness now. The people of Béziers looked to her, just as they looked to him. And until the moment came when the siege broke upon them, they would all cling to the one thing they had left.

Hope.

The midday air carried the scent of damp stone and faint traces of roasted grain from the bakeries below. Béziers continued to stir a with nervous energy, its streets now more alive with preparation, voices rising in a mix of hushed urgency and forced normalcy. The city was waiting—some for a miracle, some for a death sentence.

Adelinda climbed the last of the stairs to the top of the walls, her fingers trailing briefly along the cool stone as she steadied herself. She had walked these paths a hundred times before, watched the seasons change from this height, gazed at the countryside when the world was still peaceful. But now, the view beyond the walls churned her stomach. The camp of the host sprawled across the plains, a sea of pavilions and banners, a horde waiting for the order to arouse them.

She turned as the heavy sound of boots approached.

De Servian.

The grizzled commander moved like a man with the weight of the city strapped to his back. His shoulders, broad and stiff, bore the burdens of war and duty, the leather straps of his armor worn and creased with age and use. In one hand, he inspected an arrow, running calloused fingers along the shaft. Adelinda knew he wasn't checking for flaws—it was a habit, a thing to do while his mind churned with decisions that meant life or death.

"Sir Bernard," she greeted as she approached.

De Servian turned, his keen eyes flicking over her before nodding once.

"Lady Adelinda. You're as vigilant as our best soldiers."

She folded her arms, the breeze tugging at the loose strands of hair escaping her veil.

"I try to be useful, good sir. My, you have barely even slept since the enemy arrived."

De Servian grunted, setting the arrow back in the quiver beside him.

"The city won't defend itself, my lady. These walls will hold, but only if we're vigilant," the old soldier's gaze swept the horizon, his eyes exhausted yet observant. "Every man under my command knows it. And so must you."

Adelinda stepped closer, lowering her voice.

"Do you truly believe we can hold them back? The *milites Christi* are relentless. If they breach the walls…"

"They won't. If we remain disciplined and determined, the enemy will not get past these walls."

His voice was firm, sharp, the kind that brooked no argument. "The men are ready. The gates are reinforced. Even if they somehow manage to scale the walls, they'll meet a fight that will make them regret ever setting foot here."

She searched his face, looking for any sign of doubt. Nothing. Stone and steel, just like the walls he guarded.

"The council is prepared to assist however we can," she said. "Supplies, support for the wounded—just say the word."

For the briefest moment, de Servian's hard expression softened, if only slightly.

"Your efforts are appreciated, Lady Adelinda. The council's work has kept the people calm, and that's no small thing. Panic is as dangerous as any siege tower."

Adelinda hesitated, her gaze shifting past the battlements, past the open plains where the enemy camp lay like a storm on the horizon.

"And if the Viscount does not return in time?"

She saw it, then—the flicker of something in his eyes, a shadow of doubt, perhaps, that hadn't been there before. He turned his head slightly, looking where she looked, staring at the place where hope lay in the form of Raymond-Roger Trencavel's absent banners.

"Then we will have to stand without him," he said quietly. "But I believe he will come. He gave his word."

She nodded, though her heart remained heavy. A promise was only as strong as the army behind it.

"If you need anything," she said softly, "send for me. I'll be at the council hall the rest of the day."

De Servian dipped his head in respect.

"You have my thanks, my lady. And my respect. You've done more for this city than most men would dare."

Adelinda turned, moving back toward the steps, but as she reached the edge of the wall, she paused. The plains beyond were beginning to stir. Campfires smoldered, figures moved purposefully between tents, the unmistakable sound of steel on steel drifting through the midday air.

She looked for him.

John.

She could not see him, but she knew he was there,

somewhere among the enemy ranks. A knight of the besieging army. A man she had once loved standing among those who sought to destroy the only home she had left.

Adelinda leaned against the parapet, the summer sun warming the stone beneath her hands. If he was there, could he stop this?

Would he?

Or would he be swallowed whole by the same machine that had brought war to their gates?

The scent of crushed lavender and damp wood lingered in the air, mixing with the distant, acrid bite of smoldering firewood from both within the city and from the enemy campfires. The chants of the *milites Christi* carried on the breeze—low, rhythmic, ceaseless. Prayers for their holy conquest. Prayers for their slaughter.

Adelinda closed her eyes. Just for a moment.

She let herself imagine an impossible dream.

One where the enemy would grow weary. Their chants would fade to silence, their fervor eroded by time and failure. The walls of Béziers would stand unbroken. And when they finally abandoned their siege, she would be there—waiting. Waiting for John.

She could almost see him. Dark eyes filled with the same longing, the same memories, the same aching sorrow. He would take her hand, and they would leave this wretched war behind. No more holy wars. No more blood. Just the two of them, somewhere far away, where the past could not reach them.

A small, wistful smile flickered across her lips. A foolish idealistic vision. A lie she could not afford to keep entertaining. Daydreaming would not solve their predicament.

The clang of metal, sharp voices breaking the hush of the moment, yanked her back to reality. She opened her eyes, exhaling slowly as the city and the surrounding plains returned in all its chaotic urgency.

The walls buzzed with more movement. Defenders moved in practiced rhythm, their armor glinting under the sun, their voices a murmur of strategy and tension.

Her gaze shifted lower, to the gatehouse below.

Stefan Meric. The arrogant little whelp.

He leaned against the stone parapet, laughing too loudly, his red hair catching the morning light. His movements were loose, casual, his hands gesturing animatedly as he conversed with two young guards. One of them smirked, pulling a flask from his belt and tossing it to Meric, who raised it in mock salute before taking a long drink.

Adelinda's lips pressed into a thin line.

Drinking.

At the gatehouse. The very heart of the city's defenses, and its so-called second-in-command was acting as if they were at a tavern.

"You call that leadership?"

The familiar voice like gravel, sharp and unrelenting.

Adelinda watched as de Servian strode up the steps, his steel-plated boots striking against the stone with measured, deliberate weight. The laughter died instantly. The guards stiffened. Meric turned, flask still in hand, the easy grin on his face faltering as his commander now loomed over him.

"Sir Bernard!" Meric straightened, clearing his throat. "I was simply—"

"Simply making a fool of yourself," de Servian interrupted, voice cold as tempered iron. "These men look to you for guidance, not buffoonery."

Meric bristled, his bravado flickering back to life.

"I was lifting their spirits! Morale is important, isn't it?"

"Morale," de Servian snapped, stepping closer, "comes from discipline, not from drunken antics at the gatehouse. Do you think the *milites Christi* will wait for you to sober up before they attack? Get to your post, Meric, and act like the second-in-command you're supposed to be."

Silence.

Meric hesitated. His jaw tightened. For a moment, he looked as if he might protest.

Then he muttered, "Yes, Sir Bernard," and stalked off, his flask vanishing into the folds of his cloak. The guards, wisely, followed suit, their laughter replaced by the muted clink of chainmail as they resumed their duties.

Adelinda let out a breath she hadn't realized she was holding.

She turned her gaze back toward the plains, toward the enemy that waited beyond them. A storm was coming. The walls would hold, or they wouldn't.

Memories of Stefan Meric's reckless youth clung to Adelinda's mind like smoke that refused to clear. His pranks, his endless mischief—ducking the watch after some drunken brawl, vanishing into the maze of Béziers' streets like a stray cat. Always stirring trouble, yet somehow always landing on his feet. The boy had been a whirlwind of noise and swagger, a nuisance tolerated only because he could charm his way out of nearly anything. And because of some strong connections.

How had that boy become second-in-command?

She knew the answer—Trencavel's favoritism.

The young viscount had grown up with Meric—his friend, his shadow. She recalled seeing them together at council gatherings many years ago, Stefan lurking near the back, flashing that smug grin whenever the viscount spoke. The bond between them ran deep, too deep for Trencavel to see Meric's failings. The weight of old guilt had blinded him—guilt over the death of Meric's father, who had died fighting in service to the Trencavel family. The young viscount's father, Roger II, had vowed to care for the boy, to ensure he would never be left behind.

But placing him as second-in-command now? A fool's risk. The one decision she questioned. Adelinda's fingers dug into the railing as she watched de Servian descend the steps, his face dark with frustration. He knew. He saw what she saw—knew the danger Meric posed to the city's defense.

Bernard de Servian was iron-clad in his discipline, a man who carried the mantle of leadership like a mailed hauberk. He had prepared Béziers with precision, inspecting every wall, every bastion. But even his strength couldn't mend Meric's arrogance.

Adelinda prayed. Not for miracles, nor victory.

For time.

Time for the viscount to return. Time for the walls to hold. Time—*time* for someone to shake sense into Stefan Meric before his recklessness dragged them all to ruin. Perhaps Sir Bernard would be able to keep him in check— at least long enough for the viscount to return.

She returned her gaze outward, past the city's defenses, her eyes sweeping over the enemy encampment sprawled across the plains. Tents stretched in rigid rows—orderly, disciplined. Banners fluttered above each column, marking the presence of seasoned knights and hardened infantry.

Men drilled in tight formations, shields rising and falling in rhythm. Even from here, their precision was unmistakable—marching in perfect unison, blades flashing like scales in the sunlight. Chanting drifted over the plains, low and relentless, punctuated by the ring of hammer on iron. Armor checked. Weapons sharpened. Siege weapons at the ready.

Adelinda's gaze fixed on the men below cutting trees and hauling logs. They were building siege engines. She traced their likely plans in her mind. The gates would take the brunt. The walls—there, near the old merchant quarter, where the stone had weathered and crumbled. The enemy would find the weak points. They had studied this place. They knew what they were doing.

Efficient. Cold. Calculated.

She had learned the art of warfare from her father, the Knight William de Montaro, who served at the side of the Earl Devon.

The realization of the enemy's efficiency sickened her.

Her father's voice surfaced in her memory—a stern reminder from her childhood:

"Victory isn't won with strength alone. It's preparation that saves a city."

The invaders had prepared. They had the numbers, the discipline, the leadership. Béziers, for all its pride and resilience, lacked all three.

Of course, the population itself outnumbered the enemy—at least twice over. But they had less than a thousand men with arms.

Adelinda shifted her gaze back to the defenders on the walls. Some stood ready, eyes locked on the distant camp. But others—too many—lounged in boredom. Some leaned on their spears, laughing and trading jokes as if this were a harvest fair. A few gambled with dice, their coin scattered along the stones. One boy—no older than fifteen—dropped his bundle of arrows and stumbled clumsily as he tried to gather them. The soldiers around him burst into raucous laughter.

Adelinda's stomach knotted.

Then came Meric.

Swaggering up the steps to the parapet, red hair catching the sun. The men cheered him as if he were a returning hero. Adelinda's hands tightened on the stone. Sir Bernard had left to inspect another section of the wall—leaving Meric to play the role of leader.

He greeted the men like old drinking companions—clapping backs, trading jokes. One soldier offered him another flask. Meric snatched it with a grin, raising it to his lips with the same smug bravado that had defined him since boyhood.

Adelinda felt her nails dig into her palm.

This man will get us all killed.

"Keep up your spirits, lads!" Meric called out, his voice high-pitched and jarring. "We'll send those zealots running back to their priests soon enough!"

A few men laughed, while others exchanged uneasy glances. Adelinda noticed one veteran—a grizzled man with a scar running down his cheek—tighten his grip on his spear and turn back to the plains without a word.

"Stefan," Adelinda called sharply, stepping forward to lean on the railing overlooking their post. He turned to her inebriated with an exaggerated bow, his grin broad and insincere.

"Lady Adelinda," he replied in a mocking tone with a slight slur. "What brings the esteemed councilwoman to grace us with her presence?"

"To remind you, Captain Meric, that leadership demands more than jesting and drinking."

Her voice was firm, cutting through his theatrics as she continued.

"Our enemy is disciplined and methodical. If you continue to treat this siege like a game, you will lead these men to ruin."

Stefan's grin faltered for a moment before he laughed it off, waving her concerns away.

"You worry too much, my lady. The walls of Béziers are strong, and the men here are eager to fight. A bit of levity keeps the spirits high."

Adelinda stepped closer, her gaze piercing.

"Levity will not stop a trebuchet's stones or a battering ram at the gates. Discipline might. You are second-in-command for a reason, Stefan. Act like it."

For a moment, Stefan's face darkened, and she thought she had struck a chord. But then he smirked, lifting the flask again.

"With Sir Bernard overseeing the real work, I doubt my... levity, as you call it, will matter much."

Adelinda forced herself to swallow the sharp words rising to her lips, her fists clenching at her sides.

Not here. Not now.

Sir Bernard had left Meric in charge of this section of the wall, and though he had done so reluctantly, it was still his command. And yet, watching the young officer bask in the laughter of his men, flask in hand, she knew this was a mistake.

The viscount's favor had blinded him. Meric had been given rank not by merit, but by friendship. A boy who had never outgrown his games now stood in charge of men whose lives depended on discipline, on order. On leadership. But Stefan Meric did not lead. He entertained. He played at command.

She turned her gaze to the walls. De Servian's men stood ready. Their armor, their weapons, their very stance spoke of preparedness, of duty. But here—here, under Meric's careless watch—men leaned on their spears, their laughter an insult to the enemy that waited in perfect silence beyond the walls. The attackers would not falter. Would Béziers?

Her eyes snapped back to Meric.

"I pray Sir Bernard returns before you test the enemy's patience, Captain," she said, her voice even but cold. "These men deserve better than reckless leadership."

Meric chuckled, lips curling into that same smug grin he had worn since boyhood.

"Come now, Lady Adelinda," he drawled, lifting the flask as if to toast her. "What's a war without a bit of merriment?"

Without another word, she turned on her heel, stepping away before she said something she would regret. Behind her, the men's laughter resumed, muffled only by the distant clatter of steel and stone as Béziers braced for what was to come.

Let them laugh. Let them drink.

Soon, they would choke on both.

The city's defenses looked strong. But war was more than walls and weapons. It was men. Discipline. Resolve.

Six hundred men-at-arms stood ready beneath Sir

Bernard's command. They were trained. Armored. Capable. De Servian had drilled them relentlessly—day and night, no respite, no mercy. He understood the stakes. He understood that walls could break, that men must hold. Two hundred archers lined the parapets, their bows strung, their quivers full. Barricades of stone and timber shielded them, ready to break the storm of arrows that would soon come from the plains below.

It should have been reassuring.

But it wasn't.

Adelinda leaned against the doorframe of her home, her fingers tightening against the wood. The weight of the council's decision pressed against her like an iron vice. To stand. To endure. To wait for a viscount who may never return.

Was this wisdom? Or folly?

The besieging host was not merely large. It was something else entirely. She had seen them, studied them from the rooftops. Their precision. Their purpose. This was no band of hired blades or warring barons. This was something far worse.

An army of zealots.

She had watched them—the flagellants, driven to frenzy by the Cistercians' cries, lashing their own flesh raw as they howled prayers to a God that would soon demand Béziers' destruction.

She had seen the siege engines rising from the plains, their skeletal frames monuments to patience, to inevitability.

And the pilgrims—fanatics in tattered robes—working alongside the warriors of the Cross, their hands bleeding from labor, their voices rising in fervent hymns. This was no ordinary host. This was the sword of Rome—not the sword of justice, although many were quick to insist they were one and the same.

Adelinda exhaled, pressing her knuckles to her lips.

And we have chosen to resist it.

327

The council believed in the walls, in the men, in Trencavel's return.

But supplies would dwindle. Morale would fray. They would not be able to hold out forever at this rate.

And with Meric lounging atop the gatehouse like a boy at a festival, how long before disorder seeped through the cracks of Béziers' defense?

She drifted to the hearth, barely noticing Elizabeth's soft humming from the other room. Her daughter, oblivious to the storm that loomed outside the walls. Oblivious to the choices her mother had made.

The *Bons Chrétiens* had always preached peace, had always shunned the sword.

And yet, here they were, being defended by Catholics against their fellow Catholics, not out of shared belief, but out of loyalty to their neighbors, men who had taken up arms to protect them because they refused to protect themselves.

The thought of Berlanda Laborde, the *Bonne Femme* who had taken her in all those years ago. The woman who had given her kindness when she had none. Who had helped her bring Elizabeth into the world.

The people of Béziers stood for something greater than war, greater than Rome's decrees. But would it be enough?

Adelinda turned toward the table, hands steadying against the wood. She would cook. She would prepare the evening meal. Then—she would do what she could.

The storm had not yet come.

But she knew something horrible would happen—and soon. There would be no walls strong enough to prevent what was about to take place.

::

The laughter grated against his skull, sharp as grinding steel. John's jaw clenched as he watched the young men atop the walls—drunk, reckless, oblivious. They leaned too far over the parapets, wine-slicked hands gripping the stone, pointing down at the vast encampment below. Jeering. Mocking. Spitting insults at an army that would soon come for them with fire and steel.

Did they not see it? Did they not feel the weight of the threat which loomed beyond their walls?

Fools.

A stir below. The pilgrims had gathered, their voices rising—prayers laced with fury, pleading for justice, for divine wrath. Priests clutched their rosaries, their fingers white with tension. John exhaled slowly, his fingers curling into fists. It was an unnerving sight to behold.

A red-haired youth atop the wall stumbled forward, clearly inebriated, emboldened by the cheers of his comrades. John watched from a distance as the young man grinned down at the mass of clerics and soldiers, a sneer curling his lips.

"These are your sacred texts!" he yelled in Occitan, waving a stack of books above his head.

John stiffened. He knew exactly what was going to happen.

The pilgrims below gasped. A priest clutched his chest as if struck by a physical blow.

The red-haired youth laughed. Then—*rip*. A page tore free, caught by the wind, fluttering toward the earth. Another. And another. The parchment began scattering like dying leaves, drifting, helpless.

Screams rose.

"Blasphemy. Heresy!"

The priests wailed, their voices breaking against the walls. Some fell to their knees, arms raised toward the heavens in trembling supplication, as if calling upon divine judgment in the form of fire from the heavens. Others shook with rage, their grief inconsolable.

The youth wasn't finished.

He unfastened his belt.

No.

John's stomach turned as the boy urinated over the edge of the parapet, dousing the torn pages in filth.

The gathered pilgrims below erupted in screams.

John heard the snap of a bowstring pulled tense, stretched— but no arrow flew. A priest, face red with fury, pointed toward the wall, screaming at a group of Frankish archers.

"Loose those arrows!"

The soldiers did not move an inch.

John pushed through the formation below, his pulse hammering. With the absence of the abbot, they looked to him for command. He lifted his hand and in a downward motion signaled for them to hold their fire.

The archers stood still, their gazes fixed ahead, waiting. Disciplined. Controlled. Despite the priest's constant wailing, they knew he had no authority over them. Knew this was not the moment. But the cleric's rage was blind, his voice cracking as he bellowed, spit flying from his lips.

One arrow. That's all it would take.

One shot, and the tenuous thread of restraint holding this army together would snap.

John turned his gaze back to the walls.

The defenders roared with laughter, reveling in their blasphemy. One of them blew a mocking kiss to the clerics below. Another threw a rock—then another.

A fool's game.

The pilgrims retaliated, snatching stones from the ground, hurling them back with trembling hands. The air filled with the crack of rocks against stone, as they lacked the strength to clear the walls.

John's breath came shallow, tight.

He looked up just in time to see it—the wind catching a single parchment, lifting it high, dancing it above the chaos. It twisted, caught in the current, refusing to fall. It was like a relic suspended between two worlds.

John followed its path, his eyes tracking its slow descent. Drifting. Spinning. Falling.

It came to rest at his feet.

A scrap of parchment. That's all it was.

He knelt, fingers brushing the coarse fibers, the inked letters uneven beneath his touch. The wind stirred the edges, lifting them slightly, as if the parchment itself resisted being claimed. Around him, the din of righteous fury and drunken revelry swelled—two clashing tides, each blind to the absurdity of the other.

He smoothed out the page. Read. He paused. His brow furrowed. A ballad?

Not scripture. Not doctrine. Not some sacred passage torn from the Holy Writ. A bawdy song. A knight's misadventures with a miller's wife, each stanza more obscene than the last. A filthy jest scrawled in careless ink, now trampled into the dirt, mistaken for divine blasphemy.

John exhaled sharply, barely suppressing the bitter laughter rising in his chest. This is what they're screaming for?

"George." His voice was steady, but beneath it, something cracked.

George strode over, arms crossed, his eyes flicking between John and the wailing priests. The defenders above were still laughing, still tossing scraps of parchment like falling leaves, reveling in their drunken mockery.

"What is it, milord?" George asked, his voice laced with exhaustion.

Wordlessly, John handed him the parchment.

George unfolded it, his eyes scanning the text. A beat of silence. Then—a snort. A chuckle. A full-bodied laugh, dry and mirthless.

"This?" George said, lifting the page as though he held a holy relic. "This is what they're wailing about? A knight rutting some miller's wife?"

He scoffed, shaking his head.

331

"And here I thought they were lamenting the desecration of the Holy Writ."

John's gaze turned toward the priests. Their faces, red with righteous fury, twisted in despair, hands clutched at their rosaries, their tear-streaked eyes cast heavenward as they screamed.

Above them, the leader of the drunken rabble—his tunic stained, his footing precarious—held another book high. A mockery of reverence, he pressed it to his lips before hurling it backward, to the roaring laughter of his companions.

John clenched his fists.

"I thought this was a campaign of faith," he muttered, voice edged with disbelief. "What faith is this?"

George crumpled the parchment in his fist and tossed it to the ground.

"Faith?" he echoed, scoffing. "This isn't faith, milord. This is madness. These priests would have the archers fire on cattle if it pleased their zeal."

John's gaze returned to the men atop the walls. Wine-drenched fools, laughing at death, hurling curses at an army that would tear them apart without mercy.

"And them?" he asked, eyes dark. "They mock their very deaths."

George shrugged.

"Fools on both sides, milord," his voice was quiet, though his eyes were sharp. "But at least the fools up there have walls. What do we have?"

John exhaled through his nose.

"The will of the Lord, apparently."

Beside them, the priests' shouts dissolved into hymns. A low, haunting chant, rising like smoke from a foul incense. Pilgrims wept, some falling to their knees in fervent prayer, others hurling stones at the walls in futile defiance.

Above, laughter continued. Below, wailing prevailed. And somewhere between the two, John stood. His fingers twitched at his side, though whether to reach for his sword or the parchment at his feet, he did not know. His mind drifted past the chaos, to her.

Adelinda.

Perhaps it was the defiance he saw in her stance, the guarded hope in her eyes. The weight of all she hadn't said. He would find a way. He would get her out. Get her daughter out.

But how?

And when?

And—God help him—what if it would be too late?

He shuddered at the thought yet forced himself to refocus. He had to remain calm and collected if he were to come up with a plan. He forced a breath through his nose, glancing down at the crumpled page still lying in the dirt. A cheap, tawdry ballad. Nothing holy about it. Nothing worth killing for. Nothing worth the lives of the men in this field and those on the other side of the walls. Certainly not worth the lives of Adelinda and her child.

He turned away from the spectacle, his voice clipped.

"Come. We should return to camp. This is beneath us."

The light had changed by the time they reached the tents. The torches atop Béziers' walls burned like stars against the darkening sky, their glow stretching long and thin across the stone. Below, campfires flickered in the Crusader encampment, small circles of warmth in a sea of cold anticipation. Laughter and murmured prayers wove together in a strange, uneasy harmony. The siege would not begin tonight, nor tomorrow. Amalric would not be so fool hardy to attack this soon. There was still time.

Time.

Again, John's fingers twitched at his side. He needed to use time well.

His gaze swept over the sprawling host as he analyzed the situation. Ten thousand strong. Knights, footmen, crossbowmen. And more—camp followers, pilgrims, men who had never touched a sword yet carried banners as

333

though they were shields. A force built as much on zeal as it was on steel.

And against them?

Béziers.

A city well populated but outnumbered in trained soldiers. Six hundred men-at-arms at most, but well-drilled, armored, steady. Two hundred archers, perhaps, positioned behind their stone barricades. The walls were high, the bridge a death trap for any who dared cross it. But for how long could they hold once the siege engines were completed? Days? Weeks?

He reached his tent, but didn't step inside. Instead, he turned, looking back toward the city. The walls stood unmoved, their torches flickering, silent, watching.

Bribery. Stealth. A hidden gate. A desperate climb under the cover of darkness. He turned the possibilities over in his mind, testing their weight, discarding the ones that wouldn't hold.

There had to be a way.

And he had to find it.

John turned abruptly—a sound—boots crunching against gravel. He knew the rhythm of that step before he even looked.

Hugh.

The knight stopped a few paces away, arms crossed, expression unreadable.

"G'evening, my lord."

John exhaled.

"Evening, Hugh."

Silence stretched between them, broken only by the distant clang of metal and the murmuring of monks at their evening prayers.

"You're troubled milord," Hugh said at last, falling into step beside him. "Is it the siege?"

John hesitated. He had kept this burden to himself and even kept it from George, but the weight of it pressed harder with every passing minute. He thought of Constantinople, of Zara. Of the way a holy war had turned into something else entirely. He thought of what would happen if the walls of Béziers fell.

Hugh studied him for a moment, his sharp gaze missing nothing.

"You've faced worse sieges, milord. Acre, for one. What's different about this?"

John set his jaw, glancing around. Too many ears. Too many eyes. He pulled Hugh away from the campfire's glow, lowering his voice.

"I saw her, Hugh."

Hugh blinked, confused at first.

"Saw who?"

John's throat felt tight.

"Adelinda."

Hugh stiffened, his face contorting in disbelief.

"Her ladyship? Here?" He stepped closer, voice dropping to a near whisper. "How in God's name did she end up here?"

"I don't know," John admitted. "I saw her in the delegation that came out under a flag of truce. Talked with her for but a brief moment. Tried to convince her to leave. But she has a daughter. And now she's trapped."

Hugh's breath left him in a slow exhale. He looked past John, toward the looming silhouette of Béziers, its walls flickering in torchlight. A long pause. Then, his voice came, steadier than John expected.

"Does anyone else know?"

John shook his head.

"No. And it stays that way."

"Good," Hugh's tone was firm. "The fewer who know, the better."

He hesitated, then added, "But what are you planning, my lord? Do you mean to scale the walls yourself?"

John combed a hand through his hair, pacing a few steps

before stopping.

"I don't know yet," he admitted. "I need a way in. Something that won't compromise our position here but will give me a chance to reach her."

Hugh's expression darkened.

"This is no small task, Lord John," his voice lowered, deliberate. "You'll need someone who knows the city. Someone you can trust."

John met his gaze.

"Yes," he said. "I know."

Then suddenly—a rider approached.

John heard him before he saw him, the rapid crunch of hooves against gravel, the sharp exhale of a horse pushed too hard. The man dismounted in a rush, boots hitting the dirt with urgency. One of Amalric's scouts. His face was flushed from the ride, his breath coming fast. He reached into his cloak and pulled free a crumpled parchment, thrusting it toward John without ceremony.

"A message from His Eminence," the scout said, voice ragged. "He bids you study it well."

John took the parchment, the weight of it heavier than the paper should have allowed. He knew what it was before he unrolled it. Knew because he had already seen it once before.

The *list*.

The names were scrawled in the same careful, trembling script—the same one presented by Bishop Montpeyroux at the parley. There were no new concessions, no signs of negotiation. This wasn't a surrender. It was a statement to him. To remind him of his duty—his obligation towards penance. It was a short leash, and he was to be Amalric's lapdog.

John forced himself to breathe as his eyes skimmed the contents, searching, dreading.

Then—relief.

Adelinda's name wasn't there.

The air left his lungs in a slow exhale, but the tension in

his chest did not ease. He looked up at the scout, his expression carefully neutral.

"His Eminence entrusts you with this task, my lord," the man continued, oblivious to the war raging beneath John's skin. "When the city falls, these heretics must be dealt with. If they do not go willingly, you are to see to their...removal yourself."

He met John's gaze, his meaning clear.

"Amalric trusts you to handle this as befits a knight of his staff."

John felt Hugh shift beside him, but he did not react. Not yet.

The scout bowed his head in deference.

"I will tell the abbot you received his orders."

Then, as quickly as he had appeared, he was gone, disappearing into the tangle of tents and torchlight.

The parchment felt heavier now. Amalric's faith in him—it was a noose, not an honor.

John refolded the list, tucking it into his belt with slow precision. Hugh had been watching him, waiting.

"She's not on it," John remarked.

Hugh exhaled, rubbing a hand over his face.

"God's mercy."

John wasn't so sure. Mercy was in short supply here.

"What now?" Hugh asked, his voice cautious.

John's mind raced. Amalric had given him a mission, one that would place him at the heart of the destruction once the city fell. It was a curse, but also an opportunity.

"I'll do what is expected of me," John said, voice quiet. "At least, that is what Amalric must believe."

Hugh frowned.

"And what does that mean?"

John's hand hovered over the list.

"It means I will enter the city with the rest. No one will question it. No one will suspect anything else."

Hugh's jaw tightened.

"You mean to go through with it."

John met his eyes.

"Yes. I still mean to find her."

A long silence. The campfire crackled nearby, its glow licking at the edges of Hugh's pensive face. Then, finally, a nod.

"You'll need help," Hugh said.

A breath of tension eased from John's chest.

"I know."

"George and I—we'll stand by you," Hugh continued. "But tread carefully, my lord. If Amalric catches wind of this, it won't just be his wrath you'll face. I pray you will consider the ramifications of disregarding the terms of our penance."

John clapped a hand on Hugh's shoulder, a grim smile breaking through the weight of his thoughts.

"Thank you, my friend," he said. "I'll need your support now more than ever."

Hugh sighed.

"You always have it." He glanced at the folded parchment. "And what of that?"

John's grip tightened around the document.

"I'll present myself to the abbot in the morning," he said. "And tell him exactly what he wants to hear."

As Hugh departed to gather George, John turned his gaze back to the host. Laughter still echoed through the camp. Men boasting, singing, drinking. Their voices carried across the night, a stark contrast to the grim reality awaiting them beyond the walls.

Soon, the priests would make their rounds, walking from fire to fire, offering benedictions to those who had taken up the sword in God's name. Soldiers, half-drunk, would lower their heads, whispering prayers, gripping their weapons like talismans. Seeking solace in promises of paradise, should they fall when the assault began.

John envied them.

338

Sleep had already claimed most of his men. His tent, however, remained lit, its canvas walls shifting with the night breeze. He sat at his war table, hunched over a map of the city, though his mind was far from its fortifications. The thought of Béziers burned within him, not as a target, but as a prison. A place where fate had entrapped Adelinda and her child.

The candle on the table sputtered, its glow wavering against the night's chilly breeze. He leaned back in his chair, exhaustion dragging at his limbs, but rest would not come. Every time he closed his eyes, he saw her—saw the way she had looked at him, the emotions barely restrained behind her hazel eyes. Fear, relief, disbelief. A silent plea she dared not speak aloud.

He exhaled slowly, running a hand over his face. The torchlights atop the walls flickered, figures moving between them, shadows weaving and shifting along the parapets.

To him, they were neighbors, not enemies. Trapped like them, waiting for the storm.

His fingers drummed against the makeshift table inside his tent. How could he make this work? How could he find her, reach her before it was too late? Even if he could slip inside, the city was vast—how would he find her in the chaos that would follow the breach? If the city fell, if the host unleashed its wrath, the streets would drown in blood. He had heard it before.

The stories, the tales.

Zara. Constantinople.

The thought turned his stomach. He could not—would not—let it happen again if he could help it.

He forced himself to stand, stepping outside his tent. The night air was sharp against his skin. The stars above stretched wide and uncaring, their cold light mocking the heat of the war camp below. He turned toward Béziers, toward the walls, imagining where she might be residing.

Then—movement.

A faint shift in the torchlight. A ripple in the darkness. He narrowed his gaze.

A cloth. Hanging from the wall.

It fluttered gently, barely perceptible in the night breeze. It wasn't long enough to serve as an escape rope, nor did it wave with the careless abandon of laundry forgotten in the wind. It was deliberate.

A signal.

His breath caught. It was a signal only he understood.

Can it be her?

He took a breath. Deep, steady. His body lay heavy against the chair, the weight of exhaustion pressing down. Sleep clawed at the edges of his mind, dragging him toward its depths, but he fought it, blinking sluggishly, his thoughts slipping between past and present.

The flickering candle cast shifting shadows across the canvas of his tent, the dim glow pulling him somewhere else, somewhere far from this war-torn night.

The chapel at Breckington. Fifteen years ago.

Warm candlelight. The scent of aged wood and incense, a haze of gold in the air. Adelinda beside him, her auburn hair shimmering like molten copper, her presence grounding him even as his heart pounded in his chest.

Father Barth, old and kind, eyes crinkling with mirth as he gestured for them to sit.

John, barely nineteen, too eager, too alive to hold back.

"We were thinking of getting betrothed, Father!"

The words tumbled out, his excitement betraying him.

Adelinda's gaze flicked toward him, amusement curving at the corners of her lips. A soft squeeze of his hand. A silent chastisement.

"We wanted to ensure you would officiate," she added, her voice steady, certain.

Father Barth chuckled, the sound rich with warmth.

"A joyful occasion indeed," he studied them both, his gaze lingering before he continued. "And Sir William—has

340

he given his blessing?"

Adelinda nodded, though hesitation flickered in her hazel eyes.

"John will speak with my father by the end of the week," she said, the faintest edge of unease behind her words.

The priest folded his hands, leaning forward.

"Good, good. Let me tell you a story."

His voice lowered, reverent and solemn, as he symbolically wrapped a scarlet cord around their enjoined hands.

"Long ago, when the city of Jericho stood strong and defiant, a woman named Rahab placed her faith in the Lord of Israel. She hid the spies sent to her city, and in turn, they swore to protect her. They told her to hang a crimson cord from her window—a sign that her household was to be spared. And when the walls of Jericho fell, her section stood firm. Untouched. It was her faith, her courage, that saved her family."

Adelinda inhaled softly, drawn into the tale. John leaned closer, listening, feeling the weight of the words settle into his chest.

"That crimson cord," Father Barth continued, "became a symbol of trust. Of salvation. A signal of hope amidst destruction. May such a cord bind you both, my dear children."

Adelinda's fingers found his, warm and sure. She turned to him, and in that moment, John saw everything—their past, their future, their unshakable bond. In the candlelit hush of the chapel, they were invincible.

The vision faded.

John stirred. A rustle of fabric, the cool night pressing in. His mind caught between the past and the present, unwilling to let go of either. The distant flapping of his banner called him back to the present, the whisper of linen against stone pulling his gaze toward the city.

The cloth. Still there. Swaying in the night breeze, faintly

341

illuminated by the torches along the parapets.

His chest tightened. Could it indeed be her? He knew no other possibility—he would treat this as a certainty. He straightened, bones aching, mind churning. He would act at first light, when the night's shadows no longer blurred reason, when the weight of exhaustion no longer dulled his thoughts.

The crimson cord. A symbol of hope. Of salvation.

The memory clung to him, wrapping around his resolve, strengthening it. Whatever the cloth meant—whoever had placed it there—he would find out.

And if it was Adelinda, if she had left him this sign, he would do whatever it took to bring her to safety. If it was Adelinda, he now knew which section of the city to find her.

John exhaled, allowing the memory to wash over him one last time, a balm against the uncertainty of what lay ahead. He knew where she likely was now—near the western ramparts, close to the main gate. A sanctuary. A place of refuge.

The siege would not begin for at least another week. He had time.

He closed his eyes, surrendering to fleeting rest, knowing dawn would bring more clarity to all the chaos. Or, at least, he had hoped.

Temps de la Fin

 scarlet cloth fluttering against the dawn. Adelinda stood motionless on the small patio of her third-story home, her hands clutching the wooden railing as the scarlet cord she had woven draped downward, its rich color stark against the muted grays of the pre-dawn light.

The fabric twisted and unfurled like a living thing, whispering its silent plea to the wind. She had tied it there in the dead of night, hoping—praying—that it would be seen. That it would mean something. That he would understand.

Her gaze drifted beyond the cord to the walls of Béziers, jagged silhouettes against the pale glow of the coming morning. Torchlight sputtered along the battlements, shifting erratically as figures moved in restless anticipation. The main gate loomed ahead, flanked by the imposing towers that guarded it. Below, shadowed forms gathered in murmurs, their presence an unsettling omen.

Bernard de Servian should have been there, watchful,

343

steady as the stone walls themselves. But the commander had stolen a few hours of much-needed sleep, and in his absence, command had fallen to Stefan Meric.

A bitter twist of fate. A mistake.

Adelinda's stomach clenched as she spotted him. The red-headed fool stood among a growing crowd near the gate, his posture too relaxed, his voice carrying in shrill bravado through the cold air. Even from this distance, she could see the reckless energy in his movements, the way he basked in the attention of those around him.

Something was wrong.

She leaned forward, her breath shallow, watching the assembled mass at the gate. They were not soldiers—not Bernard's men, not the hardened defenders who had spent their days reinforcing the city's walls. These were merchants and apprentices, farmers and tanners. The desperate and the drunk. Their weapons were mismatched and pitiful—rusted swords, pitchforks, clubs scavenged from old stockpiles—all led by the reckless Meric.

Adelinda's grip on the railing tightened.

What is he doing?

A terrible feeling clawed at her chest. Then she saw it— the unmistakable movement of the massive wooden beams being lifted.

What—

Her breath hitched as she watched—unable to do anything.

No. No, no, no.

The gate creaked. A slow, dreadful groan of ancient wood and iron as it parted.

A ragged cheer went up from the gathered mob, torch flames dancing in the foggy gloom. They surged forward, spilling onto the stone bridge that stretched across the Orb River, a tide of emboldened foolishness.

Adelinda's heart pounded against her ribs.

They are going outside the walls.

344

They were walking into certain death.

She sucked in a sharp breath, eyes darting frantically along the ramparts. Someone had to stop this. Someone in the garrison had to see what was happening. But the walls remained silent, the few stationed men watching in uncertain hesitation. No one moved to halt them.

Below, a woman near the front waved a torch high over her head, her voice shrill with defiance.

"You call yourselves warriors?" she jeered at the resting invaders, her Occitan words cutting through the damp air. "Come face us if you dare!"

The impetuous mob roared in drunken agreement, their voices rising in fevered, senseless courage.

Adelinda could barely breathe.

The besiegers would not be intimidated by this. These were no common bandits lurking in the countryside. *The milites Christi* were disciplined men, trained for war, and worse—driven by zeal—most of them, anyway. They would not hesitate. They would not show restraint.

She spun back toward the doorway, her mind a whirlwind. She had to find Bernard. She had to stop this. Because if she didn't, by sunrise, the ground outside Béziers would be littered with bodies.

::

A gust of cold air. Crisp, sharp. Dawn breaking over the camp. Pale light creeping over canvas and steel. John blinked, his breath clouding in the morning chill. A brief, fleeting calm.

Then—shouting.

Distant at first. A commotion beyond the river. He stiffened. Figures moving. Shadowed in the mist. The bridge spanning the Orb, barely visible through the dissipating fog.

More shouting. Louder now.

His pulse quickened. Men—and women—spilling from

the gates of Béziers—too many to be a scouting party. Not soldiers. Rabble. Pitchforks, clubs, makeshift weapons gleaming in the damp light.

John's jaw clenched.

"What in the Lord's name are they doing?"

The words left him as a breathless whisper. He already knew the answer.

A taunt carried across the bridge, followed by a chorus of crude laughter. Townsfolk emboldened by their own bravado, hurling insults at the besieging army.

A *routier* stepped forward from the ranks of the besieging host—approaching the bridge, emboldened by either arrogance or stupidity. John couldn't tell which.

Steel glinted. A quick, ugly movement. Then screaming.

The mob closed in, their weapons descending in a chaotic frenzy. The *routier* crumpled beneath them. His body barely hit the ground before rough hands lifted it, hoisting it high, a gruesome trophy. Then—splash. The corpse vanished into the flowing waters of the Orb.

Silence. Just for a moment. A terrible moment.

Then—war cries.

The *routiers* erupted in a ferocious response, arousing quickly, ahead of the rest of the host.

Now or never…

John mounted quickly, spurring on his horse, his voice cutting through the chaos.

"To me! Breckington's host, to me!"

Hugh, George, the familiar blue and yellow banners whipping in the wind, began to emerge from their tents, rushing to form a column.

Too slow. Too late.

The *routiers* had already reached the bridge, bloodthirst in their eyes, weapons raised high. The sallying mob—drunk on their brief triumph—broke. Chaos turned to panic as they rushed to fall back back into the city.

The gates of Béziers loomed above them.

John's heart pounded hard as he watched.

A single figure ran ahead of the retreating mass. Young. Red-haired, shrieking.

"Open the gates, now! I command you!"

He seemed familiar. But John had no time to place him. He was important enough to risk the city for, as the men who manned the gates moved quickly. The gates yawned open, barely wide enough for the youth and the first wave of retreating townsfolk to stumble through.

But behind them followed their deaths.

The *routiers* crashed forward, quicker than expected, a relentless tide. John knew the moment before it happened— the second when the defenders hesitated, unsure whether to slam the doors shut or wait for the last stragglers.

A second far too long.

The *routiers* wedged themselves between the wooden doors. Then, like a dam breaking, the gates burst open under the sheer weight of men. A flood of them.

John gripped the reins of his mount, his breath sharp.

No.

The disciplined garrison atop the walls tried to stem the tide. Arrows rained down.

Futile.

The *routiers* were already in. The city, open. Open to slaughter—open to massacre.

"Christ, have mercy," John muttered as he watched, but he knew there would be none.

The world was moving too fast. This wasn't how it was supposed to happen. Not yet. Not like this. He had planned to infiltrate the city under the cover of an ordered assault. He had thought there would be time. Time to find Adelinda. He had thought—

A horn blast.

John's head snapped toward it.

Amalric.

Crimson and white. A vision of righteous fury astride his

warhorse. His voice bellowed over the field.

"Forward! Take the city! Leave none alive who resist!"

"Wait—" John mouthed with futility.

The host surged as if as one. A monstrous, living thing. Knights dug spurs into their mounts. Footmen roared. The *Vexilliferi Crucis*, "Bearers of the Cross," descended like a tide.

John hesitated. Just for a breath. Just long enough to know what he was about to do.

He had no love for Amalric's order, yet he had no choice but to urge his men forward.

Adelinda—her child—

They were in that city. He could still rescue them if he moved fast enough. He could only hope for mercy for the other residents of the city. But mercy was already dead.

What is that smell?

Steel and fire. Blood. Burnt flesh. Smoke had begun to curl into the sky, thick and acrid, clawing at John's throat as he urged his horse forward. The streets of Béziers now convulsed with chaos, violence reigned supreme. Screams clashed with the clang of steel, the guttural cries of the dying swallowed by the infernal roar of a city devoured by war.

"To me! Breckington's men, to me!"

John's voice rang sharp, slicing through the chaotic scene of death and dying.

His banners, blue and yellow, fluttered amid the sea of black, maroon, gray, crimson and white. Soldiers of the host poured through the shattered gates, an unholy tide of presumptive righteousness and plunder.

John wheeled his destrier around, seeking Hugh in the melee.

"Hugh!" His voice snapped like a whip. "Take the levy spearmen and fall in with the host! Maintain your composure—do what you must!"

Hugh's brow furrowed, but he nodded. His hand tightened on his sword.

348

"Aye, my lord." His gaze flickered, searching. "And you?"

John's grip tightened around his reins.

"I'm going after her."

Understanding dawned in Hugh's eyes. He had served John too long not to know the meaning of his words—and his facial expressions. The knight's jaw set, but he gave no argument.

"God go with you."

John turned next to George, his most trusted friend.

"With me, Sir George," he ordered. "We ride for the west quarter—to rescue a lady."

George hesitated only a breath. He already knew what was on his lord's mind.

"Aye, milord!"

He kicked his horse forward, following as John veered from the main thrust of the assault.

Behind them, Hugh led the levy into the fray, their spears locking into formation as they pressed forward alongside the soldiers of the Cross. He would do what was necessary to keep their cover intact, to keep suspicion from falling upon John's absence.

John had no interest in this slaughter—and by this time he could do nothing to halt it. He rode with a singular purpose.

Adelinda.

The city burned around him, plumes of fire licking at the heavens. *Routiers* stormed through the streets, their savage cries of plunder and conquest filling the air. They carved through Béziers like starving wolves, looting, killing, taking all they could before the disciplined knights followed to claim the city in the name of Christ.

John's destrier thundered beneath him, hooves clattering over shattered stone and broken bodies. He cut through a side street, George close behind, their path veering toward the district where he had seen the scarlet cord.

He had to reach her before the *routiers* did.

Before the fire did. Before the madness swallowed everything.

Smoke rolled through the streets like a living thing, thick and choking, curling around the dying as flames licked at shattered doorways. Béziers was breaking, its walls breached, its people screaming. The routiers flooded the city, drunk on slaughter, hacking their way through soldiers and civilians alike. Behind them, the host poured in, no longer a disciplined army, but a storm of blades, fire, and holy fury.

John rode through the carnage, sword in hand, not to kill—but to shield. A woman shrieked as a mercenary dragged her bby the hair from a burning house, his grip tight around her arm, his dagger already halfway to her throat with an intent to take her virtue—before her life.

John spurred his horse forward. One clean swing and the *routier* dropped, lifeless, into the mud.

The woman gasped, stumbling back.

"Run," John ordered, his voice sharp, urgent. He didn't wait to see if she obeyed. He was already searching, already moving.

Another *routier* had cornered a man in a doorway, laughing as he toyed with his victim, letting the poor soul scramble backward, pleading.

George moved first. His sword slashed across the mercenary's back, the blow sending him crumpling forward, dead before he hit the ground.

"We're saving more souls than these damn priests," George muttered, spitting into the dirt.

John said nothing. He didn't have time to argue with the truth. They pressed forward. A child sobbed beneath a collapsed cart, her tiny body barely visible under a sheet of dust. George leapt from his horse, pulling the debris away, scooping her up in his arms.

John's grip tightened on the reins, his gaze sweeping the

350

streets, searching.

Where are you, Adelinda?

His heart pounded as his eyes locked onto a figure—a young boy, barely old enough to hold a sword, standing in the middle of the road, a rusted blade clutched in shaking hands. A *routier* laughed as he stalked toward him, axe raised.

No hesitation.

John spurred his horse, barreling toward them.

The *routier* turned just in time to see the warhorse's massive weight crash into him, the iron-clad hooves slamming his body into the mud.

John dismounted, kneeling beside the trembling boy whose sword now rested in the damp ground, his voice low, steady.

"Go. Find your family. Find a way out of this city."

The boy hesitated, his wide, terrified eyes locking onto John's. Then, with a choked sob, he turned and ran.

George ran up beside him, the rescued girl still clinging to his arm.

"This isn't a battle milord," George muttered, watching as a group of Crusaders kicked down a door, dragging screaming townsfolk into the streets. "This is damnation."

John didn't answer. He already knew. He had known since the moment they crossed into the city.

Then he saw it.

The cord.

Scarlet against the soot-streaked stone, unfurling from a railing above, on the fourth floor, whipping wildly in the wind, made to be visible above the walls.

There.

John inhaled sharply, his hands curling into fists.

George followed his gaze, his expression darkening.

"You think she's still alive?"

"She has to be," John said, his voice barely above a whisper.

George wiped blood from his brow, exhaling hard.

"Then let's find her before this whole city burns to ash."

The two men moved, pushing against the tide of death, cutting through the madness—not to conquer, not to slaughter, but to save.

Penance be *damned*.

::

A crash.

Wood splintering in the distance. Screams. The acrid scent of smoke seeped its way into the small, darkened room where Adelinda clutched Elizabeth, shielding her from the world unraveling beyond their fragile walls.

Another crash. Closer this time.

She tightened her arms around her daughter, whispering soft reassurances even as fear gripped her. The noise outside swelled—shouts of men, the metallic clash of steel, the desperate wailing of those who had not escaped in time.

"Mother," Elizabeth whispered, her voice barely audible over the destruction outside. "Why is this happening?"

Adelinda forced a smile, one that felt brittle, unnatural.

"Sometimes, my love, there are storms we cannot escape. But we will endure. We must."

A muffled crash rocked the street outside. The scent of burning timber thickened.

Elizabeth trembled.

"Will someone help us?"

Adelinda cupped her daughter's face, brushing a stray curl away from her forehead.

"Yes," she whispered, though her voice barely carried conviction. "I believe he will."

She had draped the cord over the wall that evening, fingers trembling as she secured it, praying John would see, praying he would understand.

She had spent hours glancing toward the street, watching

for movement, for any sign that he had noticed. That hope now seemed foolish. Perhaps he had not seen it. Perhaps he was already dead. Perhaps they all would be, soon.

Then—footsteps. Heavy, urgent. Boots on cobblestone.

A pounding at the door.

Elizabeth let out a small cry, burying her face against her mother's chest. Adelinda's breath hitched, every muscle in her body tightening.

Was it them? Had the *routiers* come already? They had already pushed past the defenders at the gates. Nothing could stop them now—save a miracle.

The pounding came again, harder this time.

"Adelinda! Are you there!?"

Her heart stopped. She knew that voice. Elizabeth gasped, lifting her head, hope flickering in her wide eyes.

Adelinda's hands shook as she rose, moving toward the door as if in a trance. Was it truly him? Or had desperation conjured his voice from the chaos?

Another strike against the wood.

"Adelinda! We must hurry!"

It was him.

Her hands fumbled with the latch, throwing it open.

John stood there, sword drawn, his armor streaked with dirt and blood, his hair damp with sweat. His chest rose and fell rapidly through his blue and yellow tunic and chainmail, but his eyes—his eyes locked onto hers, and in them, she saw the truth.

He had come for her.

He came for us!

"Oh John…"

Without a second thought she rushed to embrace him.

"Thank God," he breathed, lowering his sword as he stepped forward. "Are you hurt?"

She shook her head, words failing her. Tears burned her eyes.

"You saw the cord?" she managed to whisper.

353

"I saw it."

He cast a glance over his shoulder, toward the chaos unraveling behind him.

"We don't have much time. Where is your daughter?"

"Here," came a small, trembling voice.

Elizabeth stepped forward from the shadows, her tiny frame barely visible in the dim light. John crouched before her, his expression softening.

"You must be brave now, little one. We're leaving."

Adelinda turned, grabbing the small bag she had prepared earlier, though she had barely dared to believe she would ever use it.

John reached for her hand.

"Stay close to me," he said. "And don't look back."

The streets howled with carnage as they stepped out of the house, the cries of the dying mixing with the roaring flames. Adelinda's heart pounded, her grip on Elizabeth tightening.

But John was ahead of them, a steady, unwavering force.

And he had come.

Against all odds—he had come.

::

He took a long breath. Slow. Heavy.

George de Wymondham stood in the alleyway, hand clenched tight around the hilt of his sword. His pulse quickened as the distant cries of *routiers* echoed through the streets—closer now, the sound of steel on flesh, the frenzied wails of those left behind. The scent of burning timber mixed with the acrid stench of death, curling into his lungs.

Damnations. Lord John. Where are you?

His gaze flickered toward the narrow passage where his liege had vanished, minutes that felt like lifetimes ago. The wooden doors lining the alley creaked open, fearful eyes peering out from slivers of safety. Faces pale with terror.

Whispers. Hope and hesitation.

Then—a shadow. A figure stepping into the dim light.

John emerged, his armor streaked with grime, his eyes hardened with resolve. Beside him, a woman clung tightly to his arm, her auburn hair wild and disheveled, her breath ragged. A young girl pressed to her skirts—small, trembling, wide-eyed.

George exhaled, a breath he hadn't realized he was holding.

"Thank God."

It would be the closest he would come to acknowledging a God.

"You found them," he said, half in relief, half in exasperation.

John nodded, his gaze already scanning the streets.

"We need to move. Now."

Adelinda lifted her head, recognition flickering in her gaze.

"Sir George, is that you?"

Her voice but a whisper, fragile, yet full of meaning.

George gave a small, tired smile in response.

"Aye, my lady. We'll see you and the little one out of this hell."

Then—doors opened fully. The hidden eyes became figures. One by one, residents of the quarter emerged, faces lined with fear, hands clutching the remnants of their lives. Some clung to children, others held nothing at all. They had been waiting. Watching. *Hoping*.

Adelinda turned, her breath catching as she saw them. Friends. Neighbors. The people who had given her a life when she had nothing. The weight of their silent pleas pressed against her chest, crushing, suffocating.

She turned back to John.

"I can't leave them to die," Her voice was steady.

But her eyes—Oh, her eyes were breaking.

John inhaled sharply, fighting the instinct to argue. To

beg her to move.

Instead, he looked past her, to the people who had gathered behind her like shadows, clinging to the last flicker of hope she could offer them. Fifty, maybe more. Huddled together, waiting.

His heart clenched.

Curses.

He should have known. Adelinda would never leave them behind. And he didn't have the heart *to* leave them behind.

George stepped forward, lowering his voice.

"My lord. What are we doing?"

John swallowed hard.

"I don't know, George. I honestly don't know," his voice was raw, stripped bare to the bone. "But we can't just leave them."

There was a long pause. Hearts beating fast. George sighed, pressing his lips into a firm line before nodding.

"Okay," he said quietly. "Okay, milord. Let's get them to safety."

John turned, leading them forward. One step. Then another.

They slipped through the alleyways, the scent of blood growing thicker with every breath. Ahead, a square opened like a wound in the city—bodies littered the ground, the wounded groaning in agony. Civilians fled toward the far end of the city in frantic, desperate streams.

But John's group—they were different. They did not scream. Did not break into a panicked sprint. They moved carefully, deliberately, clinging to one another, some covering children's mouths to stifle whimpers. It was as if they had been preparing for this moment all along.

John gritted his teeth. It wouldn't be enough.

The sound came suddenly—boots against cobblestone, marching in unison.

John turned sharply, his grip tightening on his sword. Not

routiers. Not looters.

At the far end of the street, yellow and blue. A formation of polished steel, spears glinting in the rising sun.

Sir Hugh Philip at the lead.

The Breckington levy.

Relief, like a knife loosening from his ribs. John exhaled. "Finally."

A rush of steel and surcoats. The yellow and blue of Breckington blurred in a wave of bodies, the pounding of boots and rattling of spears swallowing the square in an instant.

John's breath hitched.

Wait—

Hugh's sword was raised, his voice cutting through the din.

"Men of Breckington, charge!"

Curses!

John stepped forward, his hand already flying up before his mind could catch up.

"HALT!"

The shout came like a crack of thunder.

The levy faltered in their steps. Spears wavered mid-air. Their momentum stuttered, feet scuffing against stone as the surge of men hesitated at the familiar sound of their lord's bellowing command. John took another step, arms spread wide, his body a shield between the spearmen and the terrified civilians behind him.

Silence.

The square hung in eerie suspension, as if caught in the final moment before a storm.

"Lord John?" Hugh's voice, sharp with confusion, cut through the stillness. "Are you not in danger?"

John turned to face him.

"No," he said, the weight of the moment pressing against his ribs. "Stand down, Sir Hugh! These people are under my protection."

Hugh advanced, lowering his sword as he broke from the formation, his brow furrowed in wary disbelief as he removed his helm. His voice dropped, but the edge in it remained.

"Under your protection?"

His eyes flicked over the frightened faces behind John.

"My lord, these are the people of Béziers. These are heretics. The enemy. You said you would only rescue her ladyship. The legate—"

"I know what the legate commands." John's tone was as tough as iron. "And I know what my conscience commands."

He stepped forward, his gaze locking onto Hugh's.

"These people are not our enemy."

A murmur spread through the levy like ripples in a disturbed pond. The men exchanged glances, their grips tightening on spears, uncertain. This was not the charge they had been expecting.

"My lord," Hugh said, voice tense, "you know what they say about Béziers. They harbor enemies of the Church. If we don't act, we risk—"

"They harbor neighbors, Hugh." John's voice softened, though the steel remained beneath it. He gestured behind him. "Children. Families."

He pointed toward a young boy clinging to his mother's skirts, his wide eyes darting between the soldiers. An old man trembled on weak legs, a walking stick clutched as if it could protect him from what was coming.

"Tell me, do they look like a threat to you?"

Hugh hesitated. The levy wavered. Some still clutched their weapons with resolve. Others shifted uneasily, looking not at John, but at the people he was shielding.

"Stand down," John said again. Quieter this time. But there was no mistaking the command. "I will take responsibility."

He met Hugh's gaze, the finality of his next words like a

blade sliding into place.

"If the legate wishes to condemn me, so be it."

George stepped forward, his blade lowered but steady. His voice, firm yet measured, carried through the tense square.
"You heard your lord. Stand down, Breckington men! There's no blood to shed here."

Hugh let out a slow, heavy breath, his jaw tightening. His fingers flexed around the hilt of his sword, then relaxed. He turned to the levy, his hesitation evident in the slight delay before he spoke.

"Levy, rest your spears."

The command came reluctantly, his tone laced with an uncertainty that had not been there before. The spearmen obeyed, though their movements were not those of men wholly convinced. Wooden shafts clattered against steel rims, the sound echoing in the uneasy silence.

John felt the tension shift, but not disappear. It lingered, simmering just beneath the surface like embers waiting for the right breath of air to ignite again.

The murmurs came next, quiet at first, but growing, rippling through the ranks.

"Is this why we marched?" A bitter voice. John recognized it as Aldric's. "To stand here and let the townsfolk walk free?"

A younger soldier hushed him.

"Keep your voice down."

"Why? He's got no answer for this," Aldric's grip on his spear tightened, his knuckles pale. "They're sheltering heretics. What's the point of this campaign if we're not going to act *against* heretics?"

A gruffer voice interjected, this one belonging to Osric, a veteran of their ranks.

"Better to let our lord make the call. Lord John's led us through worse. Trust him."

Aldric scoffed, shaking his head.

"Trust him? He's going against the legate's orders. You think Amalric will just let this slide? What happens when we're branded traitors, huh?"

Osric's gaze hardened, his voice a low growl.

"Hold your tongue, boy. You've seen what the *routiers* are doing. You want to be like them? Slaughtering women and children?"

Aldric's mouth shut, but his sullen expression remained.

Another spearman, quieter, thoughtful, spoke next.

"I don't like it either, just look at them," he gestured toward the cowering townsfolk. "That could be my family in there. Yours. You sure you'd want to kill them because some priest said so?"

Another nod. Then another. The doubt was still there, but so was something else—reluctant understanding.

John exhaled, but beside him, Hugh remained still. Silent. Watching the spearmen's shifting expressions.

And then, finally, he approached.

"My lord," Hugh's whisper was quiet, but sharp with meaning. "We came here to save her. That was the plan. Just her."

His gaze flicked toward Adelinda, then back to John. There was no malice in it, but there was hesitation, a lingering battle within him.

John met his stare.

"I know what we came here to save." He swept a hand toward the gathered civilians. "But I also know that we're not murderers."

Hugh's throat worked, his fingers tightening around the pommel of his sword. He glanced back toward the levy, toward the men who followed him, who trusted him, then exhaled slowly.

"Then I hope you have a plan, my lord," he murmured. "Because once the legate hears of this, there'll be no going back. Are you ready for that?"

"I am. If this is what it takes to keep my conscience clean, then so be it. Let Amalric do what he will. I'll not stain my hands with the blood of innocents."

Hugh studied him for a moment, then nodded.

"As you wish, my lord. But we'll need to move quickly. This city won't hold for long."

"I know," John replied, his voice heavy with resolve. He turned to the civilians, his gaze meeting Adelinda's for the briefest of moments.

"Stay close to me. We'll find safety deeper within the city."

He turned to Sir Hugh.

"Hugh, I'm sure you remember Lady Adelinda?" John gestured toward Adelinda, who stood amidst her fellow citizens.

"My lady Adelinda, what a relief to see you," Hugh bowed respectfully as Adelinda reciprocated the greeting.

"We have no more time. Let's get these people to safety outside the city walls," John emphasized the urgency of their situation, the look on his face already seeking swift action.

The firelight flickered across pale faces, hollow with fear. The band of refugees—forty, maybe fifty souls—moved like shadows through the broken streets, their whispers lost beneath the wails of the dying. Women clutched their children, elderly men shuffled forward with slow, deliberate steps. They huddled close to the Breckington levy, the only thing standing between them and the horror that reigned over Béziers.

John rode ahead, his gaze flicking between alleyways, his fingers tight around the reins. The city was a carcass now, picked apart by the merciless scavengers they called allies. The cries of the butchered mixed with the distant clash of steel—a wretched symphony of ruin.

Beside him, Hugh marched, his drawn sword reflecting the firelight in harsh glimmers. The levy formed a tight shield around the civilians, their spears poised like the quills of a threatened beast. They moved steadily, wary of every shadow, of every distant footfall.

Then—movement ahead. A sudden shift in the dark.

John came to a halt.

Routiers spilled from a side street, laughing, dragging spoils from ransacked homes. One clutched a gilded chalice, another an embroidered tapestry stained with blood. They reeked of wine and slaughter.

Then one of them saw them.

He stopped, his grin fading. His beady eyes traveled over the refugees, then flicked toward John, toward the levy's line of shields.

"They've seen us," John muttered. His throat was dry. His fingers tightened around the pommel of his sword.

Hugh barely glanced at him.

"We won't outrun them, my lord." His voice was quiet, grim. "They'll come for the plunder. And for them."

Hugh pointed at the refugees.

John swallowed down the bile rising in his throat.

"Form a shield wall. Quietly. We'll hold them back." He turned to a nearby squire. "Then, find us a clear path to the eastern gate at the far end of the town. We're running out of time if we want to get out of here."

A barked command from Hugh, and the levy snapped into formation. Shields locked together in a bristling wall of wood and steel. The refugees pressed against them, clinging to one another, silent but for the muffled sobs of a child.

The *routiers* were laughing now. Sizing them up. One, a brute with a rusted axe, stepped forward, amusement twisting his filthy face.

Then he lunged.

John spurred forward, his blade flashing. Steel met flesh. The *routier* crumpled to the cobblestones with a wet gurgle, his blood pooling in the cracks of the street.

The laughter stopped.

The *routiers* hesitated—but only for a moment. Then, a surge forward.

362

"They're probing us," Hugh growled, stepping in to meet the next attacker, his sword cutting in a vicious arc.

"Then let's make it clear we're not going down without a fight," John shot back. He swung down from his horse, joining the front line. "Hold this position. Do not pursue. We're not here to fight—we're here to get out."

His mind raced. The alley behind them was a trap waiting to happen. The open street ahead was their only escape, but the *routiers* were multiplying, forming a wall of their own.

"Hugh," John called over the din, cutting down a *routier* who got too close. "We push forward before we're flanked. Take the left column. Clear a path. George and I will hold the center."

Hugh hesitated. His blade dripped with fresh blood, but his eyes—his eyes held something else. Doubt.

"My lord," his voice was low, urgent. "This... this is treason. These men will tell the legate what we've done. Amalric will know."

John wiped sweat from his brow, breath coming hard.

"I know."

"Your penance..."

John exhaled sharply. Then shook his head.

"If this Holy War has any righteousness left," he said, "then let me be judged by it."

Hugh's jaw clenched.

A few paces ahead, the *routiers* had finished their plundering. Bodies lay behind them in the dirt, blood painting the street. At their head stood a familiar figure, clad in black chainmail, a war hammer slung over his shoulder.

Lord Harfleur.

John met his gaze.

The mercenary smiled. Then he raised his weapon. The *routiers* surged forward.

John raised his sword.

"Steady, men! Hold your line!"

The Breckington levy obeyed without hesitation. Shields

locked, spears bristling, their blue and yellow banners hanging motionless in the thick, smoky air. No jeering. No taunts. Just the silent, disciplined poise of trained soldiers— not like the rabble before them.

The *routiers* came to a halt, intimidated by the indomitable wall of blue and yellow before them.

A spit hit the cobblestones.

"English dogs guarding the rats of Béziers," a *routier* sneered, his voice thick with contempt.

Another, lean and wiry with a scar running jagged across his cheek, curled his lip, his Frisian accent thick.

"A levy standing between us and the heretics? Ain't that something. Thought this was a holy war."

Lord Harfleur came forward.

A brute of a man with a war hammer slung lazily over one shoulder, the other hand resting on the pommel of his sword.

"They've gone soft," Harfleur muttered, scanning the levy with eyes like a butcher sizing up a slab of meat. "Might as well be heretics themselves, standing with these rats."

"Then let's kill 'em all," the scarred man said, his fingers flexing around the haft of his axe. "The levy, the townsfolk—doesn't matter. There's coin in it either way."

"They are better armed," another quipped.

"Let's take the risk! There's more of us than them—"

But then—a horn blast.

Deep. Distant at first, then rising, cutting through the clamor of battle like a knife. A shiver ran through the mercenaries as they turned, their sneers faltering at the sight of black and purple banners advancing down the main street.

The Calatravan Order.

And at their head, towering in white, the legate himself. Amalric. His retinue of knights rode behind him, steel gleaming in the firelight.

The *routiers* shifted uneasily.

"That's Amalric," one of them muttered.

"So what?" the scarred man snapped. "He's not here to stop us."

Harfleur exhaled sharply, shaking his head.

"You're a damned fool," he growled. "The levy is one thing. Amalric and his knights? They'll cut us down just for sport. You think they'll let us have our fun while they're watching? You think they care about us?"

The scarred man hesitated, his grip loosening just slightly.

"But the levy—they're protecting those Béziers rats," he argued, though his voice wasn't as steady as before. "That's defying the Church, isn't it? Shouldn't we help the legate take 'em out?"

A low, bitter chuckle escaped Harfleur's lips.

"Help?" he echoed, shaking his head. "Boy, Amalric doesn't need our help. He'll deal with the levy on his own terms. And when he's done, we'll pick over the bones. But we don't cross the Church. And we don't waste our time on trained men when the city's full of easier prey."

Silence. The earlier bloodlust in the *routiers* dimmed, replaced by something colder. Calculated.

A younger mercenary, hands trembling slightly, swallowed hard.

"So… what now?"

Harfleur turned, motioning to the homes lining the street, their doors battered open, their windows shattered.

"Now?" he said, voice low, almost amused. "Now we take what we came for. Let Amalric deal with his problem. We've got plenty of houses to loot. Plenty of soft bellies to cut."

A pause. Then the scarred man laughed, shaking his head.

"Fair enough."

One by one, the *routiers* turned from the levy, slipping back into the burning streets like wolves fading into the dark.

The citizens huddled behind the Breckington levy,

pressed together like sheep cornered by wolves. Their breath came in ragged gasps, their hands clutching at loved ones, at rosaries, at anything that might anchor them in the face of impending doom.

The *routiers* had slunk away, fading into the burning streets to indulge in their own brand of savagery. But the silence they left behind was worse.

A steady rhythm of hooves. A deliberate march of steel-clad boots. The measured, unhurried arrival of those who did not scavenge like wolves but hunted like executioners.

The Holy Warriors. The swords of the Church.

Their banners bore the cross, their armor gleamed even beneath the ashen sky, a stark contrast to the soot-streaked ruin surrounding them. The men of the Count of Nevers rode beside them, their expressions grim, their eyes hollow. Hundreds of them. Pouring into the cramped space.

And at their head—unmoving, impassive, like a statue of divine wrath—was the Abbot Amalric.

John did not move. His fingers hovered over the hilt of his sword, his stance firm, unwavering, lips pursed. The fire in his chest burned hot, but his face remained cold.

Behind him, the refugees murmured in fear, their whispers like the rustling of dry leaves before a storm.

Amalric reined in his horse, his sharp gaze cutting through the smoke and settling on John. Contempt flickered in his eyes, twisting into something resembling triumph. He did not shout. He did not rage. His voice, when it came, was far worse.

"Lord John," he called, slow, deliberate. "What madness is this? Consorting with heretics while under penance?"

The words dripped with scorn. A public rebuke. A warning.

John opened his mouth to speak—but something in Hugh's stance caught his attention.

His vassal had gone rigid, his breath shallow, his fingers flexing over his sword's hilt as if restraining himself from drawing it outright. His gaze was not on Amalric.

It was on a single knight riding among the abbot's retinue.

John followed his stare.

The man was helmetless, his young face visible, the rest of his body under polished mail beneath a white surcoat marked with a crimson cross. His bearing was one of quiet command, his posture exuding the kind of confidence that came not from arrogance, but from certainty. A man utterly convinced that he rode in the will of God Himself.

His gaze locked onto Hugh.

And he smiled.

Not a wide grin. Not a smirk. A mere curl of the lips, a movement so slight it might have gone unnoticed if not for the raw hatred simmering in Hugh's eyes.

John leaned in, his voice low.

"Who is he?"

Hugh's breath came slow, measured, as though he were forcing himself to remain still.

"Peter of Vaux-de-Cernay," he said, barely above a whisper. "The zealot I crossed in Breckington crypt, my lord."

John's grip on his sword tightened.

As if he had heard his name carried on the wind, Peter nudged his horse forward, breaking from Amalric's side with a calculated slowness. The hooves of his mount echoed against the stone, each step deliberate.

He stopped just short of them.

His gaze flicked over John, over the levy, over the huddled civilians behind them. Then back to Hugh.

When he finally spoke, his voice cut through the charred air like the first crack of a splitting tree.

"I see," he said, his tone smooth, even. "The lord of Breckington gathers the foxes, shielding them from the judgment of the Lord."

He tilted his head slightly, his smile never fading.

"How disappointing."

Hugh shifted uncomfortably, struggling to control his emotions.

"Sir Hugh," Peter continued, his tone both mocking and cold, "fancy meeting you here, amidst heretics and cowards. I see your taste for poor company hasn't changed."

"And I see your arrogance remains as bloated as ever, de Cernay."

Peter's smirk deepened.

"Ah, but arrogance is the privilege of those with righteousness on their side. Do you believe, even now, that you stand on the right side of history? Or have you finally come to your senses and joined us in rooting out corruption?"

Hugh's hand hovered near his sword though he remained silent.

Peter's eyes narrowed, his composure slipping for a moment before he turned to address the Abbot Amalric.

"Your Eminence, it seems Sir Hugh and his liege's defiance know no bounds. Even here, they ally themselves with the enemies of the Church."

"You will not insult my lord!" Hugh growled.

Amalric, observing the exchange with faint amusement, raised a hand to quiet Peter before addressing John.

"Lord John, control your man. I will not tolerate insolence in the presence of God's will."

A breath. Shallow. Tense. John's fingers tightened around his sword's hilt. The air, thick with smoke, sweat, and something fouler—fear.

The cries of the dying echoed beyond the walls, fading into the city's ruin.

"My man stands with me," John said, his voice steady, though his heart pounded like a war drum in his chest. "As do the principles of honor and decency."

His eyes swept the huddled mass behind him—women gripping children, old men with hollowed cheeks. *People*.

That's all they were. Not heretics. Not enemies. Just frightened people.

His gaze locked onto Amalric, rigid in his saddle, the crimson cross stark against his white surcoat. The embodiment of divine wrath, or so he believed himself to be. John's breath was steady, but his blood ran hot.

"These are not heretics!" he continued, his voice cutting through the growing hush. "Look for yourself—many wear the Cross of Christ! You call them enemies of God? These are the victims of your war. The garrison is broken. The city is yours. Why does the slaughter persist?"

A silence. Then—a sound that chilled John more than the screams of the dying.

Laughter.

Amalric threw his head back, the sound hollow, grating, void of any warmth. His men did not join him. Even they, clad in the zeal of their cause, did not know what to make of it. The abbot lowered his gaze, eyes gleaming with something dark, something twisted.

"What more do I seek?" he mocked, his lips curling as if the very question amused him. "Righteousness, Lord John."

A long pause. Then Amalric's hand swept toward the trembling crowd.

"They stand in the way of God's justice. Béziers' fate was sealed the moment they chose to protect heretics. Would you defy the will of Heaven for their sake?" He leaned forward, his voice dropping into something almost intimate. "Kill these heretics now, my son. Cleanse your soul."

The weight of the words crashed down on John like a war hammer to the chest.

Kill these heretics.

Cleanse your soul.

John's grip on his sword tightened, his pulse a thunderous rhythm in his ears.

"You demand I kill them, Your Eminence?"

His voice was measured, but inside, rage coiled like a

viper ready to strike. He took a step forward, meeting Amalric's gaze, searching for something—anything—behind those cold, righteous eyes.

"Tell me, then," His voice was as iron. "How shall I discern who is heretic and who is not? Can you see into their hearts? Can you read their souls?"

Amalric's face twisted, his sneer vanishing beneath the weight of his own fury. His nostrils flared. His lips curled. Then his voice thundered, filling every crevice of the broken courtyard.

"Caedite eos. Novit enim Dominus qui sunt eius!"

A breathless hush. The words themselves were as sharp as the sharpest blade. John understood them immediately.

Kill them all. The Lord knows who are His.

The world seemed to hold its breath. A terrifying chill blew right through the courtyard.

John's men stiffened, their hands gripping their weapons, their eyes darting between their lord and the abbot's men, their lives now hanging in the balance. Behind them, the refugees trembled. A child whimpered. A woman choked back a sob. They clung to each other, waiting, praying, knowing.

John exhaled, slow, measured. His horse snorted. A breath before he would respond. He met Amalric's gaze and knew, in that moment, there was no redemption for this war.

There never had been.

Another breath. Shallow. Unsteady.

John took a step forward, planting himself between the abbot's knights and his men who were shielding the huddled mass of civilians. His sword remained sheathed, his hands at his sides, but his voice—his voice cut through the thick, suffocating air.

"No."

A single word. Defiant. Unshakable.

A ripple of disbelief passed through the gathered warriors. The knights of Calatrava stiffened in their saddles.

370

The levymen shifted, uncertain of their fate. The huddled townsfolk behind John dared not even breathe.

Amalric's face twisted with rage, his lips curling into something between a sneer and a snarl. His fingers twitched over the reins, his warhorse stamping impatiently beneath him.

"You will do your duty," he spat. "Kill them, my lord baron! Fulfill your oath, your penance!"

John's voice did not waver.

"No."

The breath that followed carried enormous weight.

"You will be excommunicated," Amalric warned, his voice dripping with contempt. "Think of your men. Their families. Do you wish to see them suffer for your defiance?"

A flicker of hesitation shot through the ranks. The Breckington levy stood firm, shields locked, but John saw it—the shift in their eyes, the silent war waging under their helmets. *Doubt. Fear.* A young spearman stepped forward, Thomas, his shield still gleaming with fresh paint, the crest of Breckington stark against the grime of the city.

"My lord…" his voice was hesitant, almost childlike, "they're heretics, aren't they? The priests told us sparing these heretics is a sin."

A murmur rippled through the ranks. Hands tightened on spears.

John turned to face them, his voice calm, but edged with something deeper.

"They told you sparing heretics is a sin," he repeated, his words deliberate. "Did they tell you to slaughter women and children? Did they tell you to burn families alive in their homes? It is not the Church that carries these swords. It is not the Church that bears the weight of these shields. We do!"

His voice grew stronger, the fire within him rising.

"It is you. Men of Breckington! Men of honor, men of justice! You must choose. How do you know these men truly

371

reflect the will of God? Words matter little. Actions do! Will you strike down the helpless? If such individuals indeed worship the devil, would it not be best to leave them to the hands of God and not our own? Who are we to be the sword of righteousness?!"

The levy stood still, their formation locked, but their conviction wavering.

Thomas swallowed hard. His grip on his spear faltered. He turned, glancing back at the refugees. A woman clutched a child to her chest, shielding the boy with her own body.

"But, my lord…" Thomas' voice cracked. "If we disobey… what happens to us? To our families?"

John stepped closer to him, lowering his voice, steady but unwavering.

"You fear for your families, Thomas. I understand." John breathed deeply. "But ask yourself this—if these were your wives, your children, your parents, hiding in fear, would you want someone to turn their back on them?"

The silence that followed was thick. Even Amalric remained quiet, unsure how he would respond.

The distant screams of the dying still echoed through the city. The fires burned. The *routiers* laughed as they butchered those too slow to flee.

And then—Sir George stepped forward, his voice steady as iron.

"We are Breckington men," His words carried through the street. "We stand for more than plunder and this misplaced zeal. Look at them," He gestured toward the terrified refugees, their eyes hollow with despair. "They are no different from the families waiting for us back home."

A hundred breaths echoed. A decision was to be made.

"If you doubt our lord," George continued, "if you doubt our cause, then leave your shields and walk away. But if you are the men I've fought beside, then stand. Not for the Church. Not for a legate. But for what's right."

The levy stood still.

Then—a sudden shift rippled across the formation.

The murmurs faded. Spears, once wavering, found solid grips. The shield wall tightened. Osric, the scarred veteran, let out a slow breath, then nodded.

"We're with you, my lord," His voice was resolute. "May God help us all."

The blue and yellow banner of Breckington whipped against the smoke-filled sky, a defiant ripple in the storm. A cheer, ragged but resolute and loudly defiant, rose from the levy—shields locked, spears steady. Not a cry of victory, but one of conviction, one of conscience.

"Ha Breck!" Sir George yelled.

"Ha Breck! Ha Breck! Ha Breck!" bellowed the levymen in response, their resounding chants echoing against the crumbling buildings surrounding them.

They had made their choice. There was no turning back now.

From the ranks of the abbot's entourage, Peter of Vaux-de-Cernay leaned toward Amalric, his expression carved with disdain. His voice slithered out, low, poisonous.

"They have damned themselves, Your Eminence," he expressed in a whisper laced with malice. "They will not survive this day."

A cruel smirk tugged at the corners of Amalric's mouth. His gaze, cold and pitiless, swept over John and his men as though already consigning them to the abyss.

"They have indeed chosen their path," he murmured, his tone almost amused. "And it is a path to perdition."

Across the courtyard Hugh Philip exhaled sharply. He had known this moment was coming, had felt it creeping closer with every passing hour. And yet, standing here, hearing Amalric's final judgment, something inside him wavered.

His hand tightened around the hilt of his sword.

"My lord," he said quietly to his liege, his voice laced with warning. "This is a dangerous road you tread. This will mean certain death."

John turned to face him. Their eyes met—resolve against reluctance, iron against hesitation.

"It is dangerous, Hugh," John admitted. "And all death is certain. But if we don't stand and die for the right, we are useless alive."

Hugh did not answer. He brooded over his lord's words but did not step with the levy. Yet neither did he move to Amalric's side. He remained where he was, caught in the balance of duty and conscience, a man suspended between two worlds.

Across the courtyard, another figure observed in silence. Count Nevers, his crimson and white surcoat stark against the shifting tide of men, sat stiffly astride his warhorse. His gaze darted back and forth between the Breckington levy, their disciplined wall of shields, and the dark-clad knights standing rigid beneath Amalric's command. A muscle in his jaw twitched. John noticed.

Doubt.

Nevers nudged his horse forward slowly and deliberately, as if to buy time, the hooves clattering against the blood-streaked cobblestones. When he reached the abbot's side, he leaned in, his voice a murmur barely audible over the distant screams echoing through the city.

"Your Eminence," he said carefully, "I must caution you. The Breckington levy, though defiant, are skilled and disciplined. Losing them could weaken our position. I would advise only anathematizing the leaders."

Amalric did not look at him. His cold, calculating gaze remained fixed on John and his men, his expression unreadable.

"Do not mistake their worth for indispensability, count," he said. "The Church's cause remains strong, with or without these men. Their defiance undermines our authority, and authority must not be questioned."

Nevers hesitated. He studied the levy again, saw the

strength in their stances, the unity in their locked shields. These were no *routiers*, no rabble of the undisciplined. They were soldiers—men who had marched through wars and still stood unbroken. If they were not loyal to the Church, they were loyal to one another, and that made them a force to be reckoned with.

Losing them would be a mistake. Fighting them, even *worse*.

Still, Amalric's voice was like a blade against his hesitation.

"Dissent is a weed, count," the abbot said, his voice sharpened with finality. "And it must be uprooted before it spreads."

A cold certainty settled in Nevers' gut. The abbot would not be swayed. There would be no reasoning with him.

The choice had been made.

"It is time," Amalric said aloud. "Anathema shall be pronounced!"

A signal from the abbot. A raised hand.

John inhaled sharply as Amalric's attendants rushed forward—one bearing a great iron cross, the other a thick, leather-bound missal. Symbols of judgment. Symbols of power.

"May all of you here bear witness," Amalric's voice thundered across the courtyard, rolling like a storm over stone and flesh alike. "It is time to deliver judgment."

Steel rasped against leather as Sir George shifted beside John, sword drawn, shield raised. The levy stood like a wall, their discipline holding fast, but the weight of the moment pressed on them. The refugees huddled closer, trembling, their fate now hanging in the balance.

The air stilled. Even the distant sounds of the city's destruction seemed to fade as Amalric dismounted, his crimson robes pooling at his feet like spilled blood. The blood of the residents of the city could certainly be laid at his feet. He strode forward, his gaze locked onto John, onto the defiant men of Breckington.

"In the name of our Holy Mother Church," the abbot proclaimed, his voice rising in a slow crescendo, "and under the divine authority of His Holiness the Pope, we pronounce anathema upon John de Ontivero, Lord of Breckington, and his men."

A hushed murmur rippled through the ranks of knights and levies alike. Amalric's pronouncement was no idle threat—it was a death sentence for the soul.

"By harboring heretics and defying the Church," Amalric continued, his gaze sweeping over John and his men like a hawk surveying prey, "they have chosen the path of rebellion and damnation."

The iron cross gleamed in the firelight as the attendant raised it high. Amalric's voice was steady, reverent, but his eyes burned with righteous fury.

"These men are cast from the body of Christ," he declared. "They are stripped of all sacraments, barred from communion, and their souls condemned unless they repent."

The heavy missal snapped shut with a resounding thud. A tolling bell, a final knell.

"Anathema sit!"

The Latin words rolled like thunder, final, inescapable.

John did not flinch.

His hand shifted slightly at his side, two fingers curling inward—a sign. Sergeant Owain caught it at once and gave the subtlest nod, his eyes already moving across the courtyard, searching: alleys, angles, gaps between buildings. A narrow lane near the market arch. Two escape routes, possibly three, depending on who moved first. Only marauding *routiers* to worry about. The rest of the host was distracted with the bulk of the fleeing residents attempting to crowd into the church on the far eastern end of the large courtyard.

Beside John, Sir George adjusted the grip on his shield— not in fear, but readiness. His gaze met his lord's for a heartbeat. No words needed. The levy would hold, but they would not die without strategy—a chance for them to escape—or to fight their way out in the chaos.

They knew Amalric had no full command of the crusader host. At least not yet. But here—now—he controlled enough to strike. Nevers' men. The Calatravan knights. Enough to make it brutal, enough to make it challenging.

And so they prepared. Quietly. Calmly. The message being passed along the shield wall with subtle taps, just as they were trained. As they had used in combat in the Outremer. Like soldiers who had once stood before death before and found it wanting.

Observing John, the Count of Nevers cleared his throat. He knew that he would have a fight on his hands, even if he had almost three times the number of men as his opponent. Amalric turned to him, a measured smile on his lips.

"You have always been a stalwart servant of the Church, my lord count, but I sense unease," Amalric paused with a calculated glare. "Surely, you do not question the Church's will?"

Nevers swallowed, his jaw tightening.

"Your Eminence, I do not question the Church," he said carefully, "but the sight of our swords turned against our own men—"

"Is the will of God," Amalric cut in sharply, "and they are no longer *our* men. They are now *heretici*. If Lord John's defiance is not crushed here, what message does that send? That heretics may defy God's will without consequence?"

Nevers hesitated even longer. He was buying John and his men as much time as he could give them.

Amalric's expression darkened.

"If you will not lead your men, I will just name another to do so."

Silence. A glance. The unspoken threat of the glare. It could even make kings grovel and beg.

"And you may join Lord Breckington in anathema."

377

The count stiffened, his face contorted with horror. Then, slowly, reluctantly, he bowed.

"No, Your Eminence. I will lead."

A thin, satisfied smile touched Amalric's lips.

"Good," he murmured. "Then let us proceed."

His eyes flicked back to John, dark with certainty.

"Remember, my Lord Count: there is no mercy for heretics. And none for those who harbor them."

As Nevers turned to rally his men, Peter of Vaux-de-Cernay drew near the abbot, his calculating gaze fixed on now excommunicated men.

"Your Eminence," he murmured, "if this act of defiance were left out of my account—if the Englishmen's rebellion were erased from the record—could we not salvage their reputation for the sake of the Holy Army's unity?"

Amalric's lips curved into a faint, sardonic smile.

"Ah, Peter, I had almost forgotten that you are my chronicler. You think like a man who sees history as a ledger to be balanced."

The abbot leaned forward slightly, his voice dropping to a conspiratorial tone.

"You will write of this campaign," he said, his voice lowering to a measured, deliberate cadence. "You will glorify our triumphs. You will sanctify our cause. You will ensure that history remembers righteousness—not hesitation."

Peter gave a slow nod, though the weight of the words settled like cold iron on his chest.

"Of course, Your Eminence," he paused, a flicker of uncertainty cut across his face. "But this… this incident—how shall I write of it?"

The smile vanished from Amalric's lips. His eyes, dark as flint, bore into Peter's soul.

"You will not write of it."

The words hung between them, final as if they were a death sentence.

"The Breckington incident is a blemish. A disgrace. It will be forgotten, erased like dust from stone," Amalric continued, his voice sharpening. "Their defiance will die here, in the dirt, beside their heretic friends. And history—" he let the word settle, shaping it like a weapon, "—will remember only the triumph of the Lord in Béziers, the will of God made manifest through fire and steel."

Peter's fingers tightened on the reins. His throat felt dry with worry.

"And if others speak of it?"

A bated breath. Then after a beat—Amalric's gaze turned colder still.

"Then we must ensure all witnesses will know the cost of defying the Church, and none will speak of this in the wrong light."

Peter hesitated. Even he was stunned by the coldness. He paused for a heartbeat too long. He could feel Amalric watching, waiting.

"I understand, Your Eminence."

A curt nod, then nothing more. Peter reined his horse back, gaze flickering to the men of Breckington, standing like a rock against the coming tide. It was not defiance on their faces, not even pride. It was something heavier—*conviction*. For all his loathing of the Englishmen who ended the life of his cousin, Amalric's cold-blooded demeanor was a bit too far—even for him.

But he did not dwell on it. He would do as he was told. He always had.

Amalric straightened in his saddle, turning his attention again toward the Count of Nevers. The count lingered on the edge of the courtyard, his warhorse shifting beneath him, his grip on his sword not yet certain as he passed orders down the line.

"Summon the count," Amalric ordered. "He continues to hesitate, and I will not tolerate hesitation."

Peter, with a wordless nod, turned his horse and rode

toward Nevers.

John watched from afar. Watched as his friend, the count, nod his head somberly. Cowed to obedience, perhaps, with the legate seeing through his efforts to delay. The count reluctantly reined his mount around to follow Peter back to the abbot's side.

With the Count of Nevers now beside him, Amalric raised his hand again. This time, it was a signal to spill blood. The ground trembled as the *Bellatores Christi* advanced slowly and cautiously toward John and his men.

The men of Breckington, outnumbered yet determined, stood unmoving, their blue and yellow banners rippling in the smoke-choked air. Their lord dismounted to join the line.

John turned his head, voice steady.

"Steady men. Hold the line."

His men did not flinch.

"We stand not as zealots," he called out loud, "but as men of honor."

Spears bristled. Shields locked. The levy stood firm, their discipline a stark contrast to the chaos that reigned in the city beyond. This was what they were trained and drilled for.

The men of Nevers advanced—their march was slow, hesitant.

Their boots shuffled against the cobblestone, their approach slowing, not out of cowardice, but uncertainty. A clash of duty against conscience. Perhaps a hope that they would not have to shed the blood of their erstwhile comrades. The orders had been given, but the sight before them—the disciplined Englishmen standing in formation, not against them, but in defense of the helpless—gave them pause.

A few paces more, then a near halt.

The count himself reined in his horse, eyes narrowing as they locked with John's.

A test. One final moment. Would Nevers truly attack?

And as the banners of Breckington fluttered defiantly in

the wind, the answer was yet unclear.

The banners of Nevers rippled, crimson and white against the choking sky.

John stood unmoving, a statue behind the bristling wall of blue and yellow shields. His grip tightened on the hilt of his sword, sweat slick beneath his armor. Across from him, past the poised spears of his levy, the count lingered in indecision, his horse shifting uneasily beneath him.

John called out from behind his shield wall, voice steady but urgent.

"My Lord Count, do not do this. We do not have to kill each other."

Nevers hesitated once more. His men advanced a step, their formation wavering—not from fear, but uncertainty.

John tried again.

"What are your intentions, my Lord Count?"

A long pause. Then, finally, Nevers replied, his voice carrying across the courtyard.

"To obey my orders, young baron! You still have the chance to do the same. Turn on the heretics and be spared!"

The legate leaned forward, a subtle movement, but his presence pressed against the space like a vice. His voice, cool and smooth, slithered into the silence.

"My Lord Count, I continue to sense hesitation! You are an experienced commander. Surely, you know the consequences of delaying! Attack, now!"

As if rehearsed for intimidation effect, the Calatravan knights by Amalric's side drew their swords in unison, the glint of steel catching the flickering light of the burning city. The black and purple of their capes snapped in the wind, the pall of death floating in the air.

Nevers stiffened. Then, with the weight of inevitability pressing upon him, giving him no choice, he nodded.

"As you command, Your Eminence."

A smile curled at the corner of Amalric's lips, a predator tasting victory.

"Good," he said. "Let it be known this day that the Church tolerates no disobedience. *Deus vult*."

The words settled like iron shackles. A final sentence.

Taking as much time as he possibly could and with a heavy breath, the Count of Nevers drew his sword. The men in red and white stepped forward, methodical, measured—unyielding against the defiant wall of Breckington steel.

"I'm sorry, my friends," Nevers murmured, his voice barely discernable above a whisper. "I serve His Holiness."

He spurred his horse to a trot, not leading from the front, but commanding from behind—shielding himself from what had to be done. Then, from the shadows of the advancing line, the Calatravan knights descended from the flanks.

Leading the Iberian knights on the flanks were Nuñez and Lopez—battle-hardened, relentless, zealous, their movements precise, their approach inevitable. Their measured steps swallowed the remaining distance.

The courtyard grew smaller and smaller.

John exhaled, steadying himself, his hand resting on his sword, his heartbeat like a drum against his ribs. He was ready. His men were ready. He could feel Hugh beside him—still, silent, caught in the valley of decision.

John turned his head slightly, just enough for their eyes to meet. A question unspoken.

Hugh swallowed. Shaken by the excommunication, his stance wavered briefly. He had been a devout believer; it had molded him—defined him, even. Now, it had all been shattered. He had to chose between his Breckington, his lord, and the Church. The moment stretched thin. The enemy would be in striking distance within seconds.

The end was coming—within the city, within the courtyard, within their very souls. And Hugh Philip, Knight of Breckington had only moments to decide who he truly was.

The banners of Nevers and Calatrava fluttered closer, white, red, black and purple against the blood-drenched city.

John steadied his breath. The men of Breckington flanked him, shields tight, spears braced. They had faced Saracens, mercenaries, rampaging mobs. But this? This was different. The knights of the Holy War. The zealots. The executioners of God's will.

Nuñez removed his helmet, the air thick with the scent of smoke and blood. Scarred, battle-worn, his gaze was a dagger. Sharp. Cutting.

"*Señor* John," he called out, calm, deliberate, every word a strike. "At Citeaux, you spoke of redemption. And now? You throw it away for this?"

John said nothing. He could feel George beside him, unwavering. Hugh, still caught in his own war, a war deeper than swords.

Lopez, the taller one, the colder one, stepped forward. A wolf's grin played on his lips.

"You've damned yourself, *señor*. Not only yourself—your men, too. We fight to defend Christendom, and now you stand with those who spit on the Cross."

John exhaled slowly.

"These people are not heretics, Lopez," his voice loud and steady, but inside, a storm. "You cannot condemn an entire city without knowing who stands before you. Is this what the Church has become—an instrument of blind slaughter?"

Nuñez's expression darkened, the weight of his armor making his stance heavier.

"Innocence?" A humorless chuckle. "Innocence has no place here. Amalric has spoken. The Lord's will is clear."

Lopez smirked, resting a gloved hand on his sword's pommel.

"And what will your defiance achieve?" A tilt of the head, mockery spilled out in every syllable. "Redemption was within your grasp. Now you'll die a traitor, cast out of the Church's grace. All for the sake of these…"

The Iberian gestured toward the huddled refugees as he

advanced.

John didn't flinch.

"If that is the cost of doing what is right," his voice like steel, ringing out from behind a wall of steel, "then so be it."

Nuñez sneered.

"So be it, then."

A slight turn by the Iberian. A subtle motion. Swords scraped from scabbards. Judgment was coming.

Shields locked. Spears braced.

The blue and yellow wall of Breckington continued to stand firm against the tide of red and white surging toward them.

"Ha Breck! Ha Breck!" the levy chanted.

John exhaled, steadying his grip on his sword. He could feel the weight of every breath, every heartbeat, every life behind him. The levy tightened their ranks, the thunder of boots drawing closer, the battle cries of the Count's men colliding with the smoke-thick air.

"Deus vult!"

A chorus of voices, swelling with zeal. The enemy increased their strides. A sudden sprint of hundreds of men.

"Deus lo vult! Deus lo vult!"

Then—impact.

The first wave of Nevers' men crashed into the shield wall, the sound of iron against iron ringing through the courtyard. The outnumbered Breckington line held, absorbing the momentum, their formation shuddering but unbroken. Spears thrust forward, finding gaps in chainmail. A knight in white and red staggered back, blood spilling from his side. The Englishmen's experience, discipline and training now

John parried a strike, deflecting the blade away from his shoulder before driving his own sword into the man's unguarded thigh. A cry of pain. A collapse. Another came at him. He stepped back, countered, steel scraping against steel, sparks flashing in the dim light.

"Hold!" George bellowed, his voice raw. "Hold, damn you!"

The levy gritted their teeth, shields pressed tight, the weight of the charge bearing down upon them. They did not break.

James Nugent and Peter Marshall flanked the refugees, squires with well-tempered armor and training. Behind them, Adelinda clutched Elizabeth close, her pulse thrumming raw in her ears. The other civilians huddled together, watching with wide, terrified eyes. A boy no older than ten whispered a prayer, his hands trembling.

She could not look away.

The line faltered. A breach opened.

The Count's men surged forward, pressing into the gap, their swords flashing. A spearman fell, his shield slipping from his grasp. Another staggered back, a wound splitting across his shoulder. The wall bent, strained.

Then—a war cry.

Hugh.

He barreled into the fray, his sword a blur, his shield a battering ram.

A Calatravan knight lunged at him. Hugh met him with a brutal downward strike, sending him sprawling. Another came, but Hugh did not hesitate. His blade found its mark. Blood splattered against his blue and yellow surcoat.

The Breckington men roared, their spirits rekindled at the sight of their champion fighting alongside them. The line straightened, morale surged, shields pressing forward, boots digging into the cobblestone.

"For Breckington!" Hugh's voice boomed.

"For our lord!" the men echoed. *"Ha Breck, ha Breck!"*

The attack slowed as the defenders stiffened their resistance. The advance stalled.

John stole a glance at Hugh, meeting his gaze through the clash of bodies.

A nod.

385

Hugh had made his final choice. To stand with his men—with his lord.

The levy held. Their flanks protected by burning buildings, ash spewing into the sky. The Breckington line stood firm, but they were outnumbered and the weight pressing against them was relentless. The alley choked with bodies—steel-clad knights, spearmen, mercenaries, desperate townsfolk clinging to life. John felt the tremor in his men, the slow, insidious creep of fatigue setting in. Their breaths came ragged, their grips stiff with strain.

A crash. A cry. A shield wavered, then steadied.

Adelinda crouched low, shielding Elizabeth with her arms. The civilians pressed against the walls, clutching one another, whispering prayers that would never be heard over the roar of battle.

The flames. The smoke. The city coming undone.

Where was de Servian? Were all the defenders of the town vanquished?

She gritted her teeth, searching the ruins for any sign of the garrison's commander. There was nothing. Just bodies and burning timbers. The city was lost.

"Mother…" A small voice, barely audible over the clamor.

Elizabeth.

Adelinda turned, eyes locking with her daughter's, her fingers tightening around the child's trembling hands. The question in Elizabeth's gaze was one Adelinda had no answer for.

Are we going to die?

Adelinda forced a smile. Hollow, fragile.

"No, my love. We will make it out. I promise."

A promise made in the midst of fire and blood. A promise she wasn't sure she could keep.

Ahead, the clash of steel. Sir Hugh's sword flashed as he shoved another knight back using the momentum of his large frame, the sound of armor meeting stone ringing out like a hammer on an anvil.

"We can't hold much longer!" George called out, his shield splintered, his breath labored.

John knew it too. The levy had fought beyond expectation, beyond exhaustion. But the men of Nevers were too many, the Calatravans too relentless. The line would break. *Soon.*

The refugees behind them had nowhere to go.

John tightened his grip on his sword, his mind racing. There had to be a way. A path. An opening.

Then—movement. A blur of red and white cutting through the smoke.

John's heart clenched. The Count of Nevers.

The nobleman was now dismounted, his sword raised high, his men rallying to his side as he pushed forward through the bodies. His face was grim, his pace determined.

John knew what this meant. The final push.

The levy braced, breaths held.

Adelinda closed her eyes, whispering words Elizabeth could not hear.

The echoes of Father Armand's voice swirled in her mind.

"The tunnels beneath the council hall—they are your last recourse. If the time comes, you will know what to do."

The time had come.

Adelinda's grip tightened around Elizabeth's trembling hand. Smoke burned in her throat, screams rang in her ears, but she forced her way through the huddled civilians, her voice cutting through the fear.

"Stay close! Keep your heads low! Follow the soldiers and do not scatter!"

Faces turned to her—hollow, desperate, clinging to her words like they were the last solid thing in a collapsing world. She pressed forward, pushing through the frightened masses until she reached John.

Blood smeared his armor, his sword raised as he barked

orders to the levy. He stood at the breaking edge of the chaos, the only thing holding back the tide. His eyes, sharp and battle-hardened, softened when they met hers.

"There's a way out," she said, her voice low but urgent. "The council hall. There are tunnels beneath it. We can get the civilians out."

His jaw clenched, his mind turning.

"Are you certain?"

"Yes. We don't have time to hesitate. The enemy will break through soon."

John glanced toward Hugh, who was locked in vicious combat with another advancing knight. A quick movement—John tapping Hugh's shoulder. A moment's hesitation, then Hugh slashed his opponent aside, stepped back, and turned toward them.

"Get them moving," John ordered, his breath heavy. He looked at Adelinda again, his voice quieter. "Lead them. We'll cover the rear."

She nodded, swallowing the knot of fear rising in her throat. Then she turned to the refugees, her voice clear and commanding.

"This way! Keep moving!"

A ripple of movement, then a cluster of survivors following her through the narrow alley. Footsteps, hurried whispers, the rustling of skirts and boots over stone. She glanced back only once.

John stood with Hugh and George at the head of the levy, shields locked, spears braced. The enemy soldiers were reforming, their red and white banners shifting in the smoke-filled air, their knights wheeling around for another charge.

Hugh met John's gaze. A quick nod.

"We can't hold much longer."

"We're not supposed to be holding for long," John said. "We're just buying time."

Without hesitation, Hugh turned back to the men, his voice raw from battle.

"Hold the line! Stand your ground!"

The second wave came swift and brutal, the men of Nevers slamming into the English shields, the air thick with the grunts of struggling men and the shriek of metal against metal. The Breckington levy buckled, but they did not break. Not yet.

Adelinda reached the last of the civilians, ushering them into the alleyway. Just before stepping inside, she turned—just for a moment.

John's eyes met hers. No words, only understanding. A silent promise. He would be right behind.

Then she disappeared into the dark.

The city burned. Smoke choked the streets, twisting the familiar into something monstrous. Flames danced against stone walls, throwing jagged shadows over the cobblestones slick with blood. Adelinda pressed forward, her grip on Elizabeth never faltering. James Nugent and Peter Marshall were by her side, their swords at the ready to protect her. The council hall was close—just a little further, just a little longer.

Behind her, the cries of the wounded blurred into the clash of steel, the roar of fire, the wails of the dying.

John's voice rang out over the din.

"Hold the line! Just a little longer!"

The Breckington levy stood, battered but unbroken. Shields locked, spears braced, blue and yellow defiant against the crimson tide. Each step back was earned with blood. John caught the flicker of movement at the edge of his vision—one of his men crumbling to the ground, a sword buried in his gut. Another stepped forward to fill the gap before the shield wall could buckle.

Too many dead. Too many lost.

John's pulse hammered. The formation would give way soon; they had to move. He turned to Hugh, their gazes meeting through the smoke.

A brief lull—only seconds, but enough.

"Hugh! George! Spread the word! Follow the refugees to the council hall—controlled retreat! Shields up, protect the civilians!"

The order passed down the line, voices hoarse, weapons slick with sweat and blood. The Breckington men tightened their formation, stepping back in measured strides, keeping the huddled refugees behind them.

Then—

Screaming from the other edge of the courtyard.

John's head snapped toward the adjacent far corner of the courtyard where the church of St. Mary Magdalene stood, shrouded with smoke and dust. Its great wooden doors shuddered under the force of spears.

He saw him.

Amalric.

The papal legate sat motionless atop his warhorse, bathed in firelight and ash, his eyes burning with self-righteous fury as he focused on a large group of townsfolk retreating into the sanctuary. At his side, Peter of Vaux-de-Cernay was seen to be murmuring something to him, his gaze fixed on the scene like a scholar observing a lesson.

A local Occitan priest stumbled from the church steps, blood trailing from a wound on his temple. He held up a heavy crucifix, its gold gleaming in the fire's glow.

"Your Eminence, stop this madness! We are no heretics!" His voice cracked with desperation. "In the name of Christ, I beg you—spare us, spare the innocent!"

Amalric tilted his head. Slowly, deliberately, he exhaled.

"Mercy," he murmured. A sneer curled his lips. "Mercy is for the repentant, not the damned."

He flicked his fingers. The knight beside him spurred his horse forward. The priest never had a chance.

The spear drove through his chest with sickening ease, lifting him from the ground before he slid off like a discarded sack of grain. The crucifix tumbled from his grasp, landing in the dirt beside him.

John watched, clenching his fists.

Something inside him twisted, dark and violent, and for the first time, he wanted to drive his sword straight through the legate's black heart. Had he a bow and an arrow, he would have tried to make the shot.

The church doors splintered open.

A flood of Hospitaller knights surged inside, their black tunics and white crosses swallowed by the shadows within, their swords hacking indiscriminately without mercy.

"Holy Mother, no!"

The scream cut through everything. John turned sharply. A woman knelt in the threshold, her arms wrapped tightly around a young boy. A mother shielding her child.

Steel flashed.

John watched helplessly from a distance—as blood poured like a fountain, the crimson tide spilled down the church steps, a grotesque mockery of the vows these knights had once taken: *to protect the poor, the sick, and the oppressed.*

John gritted his teeth, as his hand tightened around the hilt of his sword. These were the men he had once admired— warriors of righteousness who had once inspired his youth, men of supposed honor and valor. Men who he had fought alongside of in the Levant, men who stood beside his father when he fell at Arsuf. Now they stood as butchers bathed in the blood of innocents, their holy vows abandoned and meaningless.

"Fall back! Keep the formation tight!" John's voice rang through the choking haze of smoke and blood, urgent, commanding.

The Breckington levy, bruised and bloodied, moved as one, their shields interlocked in a defiant wall of blue and yellow. Each step was measured, deliberate, but slow. Too slow.

John's grip tightened on his sword as he turned toward Hugh.

His vassal's eyes flickered between the carnage at the church and the desperate retreat, his arm pointing to the massacre unfolding at the church.

"My lord, what of—"

"There's nothing we can do," John bit out, the words tasting like bitter bile. "But we can still save the people who are with us."

Hugh swallowed hard. He nodded. No more words. Just grim determination to survive. The levy retreated slowly, their movements sharp despite exhaustion.

Shrieks of terror tore through the air, echoing from the distance.

John took one more glance. The church was a site of mass slaughter.

St. Mary Magdalene, once a sanctuary, was now a tomb. The doors gaped open like the maw of some hungry beast, vomiting out bodies, spilling blood down its steps. The broken altar, the fallen crucifix, the unseeing eyes of the slaughtered—John forced himself to turn away.

The taste of ash filled his mouth. This was no Holy War. No divine conquest. This was simple butchery. And they were next. A clash of steel. A cry of agony as another wave of attackers descended upon them.

The line wavered.

Nine of his men killed. Many more wounded. Some barely standing. Their once-proud formation buckled under the relentless hammering of Nevers' men and the surgical strikes of the Calatravan knights.

John raised his sword, rallying what remained of his men. They were running out of time. The screams around the church faded, smothered beneath the weight of the dead.

A graveyard in the streets.

Hundreds. Thousands. Maybe more. The cobblestone buried beneath them, lost under torn bodies and pooling blood.

The slaughter at the church was done. Now, it was their

turn to be annihilated. The Hospitallers would now join the assault against them.

Amalric sat atop his white steed, now stained crimson, his robes drenched in the blood of the townspeople. A butcher in the guise of a holy man. He returned his gaze toward the retreating Breckington men, and even from a distance, John could see it in his eyes—this was always about slaughter. Never about salvation.

This was about erasing Béziers. And more. Cleansing the Languedoc. Every soul. Every stone. A whole people, erased from the face of the earth.

"They will focus their full fury on us now," Hugh's voice was steady, but his grip on his sword was tight, blood dripping from its edge onto the already-soaked ground. "We won't last much longer in the open."

"The council hall," John said, his voice sharp, cutting through the din of dying screams. "It's defensible. Adelinda says there are tunnels beneath it. If we hold them off long enough, we can get the civilians—and our men—to safety."

Hugh frowned.

"They'll try to flank and surround us before we reach it."

John's jaw tightened.

"Then we use the alleyways. Funnel them tighter. Make them pay for every step."

He turned to his men, raising his voice over the carnage.

"Men of Breckington! Form ranks! Hold the line as we fall back! We use the alleyways!"

The response came not in words, but in action.

A deep, resounding grunt rippled down the line, a chorus of discipline forged in years of training. Shields locked together, a wall of steel and oak bracing against the inevitable onslaught. The levy moved as one, each step backward deliberate, boots grinding against the slick cobblestones, their ranks an unbroken mass of blue and yellow.

Even as the war cries of the host rose like a storm, John's

men held.

Amalric grinned.

A wolf about to sink its teeth into its cornered prey.

And then, the *Milites Christi* surged forward again. An overwhelming tide of zealots, knights, and footmen, their voices a deafening roar.

John's heart pounded as another impact came.

The third wave crashed against the shield wall, spears thrusting, swords battering against wood and steel. The Breckington line buckled but held, absorbing the assault with precise movements, their own spears stabbing out in disciplined counterattacks.

The levy stepped back, inch by inch, a dozen paces at a time.

Another charge. Another impact.

More bodies fell, many of the enemy, some of their own. But the Englishmen did not break.

John gritted his teeth, forcing another step back.

The next alley was close. Narrower, a defensible bottleneck. If they could reach it, they could further narrow the front, force the enemy into a choke point. And it led to the Council Hall looming above the smoke behind them.

Just a little further.

Another wave came. Harder. More men. Hospitaller lending their combat experience and discipline to the assault. The line trembled. They were being drained of their energy slowly, but surely.

John roared, his sword slashing through an attacker who had forced his way through. Hugh was there, cutting down another before he could reach the civilians.

The levy fell back. Step by step.

And then, finally—they found the mouth of the alley.

John's voice rang out over the fray.

"Fall back into the alley! Tighten the line! Hold them here!"

The men obeyed without hesitation, their formation

shifting, their movements honed through years of training. The walls on either side became their shield, the narrow passage nullifying the enemy's advantage in numbers.

The *Milites Christi* hesitated. For the first time, Amalric's forces faltered. They had expected to break the levy in the open.

But now, they had to bleed for every step, funneled as they would be into a tight space.

Smoke clung to the air, thick with the scent of charred wood and blood. The streets of Béziers, once bustling with life, were now a battlefield of fire and ruin. The men of Breckington enjoying a brief respite as the enemy contemplated their next move.

John's breath was ragged as he retreated backward into the alleyway, turning his gaze briefly toward the council hall, its towering stone frame barely visible through the haze. Their sanctuary. Their last stand.

A movement in the distance caught his eye—Amalric and Nevers, deep in hushed discussion. A rider peeled away from them, galloping across the courtyard toward the Calatravan's flank. John's gut tightened.

"They're moving to cut us off," Hugh muttered, gripping his sword, his gaze following the departing horseman. "They'll try to flank us from behind."

John's jaw clenched.

"We take the hall now. No more hesitation," he turned to Hugh, urgency burning in his voice. "Lead the vanguard—clear the entrance!"

Hugh nodded, already in motion.

"George," John called, wheeling to his other side. "Hold the rear! Nevers' men are coming, and we need every second you can give us. I'm going to join Hugh in clearing out the council hall!"

"Faith and Honor!" responded the vassal.

The knights' voices rose as one, their response resolute.

Hugh wasted no time. Twenty men, half of them the

Blitheful squires, surged forward in his wake, cutting a bloody path toward the looming council hall. Behind them, the civilians stumbled after Adelinda, their terror evident in their wild, darting eyes.

"Stay close! Don't look back!" Adelinda urged, her hands guiding those too weak to move quickly. Yet, her own gaze turned for a brief moment behind her, her heart hammering at the sight of the Breckington rearguard bracing for another inevitable charge.

A terrible cost, she thought.

John stayed just behind Hugh's vanguard, his eyes locking onto the heavy wooden doors ahead. So close.

Then—laughter.

Low. Guttural. Crawling out from the council hall like something rotten.

John's stomach twisted.

"*Routiers*," Hugh spat, his voice dark with loathing.

Inside, firelight flickered against the stone walls. Brigands, already within. Their jeering voices filled the chamber, crude jokes laced with the sounds of ransacking. In the corner, huddled shapes—townsfolk, alive but trapped.

John's grip tightened around his sword.

"Breckington vanguard, with me!" His roar cut through the chaos, and the levy stormed forward.

The *routiers* barely had time to react before the blue and yellow shields smashed through the doors, a tidal wave of steel and fury.

The fight was brutal.

The brigands, drunk on slaughter, swung wildly, their weapons glinting in the firelight. But they had no formation, no discipline. The Breckington men struck hard and fast, spears finding gaps in leather armor, swords cutting through makeshift defenses.

Hugh's blade was the first to draw blood, cleaving through a brigand's chest with practiced precision. Another man lunged at him—a mistake. Hugh caught him with his shoulder, sending the wretch sprawling onto the blood-slick floor.

"Push them out!" Hugh bellowed.

The *routiers*, realizing their advantage had turned to doom, scrambled for the exits. Some tried to fight, but the levy cut them down where they stood. Those who fled vanished into the streets, their howls of anger fading beneath the din of battle outside.

Silence fell.

The town hall lay in ruins—wood splintered, frames shattered, blood pooling across the floor. Smoke curled from the collapsed section in the corner. But there, among the bodies, five survivors. Wide-eyed, trembling, but alive.

Then—shouts.

"Make way! Make way!"

Down the alley, George and the rearguard were coming, the last civilians in tow. Behind them, a storm of crimson and white surged, the Calatravans and Hospitallers leading the charge.

"Let them through!" John bellowed.

The last of the refugees stumbled inside. The final line of Breckington men followed, George among them, bloodied but still standing. The enemy soldiers were seconds behind.

"Block the entrances!" John ordered.

Reggeye and Bobbeye slammed into position first, their shields locking against the splintering doorframe. The other squires followed suit, their bodies forming a desperate barricade as the first hammering blows struck from outside.

The hall was theirs.

Wood scraped against stone. The heavy thud of benches and shattered beams thrown into place. The refugees assisted in gathering debris to pile at the entrances and open windows. The council hall transformed into a fortress, its defenders moving with frantic precision.

Sir George reinforced the windows, his shield braced against the wooden shutters as arrows thudded against them, thcir shafts quivering. The doors groaned under the assault of Calatravans, Hospitallers and the men of Nevers, the hammering clash of steel on oak reverberating through the chamber.

They couldn't hold forever.

John's gaze swept the room, his men bloodied but standing, their breath ragged, their shields splintered yet still raised. They had fought harder, longer than any had the right to expect—but resolve alone would not save them.

"Adelinda!" His voice cut through the din. "We need a way out. Now!"

Adelinda, her hands trembling but her mind sharp, turned to the refugees.

"Find it!" she ordered, her voice steady despite the fear curling in her chest. "There's an entrance—there has to be!"

She moved with purpose, eyes scanning the room, fingers trailing along the stone walls. This place held centuries of secrets. Somewhere beneath them, a passage lay waiting. Father Armand had reminded her. But her memory failed her now, the weight of the events suffocating.

We don't have time.

John turned to Hugh, his voice low but firm.

"We hold this hall until she finds it. If they breach—"

Hugh wiped blood from his brow, nodding grimly.

"We make our stand."

John nodded back. No words left to be said. The hacking at the barricades grew louder. The barricades shook. The enemy was relentless, hacking with all strength.

"Search behind every piece of furniture!" Adelinda barked, urgency snapping through her voice.

Civilians scrambled, pushing over tables, pulling at torn tapestries, running their hands over the stone. Dust choked the air, kicked up by desperate hands and shifting debris.

Nothing.

Adelinda clenched her fists. Her pulse pounded in her ears. The weight of every life in this hall pressed against her like a vice.

The battle outside was inching closer, steel meeting wood, voices rising in rage and frustration. The doors of the great hall bottlenecked the attackers, nullifying their superior numbers as the defenders strained with their might to hold the enemy at bay.

But they couldn't hold forever. She had to move faster.

Past broken chairs, over splintered wood. Her breath came in quick, panicked bursts. The walls blurred.

They had a way out. But could they reach it before the barricades gave way?

Smoke. Soot. Sweat. The air was thick with it, pressing down like a weight on the lungs. The acrid sting of burning timber clung to the back of Adelinda's throat as she moved, her hands raw from clawing at the cold, unyielding stone. Elizabeth's small fingers gripped the hem of her dress, her breaths shallow but silent.

She could feel the child's heart pounding against her own, quick and frightened, as though it might burst free from her ribs. The din outside intensified—the crashes, the war cries, the relentless pounding of the battering ram—and made every moment stretch into eternity. They had to find it. The tunnel. The way out. The *last* hope.

Her voice was hoarse, but she forced it steady.

"Keep looking! The council hid it well, but it must be here!"

A frantic search. Dozens of hands scraped against mortar, nails pried at cracks. Somewhere, there had to be a hidden seam, a false panel, anything that would grant them escape. The hall was growing smaller. It was as if the walls were pressing inward. The sounds beyond them growing louder.

By the barricades, John's voice rang out above the din.

"Hold! Hold, damn you!"

A crash. The barricade trembled. The heavy thud of a war hammer striking wood, splintering it.

A grunt of pain—one of the levy collapsing, his leg

crushed beneath a fallen beam. Blood pooling, black against the firelight. But the others didn't waver. Their shields locked tighter, their spears striking out through the gaps with mechanical precision.

The bloodthirsty horde outside howled with fury. Another strike. Another push. The barricade wouldn't hold forever.

"Adelinda!" John's voice. Desperate now. "Find it!"

She swallowed her fear, pressing herself against the farthest wall where a large tapestry had been torn from the façade. A prayer caught in her throat, to God above.

Her fingers skimmed over the stone—and stopped.

A slight shift. The faintest give beneath her touch. Her breath stilled for a moment. Then, she gasped.

"This is it!"

A cry of relief rippled through the huddled civilians as she pressed her weight against the panel. The stone groaned, as if resisting centuries of stillness. Then—movement. A grinding of rock against rock. A passage revealed itself, dark and yawning, leading down into the unknown.

Adelinda turned, her heart hammering.

"John! We've found it!"

John spun, his sword dripping with blood, his breath ragged. His gaze locked onto hers, a flicker of hope breaking through the grim determination in his eyes.

"Get them inside," he ordered. "Now."

Elizabeth clung to her mother's hand as the first of the refugees hurried forward, scrambling into the darkness of the tunnel. The entrance was tiny. Adelinda ushered them through, counting each one, pushing them toward whatever lay below. It would take some time to get everyone through, especially with the wounded.

Behind her, the barricade gave another sickening crack.

The hall shuddered as something massive struck it—the attackers looking to inflict one final, crushing blow. The Breckington men braced for impact.

John turned to George and Hugh.

"Buy us time."

No hesitation. No questions. Only the grim nods of men who understood what must be done.

Grunts of pain and exertion echoed through the hall as levy spearmen and knights in blue and yellow poked at the attackers through the barricade. They could hold out for a little longer, but not forever.

John pressed his eye to a splintered hole in the barricade, the scene beyond sending a jolt of dread through his chest.

The Duke of Burgundy had arrived. Gilded armor, pristine despite the carnage, the maroon plume on his helmet barely stirred in the rising heat. He was calm. Too calm. A man who had come to finish a hunt, not fight a battle.

John could see Amalric mounted beside him, a dark silhouette against the white smoke swirling from thatched roofs kindled by the hellish torches of the attackers. The abbot's face was barely visible through the haze, but John didn't need to see him to know the expression he wore. He could hear it in the smooth, satisfied drawl of his loud voice, still audible over the din.

"A brilliant solution, Your Grace."

John's blood ran cold.

Through the hole, he saw even more torches flaring to life, orange tongues licking hungrily at the air as the Calatravans moved forward. *Lopez. Nuñez.* Their black-and-purple mantles rippling behind them like shadowed specters of death.

They were going to burn them alive.

A strangled cry rang out behind him.

"My lord John, they're going to burn us!"

Reggeye, desperate, wild-eyed, pointing at the glow seeping through the cracks in the barricade. Smoke curled like fingers through the wooden beams, slow at first, then faster, licking along the edges of their sanctuary. The air thickened, heavy, oppressive, suffocating.

John wrenched back from the barricade, turned sharply.

"Move! Get everyone into the passage, now!"

The defenders hesitated, their bodies tense, eyes darting to the blocked entrances, to their swords, to the fire creeping closer.

He didn't have time for hesitation.

"We cannot hold here anymore!" John bellowed, his voice slicing through the rising panic. "The tunnels are our only way out! Move, now!"

Adelinda had already ushered the terrified civilians through the hidden entrance, her voice steady even as her hands trembled. Elizabeth clung to her mother's dress, silent, her face pale.

John caught Hugh's eye across the smoke-filled hall.

"We have to make it look like we all died here," John ordered, urgency sharpening his tone. "We can't let them follow."

Hugh nodded, already moving. He and George began toppling shattered tables and broken beams, feeding the fire with debris to make the destruction more convincing.

The flames surged. A wave of heat slammed into them as the barricades buckled. The shouts outside—once triumphant, once commanding—became distant, muffled by the roar of the inferno.

Good. Let them think us dead.

John turned, saw the last of his men slipping into the tunnel. He was the last to enter, the heat licking at his back as he stole one final glance at the council hall. Flames crawled up the walls, consuming banners, devouring history.

And outside, through the thick smoke, he heard Amalric's voice, triumphant, exultant.

"Burn, burn, you heretics! Let the flames cleanse this city of the impious!"

John clenched his fists, resisting the urge to turn back. To strike down the man who had orchestrated this massacre. But no. That was not the battle to be fought today.

Today, survival was the victory.

With one last breath of acrid air, he slipped into the darkness, the last of the beleaguered, the tunnel swallowing them whole as the city of Béziers and its massive town hall burned above.

The air hung thick with damp and smoke, a blend of the dying fire above and the musty depths below. He wiped sweat from his brow, his breath shallow as he followed the lights ahead.

The flickering torches cast erratic shadows on the ancient stone walls, twisting their silhouettes into eerie, shifting figures. The tunnels stretched endlessly ahead, winding, narrowing, each turn pressing them further into the earth.

Carved into rock, wide enough for three men to walk abreast. Pitch black, save for the pin light torches distributed disparately across the column. Cool air—a respite from the oppressive heat from the fires above.

In front of him, Reggeye's torch sputtered, its flame licking at the damp air. The boy clutched it tightly, his knuckles white, his usual bravado dimmed by the weight of fear.

John glanced beyond. The line of survivors moved slowly, trudging through the uneven ground. The wounded groaned, their steps faltering. Two men, too injured to walk, were hauled on makeshift litters of broken wood and tattered cloaks, carried by comrades who had seen too much bloodshed for one day. Eleven more of the men leaned on each other, pressing forward with grim determination. Every man lost above haunted John's mind. The dead. The missing. His men, who had given everything, their bodies now consumed by the inferno above.

Twenty-seven. He had counted.

Curse this war. Curse the abbot.

"Keep moving," John called ahead, his voice rough from smoke and exhaustion. "Stay together."

Ahead, Adelinda moved with measured urgency,

Elizabeth wrapped in her arms. The child was silent, her small fingers gripping her mother's sleeve, her breath warm against Adelinda's neck. Even in the suffocating darkness, Adelinda carried herself with an unshaken resolve, but John had seen the flickers of doubt, the tension in her shoulders.

They were not out of danger yet. If they were not careful, this place could become their grave. The tunnels were closing in.

They twisted and branched, the pathways a labyrinth of stone and time. Some walls bore the faintest traces of old carvings, remnants of an era long past. Others crumbled beneath their fingers, damp and fragile. The passage narrowed in places, forcing them to squeeze through single file. Their torches cast fleeting glimpses of what lay ahead—another tunnel, another uncertainty.

Peter Marshall kept pace beside Adelinda, his torchlight bouncing off the walls, revealing fleeting glimpses of ancient supports.

"These passages, my lady... they must be centuries old," he muttered, his voice thick with unease.

"They lead somewhere," Adelinda said, though her voice wavered. "They have to."

But the further they pressed, the more oppressive the air became. The silence was no longer a blessing. It was heavy, unnatural. It pressed against their ears, their lungs.

A prison—or worse, a *tomb*.

John felt it too. The slow gnawing doubt. Had these tunnels collapsed over the years? Had they sealed themselves in, choosing death beneath the city rather than by fire and blade?

The column halted, and John eased his way to the front, concerned that they had hit a dead end.

Is this the end? John thought as he pushed his way beside Adelinda, who stood before a solid rock tunnel end.

No. He refused to believe that.

"This isn't where it ends," Adelinda murmured, her

words barely above a breath.

John met her gaze, the torchlight flickering between them.

"No," he said. "It isn't."

He turned back to a fork in the tunnel, tightening his grip on the hilt of his sword. No matter how deep the darkness, he would not let it swallow them. They would find a way out. They had to.

A murmur ran through the group—doubt creeping in like a poison.

John's voice cut through the uncertainty. Low. Steady. Unyielding.

"We've lost much, but we still stand. Every step forward is another step they cannot undo."

He paused, scanning their faces—hollowed by fear, streaked with soot. Their hands trembled around weapons they barely had the strength to hold.

"We are not lost," he continued, his words like a tether against the unknown. "The darkness will not claim us. There is an end to this path, and beyond it—beyond it, we live."

A single nod from Adelinda. A flicker of resolve in Hugh's gaze. The faintest tightening of George's grip on the pommel of his sword. It was enough. They pressed on.

The tunnels stretched endlessly, their path uncertain. The walls, damp and ancient, whispered with echoes of those who had walked them long before. Somewhere in the distance, water dripped—a slow, rhythmic sound that only deepened the sense of isolation.

Then—another split in the path. Two tunnels, both shrouded in the same unrelenting blackness.

Adelinda hesitated, her breath shallow. She glanced at John.

"We could be going in circles," she murmured.

John didn't answer immediately. He turned, scanning their surroundings, trying to find something—anything—that might guide them. But the tunnels offered no clarity, only endless shadow.

The murmurs began again. Fear creeping back.

"What if there's no way out?" someone whispered.

"Better to have burned," another muttered, their voice brittle with despair.

John gritted his teeth.

No. We will not die. Not like this.

He stepped forward, his voice rising—not in anger, but in certainty.

"We press on."

There was a beat of silence.

"Doubt will kill us faster than fire," he continued, his eyes sweeping over them. "We are not dead yet. And until we draw our last breath, we move forward. Trust in the path."

Adelinda's gaze met his. A flicker of something passed between them—trust, desperation, understanding.

She turned back to the tunnels, inhaled sharply, and chose.

"This way."

The group followed.

John lingered a moment, casting a glance back the way they had come. He let up a silent prayer. The faintest wisp of smoke still curled through the air, its scent a reminder of the inferno that had nearly consumed them. Above them, Amalric would be watching the flames, believing them lost.

Good. Let him.

John turned, his grip tightening on the handle of his sword, drawn and at the ready. Whatever lay in the twists and turns ahead, they would face it together.

And they would survive.

For now, however, they seemed to walk forever with no end in sight. How far? A kilometer? Two?

Surely, they would be a distance from the city's premises by now. If his reckoning was accurate.

The grumbling grew louder. Until—

Adelinda's voice broke through the murmur of shifting bodies.

"There, ahead! A way out!"

Gasps of relief. Spirits lifted. They were going to live!

The flickering torchlight caught the faint outline of an opening—jagged stone giving way to the open world beyond. A breath of wind drifted in, carrying the scent of damp earth, grass, freedom.

The line surged forward, slow at first, then with growing urgency. Whispers turned into hushed voices—muted, hoarse, but unmistakably laced with hope. The wounded were helped along, arms draped over shoulders, boots dragging along but still moving. A soldier passed a crying child into the arms of an older girl. Somewhere near the rear, an elderly man murmured a psalm, barely audible over the scuff of feet and the rustle of cloaks brushing against the walls.

Sergeant Owain moved with practiced ease through the crowd, checking shoulders, tightening sling bindings, whispering encouragement. He slowed only to help hoist a blacksmith with a mangled arm onto a makeshift litter fashioned from a broken table and two cloaks.

Just ahead, Bethan—the potter's wife—clutched her sleeping son to her chest, her face streaked with ash but set on with unshakable purpose. Beside her, old Master Guy, the baker with the bad hip, leaned heavily on a cane but refused to be carried. His lips moved in silent prayer, eyes locked forward.

George pressed toward the bottleneck near the front, barking for the pace to steady, not surge. When a girl stumbled and nearly vanished in the crush, he caught her, lifting her with one arm and setting her down beside a woman who took her hand without a word.

The corridor widened briefly where the ceiling arched higher, and torchlight revealed a procession that curved back into the shadows—faces pale, soot-streaked, hollow-eyed.

There were farmers, millers, apprentices, tanners, and widows. Noble and common alike, moving shoulder to shoulder, bound by dust and dread and now—hope.

They were a column of the broken—but still moving.

They surged forward as one, feet scraping against the uneven floor, bodies pressing toward the promise of escape. The air changed, less stagnant, more alive. And then—moonlight.

Adelinda was the first to emerge, Elizabeth clutched tightly to her chest. The girl's fingers dug into her mother's dress, but she didn't cry. She had seen too much for tears. Behind them, the others stumbled out, blinking against the silver glow of dusk. John came last, sword still in hand, his gaze sweeping the hills, the distant road, the vast nothingness that stretched before them.

The night air was sharp—cool against sweat-soaked skin, a balm after the suffocating heat of the tunnels. John sucked in a breath, his chest rising, falling, his lungs heavy from the weight of smoke and exhaustion.

They had made it.

A deep breath. The world had not yet caved in.

The fires of Béziers raged in the distance behind them, a hellish glow against the dark horizon. The city burned, its screams still carried on the wind. But here, just beyond the reach of destruction, there was silence. A fragile, fleeting silence.

John turned to Hugh, who was scanning their surroundings with a soldier's wariness.

"We can't stay here."

Hugh nodded.

"The host won't linger in the city forever. If they realize we're missing—"

"They'll come," John finished grimly.

George was already moving through the group, checking the wounded, whispering quiet reassurances to the refugees. The Blitheful Ten stood nearby, their shields battered, their weapons still slick with blood. They had made it out, but they weren't safe yet.

"We head north," John said. His voice was steady, but the weight of the past hours clung to him, settling into his bones like lead. "We find shelter, regroup. There's a town—Carcassonne. If Trencavel still stands, we may have allies there."

Adelinda turned to him, her eyes reflecting both exhaustion and determination. "And if the host goes there next?"

John didn't answer. He didn't need to. He knew she was right. But for now, he was content with the victory of survival.

The group began to move—slow at first, a quiet exodus of the broken and the damned. Behind them, in a glowing panorama of destruction, Béziers continued to burn, the fires licking the sky, sending plumes of black smoke into the heavens.

John stole one last glance at the city. It didn't strike him as looking at Sodom and Gomorrah. These people had exhibited nothing but tolerance for differing ideas—a kindness not known in a world of hubris. The horror of it all settled deep inside him, lodging itself somewhere he knew he would never be able to tear free. The Church had called this righteousness.

Amalric had called it justice.

John called it murder.

A rustle in the trees. In the darkness. A shadow shifting along the ridgeline.

"Quiet! Quiet everyone!"

Gestures all around.

John's hand flew to his sword, his body tensing, muscles screaming for one last fight. But the figure didn't emerge. It lingered, watching.

A witness. To our survival.

John was too exhausted to pursue. No one else in their

409

company had the energy to pursue. They would let the mysterious stranger leave—and inform whomever they wanted of their escape—and let the Lord decide their fate.

They were alive.

And for now, that was enough.

Fugida

July 22nd, 1209 AD

Béziers, Viscounty of Béziers

he night bore witness to the ruin of Béziers, its streets now silent save for the distant crackle of dying embers. The scent of burning timber mixed with something fouler—charred flesh, blood turned to iron in the heat.

The city, once vibrant, now lay in heaps of ruin. St. Mary Magdalene's altar, once a beacon of devotion, stood defiled in the dim glow. Defiled by violence. Bloodstained. Buried under a hill of the bodies of the damned. A throne for a butcher, not the Savior of the world.

Arnaud Amalric lingered there, his white robes sullied by soot and slaughter. He ran a gloved hand over the wooden surface, feeling the sticky warmth of spilled life. Slick and slimy.

His lips curled, satisfaction laced with something deeper. A tremor in his hands—was it divine fervor or the gravity of what had been done?

A chorus of metal on stone echoed as bodies were dragged, piled like cords of firewood. The church floor—hidden beneath a tide of the dead and a crimson layer of blood. The scent of incense long since drowned in the stench of death.

He stepped over a corpse, then another, his boots tracking blood. A final glance at the massacre he had deemed necessary. His companions waited, shifting uneasily in the dim torchlight.

"The Almighty's will," he murmured, crossing himself. His voice barely a whisper beneath the smoldering ruin—as if to convince himself of his righteousness.

"Not cruelty. Justice."

Perhaps he needed to say it enough so he could believe it. The companions nodded, as if to reassure their own selves.

"Deus vult."

Yet, the abbot's fingers tightened around the gilded pommel of his staff. The cries still rang in his ears, the screams of those who did not die so swiftly. He shut his eyes. Pushed it down. To waver now was to falter in faith. Or so he believed. He had been chosen for this. He had no right to doubt.

The hubris dug deeper and spread further like a humorous poison, permeating the air as he mounted his horse.

Outside, the night stretched on, serene in its desecration. The stars blinked indifferently, the moon casting pale light over a city silenced, as Amalric rode his mount through the city gates and over the bridge spanning the Orb.

Like a conquering emperor, with troops bowing as he passed.

The war camp beckoned beyond. Within the massive war tent and beneath the flickering glow of lanterns, maps sprawled across a wooden table, their inked borders marked with the ambition of conquest. They had begun with Béziers. There would be more.

412

Amalric stood before them, voice steady, cold.

"Tonight," he declared, "we are not merely victors. We are the Almighty's hand. His light has burned through us. And through us, justice has been served."

The warlords listened, their faces a mix of zeal and exhaustion. Some shifted in their seats, haunted by what they had wrought. Others nodded, their zeal hardened like tempered steel.

Amalric saw them all. Those who doubted, he would purge. Those who rejoiced, he would use.

Faith. Conviction. War.

The path ahead was clear. And there would be no turning back.

Flames danced against the canvas walls, their orange glow licking at the edges of the tent. A distant scream—faint, barely more than a dying whisper—was lost beneath the crackling of burning wood. The city of Béziers was silent now, save for the echoes of ruin.

Amalric turned towards the open flaps of the tent, his voice a measured calm.

"The city has fallen," he declared, gesturing toward the distant inferno. "Its defiance has been silenced. Their suffering is but a reflection of the eternal fire that awaits all who turn from His grace."

A murmur of agreement rippled through the gathered lords, though some shifted uncomfortably, their hands gripping the hilts of their swords as if seeking reassurance. The younger ones—those who had not yet hardened their hearts to the horrors of war—averted their eyes. Amalric saw it. He had seen it before.

Doubt.

A flaw to be excised before it festered.

His tone softened, though the steel within remained, his conviction a weight pressing upon the room.

"It is not for us to question the harshness of God's justice," he continued, voice low, steady. "It is only for us to carry it out, no matter how heavy the burden. This is the price of righteousness."

A gust of wind swept through the tent, rustling maps, overturning an empty goblet. It struck the ground with a hollow clatter.

No one moved. No one spoke.

For the first time since they had ridden through the gates of Béziers, the soldiers "of the Cross" let the silence settle upon them. Let the weight of it press against their chests.

Was God truly pleased with what they had done?

Amalric's fingers tightened around the gilded cross at his belt. His words had come so easily—had they not? The justification, the certainty. And yet, beneath it, something clawed at the edges of his mind. A whisper he could not allow himself to hear.

No.

He straightened, his jaw clenched tight. He fought the pull of conscience. He would fight against it. Justify what had happened.

Faith required sacrifice. Purity demanded fire. There could be no redemption without cleansing.

This was justice. This was war.

A thin smile curled his lips—though it did not reach his eyes. They doubted. They feared. He did not. And that made him stronger.

But the truth, veiled behind his righteous fury, was this: Amalric's Holy War had become a war of annihilation. The justifications—so eloquent, so certain—were a mask, a fragile cloak stretched over an unrelenting truth. He was no longer a warrior of faith. He was an executioner.

And yet, his self-righteousness gave him an answer.

Better to extinguish a thousand lives than allow a single heretic to lead others astray.

The thought burned within him, an unrelenting fever.

Like Saul of Tarsus before the road to Damascus, Amalric was a man blinded—not by light, but by the

414

darkness of his own pride. Saul had been shattered, cast down, his arrogance stripped away so that he might see. But for Amalric, no such revelation awaited. No blinding light. No voice calling him to truth.

Only *fire*.

He fashioned himself an instrument of divine will, yet the reflection he cast was something else entirely. Not righteous. Not holy.

Wicked. Demonic.

The thought did cross his mind. Yet the logic that guided him was not born of faith but of something twisted, something that festered in the unchecked corners of the human soul. In his obsession with purging sin, he had failed to see the darkness growing within himself—feeding, devouring, turning him into the very thing he claimed to destroy.

Pride.

It was his blindness. His fortress. His unbroken chain.

And as he stood in the glow of the burning city, the flames casting long shadows across his face, he was already too far gone.

He let the silence linger for a while longer, as if to let his misgivings seep into the cracks digging deep into the dry ground below him. Then, slowly, he stepped forward, his boots pressing against the dirt floor, grinding embers into ash. He would ask the men the very question that now plagued his own mind.

"Do you hesitate now?"

His voice was low, the rumble of distant thunder.

"After all we have achieved, after all you have seen?"

He gestured again toward the open tent flaps, to the ruin beyond.

"Was not Béziers a testament to the righteousness of our cause? Did not the fire itself speak of God's will?"

Again, the younger lords stiffened. Some flinched. None answered.

It was the seasoned Count of Nevers who broke the silence, his armor streaked with the soot of burning homes and the blood of the slaughtered. He scoffed, shaking his head.

"Your Eminence. They doubt because they are young," he chuckled, a dry sound, devoid of mirth. "This was their first true battle, their first real test. They have not yet learned that pity has no place in a holy campaign. What we did here was justice, not cruelty—was it not?"

A slow smile curled at Amalric's lips. He would disregard the fact that the count himself hesitated at a crucial moment against Breckington. He needed the display of resolve, to instill steel in his men. Yes, *his* men.

"Justice," he echoed. "A holy justice, ordained by God Himself."

His gaze swept over the room, pinning each man in place like a hawk eyeing prey.

"And let us not forget the agreement upon which you all joined this sacred mission. The absolution promised to you is not a gift freely given—it is earned. You swore to cleanse this land of heresy, to bring the wrath of heaven upon those who defy the Church. Do you think God's favor is won through hesitation? Through doubt?"

The younger lords bristled, their faces reddening under his scrutiny. A few lowered their gazes, ashamed. Others clenched their fists, their pride fighting against the unease in their hearts.

One of the veterans laughed outright. A sharp, biting sound that cut through the tension like a blade.

"Let the faint-hearted question, Your Eminence," he said, leaning back against a table, his fingers drumming lazily against the wood. "The rest of us know what must be done. You waste your breath on boys who still think of their homes and their mothers' prayers. The real work is done by those of us who have no room for doubt. *Deus vult!*"

A murmur of agreement swept through the senior lords.

416

"Deus vult!"

Their eyes gleamed with conviction—or something far darker. These were the men who had marched under the banner of the cross not for salvation, but for conquest. Not for faith, but for spoils. Their names would be written in the annals of history, etched in blood and fire.

For them, the screams of the dying were not a burden. They were a chorus of victory.

"Yes," Amalric declared, his tone a clarion call, like a hammer striking iron. "The work is not done. Béziers is but the beginning. The fires must spread, the land must be purified, and the heretics must be erased."

He paused, his eyes sweeping over those gathered—measuring, judging. Some stood resolute, their faces set in grim determination. Others hesitated, their gazes flickering, uncertain. It was these few that irked him, the weak, the wavering.

"To those who falter," he continued, his voice sharpening, "I remind you: absolution is the prize only for those who see this mission through to the end. To those who stand resolute—you are the true champions of God's justice. It is your swords, your faith, that will forge a kingdom free of sin."

A murmur rippled through the gathered lords. Amalric grinned as he realized his talk ignited a fire among the men. Then the murmur grew into something greater.

A *roar*.

Chairs scraped against the ground as men rose, goblets lifted high. The hesitant were drowned beneath the fervor of the zealots. Their voices rang out—bold, triumphant, drunk with wind—and blood.

"For the Church! For heaven! For victory!"

The cry echoed through the camp, carrying into the night. Amalric stood amidst it, drinking it in, his expression unreadable. Satisfaction, perhaps. Or something colder.

The hesitant few remained silent, their unease buried

beneath the fervent chorus. It did not matter. They would either learn, or they would be lost.

Amalric turned on his heel, striding toward the tent flaps. The voices behind him still rose in jubilation, but he was already elsewhere, already looking toward the next conquest.

Outside, the night air carried the acrid scent of burning flesh. The ruins of Béziers smoldered in the distance, a city turned to embers beneath the weight of righteous fury.

He swung onto his horse, his two Calatravan knights flanking him in silent vigilance. The hesitation of some of the lords gnawed at him—not because it stirred doubt, not because it made him question.

No, there was no question.

This was justice.

What unsettled him was that doubt existed at all. That any man under his command should hesitate, should falter. He denied to himself that even he entertained the notion of doubt. He was strong. God's instrument of justice.

The weak would either find conviction—or be discarded. The road ahead would allow for nothing less.

Ash curled in the wind, twisting through the ruins of Béziers like the spirits of the dead, clinging to Amalric's robes as he rode through the charred remains of the city. The fires still smoldered, embers pulsing like dying stars beneath the collapsed timbers of homes and sanctuaries alike. The streets, once alive with the hum of trade and the laughter of children, lay silent. Blackened. Coated in soot and streaked with blood.

To Amalric, it was a sacrament. A tribute to the Almighty.

The conquest of Canaan had been no different. Did not Joshua raise his sword at God's command? Had not whole peoples been put to the blade to secure His will?

This is no less righteous, he assured himself. *We are His chosen instruments, purging this land of corruption and*

418

heresy. What are a thousand lives compared to the purity of
His Church? Better that they burn than their poison spread.

He had convinced himself of this truth, steeled his heart
against the wails that had once pierced the heavens. The cries
of mothers torn from their children. The shrieks of the dying
as fire devoured them. If he let himself dwell on them, if he
hesitated for even a moment, doubt might creep in again like
rot in a wound. And doubt was the enemy.

But even as Amalric's thoughts coiled tighter around his
conviction, the truth stood as a silent witness against him,
rooted in the teachings he had long twisted—and ignored. A
theological truth that he long understood, but denied in his
pride.

The conquest of Canaan had been a singular moment in
history, a judgment decreed by the Almighty upon nations
steeped in wickedness for generations. They not simply
entertained opposing beliefs, violence was in their cultures.

It was not a precedent for men like Amalric to wield the
sword in their own time, to fashion themselves as arbiters of
divine justice. That old theocracy, that chosen nation, had
long since passed. Its purpose had been fulfilled, its role
completed.

Then Christ had come. Not as a warlord. Not as a
conqueror. But as a shepherd—and a meek and lowly lamb.

And there was another man—now miles away, riding a
different path—who understood this. John de Ontivero,
Baron of Breckington, had seen men like Amalric before. He
had watched them burn, loot, and slaughter in the name of
righteousness. He had seen what happened when faith was
twisted into a weapon, when men lost themselves in the
illusion that they could build God's kingdom with steel and
fire.

Amalric did not see the contradiction in his own hands,
clasped in prayer one moment, soaked in blood the next. He
did not see that the kingdom of God could not be forced into
existence, that it was never meant to be built through

conquest. But John saw.

John had seen it in the ruins of Acre. Heard the stories about what happened in the streets of Zara. In the hollow eyes of the broken, the lost, the ones left behind when men like Amalric marched forward in their "holy" cause.

Faith was not meant to be a banner beneath which men slaughtered.

It was meant to be a refuge. A choice freely given, never imposed. John had come to understand that God's kingdom was not one of forced obedience but of invitation, a kingdom where the walls were built not of stone and fear, but of grace. Amalric would never understand this.

For Amalric, the fire and steel were the tools of righteousness. The destruction of Béziers was not a tragedy, but a necessity. A purification. He saw no souls, only sin. No lives, only obstacles in the path of divine justice.

But John knew better. He knew that faith without mercy was not faith at all. That righteousness without love was an empty husk, as dead as the bodies strewn across the streets of Béziers.

The road Amalric rode would never lead to God's kingdom. It could only ever lead to ruin.

But John?

John would build something different. Not a kingdom of conquest, but of refuge. Not a kingdom of submission, but of faith freely chosen.

::

The wind bit deep, cold and sharp, whispering through the hills like a ghost searching for the dead. The fires of Béziers still glowed on the horizon, embers smoldering against the night sky. A ruin, a graveyard. And yet, it was not the past that haunted John de Ontivero—it was the future.

Beneath the skeletal canopy of trees, sixty-one refugees

huddled together, their breath curling in the air like fragile wisps of life. Children clung to their mothers, their small bodies trembling from more than just the cold. The elderly sat in silence, hollow-eyed, spent from the night's flight. Somewhere in the darkness, a muffled cough, a stifled sob.

John stood apart, his silhouette etched against the moonlight. His hand rested on the pommel of his sword, though it was exhaustion, not battle, that made his fingers tighten against the worn leather grip. The Breckington levy—what little remained of it—formed a loose perimeter. Sixty-two spearmen, battered and bloodied, their armor dented, their weapons dulled. A third of them were wounded, and yet, here they still stood. Then, there were his Blitheful Ten, knights and squires, bloodied, but—*Alive.*

A hundred and thirty-three souls, *alive.*

But for how much longer?

Behind him, Adelinda sat with Elizabeth curled against her side, her arms wrapped tight around her daughter. The girl had finally slipped into an uneasy sleep, her small body shivering in her mother's grasp. John's jaw tensed. She shouldn't be here. None of them should be here.

Footsteps. A familiar weight in the air as he approached. *Sir Hugh.*

John didn't turn as the knight stopped beside him, his voice low.

"What now, my lord?"

No anger. No accusation. Just quiet, grim reality.

John exhaled slowly, his breath a pale cloud in the darkness.

"I don't know," he admitted, his voice raw, scraped down to the bone. "We've lost almost half our number. What remains is exhausted. And we have sixty-one civilians, most of them unarmed, all of them looking to us for protection."

Hugh's gaze swept the ragged group.

"We can't keep running," he said. "Not like this. They are exhausted. But if we stand, we'll be cut down. You know

Amalric won't stop."

John clenched his teeth.

"I know."

His eyes flickered back to the refugees. Faces etched with fragile hope. As if he could somehow turn their ruin into salvation.

But how?

"Amalric would call this justice."

The thought burned, bitter and caustic. The kind of justice that left towns in ashes, that justified murder beneath the weight of a cross.

John had once believed in that kind of justice too. He forced the thought away.

"What am I supposed to do?" he muttered. "Abandon them? Leave them to fend for themselves?"

"No one is suggesting that." Hugh's voice was firm. "But we need a plan."

A rustle. A soft voice breaking the night.

Adelinda.

She stepped forward, her face pale but steady.

"My Lord John," she said, quiet but sure, "there are caves in the hills ahead. Deep ones. Some of the locals used them to hide during the last feudal conflict in this region. They might provide shelter. We cannot go to Carcassonne—they will head there next."

John turned to her, the words taking root, threading into the raw edges of his mind.

Shelter.

A way to regroup. Hugh crossed his arms.

"It won't last. They'll search the hills eventually."

"No," John admitted. "But it buys us time."

"To do what?"

"Find allies," he met Hugh's gaze. "Maybe the local lords will listen. Give assistance."

Hugh's expression grew dark.

"Do you think they'll listen to a disgraced noble?"

422

A long pause. A moment of silent contemplation. Then Adelinda spoke again, softer this time.

"You're not a foreign invader anymore, Lord John. You saved their people. There are witnesses. That might be enough."

John held her gaze. Had he changed? Or had he simply stripped away the illusion? It didn't matter. What mattered was what came next. He turned to the gathered men, the weary faces watching him, waiting.

"We move for the caves in the hills of the northeast," he said, his voice low, steady. A decision made. A path chosen. "We regroup. We rest. And we prepare. To rebuild—and survive."

::

Smoke coiled through the ruined streets, thick as the blood on the ground, clinging to the scorched bones of Béziers. The embers still burned, crackling beneath the weight of a city undone.

Amalric stood in the midst of it all, his white robes streaked with soot, the stench of burnt flesh thick in his lungs—yet to him it was as the pleasant scent of meat to a famished man. The fire had done its work. The purge was complete.

Or so he had thought.

A figure moved through the wreckage, stepping over corpses and shattered stone with purpose.

Peter of Vaux-de-Cernay.

His face, always joyless, was carved with something harsher tonight—urgency.

His voice cut through the silence like a blade.

"Your Eminence, the Englishmen, they've escaped."

Amalric turned, slowly, his head snapping toward Peter, his expression darkening.

"Escaped?" he spat the word like venom. "How?"

Peter inclined his head, though the tension in his jaw betrayed his own frustration.

"The fire worked to their advantage," he said. "Lord Breckington and his men found tunnels beneath the council hall. They emerged beyond our encampment, slipping away in the darkness. Sentries spotted a small formation in the firelight—men in blue and yellow—heading north, emerging from caves outside the city walls."

Silence.

Amalric's hands curled into fists. His jaw tightened, his breathing slow but sharp.

"This cannot be."

The words came low, like a prayer twisted by fury. He began to pace, boots grinding ash into the earth.

"These heretics have defied the will of God. They cannot be allowed to mock the sanctity of our mission by evading their punishment."

Peter remained still, watching. The night pressed in around them, heavy with the weight of the slaughter. Behind them, bloodied men-at-arms stood like statues, their faces etched with exhaustion, with something colder still.

Then another voice, rough and measured, cut through the tension.

"Your Eminence."

A figure stepped from the shadows of the ruins, firelight flickering against battered steel.

Guy of Vaux-de-Cernay.

A priest, a warrior, Peter's blood uncle and a man who had long since made peace with the righteousness of the sword. His armor bore the scars of past holy campaigns, his graying hair alighting against the chainmail at his shoulders.

"Give me command of the Calatravan knights," he said, his voice like grinding stone. "We shall track these heretics. None will escape the wrath of our righteous cause."

Amalric turned to him fully now, eyes gleaming.

"Ah, Guy. Better late than never to the party, *oui*?"

"I rode with haste, Your Eminence," Guy replied. His voice carried no mirth. "But it seems divine retribution moves quicker than my horse's legs. I see the city has already suffered the vengeance of God's wrath."

His eyes narrowed as he continued.

"Yet my nephew tells me some heretics live still," he exhaled, steady, unshaken. "I will execute God's judgment upon them."

Amalric took a step closer. The firelight twisted the edges of his face into something sharp, something fevered.

"You swear this?" His voice trembled—not with doubt, but with hunger. "That none shall escape?"

Guy met his gaze, unwavering.

"By my blade and my soul."

A slow smile curled at Amalric's lips.

"Yes. Of course," he exhaled, as if savoring the moment. "Then go. Hunt them like the cursed shadows they are. Leave none alive. Let them know the wrath of God."

Guy turned, the conversation already finished in his mind. The Calatravan knights awaited him, their armor polished silver beneath the cold moonlight, their banners snapping like hungry wolves in the wind.

With practiced precision, they mounted their steeds, their movements sharp, disciplined. Their mission clear.

Amalric watched them go, his hands clasped behind his back, his gaze fixed on the darkened horizon.

"The land will be purified," he murmured. "No matter the cost."

::

The wind whispered through the hills, thin and sharp, slipping past even the thickest cloaks. Cold. Unrelenting. The Breckington men and their charges huddled beneath the sparse trees, their bodies curled tight, seeking the warmth of the tiny fire. Faces pale with exhaustion. Eyes hollow.

They had been moving for hours. Felt like days.

Only the watchfires pushed back the blackness, their flickering glow dancing on wary faces, on the dull steel of spears gripped tight. The sentries stood at attention, backs stiff, shoulders tense.

Something moved.

Silent. A shadow slipping between the trees. Hidden. Watching. Then—a sound. A whistle. Soft. Deliberate. The guards stiffened, spears dropping into place.

Sir George stepped forward, his sword whistling from its scabbard.

"Who goes there?"

Silence.

Then movement. A figure emerged, hooded, cloaked, hands raised in careful surrender. The guards tightened their grip on their spears, waiting for Sir George's signal. A slow breath...

Then—

The hood fell back. George froze. His sword lowered, his breath catching in his throat as he recognized the face in the weak firelight.

Wait—it can't be.

"Ysabeau?"

His voice cracked, disbelief warring with relief. Then he moved, closing the space between them, arms wrapping tightly around the girl. Reggeye ran over, recognizing the name.

"By heaven, it's you!"

The camp stirred, weary eyes turning toward the stranger.

John stepped forward, one hand resting on the pommel of his sword, his brow knotted tight. The firelight caught her features—worn, streaked with soot and exhaustion, but unmistakable.

"Ysabeau?" he breathed, the name catching in his throat. "Is that... is it truly you?"

It felt wrong on his tongue now, like calling a queen by a

servant's name. His voice steadied, but something in his eyes flickered—recognition, disbelief, perhaps even betrayal.

"How are you here? How did you follow us?"

She met his gaze evenly, her voice clear despite the fatigue in her limbs.

"I have been following you for some time, Lord John. I was in the city during the siege."

A few murmurs stirred around the camp, heads turning.

George leaned forward.

"You were in Béziers? How did you escape?"

"The same way you did. Through the tunnels. I know them well—I played in them as a child, with my cousin who now rules the city. I slipped away while the Cathedral was defiled—murderers killing beneath vaulted ceilings. No regard even for their own sacred places."

"...my cousin who now rules the city..." John's thoughts ran wild. Could she be…

She stepped closer to the firelight now, her shadow falling long across the earth. Her tone shifted—firm, formal.

"And because I witnessed what you did—because I saw the lives you saved—I can no longer keep my name hidden."

A hush spread like fog.

John felt the hair rise on his arms. Something deep within him braced.

"I am not simply Ysabeau," she said, her chin lifting. "My true name is Philippa de Foix—daughter of Esclaramonde de Foix. Cousin to Raymond-Roger Trencavel. Niece to the Count of Foix."

The name struck like steel on a cold anvil.

George's breath caught audibly. Reggeye stepped back a pace.

John stared. The memory rushed back: rumors whispered in siege camps, noble blood vanished in the north, a name buried beneath the weight of the Church's oppression. His mind traced the implications—Trencavel's kin, the prestige of Foix. And the woman who had walked among them under a false name, now revealing the truth in a flicker of torchlight.

"Philippa…" John whispered, the word reverent, bewildered. "By God's mercy—"

She held his gaze. "The Church sought to erase us. But we are not so easily erased."

De Foix. Of course she would know the city. The tunnels. She was kin to Trencavel. But is it true? How do I know she is not some imposter playing some cruel joke to torment them?

The name carried weight. Power. History.

John's vassal knight was more pliable. Speechless, George could not believe his ears. This was not some street orphan from the streets of Brittany as he had once thought. She was nobility. In fact, much higher a station than his own.

He knew this well, being quite the student of history and politics. The House of Foix had been a pillar of Occitania, its bloodline interwoven with the heretical cause.

Esclaramonde de Foix—wise, defiant, unshakable in faith—had sheltered the persecuted, stood against the growing wrath of the Church. A legacy that earned respect. Awe.

Philippa's eyes swept across the gathered, curious faces. She did not flinch.

"When the Church turned its fury upon Occitania, my family's lands and wealth were stripped away. Our name was burned from history, our kin scattered, imprisoned, murdered."

The fire crackled, the only sound in the stunned quiet.

"My mother believed in peace," Philippa continued, her voice unwavering, "even as war swallowed our land. She hid the treasures of our house—gold, jewels, relics—to keep them from the hands of the invaders."

She took another step forward.

"And it is one of these caches that I now offer to you."

The fire crackled, throwing shadows across John's face, still skeptical. Arms crossed. Jaw tight.

"So, Ysabeau—" a pause, a shift in his stance. He would test her identity. "Or is it Philippa?"

She didn't flinch.

"If this is true, why reveal yourself now? Why help us?"

A flicker in her eyes, something softer. But her voice? Steady. Unwavering.

"Because you helped me, my lord," she said. "Brest. The port. You didn't know who I was, but you helped me anyway."

The fire popped. A gust of wind stirred the branches overhead.

"I know Amalric," she continued. "He won't stop until you and these people are nothing more than ash. You can't fight him. Not as you are now."

She shifted closer to the fire and went on.

"My family's wealth was meant to preserve hope. But this hope is running dry. Our strongholds are falling. If I can help you resist, even for a time, it won't have been in vain."

John's gaze turned to Sir Hugh. A brief exchange of expressions. A silent conversation.

Hugh exhaled through his nose. Nodded.

From the darkness, a voice rang out.

"I know her. She is who she says she is."

Adelinda stepped into the firelight, her face bathed in amber glow.

"The de Foix family has long been known for their generosity," she said. Paused briefly. Then, she lowered herself, taking Philippa's hand. "This is indeed Philippa of Foix."

"It is an honor to finally meet you, my lady."

Philippa's lips curled, a shadow of a smile.

"The pleasure is mine, Lady de Montaro."

A sharp gasp from Adelinda. Her name. There recognition.

"You—you know me?"

Philippa inclined her head.

"I have walked your town. I know of you, and of your service to these lands," her gaze softened. "You have served my people well."

John let out a slow breath, the tension in his shoulders easing. His thoughts turned over, grinding like millstones, but the weight of doubt began to lift.

He stepped forward after taking deep breath.

"My lady de Foix," his voice, measured. "I owe you an apology."

Philippa met his gaze.

"And my thanks," he added. "Not just for your courage in revealing the truth, but for giving us a chance when hope seemed lost."

He extended a hand. She took it. Her grip was firm.

"My lord John."

His eyes widened with admiration.

"If this cache of treasures can be acquired," he murmured, "it could mean the difference between survival and annihilation."

A deep breath as John continued.

"We'll follow you to retrieve it. May God grant that it gives us what we need to survive," his voice strengthened. "Shall we rest here for the night?"

The answer from the newcomer came fast. Sharp. A warning.

"We cannot stay."

The hush that followed was heavy. Philippa's voice cut through it like a blade.

"The host will be on the move soon. The Carcassonne. We must leave at once."

John frowned. Calculating.

"They'll take time to revel in their victory. A day at least. And then they'll need to pack their belongings before advancing into Trencavel's lands. We can afford a few hours of rest."

Philippa shook her head.

"No. We leave now."

A flash of irritation.

"Why?" John pressed. "As far as they know, we perished in the fire."

Philippa's jaw tightened.

"While I was searching for you," she said. "I passed a group of Frisian footmen outside the city. They were speaking of soldiers in blue and yellow escaping through caves beyond the northern wall."

John stiffened.

"A monk was among them," Philippa continued. "He was excited. Said he had to bring the news to Amalric himself."

Her voice dropped lower.

"By now, the abbot would have sent his best men to hunt you."

John felt the gravity of her words settle over him like a cloak of iron.

"Who do you think he'll send?"

Philippa glanced at the weary faces of the refugees, her expression hardening.

"Guy of Vaux-de-Cernay," she said.

A silence, deep and unyielding.

How does she know all this? John thought.

"He's been seen heading toward Béziers to meet with Amalric," she went on. "One of his most trusted lieutenants. A seasoned warrior. A man of ruthless resolve."

She paused. Then—

"If Amalric gives him the order, he won't stop," She said, her eyes grazing with certainty. "He will hunt us."

Another breath of wind and a pause, as if to listen for any distant pursuers.

"He will not stop until we are all dead."

The fire burned low, its glow casting flickering shapes against the trees. Shadows stretched long, shifting with the wind. The night pressed in, thick and heavy, a weight on their shoulders.

Sir Hugh looked uncomfortable. He took a sharp intake of breath.

"Vaux-de-Cernay..." he intoned, his voice was low, distant. "I fought a Peter from Vaux-de-Cernay. A monk, but no ordinary one."

Philippa's head snapped toward him. A flicker of something in her eyes.

"Peter of Vaux-de-Cernay is his nephew," she said, voice steady, but laced with warning. "If you crossed swords with him, he won't have forgotten. And if you killed him—"

"I didn't," Hugh cut in, his tone grim. "We dueled. We both walked away."

Philippa studied him, the firelight catching the sharp edge of her expression.

"Then consider yourself fortunate," she murmured. "Peter is well connected. Zealous. Cunning. Loyal to his uncle. And since you killed their kin—the knight Inquisitor—there are whispers that Guy is here to settle the debt."

John inhaled sharply. His mind pulled him back—to the ambush, to Galt's death and Reggeye's blind fury.

Hugh exhaled, shaking his head.

"So now it's a blood vendetta," he muttered. "Between Peter's humiliation and Sir Galt's death, the monks at Vaux-de-Cernay—especially that family—have every reason to make this personal."

Philippa nodded.

"And you should know," she said, "that Guy is not like Amalric. Amalric wields fire and terror indiscriminately. Guy is precise. Methodical. He will anticipate your every move. He will exploit your weaknesses. He will hunt you like prey," Her voice darkened. "His reputation as a tactician is well-earned. We can outsmart and outmaneuver him, but we must move, *now*."

John's jaw clenched.

His eyes flicked toward the refugees—women huddling their children close, the elderly moving slow, the few spearmen still gripping their weapons with exhaustion, but with resolve.

They wouldn't survive a chase. Not like this.

His gaze snapped back to Philippa.

"Then we move, as you desire. Now."

Philippa held his stare, unwavering.

"Can you lead us?" he asked. "To this treasure of yours? If we secure it, we might have a chance. A way to protect them—to survive the days to come."

Philippa's lips pressed together, but her eyes burned with certainty.

"Yes," she said. "But we must travel quickly. If Guy is already on the move, he won't be far behind."

John frowned.

"You speak as if you know all this for certain. How?"

Philippa's expression didn't change.

"You met me in Brest," she said. "You saw what I was. A commoner, or so you thought."

A small, knowing smile.

"I know the countryside well. I speak many tongues. I hear the rumors. The stories. You'd be surprised what men will say when they think no one is listening."

She glanced toward the darkened hills ahead, her voice quiet but firm.

"Let's keep moving until dawn's light. I'll tell you more then."

::

The night stretched wide, empty and silent, save for the steady drum of hooves against cold earth. The Calatravans rode in shadow, their black cloaks rippling in the wind, their armor whispering with every movement.

433

The moon hung low, casting its pale gaze over the fields, indifferent to the chase unfolding beneath its light.

Guy of Vaux-de-Cernay rode at the head, his silhouette sharp beneath the fluttering banner of the Calatravan Order. Behind him, Nuñez and Lopez, seasoned and merciless, flanked by four more knights, their faces hidden beneath steel, their purpose carved into their very being.

The stillness of the land mocked them. A world at peace, unaware of the judgment bearing down upon it.

Guy turned in his saddle, his voice cutting through the night.

"These heretics think they can outrun divine justice," he said before pausing, the chill air curling around his words. "They believe the shadows will shield them."

He sneered before continuing.

"They are mistaken."

His hand tightened on the reins, his eyes narrowing against the distant dark.

"Let the moon be our lantern," His voice dropped lower, the weight of his conviction pressing into the men around him. "And let our blades deliver the judgment of God."

A murmur of assent. Grim. Measured.

This was no ordinary hunt.

They were not merely tracking prey. They were pursuing defiance itself.

Each man bore the weight of Amalric's command, the knowledge that their task was more than death—it was retribution. A warning etched in blood. A message that none who defied the cleansing fire of the Crusade would live to tell of it.

Behind them, Béziers smoldered, its ruin swallowed by the night.

Ahead, the hunt had begun.

::

The night clung to them like a shroud. Footsteps muffled by the damp earth, breath held close to their chests. No sobs. No wails. Even the children—tiny feet stumbling, small hands gripping the hems of their mothers' cloaks—said nothing. They understood. Somehow.

Behind them, the horizon smoldered, Béziers still bleeding orange and crimson into the night sky. Ahead, shadows. Thickets. Narrow trails only a local could navigate. Philippa led them, sure-footed, eyes sharp, always glancing back to count the faces.

John followed near, his hand resting on the pommel of his sword, his breath slow, controlled. But his mind? A storm.

Philippa drew close, her voice just above a whisper, slicing through the darkness like a blade.

"Guy of Vaux-de-Cernay," she began, "is not just a warrior."

John glanced sideways, the name already a stone in his gut.

"He is a rhetorician by daylight," she went on, "an orator who speaks of heresy with the fervor of a prophet. Cloaked in robes. Quoting scripture. Or twisting it. Convincing even the uncertain that blood must be spilled in the name of purity."

Her voice dropped even lower.

"But when night falls—he sheds the cloth."

She looked ahead, through the trees.

"He dons armor. Polished. Silent. Deadly. He is not merely a preacher. He is a predator. The kind who smiles by day and slits throats by moonlight."

John said nothing. He didn't need to.

Philippa studied him—read the line of his jaw, the weight in his eyes. She didn't need to tell him how men like Guy thought. He already knew. He'd once been cut from the same iron.

"He'll pursue with precision," she continued. "Strike

when you rest. Corner when you scatter. He has turned the pursuit of heretics into a game of strategy—and he rarely loses."

John exhaled slowly through his nose.

"Peter?" he asked, his voice a low rasp.

"Eager. Undisciplined. But he burns with zeal. Under Guy's guidance, he'll be twice as dangerous. Twice as reckless."

Sir Hugh, trailing close behind, chimed in—grim and tired.

"He's no novice. Fought me at Breckington. Came in like a viper. Thought he'd best me. He didn't," he said, then paused. "But he nearly did. And if I'd killed him, the Church would have come for us with even more ire."

Philippa nodded once, solemn.

"They already are, Sir Hugh. Your little act of defiance in the town made you the worst enemies of the Church."

John's gaze shifted back. The line of refugees behind them—mothers, widows, farmers-turned-fighters, children too tired to cry. A handful of spearmen who still gripped their weapons like lifelines.

He clenched his jaw.

"We don't give them the chance."

He turned back to her.

"This treasure of yours," he said. "Where?"

Philippa's eyes gleamed in the dark.

"Beneath a ruined church. Not far. A sanctuary for the *Parfaits*. Guy's men were sent out before the main host and razed it weeks ago, but they never found what lay beneath."

"An underground labyrinth?"

She nodded.

"My mother ensured its secrecy. It's untouched. But you'll need me to reach it."

John nodded once. No hesitation.

"Then we move for the church. If Guy already razed this place to oblivion he won't think to look here again."

436

George, listening in, looked confused.

"How can we be so sure, milord?"

"Who hides in the ashes?" John continued, a faint, bitter smirk tugging at the edge of his mouth. "No thunder climbs the same hill twice, isn't that what the old man said?"

George shrugged, as John patted his vassal on the shoulder.

"Let's get going, George. Gather the men."

The night answered with movement as Sir George raised a hand. Cloaks shifted. Spears rose.

The hunted would not run forever.

::

Mist clung to the earth like a veil. Pale. Cold. Heavy with the scent of ash and iron.

The camp of the host stirred before the sun had fully broken the horizon. Clatter of buckles, low curses as armor was fastened tight. Smoke from dying cookfires curled into the air, mingling with the scent of sweat and boiled grain. Orders passed in hushed tones, not shouted—they didn't need to shout anymore. Béziers had made them bold.

Three days had they lingered around the pillaged city, collecting the spoils and burying the dead. A lull long enough for word of their victory to spread far and wide. But they were not done. Not yet.

Ahead—Carcassonne.

Its name passed between the men like it was an enigma. A fortress. A prize. A defiant stone heart waiting to be cracked open. It was indeed the proud citadel of the viscounts of the Midi. Certainly, the young viscount Trencavel would be fortified there.

The host was ready—and Amalric stood at the center of it all.

Still.

Eyes sharp, new robes pristine save for a smudge of soot

near the hem. A priest's robe. A butcher's stare. He gave fresh orders with clipped efficiency, no flourish. Only certainty.

His gaze drifted to the north. He could already see it, prophesied it.

Carcassonne burning.

The walls blackened. The cries swallowed by fire.

The Lord's work, fulfilled in smoke.

Then—a rider appeared from the east.

Fast. Alone. The insignia of the papal curia gleamed faintly on his cloak, dulled by road dust and urgency.

The camp paused. Just for a breath. Just long enough to notice. The rider dismounted, boots squelching in the damp earth. He bowed low before Amalric.

"Your Eminence," he mouthed, breath controlled, but tension crackling beneath every word. "I bear a letter. From His Holiness."

Amalric didn't speak. Didn't blink. He took the scroll, broke the seal. Read. His lips pressed into a thin, bloodless line. His jaw moved slightly. Grinding. A twitch. Barely visible.

Then—his face shifted. Hardened. Then twisted. In disbelief. Around him, the soldiers stilled. Instinctively. Like animals stunned before a storm.

Something had changed. They felt it. They didn't know what. But they felt it.

Amalric glared at the parchment. The letter read:

In Nomine Domini et sub auctoritate Sanctae Ecclesiae,

To Our Faithful Servant, Abbot Amalric,

The Holy Father commends your zealous efforts in leading the Holy War against the heretics of the Languedoc. The triumph at Béziers stands as a testament

438

to your unwavering dedication to the purification of these lands. Your leadership has been an inspiration to all who march under the banner of the Cross.

However, the task ahead requires a careful balance of spiritual guidance and military strategy. As such, it is the will of His Holiness that the forces of the Cross now be placed under the command of Milo, our trusted Cistercian prelate, who shall lead the army until Carcassonne is subdued. Your role as spiritual advisor remains paramount, and your counsel will continue to guide this sacred mission.

You are entrusted with ensuring that the transition is seamless and that all actions reflect the teachings of the Holy Mother Church.

May your continued service bring glory to God and deliver salvation to these lands.

Scriptum ex curia Lateranensi, anno Domini 1209.

By the Hand of Cardinal Vitale,
Secretary to His Holiness Innocent III,
Servant of the Servants of God

The parchment trembled in Amalric's grip. Not from the wind.

From rage. His knuckles whitened. Breath hissed between clenched teeth.

His face—tight, dark, like a storm about to break.

"I am to be replaced?"

Low. Venomous. Almost a whisper. But those closest heard. And they stepped back. Instinct. As if to avoid the strike of a cornered snake.

"After all I have done?" he spat. "After Béziers?"

A silence. Tense. Uncertain. One knight, bold or foolish, dared to ask, "Your Eminence… what does it say?"

Amalric's voice snapped through the camp like a whip.

"It says my service is no longer sufficient!"

His eyes burned.

"That I am to step aside. For *another* legate. For—Milo! Of all people!" he spat the name like poison.

Then—movement from an obscure corner.

Milo.

He stepped forward from the ranks, robed, composed, hands folded neatly like a man stepping into a pulpit.

He had been with the host since Lyon. Quiet. Watching. In the background preaching comfort and encouragement while Amalric had commanded flame.

"My dear Abbot Amalric," Milo said, even-toned, calm as still water. "This is not a matter of sufficiency. His Holiness seeks unity. And I have now been entrusted with that sacred task. The Holy War now requires a shepherd, not a wolf."

There was an uneasy pause. Measured. Deliberate.

"And I am here to shepherd."

Amalric turned on him like a blade unsheathed. "You speak of unity?" he growled. "You? Who's never set foot on a battlefield before this triumph?"

His hand clenched at his side.

"You think sermons will break walls? You think parchment will rout heretics? I have *bled* for this cause. Burned for it. Crushed cities beneath the heel of righteousness. I raised the Cross in Spain and tamed the Moor!"

Milo met his fury with quiet steel.

"I also know what it is to serve the will of God," he replied.

"And I know that obedience to His Holiness is not optional."

For a heartbeat—Amalric said nothing. Then another. Pride clashed with obedience. Fury with fear.

For a moment, the camp waited—Would the Abbot defy Rome itself?

Then—his shoulders fell. Slightly. He took a breath.

440

Long. Bitter.

"Very well," he muttered. "If this is the will of His Holiness… so be it."

Milo inclined his head. Not smug. Not gloating. Just resoluteness showing.

"Your guidance remains invaluable, Abbot Amalric. Together, we shall see the Holy War to its holy conclusion."

The soldiers murmured behind them. Tension cracked, but didn't vanish.

Amalric turned, mounted his horse with stiff, deliberate movements.

He did not look at Milo again. But the fire had not left his eyes. Not extinguished—only banked.

Milo mounted a warhorse brought forth by a knight. He raised his hand and the army began to move, the black line of riders stretching toward the direction of Carcassonne.

Milo rode at the front, calm. Steady. Eyes fixed forward. Amalric followed behind.

Silent. Seething. Yet the Holy Host marched on—its fire had found new places to burn.

::

The sky was bleeding gray. Dawn rising behind the hills, weak and pale. No birds. No songs. Just breath and feet and silence.

They came upon it like mourners at a grave. Charred beams jutting from blackened stone. It was the remains of a church, gutted, burnt.

What was once sanctuary, now ruin.

The fledgling group huddled at the edge of the clearing, weary, watching.

Philippa slowed. Her steps light over scorched ground. She knelt near a tangle of ash and collapsed brick, near the back of the blackened and exposed altar.

"Here," she said, brushing soot from a slab. George

groaned as he pulled on the slab. The squires Nugent and Marshall rushed to assist.

A creak as the stone shifted—A trapdoor. Hidden beneath the altar's shadow. They gathered close. The steam of their breath trailing into the cold morning air.

Beneath the door: *stairs*. Narrow. Swallowed by the darkness. Torches flaring to life in George's hands.

Philippa turned to John.

"No longer guarded by sword or flame. But by something older."

He nodded.

"Hugh, George, Hubert, Bobbeye. With me. Spearmen—secure the perimeter. Quietly."

Their descent was slow and cautious.

Cold clung to the stone. Damp and old. The air pressed in around them, thick with rot and memory.

"This was a place of peace once," Philippa whispered. Her voice echoed against the chiseled stone. "The *Bon Hommes* gathered here in secret. They prayed, they broke bread, they hid."

She paused.

"And then came the swords, the fire. Guy of Vaux-de-Cernay."

The stone church above had been burned—a decoy, a ruin dressed in ash and silence. Guy had seen to that. But what he and his men never knew, what none of the ravaging host had discovered, lay buried beneath the shattered altar and scorched beams: a corridor, long and narrow, carved into the stones of the earth, leading into darkness.

Philippa led them further into it, her torch cutting narrow swaths of light into the black. Dust hung thick. Air unmoved for years.

"This chamber underneath was the real sanctuary," she whispered. "The believers met here… long ago. Before the persecution scattered them like leaves in a storm."

442

Now, only ghosts of silence. And echoes of the past.

The small group pressed forward through the corridor. Torches flared and flickered. The damp stone drank in their heat, gave nothing back, its coldness deafening.

At the far end—a wall, blank but for an inscription chiseled deep into the rockface, and beneath it, a crude arrangement of lettered blocks inset into a slab of stone. Each one carved with a single character, worn by time, arranged in a grid of iron and granite.

No levers. No switches. No traps. Just an inscription.

Philippa stepped forward, brushing her gloved fingers across the Latin inscription, reading aloud:

QUOD SEMPER LATET, SED CUNCTA REVELAT— QUOD OMNES QUAERUNT, SED PAUCI INVENIUNT—IN CORDE HOMINUM HABITAT, SED NON VIDETUR: QUID EST?

John frowned, stepping closer. His lips moved silently as he read it again.

What always hides, yet reveals all—What do all seek, yet few find—What lives in the heart, but is not seen?

A riddle. A gate. A final guardian.

He stepped past the inscription—And the floor clicked beneath his boots. A stone shifted. And from the side of the wall, a glass bulb rotated in the torchlight—an ancient sandglass, sealed in crystal. Sand began to fall.

Grain by grain. Silent. Unforgiving.

John froze. George swore under his breath. Philippa stepped back, eyes wide with realization. She gasped as she grasped George's arm. Beside them, John breathed deeply with concern.

"It's timed," he said. "We only get one chance. When the sand runs out…"

"We'll be locked out," Philippa finished. "Forever."

John stared at the letters—dozens of them, arranged like

tiles in a mason's grid. Each of the letters could be pressed into the grid. He reached out. Hesitated. His mind raced.

"I knew there would be a test to enter, but mother did not tell me how to solve it," Philippa mourned.

"What could be the answer?" Sir Hugh asked, his mind churning.

John muttered, "*Truth?* ... Should be."

He pressed the first series of letters into the stony grid:
V-E-R-I-T-A-S

The blocks sank in. Nothing. Then—a click, and the letters returned to their original position.

Rejected.

John gritted his teeth.

"Latin's no good."

"Try French," George offered.

He did: *V-E-R-I-T-E*

Another click. Another rejection.

"Curse it."

His voice was taut and desperate. He tried again in frustration—Middle English, a tongue from his land.

T-R-E-W-T-H

Nothing. What was he thinking? He wasn't in England. The sand kept falling. Time bleeding out.

John stepped back, ran a gloved hand through his hair. His gaze swept the room. The walls. The dust. The silence. Then—

Philippa.

She stood watching him. Torch in hand. An Occitan noblewoman. Born of the land. *This* land. Of its people. Not Latin. Not French. Not Roman. Certainly not English.

What if that was the point?

He turned back to the letters. His eyes narrowed.

Not the language of kings. The language of shepherds. Of those who suffer. Of those who believed in truth—a truth that all men should have the freedom to believe what they believed.

444

His fingers moved—hesitant, then certain.

V-E-R-T-A-T

A hiss. Low. Like breath pulled through stone. Just as the sand ran dry. And the wall... moved. The sound of stone grinding against stone reverberated throughout the cold, stony corridor. Slow. Reluctant.

And then—it *opened.*

Beyond it—darkness. Dust. And the first promise of something sacred, mysterious.

Philippa exhaled, relived and awed—all at once.

John stepped through the threshold. Not as a knight. Not as a conqueror. But as a man who now understood the truth.

He stood there a moment longer, breath shallow, hand still hovering above the final stone, contemplating the significance of it all.

Vertat.

Not *veritas.* Not *vérité.* Certainly not *trewth.*

Not the words of courts, or noble scrolls, or men in silk robes. The door had opened—because he'd stopped thinking like a knight, like a noble.

That's what struck him.

Not the sound of grinding stone, or the gasps behind him, but the weight of what it all meant. The answer had always been there. Not hidden, just... overlooked. Because they'd been taught to look upward—to Rome, to Latin, to the powerful—as if truth were only found in books guarded by the clergy.

But here, beneath a ruined church, truth waited in the tongue of farmers. Weavers. Midwives and shepherds.

The people of this land.

That was the test. Not a puzzle of strength. Not a test of nobility.

Humility.

And he—John de Ontivero, once a knight sworn to the Holy cause, once proud beneath gilded banners—had only passed because he'd laid all that pretense down.

Because he'd looked at Philippa, not for what she could offer, but for where she came from. Because he had listened to conscience.

He had *listened*.

That's what he had to learn. And it would haunt him—because he knew now how much he had failed to hear before. God resisted the proud and gives grace to the humble. Father Barth's weekly homilies spoke to him even now.

Philippa stared at the opened passage, at the final grains of sand still clinging to the curve of the glass.

A breath caught in her throat. Then slowly—softly—she spoke.

Not to John. Not just to him. But to all who stood behind. Listening. *Waiting*.

"They would have failed," she said.

George looked over.

"Who?"

"The men of the host," she answered. Her voice thin, trembling with the weight of realization. "The *Milites Christi*."

She turned, faced them fully now. The light of their torches flickering on her bright-eyed expression.

"If any of them had made it this far—to this place—they would have stood here, just as we did. Read the Latin, understood the riddle. Maybe some would even guess the answer."

She paused.

"But they would never have answered it in Occitan."

Confusion rippled through the men. She pressed on.

"They would try Latin. Then French. Maybe even their own tongues. German, perhaps. Iberian, even. But not ours. Not the tongue of shepherds and seamstresses of the Midi. Not the language spoken in kitchens and vineyards."

Her eyes shimmered as she continued.

446

"To do so would require humility. The kind they crushed out of themselves with every oath to Rome. They would not lower themselves to speak the language of heretics, of peasants, of the dying south."

She looked back at the stones John had pressed.

V-E-R-T-A-T

"The truth was never hidden," she whispered. "They just couldn't bear to speak it in the voice of the people."

A hush fell. And in that silence, something deeper settled in—a truth not chiseled in stone, but a truth born between them.

John lowered his head. Just a little. Not in shame. In *understanding*.

The chamber itself was quiet. Still. The air unmoved, untouched by light for years. It wasn't grand—no vaulted ceilings, no gilded pillars. Just stone. Dust. Silence.

And at its center, set like a relic atop a raised altar—a large chest. Long as a man, like a sarcophagus. Carved with care. Symbols winding into symbols. Not just a whimsical aesthetic.

A story etched in wood. A secret buried in silence.

Philippa stepped past the threshold, her torch casting dancing light over the lid.

She looked at John, eyes gleaming not with certainty, but with gravity of what they would soon uncover.

"This chest," she said, low, steady, "was sealed by my mother's will. Not to keep every men out—but to ensure the wrong ones never got in."

She reached beneath her collar and drew the key.

Small. Wrought like jewelry, but no ornament. It caught the firelight and scattered it in strange patterns across the walls.

She knelt.

"This key opens only with trust," she said, voice barely more than a breath. "And I give it to you, my lord, at this moment—not because you command it, but because I choose you."

John gave a silent nod. That was all. No speeches. No vows. There was no need.

The silence was deafening.

John, George, Hugh and the two squires held their breath as Philippa placed the key into the lock.

A quiet click.

Then—The chest yawned open, held by Hubert and Bobbeye.

At first—gold. *Coins*. Hundreds of them. A full treasury! *Jewels*. An almost endless variety. Neatly packed leather pouches filled with stones glinting in the dark. Enough to feed, arm, and house a thousand people for years.

But John's eyes didn't stay there.

Something else lay in the chest. Scrolls. Manuscripts. Leather-bound books, wrapped in silk and sealed with wax long broken.

John reached out, reverent. His fingers brushed parchment older than war.

A Torah. A *Bon Hommes* New Testament. A Latin Vulgate marked with Waldensian notations. A Bible in Occitan, inked by hand, word by word. A Qur'an. Fragments of Zoroastrian scripture.

He stared for a moment. This was no simple hoard. This was a library of defiance.

It was not intended as a fusion of truths. But a gallery of belief—unmolested, unburned.

Philippa drew out a bundle wrapped in crimson cloth.

"Letters," she said. "From my mother, the Lady Esclaramonde de Foix."

John unwrapped them slowly. The ink had faded at the edges. The script—elegant, firm. He began to read. And the world narrowed to the page.

A *declaration*.

Written in the tongue of nobles, but for the hearts of the humble. She did not ask for unity of doctrine. She demanded freedom of belief. A society where faith did not bind the throat but freed it.

Not for the sake of blending truths.

But so each soul might hold to its own, without fear. She laid out a structure—feudal model rooted in mutual oaths of protection. Lords who defend, not dictate. Priests who preached, but did not punish with the sword.

She expected—no, invited—retribution from the Church for this. For simply reading this material, men would be sent to the pyre.

And in closing, she asked only one thing from the reader: Keep the ideas in your heart and burn these words.

John said nothing. Not for a long time.

Esclaramonde did not want the letters to incriminate her, but she wanted the ideas to live on. In *him*. Whom Philippa trusted. They were written for this very moment. He would follow her wishes, but he needed more time to study and internalize her ideas.

He touched the letters gently, then rolled them tight in canvas, wrapping them like relics.

He stood, placed a hand on Philippa's shoulder.

"These," he said, "I will guard with my life."

He paused before continuing.

"Not just for what they are. But for what they mean."

Philippa turned away, her gaze drifting to where light pooled at the stairwell.

"Occitania," she murmured. "A land of stone and soul. Where even now, the light of tolerance tries to burn through the smoke."

She paused briefly.

"I stayed within the old ways, to follow tradition and the structure of the Church," she said. "The orthodoxy. It felt… safer. Mother never forced her faith upon us. Even when she became a *perfecta*, she let us choose."

John's brow tightened.

A word lingered. Foreign. Heavy with something more

449

than language.

"*Perfecta*," he repeated. "What does that mean?"

Philippa turned to him. Her face calm, but shadowed by memory. The kind of memory that doesn't fade—only settles deeper.

"To the Church," she said, "a heretic priestess."

She paused before continuing.

"A *perfecta* is one who has received the *Consolamentum*—the final sacrament. No marriage. No wealth. No meat, no war, no ties to this world. They live for spirit alone. They care for the soul of others, not their own comfort."

John's gaze didn't move from her.

"And your mother?" he asked, quiet. "She lived that life?"

Philippa nodded.

"After my father died, she took the rite. Became... more than a mother. She became their mother. She walked from village to village. Whispered prayers where no priest would go. Gave the people comfort in their silence. Hid from the fire of the pyre. But she never hid from her calling."

She paused. Her breath caught—but she steadied it.

"When the first foreign knights came, before the full force of your host arrived at our borders, they forced us below ground. Into caves, and hillsides, and cellars. People like my mother had two choices—renounce or run."

She looked down at her hands.

"She didn't run for herself. She ran for us. She left the gold, the trappings—gave them to me. Said they'd serve better in the hands of those who still had the means to fight."

John was quiet for a moment.

Then—

"Where is she now?"

Philippa's eyes lit, just barely.

"If she's alive... Montségur. Our family's fortress. High in the Pyrenees. It sits on stone like a crown. No siege can

450

take it. At least, not for a very long time. It's where the last of faithful will go."

Silence settled in, soft but thick, as the two they made their way back up to the outside, just wind, and footsteps behind them. Hugh, George, and the squires hoisted the heavy chest. John squinted as looked out into the brightness, past the trees.

"She's not just fighting for faith," he said to a trailing Philippa, slow. Thoughtful. "She's fighting for the right to choose."

His voice sharpened, but not with anger—with conviction.

"To live. To believe. Without chains."

Philippa turned to him. Eyes shining, but not with tears.

"Yes," she said. "And that choice is worth more than any crown. Than any jewel on earth."

John nodded.

"Then we protect it."

A moment passed. Then Philippa whispered—

"With whatever it takes."

A faint smile tugged at her lips. Gratitude. Iron-willed and quiet.

"Thank you, Lord John. With men like you... maybe this land still has a future. One not ruled by fire and fear."

John looked back at the chest, then at her.

"And with mothers like yours," he said, "it has something worth building that future for."

A voice cut through the moment.

Adelinda.

"When you lovebirds are done," she called out in a mocking tone, "we still have hungry mouths and tired feet."

John smirked. A rare light in his eyes.

"I didn't know my lady was capable of jealousy."

Adelinda rolled her eyes.

"I am capable of stabbing, too."

The moment broke—but gently. John turned, shoulders

loosening.

"You're right," he said. "We camp here tonight. Let the people rest."

He looked once more toward Philippa.

"At first light. We move."

::

The sun burned high, white and pitiless. No shadows to hide in. No breeze to speak of. Just dust. Stone. Heat.

Guy of Vaux-de-Cernay crouched low, fingers brushing the earth like a man reading scripture. Not ink and vellum—hoofprints, crushed weeds, disturbed stone.

Every mark whispered. They'd passed this way. Not too long ago.

"They're close," he said. His voice didn't rise. It didn't need to. Steel didn't shout—it cut.

He stood.

Armor groaned as he moved, gauntlet pointing toward the jagged cut of land ahead. Ravines. Plateaus. A maze carved by wind and time.

"They think the rocks will hide them," he said. "Fools."

Behind him, the Calatravan knights shifted in their saddles. Mounts snorted and stamped.

Tension in the reins. Blood in the air.

Guy turned to Peter. His nephew. He saw fire in the young man's eyes. Still learning, but dangerous all the same.

"We ride," Guy said. "Three hours ahead, at most."

The order was wind and iron—the knights surged forward. Hooves thundered. Dust rose. Blades clinked against armor. The sound of war on the move.

They rode for what seemed like an eternity. Yet Guy's eyes never left the horizon. Scanning. Calculating. Hunting.

Until—

They crested a rise—And there. A flicker of movement.

Blue and yellow, small against the distant stones, vanishing over the next hill.

Guy's lips twisted.

"There," he snapped. "They run for the far side. After them!"

The chase tightened.

Horses strained, their lungs flaring with heat. The ground turned cruel. Loose stones slid under iron shoes. The incline steepened, jagged and mean. They would not be able to ride up these cliffs.

Guy reined in.

"No further," he barked. "Dismount. We climb."

The knights hesitated—then obeyed. No one questioned Guy.

Boots hit dirt. Gauntlets reached for stone. They climbed. The sun didn't relent. It burned through armor. Cooked the flesh beneath. Sweat ran like blood, pooling beneath collars, stinging eyes.

But they climbed.

Guy led. *Always* Guy. Peter followed close to his uncle, lips pressed thin, jaw tight. His youth hadn't failed him yet— but the hill tried its best.

Rocks slipped. Steel scraped.

One knight stumbled—caught himself. Cursed under his breath.

Two hours passed. No mercy from the unrelenting sun.

And then—the summit. They paused. Just long enough to breathe. To drink water from sheepskin. To look.

Below—movement.

Figures darting through the ravine. Blue. Yellow. Running.

"There," Guy said. His voice a promise. "They seek to vanish in the valley. Be prepared, as they may put up a fight."

He moved before anyone else could speak. Down the slope, loose gravel sliding underfoot. Sharp edges bit into soles, but they didn't stop.

They were close now. Closer than ever. They had them

now.

Guy's voice cracked through the air—fierce. *Final*.

"They end here! No mercy. No quarter! *Deus lo vult!*"

The knights poured down the hill behind him, a tide of iron and fury, swords drawn. The valley below narrowed.

And the gap—closed.

The hunted scattered, but it was too late. The valley had become the crucible of battle. And death was coming.

Luzbreca

July 25th, 1209 AD

Carcassonne, Viscounty of Carcassonne

he Holy host rolled forward like a tide—steel and zeal wrapped in white banners and red crosses. Dust rose behind them, fields trampled flat beneath iron hooves and pilgrim feet. This was not just an army. This was the judgment and wrath of zeal.

Ahead, Carcassonne loomed.

A wall of stone perched on the hill like a crown. Towers clawed at the sky. Double walls. Deep moats. Gates that had turned away armies of kings.

To the host—a citadel of heresy, yes. But also—a prize.

Amalric rode in silence. No longer at the front. Dismissed. Replaced.

But not erased.

He watched the fortress rise before him, eyes fixed, jaw tight. Carcassonne was meant to be *his* triumph. His sermon in stone, painted with blood.

Now another would wear the mantle. And still—he watched. Waiting for something to burn.

At the center of the swelling camp, amid wagons and hammers and raw-eyed footmen, stood Milo.

Cloaked in modest robes.

Still. Calm. Eyes sharp as any blade. No general. No warrior. But appointed. Elevated. The new legate of Rome. He stood on a plank raised over barrels. Makeshift pulpit. Makeshift throne.

Surveying the land like a man reading the lines of a sacred scroll.

Not by fire, he thought. *Not yet.*

Stone like this would laugh at fire. Milo's mind turned—calculating. Carcassonne was built to last. Even more formidable than Béziers .

But stone didn't feed the mouths of its residents. And hunger broke more walls than hammers.

The sun dipped low. The camp spread like mold across the valley. And by torchlight, the leaders gathered. Inside the largest tent, a map stretched wide on a wooden table.

Carcassonne and her veins—roads, hills, rivers, forgotten paths. A wound waiting to be pressed.

Milo stood before them, hands folded, eyes level.

"Brothers," he said, voice even. Measured. "We stand before a citadel that has defied kings. Its strength lies not in its stone… but in the confidence of those within. That confidence must break."

Murmurs passed between knights. Uncertainty.

A grizzled voice cut through—the knight Guy de Courcy, eyes narrowed, fingers drumming the hilt of his blade.

"You mean to starve them, Father?"

Milo nodded once.

"Yes. No food. No messages. No water. No hope. We will not break their walls—we will unmake their courage."

Steel shifted. Eyebrows raised.

Amalric lingered near the edge of the circle. Silent. But the corner of his mouth curled—just a little.

"Starvation and thirst," he said softly, "are a fitting punishment. A slow, holy withering. Just as the wrath of God withers the soul of the unrepentant."

Milo didn't turn. Didn't flinch. His voice carried on, undisturbed.

"And while their bellies ache, let them hear whispers of mercy. Let them believe they have been abandoned. We will plant seeds of doubt—then watch as they bloom into betrayal."

One of the younger knights leaned forward, impatience in his bones.

"And if they don't break? If they last the month? Two? This army won't sit idle forever."

Milo's gaze sharpened, slicing straight through the protest.

"Then we turn to subtler weapons," he said. "Vicomte Trencavel is within. I have no doubt. And I do not care how we reach him."

He paused.

"We will deceive. We will infiltrate. We will use every tool Heaven grants us. There is no sin in the service of the Lord. There is no wickedness in advancing His cause."

The torches flickered.

No one spoke.

Milo looked across the table, across the map, across the faces of men who had once only known Amalric's fire. Now they would learn his cold resolve.

And Carcassonne would answer. One way or another.

::

The ravine swallowed them.

Stone underfoot shifted treacherously, crumbling with every bootfall. Sunlight poured over the cliffs like molten brass—merciless, blinding.

Even the most seasoned Calatravans stumbled, sweat soaking their tunics, armor hissing beneath the weight of heat and humiliation.

Still, Guy pressed forward, leading the charge.

Eyes fixed. Jaw clenched.

Those flashes of blue and yellow—he'd seen them from the summit. A trail of ghosts darting just beyond reach.

They were close. He could feel it in his bones.

The ravine widened at the base. Jagged rock walls rose around them like silent judges. Guy's knights fanned out— silent, blades drawn, tension humming like a bowstring.

Peter moved beside him, every step a thud of rage. The young man's face twisted with fury.

"There," Guy said, pointing through the shimmering air. Movement ahead. Tunics. Blue and yellow. Darting through the large boulders.

"Take them, now!"

The knights surged forward, swords held high— desperation lending strength to their tired limbs. The clank of steel, the crunch of boots, the quickening breath of men tasting victory.

Then—

"Baaaaa..."

They halted. Dead in their tracks. No one spoke. No one moved.

Sheep.

Blue and yellow tunics draped over their woolen backs, tied with rope and sagging crookedly. The sound of bleating echoed up the canyon walls, mocking. Some sheep chewed on the disparate weeds. Others wandered. Their slow, mindless movements were exactly what Guy had chased.

Exactly.

Guy stood frozen. Incredulous. Helmet in hand. Sweat sliding down his temples, evaporating against flushed skin.

His face—a mask of disbelief stretched thin over

458

mounting rage.

"What in the name of the Holy Virgin…"

He didn't finish. Didn't need to.

Peter didn't hold back.

He slammed his gauntleted fist against a boulder—

CLANG!

The rock split, shards bouncing into the dirt.

"Sheep!" he barked. "They've dressed sheep in their colors! We've been chasing animals for miles—miles!"

The knights stood dumb, shame thick in the air. Their pride, trampled like dust under hooves. This wasn't simply an evasion. This was a humiliation.

Peter's fury cracked wide open.

"This is Sir Hugh's doing! I know it!"

He kicked a stone, sending it tumbling down the slope.

"That swine! That knight of Breckington! I swear, when I find him—"

"Enough."

Guy's voice cut through his rant like a blade through cloth. Not loud. Not sharp. But final.

Peter fell silent, chest heaving, hands trembling.

"They've bought themselves time," Guy said, voice low, cold. "But they haven't escaped. Sheep in tunics won't save them when we catch up."

Peter spun on him, wild-eyed.

"You don't understand, uncle. This isn't just a game—it's mockery. They're laughing at us. Right now. John, Hugh—every last one of them. They've made fools of us."

Guy met his gaze—unflinching.

"I understand perfectly," he said. "But curb your rage. Or it will blind you again. Today we were deceived. Yes. That is on us"—an awkward pause—"but only the desperate waste strength on mockery. The cornered kind. The kind that knows it's running out of ground."

Peter's fists tightened. His nails dug crescents into his palms.

"I'll see them dead for this," he muttered, his voice hoarse with wrath. "Every last one of them."

Guy said nothing in response. Just turned. Surveyed the ravine. The sheep wandered, oblivious.

Obnoxious. Unbothered. A sick joke. And they'd walked right into it. But in the back of his mind, something turned. This trick cost them time. Coordination. Material. Nerve. They were running out of options.

"They're close," he said at last, quieter now. Calculated. "This ruse… it cost them. They won't have gone far."

But the truth was, he didn't know how far they had gone...or where. He glanced over his shoulder.

"We press on. Faster. Harder. Let them think they've won. Let them think they've slipped free. We'll remind them—vengeance doesn't sleep."

He pivoted toward the trail to return to their mounts, cloak snapping behind him. The knights followed, their silence no longer shame, but purpose.

Peter lingered.

He glared at the sheep as if they mocked him with every step. His eyes narrowed to slits.

He spat into the dust.

Then he followed—and the vengeance within him burned hotter than ever.

::

The hills of the Languedoc loomed silent, cloaked in pine and shadow in the darkening glow of the sun.

Trees stood like sentinels. Still. Watching. Waiting.

Wind brushed the branches. The hush of a sleeping land. Or so it seemed at the moment.

They had found a hollow—clearing just wide enough for firelight to dance.

A circle of weary faces. Refugees digging out a spot for the night. Breckington spearmen, tunics shed and their

460

shields covered in sackcloth to hide the distinctive blue and yellow.

Women wrapped in shawls, cradling children too tired to cry.

Old men who had walked farther than their bones should have allowed.

No one spoke. Crackling wood split by fire filled the silence.

John stood apart.

Boots planted on dry earth. Eyes on the dark between the trees. Listening. Observing.

Sir Hugh. Sir George. Beside him, as always. But this wasn't just their council.

Not tonight.

Tonight was for the spearmen. The levy. And the refugees. The ones who bled beside him. The ones who never wore a crown but bore every cost.

He turned.

The fire cast gold across his face as darkness enveloped around them. His voice carried, low but sure.

"We must decide," he said. "Not just I. Or my knights. All of us. Every voice matters."

A ripple moved through the group. Uncertainty. Surprise. Expressions showing a look of trust. Of security in his leadership. Then one named Edmund stood. Weathered face. Salt and soot in his beard. A Norman veteran who marched to the Levant with the levy five years prior.

"With respect, my lord," he began, quiet but firm. "I've got a wife. Two sons. If there's a way to get back to them… I'll take it. My heart's there, even if my feet are here."

A few nods. Faces turned inward. Toward homes left behind. But Alan rose—young, too young maybe. Firelight in his eyes.

"What about them?"

He pointed to the huddled masses near the flame. The refugees. The forgotten. Their eyes revealed their plight.

"If we leave, who protects them?"

No one answered. Even Edmund looked down.

Sir Hugh's voice broke the quiet. Arms crossed. Brow furrowed.

"If we stay, Guy of Vaux-de-Cernay will hunt us. He doesn't forgive. He doesn't stop."

John nodded.

"He hunts what moves," he said. "But if we build—if we stay in one place—we might catch him off guard—we'll have a chance to face his onslaught together."

A few murmurs. Thoughtful. Hopeful.

Henry, a quiet and steady lad, new to the levy, leaned closer to the fire.

"We've made it this far, my lord. Together. Maybe we can find ground no one's looking for. Deep. Hidden."

"But Breckington..." another voice, hesitant. "That's home. Were our families are. How are we going to go home?"

John's gaze softened.

"I've thought of that," he said. "If we stay, any man who wants to return is free to go. Just... be discreet. The crown may not welcome us. But your families will."

Relief passed like wind through the leaves. Edmund exhaled, nodded once.

"Then I'll stay. For now. But Guy..." he added.

Philippa stepped forward then. Cloaked in stillness, contemplation. But her voice cut clean.

"The forests are vast," she said. "And Carcassonne draws the host. Amalric is no longer in charge. Replaced by Milo, as my scouts report. A priest truly cut from the cloth, not a want-to-be-warrior."

Sir George raised a brow.

"Milo? He's soft."

"No," she replied. "He's clever. He'll strike the strongholds—Termes, Minerve, Carcassonne. Not with a sword but with guile and deception."

She paused. Her eyes sharpened as she continued.

"Guy and Peter will come. But they are fewer. And we are wiser now."

Alan grinned, youth returned to his voice, chuckling.

"They're chasing shadows. Or sheep. We'll keep it that way."

John looked around the fire. Faces upturned. Hope flickering behind the eyes. He stepped forward.

"Then it is settled. We build," he said. "A haven. A refuge. A home."

Silence. Then murmurs. Then nods.

"We've bled together," John went on. "We've fled fire. But here, in the forests of the Midi, we make something new. A place where no man compels another. Where faith is free, and life belongs to us."

His voice lowered.

"We may be hunted. But we are not broken."

He looked toward the stars, now visible in the dark ink of the sky.

"They call us exiles. Let them. We are the harbingers of something better."

Silence. Then Alan leaned forward, eyes bright.

"If we build it… it needs a name."

A few chuckles. Even the grizzled Osric cracked a smile through his beard.

"Aye," he muttered. "Can't build a place with no name."

John rubbed his chin.

"It should speak to who we are," he said. "Where we come from. And where we're going."

Sir George, voice distant, whispered, "Breckington... it's still our root."

Adelinda, with Elizabeth asleep on her shoulder, tilted her head.

"But most here are Occitan. Let the name be theirs too."

Philippa spoke then, soft and thoughtful.

"The Midi holds many names. If we honor

Breckington... perhaps we soften it. We can make it *Bricaton*."

Henry scratched his youthful beard.

"Bricaton," he repeated. "Has a ring to it."

But then—a soft voice from the refugees. A young Castilian girl, a refugee, barely more than a whisper.

"*Luzbreca*."

She blushed, as all stares turned her way.

"It means...the light of Breckington."

The word hung there. Warm. Settling like a blanket across the clearing. Alan beamed.

"Luzbreca. Now that sounds like a place worth fighting for."

Adelinda leaned forward gently, placing a hand on the arm of the Castilian girl.

"How did you come up with that name, little one?"

The girl hesitated, then pointed to the toddler on her hip—her sister, no more than three.

"She cannot say 'Breckington,'" she murmured. "She always says '*Breca*.' I tried to teach her... but I like how she says it. And *Luz* is 'light' in Castilian."

John's gaze softened. He looked at the smaller child, now curled against her sister's shoulder, thumb in her mouth.

Hugh let out a breath.

"From the mouth of babes..." he muttered.

John nodded slowly.

"It holds the old... and points to something new."

Adelinda smiled.

"A place where the light survives. Even in the dark—we are harbingers of the light."

The group spoke softly now. Ideas. Plans. Dreams forming like breath in the cool air. Then John raised his hand.

"Then we call it *Luzbreca*," he said. "Let it stand for freedom. For unity. For a fire that will not go out."

Philippa met his gaze.

"A new beginning," she said. "And a name worth remembering."

The fire crackled. The wind whispered through the pines. And above them, the stars bore witness to a small, tired group, barely over a hundred, who refused to vanish.

Luzbreca had no walls yet. No homes. No towers. Indeed, it was just an idea. Yet that idea had a name. And sometimes, that's just how a world begins.

Lords of Breckington

Continued…

7. Lord John de Ontivero (1175–?)
Seventh and Last Baron of Breckington, 1191–?

A lord who was both warrior and philosopher, torn between oath and his conscience. His baryonic rule was marred by religious strife, political betrayal, and a love both lost and rekindled. Said to have abandoned his noble title in pursuit of liberty for the persecuted. He is the founder of the exilic community of Luzbreca.

> **Spouses**: Mary de Dustanville (1172–?), marriage annulled, Adelinda de Montaro (1177–?), his one true love, union by conscience and shared flight
> **Issue**: Elizabeth de Montaro (b. 1200—?), adopted

EPILOGUE

In the aftermath of the tumultuous Albigensian Crusade, the once-vibrant cultural landscape of Occitania lay irrevocably altered. The haunting echoes of the conflict lingered, not merely in the charred remnants of besieged cities but in the collective consciousness of a land scarred by the dangers of religious intolerance and the insatiable lust for control.

The triumphant Crusader lords, having subdued the dissenting voices and dismantled the foundations of religious tolerance, now found themselves rulers of a fractured realm. The theocratic dominion they envisioned came at a profound cost—the erosion of diversity, the suppression of intellectual inquiry, and the subjugation of individual freedoms beneath the heavy and oppressive mantle of Church dogma.

The once-thriving cities, now fortified bastions of orthodoxy, bore witness to the perilous price paid for the imposition of a singular belief system. The remnants of dissent, though quelled on the surface, lingered in the hearts of those who remembered a time when tolerance and diversity flourished.

As the years unfolded, the consequences of religious zealotry became increasingly apparent. The Inquisition, once hailed as a tool of divine discernment, morphed into an instrument of fear, silencing any whisper of dissent that dared to challenge the established order. The land, once rich with cultural exchange and intellectual discourse, languished in the stifling grip of orthodoxy.

The lessons of the Crusade to subjugate the Languedoc have resounded through history as a cautionary tale—a stark reminder of the perils that accompany the unchecked pursuit of religious supremacy and the lust for control. The scars of the Albigensian Crusade served as an enduring testament to the fragility of a society when gripped by the fervor of intolerance.

In the quiet moments of reflection, some even began to question the righteousness of their deeds. The once exuberant Crusader lords, now burdened with the weight of their choices, faced the realization that the pursuit of absolute control came at the cost of their own humanity. The lands of Southern France, once pulsating with diversity, yearned for the healing balm of tolerance.

Occitania, resilient in its spirit, held within its very soil the seeds of renewal. Despite the scars, the whispers of dissent found root in the hearts of those who remembered a time when coexistence was cherished, and ideas were allowed to flourish without fear. Sadly, the flames of intolerance would find its expression, not only religious zealotry, but also anti-religious fervor, as seen many centuries later in France's history, leading up to and during the Reign of Terror.

As the pages of history turned, the Albigensian Crusade stood as a violent chapter, a tale of terrible tragedy. It beckons future generations to tread with caution, to recognize the dangers that lurked in the shadows of zealotry, and to safeguard the sanctity of diversity in the face of intolerance.

The epilogue of Occitania's saga served as a poignant reminder that the true measure of a society lay not in its ability to enforce conformity but in its capacity to embrace the mosaic of beliefs, ideas, and cultures that collectively wove the intricate fabric of human existence. The Albigensian Crusade, with all its tumult and strife, left behind a legacy etched in the annals of history–a testament to the enduring struggle between the quest for control and the inexorable human yearning for freedom, understanding, and the beauty of diversity.

SOURCES

While this novel is largely a work of fiction, I endeavored to stay as close to the historical data as possible. Historical characters are reimagined, giving them life and revealing their purposes and motivations. We may never know the true reasons why certain people would be led to commit the atrocities seen in our history, but it is a lesson that is seldom heeded. This book is a memorial to those that resisted them, by voice, pen, and sword, to protect the innocent and preserve life and liberty.

To gather a general consensus of how the Crusaders thought and acted, I perused a good portion of Peter of Vaux-de-Cernay's *Historia Albigensis*, which is a valuable primary source of data concerning the Crusade. It is pointed out that the *Historia* is wholly partisan, yet in this case it is fortunately so, as it has given invaluable data concerning the motives and mindset of the Crusader side. The *Historia* so demonized the population of the Midi that it revealed the crusaders' reasoning for their unholy cause. For this reason, Peter himself is fictionally reimagined in this novel as a primary antagonist in the form of a warrior-priest, as is his uncle, Guy of Vaux-de-Cernay.

There is a scarcity of primary sources for the Cathar side, as any written information would have been likely destroyed from the purges. However, what we do know from piecing bits of historical information together is that the social culture of the Languedoc was very progressive and tolerant, especially for its day.

It should be noted that Cathars comprised only a tiny portion of the region's population, and they themselves were non-violent. Yet still, the campaign against them was especially brutal and merciless. It was up to their mostly Occitan Catholic brethren, some Waldensians and other members of various faiths to defend them with the sword, and yet we have no surviving written records from them, either on this particular event.

I am also indebted to the French novelist and historian Zoé Oldenbourg, whose literary work assisted me in the writing of my narrative. Her writings provided valuable insights into my own study and research on the subject.

A FINAL WORD

Ideological extremism, whether wrought by religion or antireligion—or some other fanatical extreme—has always been the spark that kindled the fires of humanity's darkest hours. From the burning cities of the Albigensian Crusade, the Inquisitions, the Colonial and Imperial conquests to the 20th century purges of fascist and communist regimes, history shows what happens when belief, detached from empathy, is wielded like a lethal weapon. Whether cloaked in sacred robes, flying the banners of so-called "egality" or the vain badges of ethnic and cultural "purity", unchecked zeal can justify any cruelty. Today, as culture wars deepen and polarization increases, we must tread carefully. The same contempt for dissent, the same hunger to silence rather than understand, still simmers beneath the surface. Left unchallenged, it can lead us back to the same blood-soaked ground—only with different banners.

If you enjoy this book, please consider leaving a review on Amazon or Goodreads and letting the author know what you think!

ABOUT THE AUTHOR

Lemuel Valendez Sapian is from Denton, Texas and holds a Bachelor of Arts degree in History from the University of North Texas. As a lifelong student of the past, he believes that history is more than just dates and events; it is the story of people, their choices, and the beliefs that carried them through trial. His years of historical research, ministry and service in the United States Air Force Chaplain Corps have given him a unique perspective on the courage, sacrifice, and hope that endures in the darkest hours. *Heretic Knight: Harbinger of Light* is his debut novel and the beginning of a series exploring religious liberty and resilience in the crucible of history. Through his writing, he seeks not only to tell a good story but also to inspire reflections on what it means to live with conviction in a world that is often at odds with conscience.

The saga continues!

Follow John and his band in

Heretic Knight: *Lux Lucet in Tenebris*

Heretic Knight: *Ubi Spiritus, Ibi Libertas*

COMING SOON

www.hereticknight.com